EARTH ALONE

EARTH ALONE

EARTHRISE, BOOK I

DANIEL ARENSON

CHAPTER ONE

Marco was walking home with his mother when the scum rained from the sky.

Fire melted the snow.

There was a lot of snow this winter in what remained of Toronto, fourth largest city in what remained of the North American Alliance, this ravaged continental command in what remained of the world. The trains were dead again. For long hours, Marco and his mother had been walking down the streets, heading home from the gas mask distribution center. The snow assaulted them like a second invasion, piling up at their sides, swirling around their legs, beating their faces, whipping their coats, coating their eyelashes and eyebrows, and numbing their fingers and bones and souls. It was the heart of winter. The coldest, bleakest day of the year. The coldest, bleakest century of mankind.

"Forty-three years ago," Mother had said that morning, struggling through the cold, "lights would hang on the houses in winter. A million lights all in green, red, yellow, and blue. Bells would ring and music would play, and even the trees shone with light."

Marco shivered at her side, trudging through the snow. Some days the trains still worked, screeching, clattering, spraying sparks underground, roaring forth like great tunneling worms, their insides hollowed out and filled with parasitic commuters. But most days the underground was just full of those too afraid to walk above in the world. Those who hid in shadows. Thousands. Hundreds of thousands. Hiding. Waiting for the rain.

"I don't believe you," Marco said. His cardboard box banged against his hip as he walked, hanging on a plastic strap. Every winter—a fresh cardboard box, fresh filters and lenses and needles and rubber, fresh life. "There wouldn't be enough power in the world."

"The world was different." She stroked his hair. "The world was good."

No, Marco did not believe it. Forty-three years ago? Before the Cataclysm? Almost nobody was still alive from that time. Marco was eleven years old; his mother was thirty-six. All they had ever known was this. Cold. Snow that stung and clung to your skin like frozen leeches. Subways shrieking and dying in underground tunnels full of huddling masses and white, terrified eyes and whispers and prayers. Aching legs. Old stories. All they had now was old stories. Lights? Warmth? Fairy tales. Marco was the son of librarians. He knew something of tales. Of lies.

"The world was good," his mother whispered again, holding his hand as they trudged down the ruined street, moving between the snowdrifts, between the shells of old cafes, restaurants, bars, strip clubs, offices, tattoo parlors, the ghosts of old generations. Their cardboard boxes dripped water, withering away, hanging against their hips, constant companions. "The world was good."

A mantra. A dying dream. If the world had been good, it was forgotten. Today there was only snow and fire.

And as they crossed an icy road, the sky opened and the snow stormed and swirled aside like curtains parting on a stage. And the fire blazed. And they came.

Across the road, the handful of others who had braved the snow paused, pointed, shouted. Their voices flowed through the storm.

"Scum!"

Marco stood still. The snowy wind whipped his face, tore off his hood, and streamed his hair. He stared up at them, at a sky that cracked open like a womb to spill its festering, writhing eggs. Five of the pods streamed down, pulsing, purple fringed with orange flame, ionizing the air, cauterizing the clouds, screaming, blazing with heat. One pod slammed into a building. Bricks rained. Flames roared. Creatures squealed. Another pod slammed onto the street ahead of Marco and his mother. It was as large as one of the rusty cars you could still find alongside the frozen highways. The snow melted beneath it, turned to water, then to steam. Asphalt cracked. The egg began to bloom open.

The sky shattered behind them. Marco spun to see more fire, more twisting indigo balls falling.

Scum. He couldn't breathe. He couldn't move. *Scum.*

The rancid lavender miasma seeped into the air.

"Marco, your mask!" Mother pulled her box open so violently she tore the cardboard. The gas mask gazed from within, its eyes glassy and condemning, its mouth thrusting out, round and bulging like the mouths of tribesmen Marco had seen in magazines, plates stretching their lips to obscene sizes. As the lavender gas crept, Mother pulled the mask onto her head. She tightened the straps so hard she ripped her hair. Her breath rattled through the filter, and her eyes were huge, round black pools. She had become something no longer human. Something hurt. Haunted. Ancient and scared, a deity of glass and rubber.

Fingers numb, Marco opened his own cardboard box, pulled out his own gas mask. He had worn a gas mask countless times. Sometimes he wondered which was his true face—his face of skin or this face of rubber, which eyes were his true eyes, which voice was the true voice of his childhood. He put on the mask and gasped for air. The alien pods rained down. The miasma wafted around them, the disease that withered your balls, that made your babies born with shrunken heads, that clung to your clothes and frothed your shit, that smelled like cotton candy and forgotten summers if you caught but a whiff, that turned to rot like childhood's end.

They ran.

They ran as the fire rained from the sky. They ran as the snowdrifts collapsed. They ran as buildings crumbled. They ran as those glowing, twisting, purple pods fell, as the smoke rose, as people fled, seeking manholes under the snow, seeking pathways into the darkness. They ran as the massive ship of the creatures blocked the sky, hid the sun, birthed its eggs, and laughed with guttural, mocking, organic engines like valves opening and closing in a throat.

"There, ahead!" Mother's voice emerged from her mask, deep and metallic. She pulled Marco along. He slipped. She yanked him up. They ran onward. "Do you see the sign? A pathway underground! Come—"

They were racing along the sidewalk when the pod slammed down before them, shattering and spilling its slime and smoke, and the creature emerged from within.

Marco froze and stared.

The scum. The *scolopendra titaniae*. The bastards that had ravaged the world over forty years ago, slaughtering most of humanity, that had taunted and brutalized humanity since. In the flame and smoke and steam, Marco saw only a shadow, then glimpsed rows of claws like spikes on fences, like swords in an armory, like the pikes of ancient warriors, and twisting, flailing segments all in armor, a great centipede, ten feet tall and rising, a god. A god of the darkness. A god from the stars. A god of wrath. Baal. Lord of flies. Crying out in the snow, born into the world hungry, so hungry, every twitch of it, every hiss, every clack of its mandibles screaming of hunger.

Its fumes flowed, and it leaped toward Marco and his mother.

"Fire!" rose a distant voice, and hundreds of boots thudded, and machine guns blazed. Halos of flame burst around the muzzles of hundreds of guns, and jets screamed overhead, charging across the sky like dragons in old books with crumbling yellow pages. Armored vehicles rumbled in the distance, cannons firing, and buildings tumbled. *Fire! Fire! Scum. Scum.*

"Mother!"

Marco pulled her hand.

The creature slammed into her.

Those claws drove forth, cutting through flesh, impaling, emerging slick with red blood and steam that soon froze, wafting away, wisps of frost like fairies, like her soul fleeing.

The scum pulled its claws free, and Mother fell onto the snow, her blood red in the white like poppies.

"Fire!"

Machine guns—pattering. Jets—screaming. Hot, searing metal blasting forward, and the smell of it. Of gunpowder and war and smoke. The great centipede seemed almost to dance as the bullets tore into it, cracking armored segments, bursting out with yellow blood. The arthropod fell as its comrades scuttled along the street, and the soldiers of the HDF ran and fired their guns and streamed across the sky in their machines.

Mother . . .

Marco knelt above her, tears in his eyes, the lenses of his gas mask fogging up. He clutched her hand. It was already growing cold. He touched her rubber cheek.

"Mother . . ."

The holes gaped open across her torso, four of them, a neat row like oversized red buttons. She leaked into the snow. There was so little blood this way, only poppies and frost.

"Mother!"

Marco tore off her gas mask, exposing her pale face, her staring eyes, and her hand was frozen in his. He tugged her hand. He pounded her chest.

Wake up. Wake up!

Dead. Dead.

In the snow ahead, creatures stirred. Creatures rose. Two of them, claws sinking into the snow, long as swords, curved, moving together, propelling forward on segmented, armored bodies, mandibles dripping. So hungry. Moving toward their prey. They would scavenge if they could not hunt. They approached.

Marco rose to his feet, breathing heavily through his gas mask. He stood over his mother, fists clenched.

"You will not take her." His voice shook, and tears clung to the lenses of his mask. "You will not eat her. You will—"

He gasped as something grabbed him from behind. He spun around, heart leaping, and saw her there. A girl in the snow, perhaps eleven like him, maybe twelve, tall and skinny and blond, peering at him through a gas mask.

"Come with me, idiot." She pulled him.

He recognized her. Addy Linden. A girl from his school, one from the "troubled children" classroom, that room at the back the other students feared. Her father had just come out of prison, they said, a truck driver who had crashed while drunk, killing two kids. Addy was wild and troubled, a girl who laughed too loudly, who fought in the halls, who smoked in the bathroom, who always bled from skinned knees and elbows and made others bleed.

"My mother—" Marco began as the creatures scurried closer to the corpse.

"She's fucking dead, you idiot." Addy yanked him. "Come with me or die with her."

He slipped in the snow. Addy pulled him onward, moving away from his mother. The scum scuttled toward the body, ready to feed, and their claws rose, and their mandibles descended, and Marco cried out and tried to free himself.

"Addy, I need to go to her." He tried to run back. "She might still be alive. She might still need me. She—"

"They're dead." She slapped him hard, cracking the lens of his mask. "They're fucking dead. All of them. Our parents are dead. Come with me. Come with me and live."

And then Marco saw them behind Addy, only a few feet away. Two corpses, tall and burnt, their skin peeling and fluttering like scraps of charred paper, their gas masks melted, their blond hair caked with blood. A dead centipede lay beside them, ten feet of armor and claws, curled up and riddled with bullets.

Her parents.

Marco nodded. Hand in hand, Addy and he ran.

They leaped over strewn bricks, fell into snow, rose and ran again. Above, the dark ship vanished into the clouds, the last of its eggs spawned onto the world, but the jets of the Human Defense Force still screamed, and their missiles still streaked down like comets. Another building fell, and soldiers in white uniforms ran, firing their guns, tearing down another scum, and a man shouted, "One missing! One fled down 7th!" And a hundred soldiers ran. And Marco and Addy ran the other way.

A sign rose ahead from the snow, red and blinking and glowing like those lights from the old stories. The snow had melted to reveal the stairs plunging underground. Marco and Addy ran so quickly into the darkness he slipped on the wet steps, would have fallen had Addy not held him up. At the bottom of the staircase stretched the tunnel, the place where the trains sometimes ran, where thousands now crowded together, thousands of rubber faces with glassy eyes, thousands of round mouths, thousands of breathing damp souls in gas masks, staring, the flickering neon lights reflecting in the lenses.

Addy and Marco wormed their way through the crowd. They stood against a wall, waiting, silent. The people pressed against them, silent too. A radio crackled to life. A man spoke through speakers on the ceiling, comforting, voice deep and smooth, the man Marco had grown up with, the man he had never met, the man whose voice he had heard more than his own.

"Fifteen pods landed on Yonge Street, Toronto. Fifteen *scolopendra titaniae* exterminated. All clear. All clear." Following his voice sounded a long, mourning wail like a life-support system after the patient had died. All clear.

The people pulled off their gas masks, faces and hair damp with sweat. A few laughed. Two teenagers kissed deeply, pawing at each other, and an old man grumbled. A couple of women in ragged cloaks chattered in a foreign language and argued over a bag of clams. A few people climbed back into the world, and a train screamed along the tracks with a fountain of sparks and light and smoke and rust, and hundreds boarded. Life resumed in the cold, in the heart of winter, in what remained of the world.

But not for us. Not for my mother.

Marco's eyes swam with tears. Addy pulled off her gas mask and glared at him with hard red eyes, but then her lip quivered, and she pulled him into her arms. They held each other in the subway station, nearly crushing each other, eleven years old and lost as the world clattered and grumbled on.

CHAPTER TWO

He walked through the library on his last day of freedom, seeking a book to take into hell.

He was eighteen. He was that horrible age. He was that age they all dreaded, the birthday nobody celebrated, the number they whispered with the voice of mourners. *Eighteen.* Two syllables. A breath at the back of the mouth, a tap of the tongue on the palate, a shiver down your back. Eighteen. The day they came. The day they took you away. The day you left home and entered the inferno.

Marco walked between the bookshelves here in his library, the last library in Toronto, among the last in the world. For eighteen years—that horrible number again—he had lived in the apartment above this library. He and his family were stewards to these books, generational librarians like an ancient dynasty tasked with maintaining a crumbling kingdom long past its golden age. The bookshelves stretched alongside Marco, forming canyons in the shadowy hall. Books stood on the shelves like soldiers, like the soldier Marco would become tomorrow. Small, dusty paperbacks. Heavy hardcovers with torn jackets. Leather-bound tomes with golden spines. Most were from before the Cataclysm fifty years ago, before the skies had opened, before the scum had ruined the world. Marco had read hundreds of these books, had spent his life reading them. Most books written before the Cataclysm were funny, exciting, scary, delightful. Those written in the past fifty years were mournful, tears watering every word like rain brings forth every flower.

He walked, passing his hands over the familiar book spines. It was Sunday. The library was closed. The library was almost always closed, even when the doors were unlocked, even as the world rolled by outside and light shone and some semblance of joy filled the city. Barely anyone read books anymore. They stared at their phones and listened to their headpieces and looked through their glasses of augmented reality, and mostly they forgot. Forgot what it meant to be human. To have humanity. Some days Marco barely knew the difference between the normals and those born to parents who had inhaled the miasma of the scum, born with shrunken skulls, dead eyes, pendulous lips.

"A funny book." He paused by a shelf. "A book full of jokes and anecdotes and life and laughter. I'm going into hell. Let me bring a little piece of heaven."

Hell? He inhaled deeply, thinking of those he had seen come back from that realm, five years older on paper, five centuries older inside. Some had returned missing limbs. All had returned missing their joy. Many never returned at all. Hell? Yes. The HDF. The Human Defense Force. The global military created to fight the scum. The gauntlet all humans from every last corner of this ravaged Earth entered at eighteen, then spent five years in the fire.

Marco inhaled deeply and placed his hand on a book. Five years? How to choose one book—just one title—to carry in his pocket for five years? How to—

The library doors creaked open, and sunlight washed the library.

"Marco?"

He turned around and saw her enter, bringing with her the sun and air. Within an instant, Marco's anxiety faded, the visions of war retreating under her light.

"Kemi," he said, walking toward her.

She smiled at him, her teeth bright, her cheeks dimpled, the smile he loved. The granddaughter of Nigerian immigrants, Kemi Abasi had soft brown eyes and a mane of curly hair. She wore a gray sweater vest over a white collared shirt, charcoal trousers, and the necklace he had bought her last month for her own eighteenth birthday. The silver amulet was shaped as the Greek letter pi. He loved words; she had always loved numbers. He was writing a novel; she dreamed of charting the distant galaxies. Her cardboard box, containing her gas mask, hung against her hip. She had painted it blue and decorated it with golden stars. Most youths their age decorated their government-issued boxes, turning them into elaborate cases that shone and jangled. Marco's was still plain cardboard.

He wrapped his arms around Kemi, and they kissed.

"Hey, silly." She mussed his hair. "It's your last day with me. Why are you lurking in the shadows like Gollum?"

"What's taters, precious?" he asked her.

She laughed but Marco cringed inwardly. Her words lingered. *Your last day with me.*

"Come, you hobbit." She held his hand and tugged him. "I have a gift for you."

As she turned and pulled him toward the door, Marco winced.

Fire flashed before him.

Snow stung him.

She's fucking dead! Bullets rang and Addy grabbed his hand, yanking him. *Come with me or die with her!*

"Marco?" Kemi turned back toward him, wreathed in sunlight. "You coming?"

He nodded, letting those memories fade. It had been seven years since that day, and still whenever somebody pulled his hand, Marco was back there in the snow and fire.

Holding hands, Marco and Kemi stepped out of the library onto the city street. Maple trees grew along the sidewalks, and red and golden leaves rustled and glided down. Despite the chilly air, many people walked outside. It had been several days since the last scum attack—several days to breathe without a gas mask, to feel the sunlight, to live again upon the surface of the world and not in bunkers and subway tunnels. Before the Cataclysm, Marco knew, twice as many people had lived in Toronto. Twice as many people had lived in the world. These streets had brimmed with cafes, restaurants, pubs, theaters, pockets of laughter and life. Today, many of those old buildings housed garrisons of the HDF. Soldiers stood on rooftops, peered from windows, and patrolled the streets. A massive transporter rumbled down the street, carrying two tanks on its back. The city shook as a sonic boom rattled windows and silenced all sound, and a jet streamed overhead, missiles thrusting forward like fangs.

Toronto. It was past its golden age but still home to three million civilians and soldiers, among the largest cities left in the North American Alliance, a bastion of civilization and might in a crumbling world. It was the only city Marco had ever known, the city he would leave tomorrow at dawn, would not see for five years, perhaps never again.

"So where's my gift?" Marco asked.

Kemi still held his hand. She gave him that smile again. "Not yet. First we eat." She patted his belly. "It might be a while until you enjoy a good meal again, so I'm fattening you up today."

They walked through a playground, past swings, laughing children, maple trees, and soldiers with machine guns and hard eyes. She took him into *Siddhartha*, one of their favorite haunts. Two burly guards stood at the door, machine guns in hand. They gave Marco and Kemi cold looks, seeking the lavender curse, then nodded and stepped aside. Marco held the door open for Kemi. The scent of curries and fresh naan bread greeted them, and they entered to find a golden statue of Ganesh, artwork of the Hindu pantheon, and a smiling server in a white apron. For two hours, they ate, stuffing themselves with butter chicken, tangy mutton stew, and steaming flatbread, ending their meal with green tea ice cream.

"I'm so stuffed I won't need to eat for five years," Marco said.

Kemi nodded. "Mission accomplished."

Marco looked around him, then back at her, and his eyes stung. "I'll miss this place." He reached across the table and touched her hand. "I'll miss you. I wish that . . ." He lowered his head. "I wish we could run. Just you and me. Before you're drafted too this winter. Run to the south and—"

"Marco!" Her eyes flashed, and she glanced around nervously, then back at him. "You shouldn't—" She sighed. "I know you're scared. I'm scared too. But we're going to be amazing, Marco. We're going to see the stars."

He smiled mirthlessly. "You will. They'll send you to fly a fancy spaceship and patrol the solar system. I'll end up cleaning latrines somewhere on a desert base surrounded by inbred mountain men."

She laughed. "Good. We need somebody to defend the world from inbred mountain men." She blinked tears away. "Come with me, Marco. No fear today. No tears. I want our last day to be good. To be happy. To be a day to remember."

Bullets blazed. The scum fed on his mother. Addy gripped his hand. *She's fucking dead, she—*

He swallowed hard, shoving the memory aside.

No fear today, he thought. *No tears.*

They walked outside again, passing by more soldiers, by civilians carrying their cardboard boxes, by schoolchildren who ran and laughed, by racing dogs. Several days since the last attack, and on a cold autumn day, the city flourished. Marco tried to imagine what it had been like here before the Cataclysm, before Earth's first contact with an alien species, before the *scolopendra titaniae*—the scum from space—had slaughtered sixty percent of the world's population and plunged humanity into this war. It must have looked, he imagined, a little like this fall day.

Marco and Kemi were walking by an old movie theater when an orange blaze filled the distant sky.

Sirens blared.

They froze, opened their boxes, and pulled on their gas masks. Across the street, people pulled back manhole covers and leaped into the public bunkers. Every city block these days had a public bunker. Soldiers wore their own masks and loaded their guns. Kemi made to race underground, but Marco held her hand.

"Wait." He pointed. "It's just three pods. Far. By the lake."

They stood together outside, only soldiers remaining around them. The sirens still wailed, rising, falling. The first pod streamed down toward the city and fell with a crash that shook the streets. Even here, a good two kilometers away, the buildings trembled and the ground cracked and Marco's ears rang. Another pod slammed down. Another. Windows rattled and one shattered nearby, spraying glittering shards. Gunfire sounded in the distance, and fighter jets streamed overhead.

"Just three pods," Marco said again. "Just three scum inside."

Across the streets, the soldiers' radios crackled to life. The deep, soothing voice emerged, that voice Marco had grown up with. He heard snippets. Three centipedes. Battle raging. Casualties. Fifty-two civilians breathed the miasma. Twenty-three civilians and four soldiers slain. Battle raging. Battle raging. All the scum are dead. All is clear. All is clear.

Across the city, the siren smoothed out, becoming a long wail with one note, then fell silent. All was clear. The people emerged from the bunkers. The city lived on—harder, quieter, colder now. Twenty-three people fewer. No more laughter sounded.

"It was five days," Kemi said, voice strained, and her hand tightened around his. "It was five fucking days they gave us. They couldn't even give us a week?" Her eyes dampened. "For once, they couldn't give us just one week?"

Marco stroked her hair and kissed her cheek. "Remember what you told me. No tears today. Today is for us."

She nodded, sniffing, and embraced him. "Today is for us."

They walked on through the city's oldest cemetery, many of its graves dating back to the nineteenth century. There were no parks in the city anymore, not like in the old days. They had all been converted into military bases. Mount Pleasant Cemetery was the only green lung left in Toronto, and countless trees grew along its pebbly paths: purple Japanese maples, rustling elms, birches and ash trees with white bark, twisting oaks, proud pines, and many other species. Statues of nymphs and angels frolicked between the ancient graves. Those slain in the war rested in smaller, crowded cemeteries outside the city. Here was a place for old souls, old ghosts from long before humanity had ventured into space, had found terror among the stars. Aside from the library, it was Marco's favorite place in the city. Like the library where he lived with his father, here was a place of old stories, old lives, memories from a better era.

As Marco walked, holding Kemi's hand, he thought about the tales the elders told. How the scum had ravaged the world in a massive assault, bombing and gassing city after city, wiping out billions—a year of inferno, of death, of humanity hurtling toward extinction. The elders still spoke with pride of how humanity had scrambled, bonded together, and launched their own warships into space. How ship after ship had perished until one intrepid pilot, the hero Evan Bryan, had launched a nuclear bomb against the scum's homeworld, slaying millions of the centipedes. The Cataclysm had ended that day. Humanity had emerged from the flames stronger, a civilization with the power to ravage distant worlds, to face its enemies in the depths of space and defeat them.

That day, the genocide had ended, and the long War of Attrition had begun.

They don't dare destroy entire cities anymore, Marco thought, looking around at the trees, trying to imagine that day when the fire had lit the world. *They know we'd nuke them in retaliation. They know that if they destroy us, we'll destroy them. So they simply hurt us. They torture us. Week after week, year after year, decade after decade, they decimate us. They cannot stab a sword into our heart, so they will torment us with ten thousand smaller cuts.*

A mother came walking down the pebbly path toward them, pushing a stroller. Inside drooled a baby with vacant eyes, his face the normal size but the head too small, the skull tapered. Those who breathed the gas that emerged from the pods often gave birth to these poor souls. Yet even these parents were the blessed ones. Usually, if you stood close enough to a pod to inhale the fumes, the scum's claws got you long before you could give birth. Marco knew that all too well. He knew that every night as he awoke washed with sweat from his nightmares.

Every hour the scum take a life somewhere in the world, Marco thought. *They kill us. They deform us. They dare not trigger mutual destruction, but oh, they can hurt us.* He inhaled deeply and raised his head. *And tomorrow I will learn how to hurt them.*

Marco and Kemi bought giant cups of coffee topped with whipped cream, and when it began to rain, they ran toward Kemi's apartment building. It rose ten stories tall, its bricks brown and its balconies white. As jets screamed overhead, they took the elevator to the top floor. They entered an apartment, elegant and clean and sparse. A family photo hung above the leather couch, showing a gray-haired man in a suit, a radiant woman in a red dress, Kemi in a sweater vest, and her older brother in his HDF uniform. Windows stretched from floor to ceiling, showing the city skyline. Smoke still rose by the lake where the pod had landed, where twenty-three people had died only an hour ago.

"My parents are in Colombia again," Kemi said, her voice quiet yet seeming too loud in the silent apartment. "It'll be four years this Tuesday."

Marco looked toward a bedroom off the hallway. Inside, he could see a poster of the Toronto Blue Jays, a globe, and a model of a Firebird starfighter, the model Kemi's brother had flown. Marco had never met Kemi's brother, but he had walked by his room many times, had looked at the photograph of the handsome, uniformed pilot whenever he visited the apartment. Ropo Abasi now rested in a military cemetery in South America with hundreds of other soldiers who had died that horrible day four years ago, their base attacked by a rain of scum plasma.

"You didn't want to go with them this year?" Marco said.

Kemi shook her head. "I went the first three years. I only have another two weeks until I myself enlist. And I only have this last day with you." She held his hands and kissed him. "I wouldn't miss it."

Enlist, she had said. Not drafted. *Enlist.* Every year, the HDF drafted millions of youths across the globe. Those who refused service were cast into a prison cell for their five years of service. Marco wasn't going to enlist tomorrow morning. "Enlist" implied a choice. Marco didn't want to fight. He didn't want this endless cycle of violence: attacking the outposts of the scum, blasting their organic starships like floating sacks of meat, firing at their pods whenever they landed on Earth. He wanted to remain in his library, to keep working on *Loggerhead,* his novel, to mourn his mother rather than avenge her.

He wanted to say all of this to Kemi. But he felt like a coward. He felt like a traitor. He knew that she wanted to fight, to carry on the family legacy, to excel in the military like she excelled at school, like her brother had excelled. So Marco said nothing. She smiled and kissed him again.

"What about that gift you promised me?" he said, voice a little too low, a little too hoarse, and he hoped she didn't hear the pain, the terror of what awaited him tomorrow, the mourning emptiness of losing her for five years.

Kemi pulled him down the hallway, past the bedroom with the Blue Jays poster, and into her own bedroom. Classical music from the late twentieth century was playing—her favorite era of music, one all but forgotten by now, nearly two centuries later. She pulled the curtains shut, then pulled off her sweater vest, collared shirt, and trousers. She stood before him in flaming red undergarments that crackled like real fire, and by all the stars above, she was beautiful. She was so beautiful that it hurt him. She was so beautiful that Marco could barely breathe.

She kissed his lips. "I am your gift," she said. "I want us to finally do it. To finally make love. I want to send you off with this memory."

Marco had kissed Kemi many times since meeting her three years ago, since that day in math class when she had helped him with his equations. Over the past year they had begun to make out under the blankets, naked, always shying away from the full act. Today they kissed hungrily, and he pulled off his clothes, and he stroked her cheek and gazed into her eyes. She smiled at

him, eyes damp. Her playlist reached an old favorite of theirs—
"Lavender" by Marillion—and the irony of its title, the same color
of the scum miasma, did not evade Marco.

"I'm scared," Kemi confessed, naked in his arms.

"You're the most beautiful woman in the world," he said.
"And I love you."

She caressed his hair. "I love you, Marco."

They kissed again—a kiss that tasted of her tears, and their
bodies pressed together, and they did what they had never dared,
joining together on this last day. Marco could never afterward
remember how long it had lasted, whether they had sex for two
minutes or two hours. It passed in a heady blur of heat and lust
and nervous laughter, and when it was done, they lay side by side
on the bed, the blanket pulled over their nakedness, and sweat
coated them.

"That was amazing," Marco said.

She gave him a sidelong look. "You sound surprised."

"Whenever you hear stories about the first time, it's about
how awkward it is, how it never works, but that was . . . amazing."

He lay on his back, and Kemi rolled onto him and stared
into his eyes. She cupped his cheek in her palm. "When you're out
there, Marco, no matter what happens, no matter how scared you
are, no matter how hard things are, remember this time we had.
Remember my kiss." She kissed his lips. "Remember we had this
last good day." Her tears fell. "Goodbye, Marco."

Marco frowned. Journey's "Separate Ways" came onto the
playlist, the bass and drums pounding.

"Not our last good day," Marco said. "We'll have many more good days. This isn't goodbye forever."

She looked away from him, a tear on her cheek. "Oh, Marco. I love you so much." She looked back into his eyes. "Listen to me. If you meet another girl in the army, you can love her like you love me. You can make her happy, like you make me happy."

His frown deepened. He rose in bed, and she rolled off him. They sat side by side, still naked, the blankets around their waists.

"Kemi, what the hell?" He held her hand. "I'm going to make *you* happy. I'm going to love *you*. I don't want anyone else. It's goodbye for now, but you'll be joining the HDF in just two weeks." He attempted a smile. It tasted sour. "Who's to say we won't be stationed on the same base?"

Her long, curly hair hid her face. She spoke softly. "There are three hundred million soldiers in the HDF, Marco. The odds of us meeting there aren't good."

"So we'll wait five years." He took a deep breath. "We'll write to each other. We'll talk on the phone whenever we can. When we're out, we'll only be twenty-three, and—"

"Marco." She leaned against him. "Marco, I have some news. I was accepted to Julius Military Academy." She glanced up at him, half-afraid, half-excited. "I was in the top five percentile of applicants. I won't be enlisting with everyone else."

Marco's eyes widened. Julius was among the most prestigious military academies in the North American Command.

They had trained most of the famous officers, generals, and war heroes. Few were accepted to Julius. Fewer graduated from it.

"That's fantastic," he said. "I'm proud of you."

She blinked, eyes damp. "If I graduate from the Academy—and I will graduate, Marco—I'll be an officer, not an enlisted soldier. I'll have to serve for a minimum of ten years. Maybe even twenty." Her tears flowed again. "I'm sorry, Marco, but . . ." She embraced him. "We may never see each other again. I'm so sorry. I love you so much."

Marco stared at her, silent, and outside the jets screamed, twenty or more, racing past the window, ripping through the sky, roaring, howling, booming, and the windows rattled and the shelves shook and a book fell, and the music drowned under the roar. The lights flickered, vanished, flared again with white, searing intensity like sunlight on knives.

Marco rose from the bed. He dressed quickly, fingers numb.

"Marco." Kemi rose to her feet, the blanket wrapped around her. "Please. Don't leave mad."

He left the bedroom. He walked through the apartment, passing by the photo of her family, of her brother who had fallen in the war, of the family he had wanted to join, of a life ending, his life—his old life, who he had been for years, torn away in the searing light, washed away in the sound and fury.

When he reached the front door, Kemi caught his arm. She stood wearing a long T-shirt showing Hendrix in purple haze.

"I love you," she said.

He wanted to leave. To storm out. To walk down the street, empty, leaving the shrapnel of his heart here in this apartment like shards of glass, to let her step in them, cut herself, forever hurt for what she did to him. But he looked into her dark liquid eyes, and damn it, he shouldn't have looked, because now all his rage melted away, and damn it, he loved her, and damn it, he couldn't breathe again, and damn it, it hurt too much. Too much. He held her close, and she wept against him. He kissed her forehead.

"Goodbye," he whispered. "I'm proud of you. I love you. Always. You're going to be amazing."

He pulled back slowly, their bodies parting until only their hands touched, then their fingertips, arms reaching out as if neither could tolerate breaking contact, and when their fingertips finally parted, it was like breaking electrical circuits, like light and heat and air fading, like a perfect machine collapsing, like civilizations dying, like realities fading into emptiness. His last vision of Kemi was her standing in the doorway in her Hendrix shirt, hair disheveled, lips trembling, her fingers still reaching toward him.

He walked down the street at sunset. The radios crackled in the storefronts and apartments all around him, a tunnel of deep, calming serenity. All was clear. All was clear.

CHAPTER THREE

At sundown Marco stepped into his home, the apartment above the city library, only for a beast to leap onto him and knock him down.

He banged his hip on the floor. Weight shoved against him, pinning him down.

"Marco Emery, you son of a bitch!" The shout rang in his ear. One strong hand twisted his arm behind his back, and knuckles rapped against his head. "Are you ready to kick scum ass with me tomorrow, you filthy alien killer?"

Marco groaned. "Get off!" He shoved her away. "Addy, for chrissake. That hurt."

Addy grinned, her blond hair wild, her blue eyes bright. "Good!" She rose to her feet and placed her hands on her hips. "You need some pain. You need to toughen up. We're going alien hunting tomorrow morning, my friend." She drew the gun at her hip, pointed it at him, and pulled the trigger. It clicked and she laughed. "Don't worry. No bullets. Yet."

"Damn it!" He stood up and shoved her gun away. "You don't do that. You pull that shit in the military, they'll toss you into the brig."

Addy breathed heavily through her grin. Seven years ago she had saved his life, pulling him away from the scum that had slain his mother and her parents. Since then, Addy had lived with Marco and his father here above the library. The scrawny eleven-year-old kid with skinned knees had grown into a tall, wild woman. She wore cargo pants, heavy black boots, and a white tank top that revealed a blue maple leaf tattoo on her arm—logo of her favorite hockey team. A hockey stick hung across her back, the same one she used on the ice every day, playing for a local team—and spending most of her time in the rink punching her fellow players.

Marco sighed. Seven years of living here above a library, the adopted daughter of a studious librarian, had done nothing to soften Addy. She was still as fierce as the girl who had saved Marco, just taller, stronger, and armed.

"Oh, don't worry, little brother," she said. "Once I'm in the HDF, I'm going to point my gun only at scum. I'm going to blast them away."

She holstered her weapon, pulled her hockey stick off her back, and swung it wildly. Marco leaped back, and the stick slammed into a shelf, knocking over a jug. Marco caught it before it could shatter.

"Careful!" he said.

Addy ignored him, swinging her hockey stick. "That's right, little one. Pow!" She swung the stick at a plush scum on a shelf, knocking the fluffy centipede onto the floor. "I'm going to kick their asses." She kicked the toy, and it squeaked.

"I'm not sure they have asses," Marco said.

Addy shrugged and kicked the toy. "Then I'll kick them in their . . . thoraxes. Better?" She spun toward him, grabbed his arms, and hopped up and down, grinning wildly. "We're going to be soldiers tomorrow, little brother. You and me! We're going to finally have vengeance." Her eyes shone. "We're going to blast those fuckers off the face of the galaxy."

Marco sighed. Addy was two days younger than him, which didn't stop her from referring to him as her "little brother." For years now she'd been talking about joining the HDF, about avenging her parents. When she and Marco had received their draft notices earlier that year, her excitement had only grown. They were to be drafted on the same day, along with hundreds of other youths across the city. But while Marco had spent the year afraid, Addy had spent it beating up toy scum and firing unloaded guns at anything that moved.

"Get out of the way, Addy." Marco tried to shove past her. "I'm going into the kitchen to find some food."

But she blocked his way, arms crossed. Addy was as tall and heavy as him, and she spent her days slamming into men twice their size. Marco wasn't going anywhere unless she moved.

"Wait a minute." She frowned. "You were out all day. Did you see . . . your girlfriend?" She sniffed him, then gasped. "You did! I smell her perfume. Did you finally sleep with her?"

"Addy!" He shoved her. "For God's sake. Shut up."

She covered her mouth, then leaped up and down. "You did. You did!" She leaped onto him, twisting his head, and mussed his hair so violently he thought his scalp would tear off. "I'm proud of you. You're a man now. A man who fucks girls and will kill scum and—"

"Enough!" He shoved her with all his strength, finally knocking her off. "I don't want to talk about Kemi. I don't want to talk about scum. Just . . ." He sighed. "Please, Addy. Give me some space tonight."

But she slung her arms around his neck, jumping up and down. He trudged toward the kitchen with her hanging off him like a tenacious monkey.

The kitchen was small, its cabinets cracked, its counters cheap laminate. An animated painting hung on the wall, depicting a hand cracking an egg over a frying pan, only for a chick to emerge and flee. Over and over, millions of times, that chick kept emerging and fleeing, only for the egg to seal itself up again. *Which came first?* read a caption below the animation. Marco hated that painting. He knew that his father hated it too. His mother, however, had delighted in kitsch, and they'd never had the heart to throw out her belongings. Her cat clock still hung on one wall, tail and eyes moving, while a golden statue of Michael Jackson and his pet chimp, Bubbles, stood on a shelf. Every time Marco stepped into this kitchen, he winced to see the awful artwork, then smiled to remember his mother.

Marco's father stood in the kitchen, frying burgers. Even in the hot kitchen, he wore corduroy pants and a woolen vest. His hair was shaggy, his mustache bushy, and round spectacles hung on his nose. Marco's hair was shorter, his face smooth, his eyes sharp, but many people said he looked like his father. Certainly he was more like the rumpled librarian than his mother. Grace Emery had been a ray of sunshine, red-haired and silly, while Marco had his father's brown hair and somber eyes that loved to gaze into books.

"Where's the beer?" Addy yanked the fridge door open, nearly tearing it off, and began tossing out tomatoes and apples. "Junk, junk—ah! Here we go." She pulled out three beer bottles, pulled the tops off with her teeth, and slammed them onto the table. "Drink with me, boys."

Father slid the burgers onto buns and placed three plates on the table. He looked over the tabletop at Marco, saying nothing. Marco stared back, silent. They rarely talked to each other, but they communicated volumes with their silence. It had been so since Mother had died.

It's funny, Marco thought. *I'm writing a novel, and Father is steward to billions of words, yet we can barely string a sentence together to speak to each other.*

Addy raised her bottle. "To kicking scum ass!" she said.

Marco and Father raised their own bottles. They drank. Father had always preferred rye or wine to beer, but tonight he too drank. Molson beer. Addy's favorite. Both she and Marco were too young to legally drink, but Marco figured that if tomorrow they were old enough to fire machine guns and starship cannons at man-eating aliens, a beer wouldn't hurt them.

When their bottles were empty and their plates clean, Father finally spoke.

"It will be all right." His voice was soft, calm, but Marco knew that the librarian was struggling to keep it steady, to keep his eyes dry. "I survived it. I did my five years, and I was fine. I still have some friends who have friends in the HDF. If you get stuck in some hole, in Ganymede or Titan or North Africa, I'll make calls. I'll—"

Addy snorted. "We'll be fine, Carl. Marco and I aren't going to be stationed in some shithole like Ganymede, guarding latrines for five years. No, sir." She brandished a knife. "We're going to fight on the front lines, both of us—right there in the Scorpius constellation. We're going to fly right at those scum and fire our bullets into their stinking thoraxes." She slammed the knife into the tabletop. It stayed standing, quivering.

"Addy, this table is real oak," Marco said. He turned toward his father. "We'll be all right. We'll have fun. I want to do this."

He was lying. This was not all right. This was not what he wanted. He had left his heart in Kemi's apartment, he had left his soul in the bloody snow seven years ago, and he wanted nothing more than to crawl down into the library, to feel the comfort of the books around him, to read, to work on the next chapter in *Loggerhead*, to drown himself in ink and paper and other worlds. Old worlds. Worlds better than this one where giant bugs rained from the sky, where lavender poison polluted your balls and made your kids born deformed, where healthy kids got carted off to war, where every day that soothing voice on the radio spoke of those who had died. It was all wrong. It was nothing he could change. It cracked him apart.

"Don't worry, pops." Addy slung her arm around Marco's neck, pulling his head against her. "I'll look after him. If he does anything incredibly stupid, I'll save his ass and win a medal." She nodded, growing somber. "This war's about to end, boys. We're going to win it. I'm going to be the one to fire the winning bullet and slay the scum emperor."

The food soured in Marco's belly. He had eaten too much, and only one bottle of beer spun his head. He rose from the table, excused himself, and went into his bedroom. He closed the door.

The room was small and comfortable. A window above the bed showed a view of treed residential streets behind the library, and three of his paintings hung on a wall. Several books rested on his bedside table. They told him he wouldn't have time to read in the army, wouldn't have room for books, but he would take just one, just one, small enough to squeeze into his pocket. He picked up a paperback in his room, a copy of *Hard Times* by Charles Dickens. He had read a few Dickens novels this year— *David Copperfield* was his favorite—and had been meaning to read this one, but he'd always found himself stuck on the first chapter. He nodded.

"This is the one. *Hard Times*." He smiled thinly. It was a bit melodramatic, perhaps. But he wanted this book less for its title, more for what it meant. It meant home. His old life. The authors he loved. He placed the book on his desk atop the pile of notebooks where he was writing *Loggerhead*, his first novel. He didn't know if the HDF would let him keep the notebooks, didn't know if he could fit them into his backpack, but if he could, perhaps he would spend the next five years writing. At least when he wasn't dodging scum claws, and worse—dodging Addy.

His eyes strayed toward the framed photograph on his desk. It showed Kemi last summer, leaning against a lion statue, one eyebrow raised and a smirk on her face. Kemi had always hated the photo, claiming Marco had caught a silly facial expression, but Marco loved it enough to have framed it, to look at it every day. To him, this was Kemi—quizzical, cynical, intelligent, both silly and smart.

Now, looking at the photo, he wanted to smash the glass, to rip the photo, to toss it out, to forget her. He lifted the frame, clutching it so tightly he thought it would shatter. Finally, delicately, he pulled the photo out from the frame, then slid it into his paperback copy of *Hard Times*.

He stripped down to his boxer shorts, turned off the lights, and lay in bed. For a long time he stared up at the ceiling, thinking about tomorrow, uncertain what to expect. His father had been born with a heart murmur; he had avoided boot camp and combat duty, instead spending his service in the HDF archives. Marco hadn't grown up hearing tales of war. Kemi's brother had been a great soldier, but he had died before Marco could meet him. As the apartment and city outside grew silent, as the night stretched on, Marco couldn't silence his mind. Again and again he saw Kemi reaching to him, eyes damp, saw Addy firing her blank gun, saw the pods raining down toward the lake, saw his mother in the snow.

Finally he drifted off into a dream. He was back in the kitchen, staring at his mother's animated painting of a chick emerging from the egg, at the cheeky *Who came first?* caption. But in his dream, when the egg cracked open, a centipede emerged, its body black and segmented, each segment sprouting two claws. The creatures kept fleeing the painting, more and more of them each loop in the animation, covering the floor, filling the pots, and Marco tried to fight them, but they kept climbing his legs. They all had his mother's face.

A sound roused him. A soft light fell on his face.

Marco froze, lying on his back. He opened one eye and saw his door creak open, revealing light in the hallway. Addy stood there in her pajamas, her hair pulled into a ponytail. Marco stiffened, ready to leap out of bed, to defend himself if she tried to bend his arm again, to knuckle his head, to wrestle him. But Addy only tiptoed into the room, closed the door, and stood for a long moment over his bed. Marco lay very still, eyes narrowed to slits, pretending to still sleep.

Addy was shaking. A tear glistened in the moonlight that streamed through the window.

As Marco lay very still, she climbed into bed with him and wrapped her arms around him.

"I'm scared," she whispered, her tears dampening his cheek. "I'm scared, Marco. I'm so scared. I'm so scared."

He remained with eyes closed, feigning sleep. He knew that in the morning Addy would be her old self, swinging her hockey stick and vowing death upon her enemies. Or no, perhaps not her old self, not her true self, but the old mask, the old armor. With his eyes closed, Marco rolled to face her, and he slung an arm around her. She nuzzled close to him, crying softly, and he held her against him until she slept. He slept only fitfully until dawn, her breath soft against his neck.

CHAPTER FOUR

It was unusually hot the day Father drove them to the HDF spaceport. The sky was pale blue, and the sun beat down even as dry leaves still fell from the maples and oaks that rose among the city's skyscrapers. They took the 404's lowest level through the urban jungle. The second, third, and fourth layers of the highway stretched above them, rattling under the weight of their own cars. Marco rode shotgun while Addy sat in the back, legs stretched out and slung over the gearbox, a cigarette dangling from her lips. The family car was a dented, rusty Toyota Feline, a model that had gone out of style the moment it hit the assembly line. It stank from tobacco, and the floors were still stained with last winter's salt and sludge, but Marco would miss riding here. He stared ahead, watching the soldiers in the armored jeep before them, machine guns slung across their backs. He could barely believe that in a few hours he'd be a soldier too.

Nobody spoke.

Once past the downtown core, the highways spread out into a single, flat, massive road. They drove now through the industrial complex, the sprawling machinery that operated the city. Factories, warehouses, airports, and row after row of barracks rose around them, a hive of concrete, barbed wire, guard towers, and smog. No more trees grew here. A fighter jet flew overhead, so low over the highway that Marco could see the pilot as the plane tilted. Its fuselage displayed the symbol of the Human Defense Force: a flaming phoenix rising from ashes, symbolizing Earth rising from the Cataclysm. The jet soared with a sonic boom that rattled the windows and elicited honks from the thousands of drivers.

"I've always loved that logo," Addy said from the back seat. "The phoenix. Fierce."

"I've always thought they should just show a picture of the Earth," said Marco.

Addy snorted. "It's the Human Defense Force, Poet. They defend humans everywhere in the galaxy, not just Earth. But if you like, you can just serve in Earth Territorial Command and stay here planetside. But not me. I'm going to blast scum in space. I'm joining the STC, the Space Terri—"

"I know what STC means," Marco said.

Addy was talking too fast again, bragging and puffing out her chest, a sign of her fear. Marco was afraid too, but he preferred to deal with his terror in silence. He checked his backpack for the hundredth time. He had bought only a couple of days' worth of clothes, a toothbrush, his book with the photo of Kemi inside, pens, and a few notebooks—one with the first few chapters of *Loggerhead*, the rest still empty. Addy hadn't even taken a backpack, just a toothbrush and pack of cigarettes in her pocket, and she had spent the morning scoffing at Marco and telling him that the HDF would give them everything they needed. Marco didn't need much more than reading and writing—and perhaps Kemi, but that was a part missing from him now, still painful like a phantom limb.

He could see the spaceport in the distance now. Fifty-odd rockets rose like skyscrapers, their surfaces shimmering in the sunlight, dwarfing a complex of warehouses, offices, and scuttling cars. Traffic slowed them down as hundreds of cars waited to enter the port. While Addy chewed bubblegum and prattled on about blasting aliens, Marco looked into the other cars, saw other parents, other children, more recruits, more fodder for the war.

It was another hour before they reached the gates. Several female soldiers stood here, hair pulled into ponytails, berets on their heads. They wore olive-green uniforms, their pants bloused above heavy boots, and T57 submachine guns hung against their hips. They looked no older than eighteen or nineteen. Marco stared at the insignia on their sleeves, unable to interpret it, wishing he had spent time studying HDF hierarchy.

One soldier tapped the window, and Father rolled it down.

"Here for recruitment," Father said.

"Trunk," said the soldier.

Father nodded and popped the car's trunk, and two more soldiers rifled through it as Father handed over Marco and Addy's paperwork. The soldier studied the papers, eyes stern, then gave the inside of the car another look. In recent years there were stories of scum loyalists on Earth. The wilder stories claimed the loyalists were clones, grown on the scum's planet using human DNA. Marco still remembered how an alleged clone had blown up an armory a couple of years ago, how he could see the mushroom cloud from home.

"Terminal 7B. Go," said the soldier, and they drove onward, entering the spaceport.

Marco tried to ignore the horses stampeding through his stomach.

They drove between smaller rockets, heading toward 7B and the massive chrome rocket that rose there, twenty stories tall, the logo of the phoenix plastered across it. Technicians stood on scaffolds, and service cars zipped back and forth. A metal fence rose around the rocket, and a few hundred people stood in a courtyard by a car park. A sign stretched across a squat concrete building: *HDF Recruit Terminal 7B.*

They parked and emerged into the heat. A couple hundred youths stood here, carrying backpacks, their families and friends with them. A few girls were crying and hugging while a few boys stood together, chests puffed out, speaking of how many scum they'd kill. One boy stood on a platform outside the building, doing his best attempt at an Elvis impersonation, singing "Hound Dog" and swaying his hips. Several youths scoffed while watching the show. A few soldiers, looking bored, guarded the fence that surrounded the rocket. That metal edifice soared above them all, reflecting the sunlight.

We're not blasting into deep space yet, Marco reminded himself. *This is just a suborbital rocket to take us to another place on Earth. They don't train soldiers in space. It won't be months until the darkness.*

He had never been to space before. Space was dark and cold and dangerous, and few civilians lived out in the colonies. Millions of civilians had once lived across the solar system and the stars beyond. Millions had died in the scum attacks. Today there were still millions of humans in space, but they were now soldiers of the STC, the space corps of the Human Defense Force.

Most soldiers, blessedly, simply served on Earth. Marco wasn't sure if any gods existed, but right now he prayed that he'd end up serving Earthside. He looked at the soldiers guarding the fence—just boys and girls, probably not yet twenty. Maybe they'd let Marco serve here in Toronto, guarding some rocket or roadblock. Maybe on weekends they'd let him go home, back to his library to keep working on his novel. That wouldn't be too bad.

He turned toward Addy. She still wore her cargo pants and the white tank top that revealed her blue Maple Leafs tattoo, a fresh cigarette dangled from her lips, and her hockey stick still hung across her back.

"I don't think they'll let you take your stick," Marco said. "You better—"

A screech and smell of burnt rubber interrupted him. A blue sports car halted with a puff of smoke, and four hulking teenagers leaped from within, all wearing hockey jerseys.

"Addy, you scum-killing bitch!" one of them shouted. "You weren't going to go butcher aliens without saying goodbye, were you?"

All four boys leaped onto Addy, and soon they were laughing and swapping punches. One of the boys pulled out cigarettes and a pack of beers, and they cracked open bottles.

Marco sighed. Smaller and quieter, he had never felt comfortable among Addy's towering, drunken friends. Thankfully, the brutes ignored him, and when one of the boys—a beefy giant with shaggy brown hair—locked lips with Addy, Marco turned aside. He felt queasy. He knew that Addy had been dating a fellow hockey player this year, but the sight of them kissing disturbed him. Strangely, Marco felt jealous. He didn't have romantic feelings for Addy—the girl was like a sister to him, had been living in his home for seven years now. And Marco loved nobody but Kemi, wanted no other woman in his life. And yet . . . Yes, that kiss hurt him to see. He thought of how Addy had lain in his arms last night, how they had slept holding each other, and oddly, again he felt his heart cracking, like he had felt yesterday when Kemi had broken it.

He forced the thought out of his mind. In a few moments he would join a massive, galactic army dedicated to fighting vicious, superintelligent alien centipedes with claws like swords. He had greater worries than who Addy kissed.

He looked around him at the other recruits, seeking familiar faces. He knew a handful of these boys and girls from school, by face if not by name. A few girls stood in a circle, holding hands, praying softly. One boy was brandishing a plush scum doll, similar to the one Addy had at home. Another boy, scrawny and balding at eighteen, stood apart from the crowd, reading *Lord of the Rings* through massive spectacles. A few girls and larger boys were pointing at the bookworm and scoffing, and Marco felt both pity and relief—pity for the outcast, relief that he himself was not, perhaps, the most awkward recruit here.

They take everyone, he thought. *Hockey brutes and bookworms. The strong. The scrawny. The brave. The frightened. Fighters and singers and nerds. If you can pull a trigger, you can kill the scum. If you can't, you're good fodder.*

Marco stepped closer to his father. They both pointedly ignored Addy who still seemed determined to suck out her boyfriend's tonsils.

"Remember, the thriller and mystery shelves are still out of order," Marco said.

Father nodded. "They'll be sorted by the time you're back home."

Marco wanted to say so many more things. He wanted to tell his father that he loved him. To hug the old man. To talk about Mother. To talk about how he was scared. But the words all jammed in his throat. He could say nothing, only stand there, awkward and stiff, his stomach twisting. He tried to curb the instinct to run. You couldn't run from the HDF. If you tried to dodge your draft, they found you. They always found you, and you spent your five years rotting in a dungeon. If Marco had to rot away, he would prefer rotting in the belly of a scum. At least it would be warm.

"Nice Elvis," he finally said, and for a few moments father and son stood still, faces blank, watching the boy in the leather jacket who was still swaying his hips on stage. He was singing "Jailhouse Rock" now, largely ignored by the other recruits and their families.

"Hello, ladies and gentlemen!" A voice rang through a megaphone, and a soldier stepped onto the stage, shooing the Elvis impersonator back into the crowd. "Welcome to the HDF Recruit Terminal!"

The speaker was a young woman, perhaps in her early twenties, with dimples and a brown ponytail. She too wore olive fatigues and boots, and a handgun hung from her hip, similar to the one Addy kept at home. A golden pendant shaped like a butterfly hung around her neck. Scattered applause sounded as the crowd turned toward her.

"I'd like to give out a warm welcome and hug to our new recruits!" The soldier with the butterfly pendant reached out her arms, her smile growing. "Today you begin a new part of your lives. Today you begin a journey to become all that you can be, to make your planet proud. Thanks to your courage, your families and friends can sleep well tonight, knowing that you will protect them. Welcome to the HDF!" The soldier paused for more scattered applause. "At this time I ask all family and friends to take a moment, to part from your brave recruits, and to return home with the knowledge that your loved ones join the warm, loving family of the Human Defense Force."

Marco looked at his father. For the first time in his life, the rumpled librarian hugged him. And for the first time in his life, Marco saw tears in his father's eyes.

"It's not forever." Father's voice choked, and he held Marco close. "It's not forever. Remember that. It's not forever."

Marco blinked, overwhelmed, confused, unable to speak. Sniffing and drying his eyes, Father hugged Addy next, then left with the other families and friends. One by one, the cars left the parking lot, leaving only a couple hundred recruits on the pavement. The rocket loomed above them.

The pretty, smiling soldier with the megaphone retreated into the concrete building. Several tall, powerful men in uniform emerged to replace her, holding electric batons.

"All right, you sons and daughters of whores!" shouted one soldier, his arms massive, his eyes blazing with malicious amusement. "Your mothers are gone now. The HDF is the only mother you have now. Form three lines! Go!"

"That's more like it," Addy muttered, moving closer to Marco. "I was about to hurl when Ms. Butterflies gave us a hug."

"Move!" shouted another soldier, stepping toward the recruits. He raised his baton, and the tip crackled with electricity. "Three lines, you fucking maggots!"

"Marco is more of a larva than a maggot!" Addy said.

Marco cringed. "Addy, shush."

A few recruits smirked. One was trembling and weeping. Most were silent and pale. Marco tried not to worry. He had seen enough drill sergeants in movies to realize this was just an act. The recruits formed three lines in the courtyard, facing the fence and the rocket beyond. A handful of recruits still lingered outside the formation, talking amongst themselves.

The soldiers moved in, batons raised.

A boy screamed as a baton drove into his stomach, crackling with electricity. Another soldier drove his baton into a girl outside the lines. She fell, and a boot slammed into her belly.

"Up!" a soldier shouted.

"Move, worm!" roared another, shoving a boy forward.

"Form the lines!" a third soldier roared, spraying saliva.

So much for it being an act, Marco thought.

"Do you think we are your teachers?" shouted a towering soldier with short red hair, swinging her baton. "Do you think we are your mothers? Your days of fun are over! You're soldiers now. Move! Move or we will shove these cattle prods so far up your asses your teeth will melt. Move!"

A soldier opened a gate in the fence around the rocket. Marco cringed as the three lines of recruits began to march, moving through the gate. A girl beside him was weeping. A few other recruits were still chuckling, trying to hide their laughter behind their palms. Behind Marco, Addy whispered, "I'm going to have fun here, I think."

"Silence!" shouted a soldier.

"Cry and we'll dry your tears with our shockers!" a soldier shouted in the face of a weeping girl.

The batons crackled, goading the recruits onward, shocking anyone who slowed down, spoke, laughed, wept, or did anything but march silently. The weapons weren't lethal, but when Marco lost his step and one drove into his side, he ground his teeth together so hard he thought they'd crack. It fucking hurt.

Addy was having the time of her life, judging by her smile and shining eyes, but Marco much preferred Ms. Butterfly's style.

They walked across the tarmac and climbed a staircase into the rocket. A vertical fuselage greeted them. Ring after ring of seats rose in many tiers, filling the rocket. Marco counted twenty stories before the seats faded into shadows far above. A ladder rose in the center of the rocket, allowing the recruits to climb. Marco climbed high, preferring to sit as far away from the engines as possible, finally finding a seat near the top of the rocket. Addy sat down to Marco's right. Marco imagined that his face was pale, his eyes sunken, but Addy positively beamed.

"Almost time to kick scum thoraxes," she whispered, eyes alight, but Marco didn't miss her fingers nervously clutching her pants, and he did not forget her tears and trembling last night.

More and more recruits came climbing up the ladder and taking their seats. Several girls sat across the rocket's fuselage ahead of Marco. Their eyes were red, and one was rubbing her side where her clothes were singed. That was a baton's mark, Marco realized. Another girl, tears on her cheeks, kept talking about how her father was wealthy and powerful, how he would save her, but she fell silent when a soldier glared at her from below.

The seat left of Marco creaked, and the entire tier of chairs jostled. Marco turned his head to see the oddest boy he'd ever seen settling down beside him. He barely looked human. The boy's brow slanted backward, his jaw thrust out in an underbite, he had no chin to speak of, his nose was squat and heavy, and thick eyebrows shadowed beady black eyes. His legs were stubby, but his torso and arms were massive. He looked, Marco thought, like a Neanderthal. The boy stared ahead with blank eyes, silent, lips tight.

Marco was about to introduce himself when soldiers came climbing the ladder.

"Silence!" one soldier shouted.

"Any one of you maggots talks, I bash out your teeth!" bellowed another.

The tall female soldier with the red hair smirked. "Fasten your seat belts, you pretty little whores, or we'll be mopping you off your friends' laps in about thirty seconds."

Marco and Addy fastened their seat belts. When Marco glanced to his left, he saw that the brutish boy with the heavy brow was still staring ahead, silent, hands clasped together.

"Your—" Marco began, then bit his lip as a soldier climbed toward them. Gulping, Marco reached over and silently fastened the Neanderthal's seat belt.

No sooner had Marco pulled his hands back when the engines roared.

The rocket trembled.

Marco inhaled deeply. Addy reached out and clasped his hand.

"I'll look after you, Marco," she whispered, squeezing his hand, blanching. "I promise."

With a deafening roar and screaming flames and shrieking metal, the rocket launched. Marco closed his eyes, jostling in his seat, and pressed his head as hard as he could against the headrest. He clenched his jaw and prayed to keep his breakfast down. As they soared through the atmosphere, as the rocket rattled and blazed, he clutched Addy's hand.

Goodbye, Father, he thought. *Goodbye, Kemi. Goodbye. Goodbye.*

CHAPTER FIVE

There was only one window in the rocket, a narrow slit above the rings of seats near the cockpit doors. Sitting at the top tier, Marco watched the blue sky fade to black and stars appear. His gut calmed as weightlessness filled the rocket. If not for their seat belts, the recruits would have floated out of their seats.

Personal items—cigarette packs, toothbrushes, travel-sized bottles of shampoo, even a dirty magazine—floated out from recruits' backpacks and filled the fuselage. Marco tightened his own backpack, mortified at the idea of his *Loggerhead* manuscript ending up in another recruit's hands. A hockey puck floated out of Addy's pocket. Marco caught it for her. A soldier climbed the ladder in the center of the rocket, collecting the floating items and stuffing them into a vacuum bin, eliciting groans from those recruits who lost their possessions. Addy elbowed Marco hard in the ribs, pointed, and grinned at a floating, elongated toy that made Marco blush.

When the last of the items was retrieved, silence fell, and for long moments the rocket floated above the atmosphere. When Marco craned his neck back, gazing toward the viewport, he could see the rocket turn, and the stars gave way to the curve of the earth, then patches of blue and white as they floated above the ocean. They were several hundred kilometers up, it seemed, somewhere among the satellites. This was not a starship. This rocket could not take them into deep space. It was far too small, far too simple a machine. Here was a suborbital carrier, designed to travel between continents, able to arrive anywhere on Earth within half an hour.

For a few moments they floated just above the sky.

The heavyset boy beside Marco, the one with the slanting brow and underbite, sat very still, stiff, and silent, his bushy eyebrows pushed over his beady eyes. Suddenly he whipped his head around toward Marco and grinned—a huge, joyous grin, full of crooked teeth. His hands pressed together in delight.

"If I were in the Amsterdam Floating Flower Market right now," the boy said, voice slurred, "I would buy such a bouquet!"

Marco smiled thinly. "That's ni—"

"Silence!" shouted a soldier, floating up toward them, electrical baton raised. Marco and the boy beside him shut their mouths.

After only a few moments in space, they began to descend, and incredible g-forces yanked at Marco. He gritted his teeth, struggling to remain conscious. Flames blazed outside the viewport as they reentered the atmosphere. Farther down the fuselage, a boy lost his breakfast, eliciting cries of disgust and laughter from the recruits as the goo floated up. The rocket rattled, screamed, blazed, spun, and the fire vanished, replaced with blue skies. They seemed to be slowing down, and Marco threw up a little in his mouth, gulped hard, and winced. He groaned, wanting to lie down, curl up, and shudder for hours. A few recruits seemed to have passed out.

A few moments later smoke covered the viewport, and the rocket shivered, swayed, and finally thumped down. Scattered applause rose through the fuselage. Shouting soldiers and buzzing batons silenced them. The entire trip couldn't have been longer than half an hour, Marco estimated, but with suborbital flight, that meant they could be anywhere from Africa to Fiji.

Or maybe, he thought, glancing at the boy at his side, *Amsterdam.*

They emerged from the rocket into chaos.

Hundreds of other rockets rose around them, and thousands of recruits—still in their civilian clothes—were spilling out onto the hot tarmac. Jungles rustled around the spaceport, and the caws and squawks of birds were so loud they nearly drowned the engines. Marco had thought the day warm back in Toronto, but the heat here pounded against him like blasts of air from a hot bellows. When he took a few steps, it felt like walking through soup, and sweat soaked him.

Addy stepped into formation ahead of him. The recruits formed three lines as the soldiers patrolled with their batons, shocking anyone who fell out of formation. Across the tarmac, other groups were doing the same. Fire blazed in the sky, and flame and smoke enveloped the world, and engines roared, and another rocket landed on the tarmac. More recruits spilled out.

"March!" shouted the red-haired soldier, the one who had shocked Marco back at Toronto. The recruits began to move.

A concrete wall rose ahead, topped with barbed wire. A sign above the gateway read: RASCOM.

As she marched, Addy looked over her shoulder at Marco. "RASCOM!" she said, eyes shining. "Reception and Sorting Command. We're in Chile!" She bit her lip, looked forward, and kept walking as the red-haired soldier moved closer.

Marco marched behind her in formation. He'd heard of RASCOM, but just snippets of hushed conversation back home. Veterans didn't like talking about this place. He had heard scarred, battle-hardened men say that RASCOM—where soldiers were first welcomed into the Human Defense Force—had been the toughest few days of their service.

The recruits marched through the gates, entering the sprawling military base. Marco's eyes widened. The base was massive. It spread for kilometers ahead, an entire city of barracks, towers, hangars, and armories. Jets streaked overhead, and armored vehicles clattered down the streets on caterpillar tracks. The flags of the HDF thudded in the hot wind, proudly displaying the phoenix. The recruits halted as lines of uniformed soldiers, several hundred strong, marched across an intersection before them. In a dusty field on the roadside, hundreds of recruits shouted "Yes, Commander!" at a soldier, faces red and chests thrust out. It felt even hotter in here, insects buzzed everywhere, and sweat stained Marco's clothes and dripped down his legs and back.

They marched through the base, three lines of recruits, following the red-haired soldier. Several other soldiers moved at their sides, batons ready to goad them back into formation. Marco wished he could think of them as more than just "soldiers" and identify their individual ranks. Over the past few hours, he'd heard talk of "sergeants" and "lieutenants" and "corporals" and "privates," but he didn't know what those meant. He couldn't interpret the insignia he saw on the soldiers' uniforms, wouldn't understand the hierarchy even if he could. To him, he and his comrades were recruits, still in their civilian clothes, and everyone else in this base was a different breed, as alien to him as the scum.

Speaking of scum, he thought, gazing ahead at a massive scum that rose in a small fenced yard. His heart leaped before he realized it was just a stuffed specimen. Even so, it was damn imposing. It had been mounted on metal rods into a rearing position, like a cobra about to strike, twice Marco's height. Its body's segments were black and shining. The exoskeleton was harder than steel, he knew, impervious to all but the most powerful weapons. But worse than its size or armor were the legs. Thirty-six of those legs thrust out from its sides, two sprouting from each segment, tipped with claws as long and sharp as scimitars. The mandibles that crowned the creature seemed tame by comparison to those rows of blades.

Looking at the dead alien, it was easy to mistake it for just a big bug, but these bugs were sentient, as intelligent as humans if not smarter. With their mandibles they could construct organic starships composed of sticky membranes and hardened shells, could clone human spies, could control technology even humanity hadn't yet developed.

The *scolopendra titaniae*. The scum. They were a race of apex predators who had been sweeping across the galaxy, destroying civilizations in their path. And now Earth lay on that path. Fifty years ago they had nearly destroyed Earth, killing billions of humans in the Cataclysm, reducing the population by sixty percent. The Cataclysm had ended with the nuke lobbed onto the scum's planet, but the War of Attrition raged on. The scum had not forgotten their quest to destroy humanity, even if they had to destroy it one human at a time.

Fifty years ago we nuked them, Marco thought. *We killed millions of them. We showed them that we will not die easily. That if they destroy one of our cities, we can destroy one of their hives. And still we fight.*

And strangely, for the first time that day, Marco felt his fear fade, felt some pride in humanity. Service would not be easy. The next few days, maybe even the next five years, would be hellish. But damn it, here—all around him—was humanity fighting back against the bugs. And Marco would be a small part of that. He was only a writer, not a warrior, but if he could do his part to stave off the scum, he would give it his all.

Though if I could still serve in the archives like my father, instead of actually firing guns at these bugs, that would be preferable, he thought as they walked by and the scum's shadow fell onto him.

They had to leap to the roadside as several tanks rolled by. Farther down the road, monkeys swung from towering pehuen trees, hurling nut shells down at the recruits and hooting in laughter. Soldiers stood outside concrete barracks, gazing at the new recruits. One soldier whistled and hooted. The recruits walked on. They passed by a yard where a hundred uniformed soldiers congregated. They looked like fresh-faced recruits who had just received their uniforms—there was no insignia sewn onto the sleeves—which didn't stop them from scoffing.

"Look at the fresh meat," one soldier said.

"Scum fodder!" cried another soldier.

The group laughed, then fell silent and stood at attention as a ranked commander approached. Soon the group was shouting "Yes, Commander!" and drilling in the dust.

Marco noticed that, despite the thousands of soldiers he passed, he barely saw any guns here. Only the ranked soldiers, those with bars or stars or chevrons stitched onto their uniforms, carried weapons. The vast majority of soldiers here were mere recruits. They wore uniforms, but they had no insignia or guns. Some must have been here for only days, maybe just hours.

Marco noticed, too, that the uniforms here were different than those he had seen soldiers wearing back home. The soldiers who patrolled Toronto's streets wore finer uniforms, the green cotton ironed, the buttons polished, and they wore berets. The uniforms here looked like . . . well, they looked like rags. Holes had been cut into the armpits. The fabric was tattered, sometimes threadbare, the color all but washed away. Barely anyone wore anything that fit. Marco saw soldiers with baggy uniforms and some with uniforms so tight they threatened to pop their buttons. Their berets hung under straps on their shoulders, not on their heads.

"Addy," he whispered as they marched, leaning toward her. "What's with the ragged uniforms everywhere?"

She glanced over her shoulder at him. "BDUs. Battledress. Rags. Fatigues. Call them what you like. It's what the HDF wears in their bases." She grinned. "Soldiers only wear the nice stuff in public. Sort of how you wear pajamas at home but pull on your old man corduroys when you go to the coffee shop."

"They're not pajamas," he said, "they're sweatpants, and—"

He grimaced as electricity crackled across him. The tall soldier with the red hair dug her baton into his side, snarling. "I hear you talk one more time, soldier, you'll spend the next week rotting in a dungeon. March!"

The soldier pulled back the baton, and Marco marched on, wincing. Addy flashed him a quick grin and winked.

You're loving this, aren't you, Addy? he thought, and suddenly a lump grew in his throat. After his brief moment of patriotism, an icy blend of fear, homesickness, and despair flooded him. He couldn't even imagine doing this—marching, shouted at, shocked—for the rest of today, let alone the next five years. When he passed by a public clock, he learned that, despite everything he'd been through today—and it felt like ages—it was only 8:14 in the morning.

Normally I'd still be asleep, he thought. *And here I am, tasered and shouted at and marching through a massive military base in South America.*

They marched by concrete barracks, electrical towers, and a yard of armored vehicles topped with machine guns. Ahead in another fenced yard, Marco saw a sight even more impressive than the dead scum farther back. Two spaceships sat in the yard, both burnt and dented yet—judging by the fence and armed guards—still quite valuable.

Marco recognized one of the vessels at once. It was an L16 Firebird. An actual L16 Firebird, and one that had seen service, judging by the burns and dents and scrapes. Marco had owned several Firebird models as a child, but he'd never seen one in real life. These weren't like the jets that constantly screamed over Toronto, defending the North American Command's skies. No. While Firebirds did sometimes fly in Earth's skies, they were primarily space fighters, single-seater assault spaceships, the deadliest weapons humanity had. An early-model Firebird had nuked the scum's planet fifty years ago, ending the Cataclysm and ushering in the ongoing War of Attrition. To this day the Firebirds and their brave pilots battled the scum as part of the STC, the Space Territorial Command. Marco had never even met anyone who'd served in the STC, only soldiers of the Earthbound ETC. Only the elite fought in space, hitting the scum in their own backyards.

He turned his eyes toward the second craft in the yard. He couldn't help but shudder as he marched by. This one was a scum ship. It barely looked like a ship at all, more like an organic, veined egg. The scum didn't use metal for their crafts but pliable materials they spewed from their own bodies, the way spiders could excrete gossamer and clams could produce pearls. The walls of these alien pods looked like skin, but they were harder than steel.

"Looks like a giant, purple testicle, doesn't it?" Addy asked.

Marco dared not reply, not after suffering a shock last time he had spoken, but he was inclined to agree.

Firebirds. Scum pods. War in space.

As Marco kept marching, he just prayed to stay on Earth, as far away from the scum as possible.

* * * * *

The chirps of insects grew, but whenever a recruit tried to swat the tiny bugs away, they earned an electric shock. Marco resigned himself to tolerate the biting critters. Finally they reached yet another squat concrete building, one of thousands that filled this base. Brutalism—an old and much-reviled architectural movement, mostly involving blockish buildings of raw concrete— was obviously still in style here in the HDF.

With shouts and electric prods, the commanders hustled the recruits through the doorway. A crowded, stifling room awaited them. The ceiling fans did nothing to cool the room; they just roiled the heat and stench of sweat. Hundreds of recruits stood here, stripped down to their underwear, both male and female. A few soldiers in drab uniforms were shoving carts full of civilian clothes.

"Strip!" shouted the red-haired commander, her crackling baton raised. "Clothes and shoes in the carts, now! Keep your underwear only."

"What if somebody's going commando?" asked a recruit, a tall boy with spiky dark hair.

"You've got hands, right?" the soldier said. "Cup 'em!"

Reluctantly, Marco removed his corduroy pants and T-shirt, remaining in his boxers. He couldn't help but sneak a glance—just a glance!—toward Addy. Back home, she had never let him see her unclothed, and he couldn't help but notice her—

No. He shook his head and looked away. Ridiculous. He would not think of Addy that way. Especially here, he had no time for such thoughts.

"Men to the left, women to the right!" barked a balding, paunchy soldier in a corridor. "Line up for inspections! Go!"

"Now!" shouted the red-haired soldier.

Addy poked Marco's naked chest. "Maybe you'll grow some hair in the army." Before he could reply, she winked, stuck out her tongue, and went to line up with the girls.

It was a long, hot, miserable wait among thousands of other eighteen-year-old boys. All stood in their underwear—aside from one boy who kept his hands firmly on his privates. Some tried to talk, only to be silenced by the uniformed commanders. Finally, when Marco felt ready to faint from the heat and thirst, they rushed him into a small room. A heavyset, bald doctor sat there, looking utterly bored. The man checked Marco's vitals, then had him drop his boxers. Marco cringed as the doctor squeezed his balls, but he thanked God that the HDF didn't yet require prostate exams.

As miserable as Marco felt with a strange man grabbing his little scum pods, he thanked his lucky stars. *I'll probably just spend the next five years battling giant centipedes, not spending every day in a sweaty room grabbing balls.*

In the next room, a technician sat Marco down in a chair and covered said balls with a lead apron. The man then wheeled a massive, clicking machine toward Marco. The machine featured a large cone, like those in old barbershops.

"What's this?" Marco said.

The technician was a wiry man in an olive-green uniform, missing one leg. "We just need to x-ray your teeth."

Marco frowned. "Why? My teeth are in perfect health."

The technician nodded. "And they might be the only thing left after the scum hit you. If you want your grave to feature your name, we need to recognize you by your teeth." He gave Marco a sparkling, toothy smile.

Marco cringed. "If the teeth are the only thing left, how would you even bury me?"

"Well, sometimes there's a bit more left, but we'll need a mop and a bucket." He plunked the cone down around Marco's head like a helmet. "Say cheese!"

Marco smiled grimly as the X-ray machine clattered and hummed.

As he moved room to room, subjected to test after test, poked and prodded, Marco wondered how he'd ever find Addy again. Countless recruits were moving through these halls in their underwear, and whenever they herded him to another room, Marco scanned the crowd for a tall, blond girl in Maple Leafs underwear, but to no avail.

Goddammit, he thought, ice washing his belly. Addy was the only person he knew in this military of three hundred million soldiers. If he couldn't find her now, he might not see her for years, just like Kemi.

Kemi.

As Marco sat in a chair to have his hair buzzed off and inspected for lice, he thought back to his girlfriend. His ex-girlfriend now, he supposed. He thought of Kemi's mane of black curls that always smelled so good, her smiling lips that he loved to kiss, her warm eyes, her fierce intelligence, how she could speak for hours about math, classical music, and space yet still enjoy a cold beer on the couch and an episode of *Robot Wrestling.* He missed holding Kemi, kissing her, reading to her the latest chapter of *Loggerhead,* dreaming of a future with her. Again his damn tears stung his eyes, and the lump grew in his throat. He had to swallow hard, to remind himself that he was a soldier now—or about to become one somewhere in this maze they called RASCOM—and would fight the scum. What kind of alien-killing warrior cried from homesickness and a broken heart?

The examinations continued. In a crowded room full of hundreds of recruits, a soldier moved between them with a clipboard, examining and taking notes of their levels of acne. In a room full of teenagers, there was a lot to go around. When he was done, the soldier with the clipboard stood at the back of the room, calling out different maladies, asking recruits to raise their hands if they had ever suffered from them.

"Syphilis!" the soldier called. "Shingles! Herpes!"

Chuckles sounded in the room as a few soldiers, faces red, hesitantly raised their hands. The soldier kept calling out illnesses, marking down names on his clipboard. Marco hadn't even heard of many of those diseases.

"Hemorrhoids!" the soldier called out. "Has anyone here ever had hemorrhoids?"

Awkward laughter rolled through the room, amplified when one recruit, cheeks crimson, sheepishly raised his hand.

"What's hemorrhoids?" asked a massively muscular, bald recruit, speaking with a heavy Russian accent.

"If you had them, you'd know," answered the soldier with the clipboard.

"I had lots of things, how can I know?" said the bald Russian. "What is it? What is hemorrhoids? Why you no tell me?"

The soldier with the clipboard seemed suddenly embarrassed, but another recruit groaned beside the Russian.

"It's when your ass hurts and you can't sit down," the boy said.

"Ah!" said the Russian. "No, ass is okay. *Niet problema*."

Finally the interrogation was completed. With shouts and crackling batons, soldiers herded Marco out from the crowded room.

He found himself trudging through an open courtyard—barefoot and still wearing only boxers, his hair shaved down to stubble. Soldiers stood around the perimeter, guns in hand, while hundreds of half-naked recruits stumbled across the hot asphalt toward a second concrete building. Monkeys hooted from a tree as if mocking these poor, naked apes. One of the guards whistled appreciatively at the "fresh meat." The girls rejoined them here, their own hair spared the razor. Marco sought Addy in the crowd but couldn't find her.

The new building was a massive warehouse, large enough to store rockets in, filled with row after row of shelves and counters. Millions—it had to be millions—of uniforms covered the shelves, a sea of olive green. Higher up, countless black boots spread across wooden shelves, enough boots to blister the feet of nations.

"Recruits!" shouted a tall soldier with tanned skin and one arm. "Grab a duffel bag, two uniforms, and boots—then out into the yard."

"Yes, Sergeant!" a handful of recruits replied.

Sergeant. Marco stared at the one-armed soldier. He saw three chevrons stitched onto the man's single sleeve. He remembered seeing some soldiers with one chevron or two chevrons.

So sergeant is the third rank, Marco thought, wishing he had spent less time reading Dickens and writing *Loggerhead* and more time researching the military. He bet that Kemi knew all this and more. Addy too, probably. Everyone but him, the bookworm son of a librarian with that lump that wouldn't leave his throat.

"Duffel bag! Uniforms! Boots!" shouted a man behind a wooden counter. "Move, damn it, ten minutes and out in the yard!"

Marco crowded with a hundred other half-naked, sweaty soldiers, both male and female, struggling to reach the counter and grab his supplies. All the while the sergeant shouted, pestering them to move faster, to step out into the yard or end up in the brig. Finally, blessedly, the one-armed soldier moved toward another counter to howl at the recruits there.

Marco rifled through the uniforms on the counter, finally finding pants and a shirt his size. Both were, as Addy had put it, indeed rags, stained with years of sweat, the armpits split open, the hems frayed. At another counter he grabbed leather boots that were horribly uncomfortable, and he could already imagine the blisters they'd give him. He watched a few other soldiers, then imitated how they bloused their pants, rolling the hems inward into rubber bands—supplied along with the pants—leaving the entire length of the boot exposed. Finally he grabbed a green beret.

Next, he approached a counter where a soldier was distributing duffel bags. Marco grabbed one. It was essentially a sack with a single shoulder strap, olive green and so large Marco could have fit inside. It was heavy. When Marco opened the duffel bag, he found it stuffed with supplies. There was shoe polish, a sturdy brush, a few pairs of underwear and socks, an empty canteen, a bar of soap, a flashlight, a gas mask, a first aid kit with some disturbingly large bandages, and possibly more items lurking beyond Marco's reach. Everything aside from the bandages and soap looked secondhand, and he wasn't so sure about the soap.

Marco stuffed his own backpack from home into the duffel bag. But he stored his copy of *Hard Times*—and the photo of Kemi inside it—in his back pocket. He wanted to feel that book and that photo close to him, to remember that even here, with all this madness, there was a better world somewhere, a world of civilization and of love. Dickens had died centuries ago, and perhaps Kemi was as good as dead to him, but this book and photo still symbolized to Marco that humanity was capable of more than this, that the human spirit could achieve more than warfare, more than pain and fear and loneliness. He vowed to keep book and photo in his pocket at all times.

At his last stop, Marco approached a wooden crate filled with helmets—thousands of olive-green military helmets like horseshoe crab shells. Nettings topped them, perhaps to hold twigs and leaves for camouflage, and leather straps dangled from them. Hundreds of soldiers were clambering for helmets, and a sergeant was shouting at them to move, damn it, faster. Marco could barely even see the crate through the crowd, let alone browse for a helmet that fit. He simply reached between the other recruits and grabbed the first helmet he could reach. Nobody was even trying them on.

"Helmets into your duffel bags!" shouted a sergeant. "Move, move, clear room!"

Hoping his helmet would fit, Marco stuffed it into his duffel bag. He moved away from the crowded crate, desperate for air, and walked between shelves topped with blankets and sleeping bags, which nobody seemed to be taking.

Well, he thought. *Uniform. Boots. Duffel bag with supplies. Helmet. All I need now is a gun, and I'm a soldier.* He wasn't sure he liked that thought.

He was about to leave the warehouse, to find out what awaited him outside in the courtyard, when the voices rose behind him.

"Hey, you fucking caveman." A guffaw rose. "Look at the goddamn caveman."

Another voice snorted. "Looks like one of those homo erectus things."

A wail of fear rose, so loud dozens of heads turned— Marco's among them.

The boy who had sat beside Marco in the rocket was here. He was a towering beast, all fat over muscles, hunched over as if ashamed of his size, his neck thick, his head lumpy. Despite his mass, he wailed in fear, drooling, trying to fend off a group of smaller boys. When Marco had first seen him—the shelf of a brow, the sliding chin, the heavy lips, the beady eyes—he had instantly thought "Neanderthal," and now guilt filled him. Now he saw the humanity in the boy's eyes.

"I'm not a caveman!" he howled. "I'm Bruno. Bruno Fabian. I'm not a caveman."

"Maybe you're an ape," said one boy, smirking. "I didn't know they let apes into the army. Maybe they want to feed apes to the scum."

The smirking boy was among the shortest, scrawniest people Marco had ever seen. Marco himself wasn't very tall, but this boy barely stood taller than his shoulders. His teeth were crooked and protuberant, his cheeks sunken, his black hair spiked. But if the small bully's physique was not intimidating, his eyes were. Those eyes were black as deep space and cruel as the horrors that lurked in its shadows. If Bruno looked like a caveman, this diminutive boy looked like a wicked goblin from a fairy tale to give children nightmares.

"Good one, Pinky," said a girl with a mop of brown hair. "He does look like a fucking ape."

The short, scrawny boy—Pinky must have been a nickname—stepped closer to Bruno and kicked, hitting the larger boy's shin.

"Cry, Caveman!" Pinky laughed and shoved the larger recruit against the wall. "Go on, ape. Cry. Let's hear you cry for your mommy."

Marco had heard enough. He placed down his duffel bag and stepped toward Pinky.

"All right, guys, he's had enough," Marco said. "Let him be."

The bantam bully raised his eyebrows, those cruel eyes widening. Marco's suspicion had been correct; Pinky barely reached his shoulders.

"Well, looks like Princess Caveman found a knight to defend her!" Pinky placed his hands against Marco's chest and shoved.

Marco stumbled back, shocked at the little bastard's strength. He managed to steady himself and remain standing. Pinky stepped closer, raising his fists, and when his sleeves rolled back, Marco saw that those arms were all coiled muscles, tense and scarred. The tendons rose on Pinky's neck, and his crooked teeth thrust out in a snarl. His friends gathered around him—the girl with the brown hair and a handful of others, all tall and hulking yet clearly subservient to their Lilliputian lord.

Marco raised his open hands before him. "Hey, buddy, I'm not looking to fight you."

"Oh, but I thought you wanted to defend your lady caveman love." Pinky smirked at his own joke. Bruno, meanwhile, had fled the scene, and no sergeant was to be found. "Maybe you love fucking shaved apes." Pinky shoved Marco again, even harder this time, slamming him against a wall. "You might not want to fight me. You might think I'm weak. I know your type. Rich man's kid. Let me tell you something. Nobody fucks with Peter Pinky Mack. You got that?"

The boy swung his fist, aiming for Marco's jaw. Marco hadn't fought another boy since the third grade, but his instincts kicked in, and he blocked the punch on his forearm. It hurt like Planet Scum slamming into his bone.

"What's your problem?" Marco said. "I did nothing to you."

Pinky grabbed Marco's shoulders, yanked him forward, then slammed him into the wall again. "You mocked me. Your eyes mock me. You thought you could challenge me. You thought I was weak. You thought you were better than me." He punched again, and again Marco blocked the blow. "I'm going to teach you that no fucking rich boy can—"

Hands grabbed Pinky from behind and yanked him backward.

"Hey, pipsqueak!" Addy said, towering over the boy. "Why don't you pick on somebody your own size like a rat or cockroach?"

"Addy!" Marco said, relief flooding him. "I thought I'd never see you again."

He cursed his words as gales of laughter sounded from the bullies—and many of the onlookers.

"Oh, college boy found his own savior!" Pinky said. "A girl with sweet tits and—"

Addy's hand flew, slapping Pinky's cheek. The boy snarled and leaped toward her, fists flying. He managed to land a blow on Addy's jaw, and she growled and kicked him, knocking him back.

Marco took a deep breath. *Fuck.* Legs shaking, he acted against every instinct in his body. He leaped into the fray, reached for Pinky, and attempted to land his own blows. Damn it, for the first time since third grade, he was fighting, and—

"Enough, boys and girls, enough!" said a fellow recruit.

"You're gonna land us all in the brig!" said another. "Sergeant's coming over."

Quickly, a sea of recruits pulled the combatants apart. Pinky smirked as several recruits pulled him away. He spat and gave Marco and Addy a crooked smile.

"Pray you never see me again," he said. "Or my gun might just empty into your guts instead of the scum."

With that, Pinky shook himself free and marched off.

"Yeah, go run to your mommy, you fucking little cockroach!" Addy shouted after him, still gripped by a few large boys. "You try to attack Marco again, I'll fuck you up!"

"Addy, please," Marco said, keenly aware of the smirks around him, and he could just imagine the teasing he'd have to endure for the next five years. "It's all right. I was handling myself."

"Let go, let go!" Addy said, wrenching herself free from the recruits holding her. She turned toward Marco. "What a fucking cockroach."

Marco nodded. "Yes, well, we managed to defeat the evil Pinky. Good practice for the scum, and I can't imagine them any more loathsome." He looked around. "Anyone see where Bruno went?"

"The caveman?" said Addy. "Out in the courtyard already. Come on, Poet." She grabbed his hand. "Let's get going. I see the sergeant, and he looks more pissed off than Pinky trying to reach a urinal."

They stepped out into a massive asphalt courtyard, where thousands of recruits gathered in the searing sunlight, all wearing their rags and new boots. They waited in the heat as a potbellied, mustached soldier stood at a podium, calling out names through a megaphone. As each name was called, a soldier stepped up, shared a few words with the man, then hurried off down a road. Marco and Addy stood side by side, waiting for what felt like years.

"What's going on?" Marco whispered to her. Addy hushed him. Those damn sergeants were patrolling the courtyard with their batons, shocking anyone who spoke or so much as swatted a fly. Marco desperately needed to scratch the bug bites, but when he saw a recruit hauled off to the brig—all for the crime of scratching his nose—he remained standing at attention. The names kept ringing across the courtyard.

Marco realized that despite RASCOM being in South America, and despite the suborbital jets able to travel anywhere on Earth within half an hour, everyone here seemed to speak English. The Human Defense Force was a global military. Where were all the Chinese speakers, the Indians, the Africans, the *world?* He saw Americans, Brits, Australians, Jamaicans, a few Kiwis, even a few other Canadians, but that was about it, only a thin slice of the world's pie. He supposed that other cultures had their own units, that RASCOM only served those who could speak English,

Earth Alone

who could obey English orders. There must have been many sorting centers across the globe to recruit soldiers from the rest of the world's nations.

Finally the mustached man with the megaphone cried out, "Addy Linden!"

Addy gave Marco a look—a look that spoke volumes, that said *goodbye* and *I hope we meet again soon* and *I'm scared* and *goddamn this fucking war* and a million other things. Then she turned and walked toward the man at the pulpit. Addy spoke to him, but with the megaphone lowered, Marco couldn't hear, then she took something from the man. She gave Marco a last look across the courtyard, then raced down the road.

Marco felt empty.

A few more names rang out.

Finally—"Marco Emery!"

He left the crowd of thousands and approached the man. The heavyset, mustached soldier had three chevrons and two semicircles on his arms, a rank Marco didn't recognize.

"Marco Emery?" the man said, megaphone lowered.

Marco nodded. "Yes, sir."

"I'm not an officer. Don't sir me." He shoved dog tags into Marco's hand, then checked his notepad. "2nd Brigade, 5th Battalion, 42nd Company, 4th Platoon, 3rd Squad. Remember, that's two, five, forty-two, four, three. Down the road to the left. Go."

"2nd Brigade, 5th Battal—" Marco began, struggling to remember it all, but the soldier raised his megaphone and already

77

called out the next name. Marco cringed, his ears ringing. He hurried down the road, leaving the courtyard behind, uncertain where to go or what to do.

Two, five . . . what?

As he walked, Marco looked at his dog tags. Two metal disks on a chain. On each disk appeared his name and serial number. The number was larger. That's all he was now, he supposed. An X-ray of his dental signature. Metal dog tags and a number. Awful boots and rags. And in his pocket—a book from home and a photo of the girl he loved. Fodder for the scum. A cog in this machine of three hundred million centipede snacks.

He placed the dog tags around his neck and walked onward, seeking Addy.

CHAPTER SIX

The road led Marco toward a dusty field in the center of the base. Concrete buildings, guard towers, and barbed wire fences rose all around, framing the field, and jets roared above, leaving white trails across the sky. As morning gave way to noon—by God, had it only been a few hours since he had left his home in Toronto?—the sun beat down with extra zeal, and soon Marco's fatigues were soaked with sweat. Thousands, maybe tens of thousands, of recruits stood in this square, organized into units.

Marco tried to remember what the paunchy soldier with the megaphone had told him. 2nd Brigade, 5th Battalion, Company . . . 42? He cringed, not sure what a brigade, battalion, or company even meant. Again he wished that he had spent less time writing *Loggerhead* this past year and more time researching the HDF. A few other recruits joined him from the road, looking just as perplexed. There must have been a hundred different units ahead of him, slowly filling up with more recruits, and Marco had no idea where to go.

"Recruit, move!" a sergeant—Marco recognized that rank now, three chevrons on the sleeve—shouted at him.

"Sir, which—" Marco began.

"I'm not an officer." The sergeant raised his electric baton. "To your unit, now, or to the brig."

Marco looked ahead again, and he noticed that several flags rose in the field, displaying symbols and numbers. He walked between the units, looking at the flags. He saw pictures of jets, of planets, of moons, of swords, beneath them numbers. Finally he saw a flag labeled *42nd Company: Starfire,* which displayed a burning planet. A couple hundred soldiers stood here, organized into smaller units, perhaps fifty soldiers in each. In each unit, one soldier held a military standard.

4th Platoon. The words returned to Marco. He saw a standard displaying a black dragon on a red field over the words *4th Platoon: The Dragons.*

Marco stepped toward them, his eyes widened, and waves of relief flooded through him.

A tall girl with blond hair stood in the platoon, wearing olive fatigues, her duffel bag slung across her shoulder.

"Addy!" he blurted out, unable to help himself.

Oh thank God and the planets and the stars! Addy was assigned to his platoon! How was this possible? Was it because they had been born only a day apart? Because they had enlisted together? Because some kindly soldiers had done a background check and had known they were friends? Or just because they were damn lucky? Marco didn't know, but by the heavens, Addy was with him again, and in this strange, terrifying place, that was a blessing.

As Marco walked toward her, he saw that the platoon was divided into even smaller units—squads. He wasn't sure which squad to join, so he simply walked up to Addy and stood beside her.

"Hey, Poet," she whispered.

"Is this squad three?" he whispered back. He thought that's what the potbellied soldier had told him.

"Did you even choose the right company, or did you just walk right up to me?" she asked.

"5th Battalion, 42nd Company, 4th Platoon," he began, then realized he hadn't even checked the brigade. Damn it! He seemed to have gotten the battalion, company, and platoon numbers right, but . . . had he chosen the right brigade?

He was about to ask Addy when another recruit walked up toward them, and Marco's breath died. All his relief vanished.

Oh, fuck.

Pinky—that little bastard, Peter "Pinky" Mack—walked up right to their platoon and joined their squad. The snaggletoothed soldier gave Marco a look that dripped hatred, then stared forward again.

Fuck fuck fuck, Marco thought.

A few more recruits came to join the Dragon Platoon. Marco recognized a few familiar faces.

One was Bruno Fabian. Marco was a little embarrassed that he immediately thought "the caveman." The hulking soldier wore a baggy uniform and, despite his girth, swayed under the weight of his duffel bag. He came to stand in formation near

Marco, eyes dark, mumbling under his breath. Marco heard something about his daffodils back home needing plant food.

Marco also recognized the massive, hulking Russian from the medical building, the one with, apparently, no hemorrhoids. The recruit was huge, dwarfing even Caveman. His bald head was like a boulder, and his arms seemed the size of Marco's entire body.

"Hey, Beast," Addy said to the Russian.

The giant grunted at her. "*Zdravstvuy*, Canada."

Beast indeed, Marco thought, covered by the Russian's shadow. *He won't even need a gun. Can just crush scum in his bare hands.*

The last familiar face surprised Marco. It was the Elvis impersonator from back in Toronto, the one who had performed for the crowd that morning. The boy was shorter and thinner than the real Elvis had ever been, and somebody had shaved off his pompadour, but Marco still recognized the long sideburns. The recruit saw Marco looking and gave him a nod.

"Canada," Marco said. "Toronto. You sang."

The Canadian Elvis nodded. "Ain't nothin' but a hound dog." He gave a little karate chop.

The platoon seemed full now. Marco counted twice, once counting forty-five soldiers, another time forty-six. The flow of new recruits continued across the field, the other platoons, battalions, and brigades growing. Marco estimated that a platoon included about fifty soldiers, and four platoons formed a company. Battalions were huge, and brigades seemed massive. Marco saw only two brigades in the field, thousands of recruits in each one. He was thankful. That meant his odds of having chosen the right brigade were pretty good.

When the flow of new recruits into the field finally died down, and everyone seemed to have found their spots, a soldier—not a recruit but a real soldier with insignia on his sleeves—marched toward Dragon Platoon. He was a tall man with brown skin, heavy black eyebrows, and a turban. He wore a beard—the first soldier Marco had ever seen with a beard. His insignia displayed three chevrons—a sergeant. A rifle hung across his back, and a curved knife hung from his belt, the sheath gilded and the handle jeweled.

"Platoon Four!" the turbaned sergeant shouted with just the hint of an Indian accent. "Form ranks—trio formation!"

"Yes, Commander!" shouted a few recruits in reply.

The platoon formed three rows and stood at attention. Addy took the front row, Marco stood behind her, while Elvis—if he had a real name, Marco didn't know it—stood behind him. Other units of three stood at their sides. When the rows were all formed, the sergeant spat.

"Break apart!" he shouted. "Again! Faster! Three rows!"

The soldiers formed rank faster this time, snapping into place. The bearded sergeant nodded.

"My name is Sergeant Amar Singh," he said. "But to you I am more than a commander. I am your mother. Your father. Your god. Your devil. To you I am the entire world. Do you understand?"

The platoon shouted that it did, indeed, understand.

Sergeant Singh nodded. "Forget about your homes, boys and girls. Forget about your comfy beds, your boyfriends and girlfriends, your mommies, your cozy little lives on the outside. For the next five years, your asses belong to the HDF, and you are nothing but scum-killing machines. Understood?"

More shouts indicated understanding. Marco, however, doubted he could kill any scum. He thought back to those scum he had seen—the dead one here in RASCOM and the live ones that had slain his mother and Addy's parents. The aliens were terrifying, and while Sergeant Singh's gun was four feet long and impressive enough, it seemed like a mere slingshot by scum claws. Marco loathed the scum. He loathed them with every cell in his body capable of loathing. But perhaps killing them was best left for strong, wild warriors like Addy or intelligent, ambitious future officers like Kemi. Marco was just a writer, and not even a published one. Perhaps, he dared to hope, they'd let him be a war correspondent, and he could hone his writing skills reporting from battlefields rather than fighting in them.

Sergeant Singh pulled on augmented reality shades, tapped a button, and began calling out names.

"Recruit Peter Mack!"

Pinky—shorter than anyone else in the platoon—raised his hand. "Yes, Commander!" he cried out hoarsely, still smirking.

"Recruit Bruno Fabian!"

Caveman nodded. "Yes, Commander!" he rumbled.

"Recruit Benny Ray!"

This time Elvis—he had a real name after all—responded.

"Recruit Addy Linden! Recruit Marco Emery!"

Both replied, and Marco was relieved; he was in the right place after all. Two other recruits had ended up in the wrong platoon, and the sergeant sent them racing to another platoon in the field.

At least I'm not the only clueless bugger here, Marco thought.

Marco had counted forty-four names when the sergeant cried out one more: "Recruit Lailani Marita de la Rosa!" A pause. Nobody replied. The sergeant tried again. "Recruit Lailani Marita de la Rosa!"

"Now that's a mouthful," Addy muttered under her breath.

"Recruit Lailani Ma—"

"I'm here, Sergeant! I'm here!"

A recruit came jogging toward them. He was a young Asian boy with a buzz cut, a delicate face, and light brown skin, perhaps Indonesian or Thai. He seemed too small, too young for this army, a mere child. His green fatigues were extra small but still hung from his frame, and his duffel bag was larger than his body. The boy stood a couple of inches shorter than five feet, scrawny as a twig. Even Pinky seemed large by comparison.

"I'm here!" the recruit said again, and Marco realized that no, this wasn't a young boy. Lailani de la Rosa was a woman.

"Fucking dwarf," Pinky—himself barely taller than five feet—muttered. Marco gave him an incredulous look.

"Where the fuck were you, de la Rosa?" the sergeant said.

"Sorry, Sergeant!" Lailani shouted. For such a small woman, her voice was powerful. "Wrong brigade, Sergeant, but I'm here and ready to kill fucking scum."

The sergeant pointed at the ground. "You are here to drop and give me thirty for your tardiness."

"Yes, Commander!" Lailani dropped her duffel bag and gave thirty quick push-ups. She leaped back to her feet. "Now can I kill some fucking scum, Sergeant?"

"Oh, I like her," Addy whispered.

The bearded sergeant seemed to stifle a smile. "First you train, de la Rosa."

"Yes, Commander! I'll train to kill as many fucking scum as I can, and I'm happy to die for Earth." She grabbed her duffel bag and joined the ranks of recruits, standing in the column by Marco. The top of her head was shorter than his shoulders, which didn't stop her from raising her chin high and clenching her fists, a little warrior ready to fight . . . and die.

Marco's amusement faded when he saw Lailani's wrists.

Long, pale scars covered those wrists, crawling across the veins.

Fucking hell, he thought.

Lailani looked up at him, chin raised, eyebrow cocked. Marco quickly looked away.

Marco now thought the platoon complete: forty-five recruits and one sergeant. But the sergeant turned toward them, and he shouted, "Attention! Platoon Commander approaches!"

The recruits all stiffened, and the sergeant himself turned forward, slammed his heels together, and saluted.

Silence fell.

A new soldier approached the platoon.

She was a young woman, about twenty years old. Her blond hair was pulled into a ponytail, and a beret rested on her head. She too wore dusty olive fatigues, but she carried a different type of gun, this one shorter, slimmer, more elegant. This gun didn't fire bullets like the other weapons Marco had seen here. It was a costly plasma rifle, rarer and deadlier by far, able to blast holes through a tank. The woman had no insignia on her sleeves like the sergeant. Instead, a golden bar gleamed on each of her shoulder straps.

An officer, Marco thought. He didn't know much about the difference between regular soldiers and officers, but he remembered what Kemi had told him. Officers weren't just enlisted soldiers like him, like Addy, like the rest of the recruits here, even like Sergeant Singh. Officers had gone to a military academy, had trained for command. If regular, enlisted soldiers were the grunts of the HDF, the officers were the leaders.

If we're the peasants, Marco thought, *she's nobility.*

"Ensign Einav Ben-Ari!" Sergeant Singh said, facing her, still saluting.

The young officer turned her green eyes toward him. For a long time, she merely stared at the bearded sergeant. Finally the platoon commander returned the salute.

"At ease, soldier," she said, a faint accent to her voice.

Marco noticed that a Star of David pendant hung around her neck, and he recognized her accent. He had heard it before in Toronto.

She's Israeli, he thought, surprised. Few had suffered the brunt of the scum attacks like the Israelis. They had lost their entire country in the Cataclysm fifty years ago. Their surviving soldiers had scattered across the world, absorbed into the newly formed HDF. Some people still spoke of them in hushed wonder, these shadow warriors with no homeland. Many Israelis now lived for nothing but war, ubiquitous in military academies across the world, dedicating their lives to military careers. With their country gone, all they had was the HDF, the hope to someday find vengeance, to destroy the scum like the scum had destroyed them.

Ensign Ben-Ari stared at her platoon silently, passing her eyes over row by row. She made eye contact with Marco for a split second, and within that instant, years of pain, grief, determination, and bittersweet loss flooded him, all with just the glance of green eyes. Then the officer passed her eyes to the next recruit. Finally she turned away. Wordlessly, she left the field.

"Goddamn," Addy whispered over her shoulder to Marco. "That one is cold as polar bears fucking on winter solstice in a snowstorm."

Sergeant Singh walked toward her, fury twisting his bearded face. He pointed at Addy. "Kitchen duty tonight. One hour."

"What—?" Addy began. "I—"

"Three hours!" the sergeant barked. He pointed at Marco. "You too."

Marco gasped. What? It wasn't fair! He hadn't asked Addy to talk to him! He opened his mouth to object, but seeing the sergeant's fury, he just nodded. "Yes, Commander."

From the corner of his eye, he saw Pinky smirking. Marco was not a violent man, but if he had a plasma gun, he'd be very tempted to melt Pinky's head off.

Sergeant Singh began to walk across the field. "Platoon Four, follow! March in two lines. Silently!"

They formed two lines and marched after their sergeant. Other platoons began to leave the field too, following their own commanders. As they walked, Marco glared at Addy.

"Thanks," he mouthed at her.

She grumbled something under her breath and wouldn't meet his eyes.

Pinky marched ahead of him. The tiny recruit looked over his shoulder at Marco, that toothy smirk on his gaunt face. "Nice one, asshole."

Marco noticed that a handful of big, brutish recruits walked around Pinky, and he recognized a couple of the boys who had assisted Pinky back in the supply warehouse. Marco's heart sank. Addy was in this platoon with him, but right now she seemed more trouble than she was worth. As for the rest of them . . . Marco was stuck here with an Elvis impersonator, a caveman, a Russian the size of a starship, a tiny firecracker with scars on her wrists, and a gang of hoodlums whom—Marco had to admit—he wouldn't mind seeing fed to scum. He sighed. It was already the longest day in his life, and when he glanced at a clock, he could barely believe it. It was only 3:00 p.m.

The sergeant marched them toward yet another concrete building, as square, squat, and ugly as the thousands that filled this base. He turned toward them in the dust.

"All right, soldiers," Singh said. "It's chow time. You eat with your bellies, not your eyes. You got fifteen minutes, so make 'em count. It's going to be a long day, and you're very, very lucky if you'll get any food or rest for twelve hours after this meal. Leave your duffel bags outside. Go."

The sergeant stepped aside, and the recruits entered the building, discovering a massive mess hall full of thousands of recruits.

And, blessedly, thousands of voices.

"Finally we can talk!" Addy said, then raised her voice to a shout. "We can talk!"

Heads turned toward her.

"We can talk quietly," Marco said.

She grinned at him, a huge grin, eyes alight. "I'm having *fun* here, Poet. Are you having fun?"

"I'm sure I'll have even more fun tonight at kitchen duty." Marco glanced toward the back of the hall. Past a counter, he could see soldiers toiling in the kitchen.

"That's the spirit!" Addy grabbed his hand. "Let's eat."

They lined up. The queues took them by plastic shelves, from which they took plastic trays, plastic plates, and plastic mugs.

Marco cringed. He couldn't find a single mug which wasn't stained with old tea and coffee, and every plate displayed remnants of past meals. But the queue kept moving, so he resigned himself to a splotchy mug and a green plate coated with crumbs. He fished out oily cutlery from a bin.

Addy and he made their way toward a counter. A row of soldiers stood here, looking miserable, dumping food onto each recruit's tray. Marco received a sticky ball of rice, a slice of fried Spam as thick as his thumb, a scoop of corn, and something that might have been dessert but looked more like a sponge. Addy and he sought a table—many filled the hall—and finally sat near the back, where they recognized some faces from their platoon.

"Fucking shit!" Pinky was shouting at a nearby table, gesturing at his tray. "I can't eat this crap."

"What's wrong with it?" asked another soldier, one of Pinky's hulking henchmen.

"This ain't food." Pinky spat on his plate. "Give me pizza, give me French fries, give me some deep-fried chicken wings."

"Very healthy," said the henchman—the beast was easily thrice Pinky's size, which didn't stop the smaller soldier from slapping the brute.

Marco looked away from that table. It was bad enough he served in the same platoon as Pinky and his gang, he didn't have to look at them while eating. He reached across his own table for a loaf of bread and a packet of jam; they seemed more palatable than his Spam, sticky rice, and sponge. The recruits all ate with gusto, speaking between mouthfuls.

"Jesus H. Christ!" Elvis said, reaching for a tin of yogurt. "Did you see our lieutenant? Hot mama! I should show her my dance moves." He rose from his seat and swayed his hips.

"She's not a lieutenant," Marco said. "She's an ensign." He felt rather proud of himself for remembering that.

Addy nodded, pointing her butter knife at Elvis, and spoke through a mouthful of Spam. "This ain't the battlefield, Elvis. Lieutenants command soldiers in battle. Hot blondie is just a fucking recruit like us, fresh outta officer school. An ensign to officers is like a private to soldiers—fresh meat."

"Swallow before you talk," Marco said.

She stuck her Spam-covered tongue out at him. "Maybe you can write about Hot Blondie in your book, Poet."

Elvis looked at him, eyebrow raised. "You writing a book? What, poetry?"

"Not poetry," Marco said.

"It's about a turtle," Addy said. "Can you believe it? A fucking jarhead turtle—"

"A loggerhead," Marco said quietly. "And it's not about the turtle."

Elvis whistled appreciatively. "Turtle poetry. I dig it, man. Could make good lyrics. I ain't nothin' but a hound turtle . . ."

Marco felt his cheeks flush. He didn't like anyone talking about his novel here. He doubted that these were exactly the literary types.

"Addy plays hockey," Marco said, desperate to change the topic. "She dreams of playing for the Maple Leafs, even though they haven't won the Stanley Cup in almost two hundred years, not since 1967. She even has a Maple Leaf tattoo on her arm. Roll up your sleeve, Addy. Show 'em."

"They'll win this year," Addy said, displaying her tattoo and flexing her muscles.

"Hey, so what's that sergeant anyway?" Elvis said. "With his beard and turban. Is he a Muslim? I thought the Muslims served in the Eastern Command."

"He's Sikh," Marco said.

"The fuck is that?" said Elvis. "Like a Muslim sheik?"

Addy groaned. "You really are a retard." She leaned toward Marco and whispered, "What's a Sikh?"

Before Marco could explain, Elvis swallowed a last bite of food and rose to his feet. "All right, listen up, Poet and Maple, my fellow Canucks. Tips from my older brother; he went through this a few years back. You don't get many chances in the army to pee or take a shit. If you gotta do either one, you got . . ." He checked his watch. "Five minutes left. Once that sergeant grabs us again, he'll ride our asses for the next twelve hours. Say goodbye to your bladder if it's still full by then."

Marco was exhausted. He had barely sat down since dawn, and he couldn't imagine this day stretching on until three or four in the morning. But if Elvis was right, Marco had some business to attend to. Addy rose with them. The three Canadians began heading toward the door, seeking a latrine. Behind them, Caveman followed, lumbering between the tables, nearly knocking them over. They placed their empty trays on a rack, then headed toward the exit.

A bored-looking soldier stood there, leaning against the wall, an assault rifle slung across his back. "Where you going, recruits?"

"Got to go piss, Corporal," said Elvis. "Our sarge says we got five more minutes."

Corporal, Marco thought, taking a mental photograph of the soldier's insignia—two chevrons on the arm. If Sergeant Singh had three chevrons, that meant corporals were one rank lower. Marco hadn't yet seen anyone with a single chevron on their sleeve. None of the recruits wore any insignia yet.

The corporal yawned and pointed at a few outhouses in the yard. "Knock yourselves out."

"I got to pee so bad it's coming out of my nostrils!" Caveman announced—loud enough for a crowd of soldiers in the yard to hear—and raced toward one latrine. Marco himself had been holding it in for hours. He waited at another latrine until the wooden door opened with a blast of stench, and a wheezing, pink-cheeked soldier emerged, glasses fogged up.

Marco stepped inside and nearly fainted. He had seen scum up close. This was worse. There wasn't a toilet or sink, just a hole in the filthy floor. A roll of blue toilet paper hung on a roller. At least Marco thought it was toilet paper; it could easily pass for sandpaper. Flies buzzed. Holding his breath, Marco peed into the hole, trying not to look inside. He didn't even want to contemplate the next time nature called for something more serious than a piss.

He burst out of the latrine and finally inhaled, thanking Sergeant Singh with all his heart for assigning him kitchen duty that night. He pitied whatever poor soul got latrine duty. The only way to properly clean these facilities would be to nuke them from orbit.

By the time Addy, Caveman, and Elvis emerged from their latrines—green in the face—they were a minute late. They ran back to find their platoon already gathered outside the mess hall. Ensign Ben-Ari was nowhere in sight, but Sergeant Singh was waiting. Tardiness earned Elvis and Caveman kitchen duty that night as well, and all four of the latecomers ended up giving their sergeant thirty push-ups. While they strained, that bastard Pinky smirked down at them. Once, when the sergeant turned his head, Pinky spat, and the sizzling globe landed between Marco's hands. He grimaced, fighting down the urge to leap onto Pinky, and finished his push-ups.

The day stretched on.

The sergeant had them work in a field for three sweaty hours, clearing out stones and thorns. As the sun set, he had them hauling boxes out of a warehouse, only to haul them back in once their work was done. The sergeant never tired of shouting, brandishing his baton, and commanding recruits to fall into the dust and give him thirty. Marco was constantly thirsty, sweaty, dizzy, and exhausted. At 8:00 p.m., they finally returned to the mess hall for another fifteen minutes.

"What's with this shit?" Elvis grumbled as he shoved a hard-boiled egg into his mouth. "We're sorted into our platoon already. Why are we hauling boxes and clearing vegetation in RASCOM instead of heading off to boot camp?"

"I thought this was boot camp already," Marco said, instantly regretting it. Gales of laughter assaulted him from across the table.

"Poet, you crack me up," said Elvis. "Crack. Me. Up. This ain't boot camp. Oh, once we're in boot camp, you'll miss RASCOM. This place is a whorehouse compared to boot camp. A whorehouse, I tell you. They're just killing time here with us, waiting for some boot camp base to become available, maybe for room on a rocket."

"If boot camp is so bad, why are you eager to go there?" Marco said.

"Because I want to get the fucking thing over with already! That, and boot camp will have actual toilets, I hope, and squatting once over a hole in the ground is enough for a lifetime." Elvis reached across the table for a pitcher of lukewarm tea. "Poet, dear old friend, boot camp ain't nothing like RASCOM. Here they're just processing us, giving us our X-rays and dog tags and shit. Once we hit the actual camp, they'll train us. Train us to kill scum, not just haul boxes and trim the hedges. Get ready for the ten toughest weeks of your life."

"I feel like just today has been ten weeks," Marco said. "I can't believe that just this morning—today, the same day!—we were back in Toronto." He sighed. "I'm homesick already."

Elvis seemed ready to snort, then nodded and lowered his head. "Me too."

Even Addy nodded. "Me too."

Caveman actually began to weep. He blew his nose into a napkin. "I miss home."

Awkward silence fell across their table, and Marco hoped that Pinky and his gang—sitting at the next table over—hadn't heard.

A soft voice broke the silence. "I like it here."

They all turned their heads. Marco hadn't even noticed that Lailani had joined their table. The diminutive recruit was so small she could barely reach the tabletop. With her buzz cut and thin frame, she looked like a schoolboy in her father's uniform. When she reached across the table for a drink, Marco again noticed the scars across her wrists.

"Lailani Marita de la Rosa," Marco said. "Did I get that right?"

She nodded. "That's me. Lailani Marita de la Rosa, scum killer extraordinaire." She aimed her butter knife and pretended to fire. "Pew pew pew."

"What's your name, Spanish?" Addy said. "You Mexican?"

Lailani shook her head. "Filipino. I'm from Manila, capital of the lovely, sunny islands of the Philippines. Come for the sun and palm trees. Stay because your passport was stolen."

"Bullshit," said Elvis. "Philippines is the Eastern Command, like the Muslims. Or Sikhs. Or whoever the fuck those guys are."

Lailani snorted. "I don't look it, but I'm half American. That's right. My pa was wholesome all-American like white bread, baseball, and clogged arteries. Probably loved Elvis too. I just happen to look like a lovely, exotic flower of the Orient. You better not have any yellow fever, white boys, or I'll chop off your balls." She sliced her knife through the air.

Marco glanced at her wrists again. It seemed like balls wasn't the only thing Lailani liked to slice.

"I like this one." Addy nodded, pointing at the girl. "I think we'll call you Tiny. If I'm Maple, Marco here is Poet, and this lovely specimen with jam all over his uniform is Elvis, you'll need a nickname too. Tiny it is."

Lailani leaped onto her chair. "I'm not fucking tiny!" She bared her teeth. "I might only be five feet tall—okay, four feet eleven—all right, four feet ten!—but I'm still tough enough to slice through you, and—"

"Recruit!" shouted a sergeant, marching toward them through the mess, and pointed at Lailani. "Kitchen duty tonight. Now sit your ass down."

Grumbling, "Tiny" Lailani sat her ass down. The sergeant marched away.

"Fucking fascist scum," she muttered.

As they swallowed their last bites, Marco glanced aside. Across the mess hall, Sergeant Singh returned to his own table, which was set across a barrier. The ranked soldiers and officers sat there, eating from a different kitchen. A few of them—corporals and sergeants—were laughing as they ate. Marco glimpsed Ensign

Ben-Ari sitting among them. The Israeli officer was listening to Sergeant Singh tell a story, smiling thinly, yet it seemed to Marco, even from this distance, that there was sadness in her eyes. She was the commander of the Dragons Platoon, but aside from that brief encounter a few hours ago, they hadn't seen her up close. It seemed that officers were too lofty to mingle even with their own soldiers.

"She's a goddess and Singh is her angel of retribution," Marco reflected absentmindedly.

Addy sighed. "Oh, Poet." She cringed as a bell rang. "Dinner's over. Time for our kitchen duty." She waved a slice of Spam at him. "Thanks to *you*."

Lailani groaned. "Fuck me, I'd rather be killing scum."

CHAPTER SEVEN

They stood in the kitchen—Marco, Addy, and Lailani Marita de la Rosa—as the trays piled up into plastic skyscrapers.

Before the three recruits rose metal shelves, row by row. Through them, like prisoners gazing through horizontal bars, they could see the mess hall where thousands of soldiers were leaving their seats, trays in hand. The recruits slammed those trays down onto the metal shelves, spraying bits of food.

Addy groaned. "Gross!" She pulled chicken skin out of her hair. "Makes me want to barf."

More and more trays kept piling up. On them, plastic plates and mugs rattled.

"Come on," Marco said. "Let's wash them. It'll be over quickly. We've got the dishwasher."

As the trays kept piling up, he gestured behind him. The room was about the size of a typical living room. This wasn't the kitchen where the food was cooked, just a scullery where the dishes and pots were washed. Several of those massive pots already stood on the tiles. Between them, a conveyor belt moved across the room. Halfway along its journey, the belt passed through something that looked like a car wash. Water sprayed within.

"All right, girls," Marco said. "Let's get the dishes on this conveyor belt and run 'em through the wash."

They began to grab the trays and place them onto the belt. The belt clattered onward, moving inch by inch, taking the trays of dishes into the square spraying structure. It reminded Marco of the belts that ran suitcases through X-ray machines at airports. The trays emerged from the other side wet . . . and still dirty.

"There's still bits of food all over this!" Addy said, raising a plate.

"More trays piling up!" Lailani called. "The whole structure's about to collapse!"

Marco returned to the shelves. More and more soldiers in the mess hall were slamming down their trays. Plates and mugs wobbled on them. Lailani was busy lifting the trays, trying to carry them to the conveyor belt, but they were piling up too fast. Finally the three recruits were reduced to placing the trays on the floor, only for more trays—hundreds of them—to instantly replace them on the shelves. There was no time to even take the three steps toward the conveyor belt, let alone wait for it to run through the wash. The trays stacked up on the floor, rising to their hips. Plastic mugs rolled across the dirty floor.

"Fuck me, no wonder the dishes are always so dirty," Addy said.

Lailani was stacking trays on the conveyor belt, desperate to fit them all on, but her wobbly towers couldn't fit through the little car wash, and the structures collapsed.

"There's no way this belt will wash things fast enough," the tiny recruit said. "Not if we want to be done by breakfast, and those fucking trays are still piling up."

Indeed, trays now rose in wobbling minarets on the shelves. One structure collapsed, and Marco ran to catch the falling trays. Soup and crumbs spilled over him. Addy cursed as condiments sprayed her.

"Fuck this shit!" Addy grabbed a knife and brandished it at nobody in particular. "I didn't sign up to clean plates but to kill aliens."

"Pretend the trays are scum," Marco said.

"They are!"

A hoarse voice rose from the mess hall. "Hey, kitchen slaves!" Pinky's ugly mug appeared behind the shelves. "Wash these." The recruit placed his tray down atop a pile of them, then shoved. A hundred trays and plates clattered onto the floor. Smirking, Pinky walked away.

"Joke's on you!" Addy shouted after him. "We were putting the plates on the floor anyway!"

Lailani walked toward the back of the room, then returned carrying a hose. "Guys," she said, "you know, there's probably a reason somebody installed this hose here."

Marco cringed and pointed. "There's another hose there. I think people figured out ages ago that the dishwasher is for show."

Addy was wobbling under a pile of trays. "Hose these damn things!"

Marco and Lailani turned on their hoses. Icy water blasted out, spraying over Addy, over the trays on the floor, the shelves, the entire kitchen. Whoever had installed the hoses must have installed the grates on the floor too. The dirty water trickled away.

"So the kitchen is a giant shower?" Marco said over the roaring water.

Lailani nodded. "At least we'll get to wash up." She sprayed Marco with her hose.

He yowled. "It's cold!" He sprayed her back, and Lailani squealed and ducked for cover behind the conveyor belt.

For two more hours, they toiled. Addy kept pulling trays and dishes off the shelves and onto the floor, while Marco and Lailani hosed them down. When the trays and dishes were finally clean—or at least, as clean as possible under the circumstances, which wasn't very clean at all—they got to hosing and scrubbing the giant pots. Addy sang as they worked, old songs from home, and Marco and even Lailani joined in.

Finally, at 10:30 p.m., they emerged dripping wet into the hot, humid, South American night.

Sergeant Singh awaited them there beside their duffel bags. The tall, turbaned soldier glowered at them. The moonlight shone on the curved *kirpan* blade that hung from his belt.

"You will stand at attention when you see your commander," he said, "or you'll do another two hours after breakfast."

Addy, Marco, and Lailani stood at attention, heels pressed together, backs straight, chins raised. Water dripped off them into the dust.

The sergeant nodded and checked his wristwatch. "You wet worms are just on time. Follow me."

Marco hoped, prayed, yearned for sleep, but it was not to be. The sergeant led them to—surprise, surprise—another squat concrete building. They entered to find a gymnasium with a stage at the back. Thousands of soldiers stood here, facing the stage. Marco spotted his platoon, and they headed over to join the rest of the Dragons.

A soldier stepped onto the stage.

"Fucking hell," Addy muttered. "It's Captain Butterflies."

Marco recognized the smiling, perky soldier from the spaceport back in Toronto, the one with the butterfly pendant. The young woman gave the crowd of recruits a huge, glistening smile that practically blinded Marco.

"Welcome, recruits, to the Human Defense Force!" she said into the microphone. "We here at the HDF hope you've been enjoying your first day as soldiers. Your service and sacrifice keep Earth safe! I'd like to extend my welcome with a little gift—from the HDF to you."

A military band stepped onto the stage. They began to play a marching song—deafeningly loud, the speakers thrumming across the gymnasium. As the music blared, a projector displayed images on a screen, showing HDF soldiers spraying scum with bullets, Firebird starfighters blasting scum ships, and military marches across the world's capitals. The flags of the HDF, displaying a phoenix rising from ashes like humanity rising from the Cataclysm, waved in the background of every image.

"I'm tired," Marco said to Addy. "It's late. Why are we subjected to this?"

"What?" she shouted.

"I said I want to sleep!" he shouted back.

"Stop being an old man!" Addy replied, then turned back toward the stage and sang with the choir. "Kill the scum, kill the scum, kill the evil scum . . . For Earth's glory, beat the drums! Kill the scum, kill the—"

Marco covered his ears and closed his eyes. He tried to take deep breaths, to ignore the noise as best he could, and he thought of Kemi. Of her smile. How they would walk through the cemetery together, the last green space in Toronto. But even those thoughts turned sour, and again he saw her reaching to him, tears in her eyes, telling him she'd be away for ten years, maybe more.

What are you doing now, Kemi? he thought. *Are you thinking of me too?*

"Play 'Freebird'!" Addy shouted at the band.

Finally, at midnight, Sergeant Singh led them out of the gym. As they marched down the road, limbs aching, Marco prayed to see another squat concrete building—this one full of beds. He didn't expect military cots to be particularly comfortable, but he had barely sat down since dawn. It still seemed ludicrous, unthinkable, had to be a mistake, that this had all been just one day, that this morning—this same day!—he had been back home with his father. Surely time was different here in the HDF, and he'd already been a soldier for weeks.

They marched toward concrete barracks. Through the windows, Marco saw rooms full of cots, and he breathed a sigh of relief. Finally—bed. Yet Sergeant Singh marched them past the barracks, ignoring the groans of protest, and they headed down a path between trees toward a rocky field.

More cardboard boxes awaited them here.

"Trio formations, soldiers!" Sergeant Singh barked. They formed rank—too slowly. Again and again, Singh had them take formation, checking his stopwatch. When finally he was satisfied, he pointed at the boxes.

"Open them," he said. "Inside you'll find tents. Raise them. But not before you clear this field of stones. Go."

Tents? Marco groaned, but beggars couldn't be choosers. Clearing the field of stones was long, laborious work. Marco was ready to sleep on nails, but Singh drove them onward until finally the field was cleared. Then another task awaited them: constructing the tents. This involved hammering pikes into the ground, raising metal frameworks, and snapping drab sheets into place, then constructing hard metal cots within.

It was 2:00 a.m. before the work was complete.

"All right, soldiers," Sergeant Singh said. "Get some rest. You've earned it. I'll see you at 4:30 a.m. for morning inspection. I want everyone with polished boots, tidy uniforms, and helmets on heads. Maybe then we'll finally ship your asses off to boot camp."

This elicited more groans. Only two and a half hours of sleep?

"Fuck me," Elvis muttered as Singh marched away, leaving them in the field. "Let the scum kill me. I'm ready."

Lailani nodded and pulled off her fatigues, remaining in a tank top and boxer shorts. A rainbow tattoo lit up one of her arms. A dragon tattoo coiled up her other arm, sneaked under her shirt, and poked its head over her collarbone—appropriate for the Dragons Platoon.

"I'm ready to spend eternity sleeping in the digestive tract of a scum," she said.

Marco stepped into one of the tents. Fifteen cots were pressed together like seats in a subway car.

"Boot camp will be easier," he said, trying to ignore the laughter of his fellow recruits.

"I'm telling you, Poet," Elvis said. "RASCOM is a whorehouse. You'll miss it."

Marco flopped down onto one cot. Addy and Lailani took the cots at his sides. The recruits of the Dragons Platoon were soon fast asleep—all but Marco. Despite his exhaustion, his mind kept racing. The old images kept flashing before him: his mother's corpse in the snow, the scum rearing above her, his father's tears at the funeral, Addy afraid in his bed, and always Kemi's face. He pulled the book out from his back pocket, and Kemi's photo dropped onto his chest. He looked at her—that quirky expression, one eyebrow raised, lips smirking, the photo she hated and he loved. He put it back into the book and closed his eyes. Finally, with an hour before wake-up call, he drifted off to sleep. His first day as a soldier ended.

CHAPTER EIGHT

"Inspection!"

Sergeant Singh's voice rang through the night.

"4th Platoon, inspection!"

Marco leaped from his cot. He checked his wristwatch. 4:30 a.m., an hour since he'd fallen asleep.

"4th Platoon, damn it, line up for inspection!" Singh pulled open the tent flap. "Uniforms tidy, boots polished, helmets on head, faces shaved, now!"

They scrambled. Marco had been so exhausted last night he had fallen into bed in his fatigues. Other recruits had stripped down to their underwear. Some wore pajamas brought from home; Caveman's pajama pants featured tiny fire trucks and dogs. Outside the tent, Singh was counting down seconds.

Marco pulled on his boots, gave them a quick rub against the back of his legs, and passed a hand across his cheek. Thankfully, his beard was naturally thin, and stubble barely covered his cheeks, though other recruits—like Elvis—were already showing a deep shadow.

"Three, two, one—out, now, form rank!"

They rushed outside the tent, slapping on their helmets, and lined up in the darkness. Sergeant Singh marched across their lines, holding a flashlight. Disgust suffused his face.

"Is this how you present yourselves?" he shouted. He paused before Addy and pointed at her uniform. "Shirt not tucked in."

"Sorry, Commander!" Addy said. "I'm used to hockey jerseys."

With a grunt, the sergeant turned toward Beast, the massive Russian recruit. He pointed the flashlight down at his legs. "Pants not bloused."

"*Eezvinite*, Commander," Beast said, accent thick. "Sorry. Pants too small for me."

Next, the sergeant approached Elvis and stared at the boy's face. "Stubble on your face. And shave those sideburns."

Indignant, Elvis touched his cheeks. "These babies? But—" He gulped seeing the wrath on Singh's face. "Yes, Commander."

The turbaned sergeant turned toward Marco, frowning down at his boots. "You call those polished?"

"Sorry, Commander!" Marco said, wishing he'd had time to polish the boots with actual shoe polish, not just brush them against his pants.

The sergeant moved on and paused by a tall, lanky recruit. He frowned at the soldier's helmet. With a thick black marker, somebody had drawn a star and the word *Sheriff* on the helmet.

"Did you draw that, recruit?" Singh said.

The gangly recruit gulped. "Yes, sir—"

"I'm not an officer." The sergeant's face reddened. "Don't you sir me. I work for a living. Did you deface military property?"

The recruit—Marco knew that from this moment, he would be known as Sheriff—nodded. "Yes, s—I mean, yes, Commander." He spoke with a thick Southern drawl. "It's tradition, Commander! To write on your helmet. Born to kill. War is hell. That sort of thing."

"Well, wipe it off," Singh said. "You don't want Bob Marley to shoot you, do you?" Laughter sounded across the platoon, and the sergeant growled. "Shut it! All of you, silence!"

Singh kept walking and paused in front of Lailani. His eyes widened. "Fuck me. Another helmet-scrawler."

Marco glanced over at Lailani. She too had drawn words onto her helmet with a permanent marker: *Life is a bag of dicks with syphilis.*

"Sorry, Commander!" Lailani said. "Sheriff told me it's tradition."

Marco could swear that the bearded sergeant was struggling not to smile. "Wipe those words off, recruit, or I'll make you wish life were that easy."

"Yes, Commander!" Lailani said.

The sergeant turned toward Caveman, and his eyes widened further. The beefy recruit was still wearing his fire truck pajamas.

"Sorry, Sergeant!" Caveman said. "I didn't have time to change."

"You didn't have time?" Sergeant Singh roared. "Do you think the scum will give you time next time they invade? Do you think the fucking scum will wait while you pull off your fire truck pajamas, soldier?"

"No, Sergeant!" Caveman shouted, face red, spraying saliva.

Singh spat and marched across the ranks. "Not one of you little shits is presentable. If this is how you prepare for me, how the fuck will you prepare next time the scum attack? Return to your tents! Back here in thirty seconds, and you better look like soldiers, damn it. Go! Thirty! Twenty-nine! Twenty-eight!"

They scrambled back into the tent. Marco grabbed his shoe polish and gave his boots a few quick scrubs. Addy tucked her shirt into her trousers, while Caveman stumbled for his uniform, falling over as he tried to pull off his pajama pants. Elvis groaned as he splashed water onto his face from his canteen and searched for his razor.

They rushed back outside, formed rank, and again miserably failed their inspection. Caveman had his pajama pants around his ankles, while Elvis's face was covered with shaving cream. Marco honestly doubted that the scum would care what pants they wore or how stubbly their faces were, but Singh seemed to think they could defeat the aliens with polished boots and a clean shave. Finally, on the third attempt, Singh grunted and nodded.

"Pathetic," he said. "I'd have you all pulling latrine duty, the lot of you, but a rocket is waiting to take you someplace far,

far worse than RASCOM. Follow me. And any one of you cockroaches falls out of rank, my prod falls into your gut."

They marched behind him through the darkness, lugging their duffel bags. Already, across the base, entire companies were drilling, marching, and shouting "Yes, Commander!" like it was a battle cry.

As they left RASCOM and headed back into the spaceport, Marco hoped he'd never see that jungle of concrete and barbed wire again.

* * * * *

As dawn rose, Marco, Addy, and the rest of the 4th Platoon stepped into the suborbital rocket. Their time at this sprawling Chilean labyrinth was ending. They were soldiers now, about to blast off toward their training. As Marco took his seat—again he sat near the top of the rocket where he could peek through the narrow viewport—the damn song from last night kept ringing through his ears. *Kill the scum, kill the scum, kill the evil scum. For Earth's glory, beat the drums!*

Marco sighed. "For Earth's glory, can I have a cushy job in the archives?" he muttered under his breath.

"What's that, recruit?" barked Sergeant Singh, climbing the ladder toward the top tier of seats.

"I said I can't wait to kill the scum, sir!" Marco said.

The sergeant glared at him. "I told you, recruit, I'm not an officer."

"Sorry, Sergeant. Too excited about the prospect of killing scum, si—Sergeant."

Rings of seats filled the rocket, spreading from engines below to cockpit above, like some towering, narrow amphitheater. The other platoons of the 42nd Company filled the rocket along with the Dragons Platoon. Soon four platoons, the entire company, filled the rocket—nearly two hundred soldiers. Sergeant Singh settled into a seat across from Marco, who instantly regretted sitting near the top. With the sarge nearby, conversation during the flight seemed unlikely.

When all the soldiers were seated, the officers entered the rocket. Four ensigns were here, the platoon commanders. Each had a single bar on their shoulder straps. Ensign Einav Ben-Ari climbed the ladder at their lead, face blank. As Marco looked at her, he thought again about the old stories from the Cataclysm, how Ben-Ari's country—that tiny stretch of coast called Israel—had been destroyed by the scum, how the nation's survivors found a new home in the HDF, dedicating their new lives to military careers.

When Ensign Ben-Ari passed by him, Marco made brief eye contact with her, and he saw cold determination . . . but also fear in her green eyes.

She's new to the military too, he thought. *She's just a fresh graduate from military academy who's never seen battle.* It was strange to think that in a year or two, Kemi would be an ensign as well, perhaps commanding a platoon of her own.

The ensigns climbed through a hatch, entering a higher level in the rocket.

"The officers fly first class," Addy whispered, leaning toward Marco. "Same as they eat from a better kitchen and sleep in comfy beds. Fuck me, I should go to military academy."

"You need good grades to get into military academy," Marco whispered back.

Addy bristled. "I got an A+ in gym!"

They fell silent at a glare from Sergeant Singh.

Following the ensigns climbed another officer, this one a few years older. He was a muscular, black-haired man with heavy eyebrows, and insignia on his shoulders displayed three bars.

"That's a captain," Addy whispered as the officer entered the chamber above and closed the hatch behind him. "That's the highest-ranking officer we've seen so far. He must command this entire company."

Marco thought it strange. Here in the military, nobody seemed to care who you were on the outside. Nobody cared if Marco was writing a novel, if Addy excelled at hockey, if Elvis could sing. All that mattered was the insignia on your sleeves or shoulders. That was all. Who you were, what you were worth—all just a few chevrons or bars. It was a depressing thought.

With blasting flame and smoke and roaring metal, they took off.

As the rocket soared, the g-force pressed down on them like the weight of scum queens. Again Addy clasped Marco's hand, her face pale. At his other side, Lailani hooted and cried out, voice nearly drowning in the din, "Yeah, time to go kill the scum!"

The sound died and the pressure eased as they breached the atmosphere. As the rocket leveled off, Marco stared out the viewport. Endless stars spread above. Below, he could see the coast of Chile and the curve of the ocean beyond. They were heading east, soon crossing South America and heading over the Atlantic. By the time they reached Africa, the rocket turned, taking Earth out of view. Marco saw nothing but stars.

They began to descend.

Fire obscured the viewport.

Surrounded with smoke, they slammed down onto the ground. Marco had no idea where they were, but judging by the last image he had seen, they were somewhere in North Africa.

They emerged from the rocket to find a desert.

Marco had thought that Chile was hot, but even that soupy land had not prepared him for *this* heat. Waves of dry, searing air hit him like blasts from an oven. Whoever had said that dry heat was tolerable had obviously never been to this place. The sun baked his hair, and the tarmac of the small spaceport shimmered.

Dunes surrounded the landing pad, and the sky had never seemed larger, a massive bowl of pale blue. A path led toward a metal fence topped with barbed wire and lined with guard towers.

A flag of the HDF hung above the metal gates. A few guards stood there, helmets on their heads and submachine guns in hand. A sign above them read: *Fort Djemila Basic Combat Training.*

The recruits took formation on the tarmac, each platoon joined by its officer and sergeant. One by one, the platoons marched into the military base. As the Dragons Platoon passed through the gates, one of the guards muttered "Fresh meat" to his friend. Marco had heard that phrase too many times these past twenty-four hours. He imagined that in a military that served Spam with every meal, fresh meat was simply an appealing concept. He looked to check the guards' ranks but saw none; their sleeves and shoulders were clear of insignia.

They're just recruits, Marco realized, looking at those helmets and guns.

Gunfire sounded in the distance, interrupting his thoughts. Marco stiffened, wondering if the scum were attacking. More and more machine guns blazed.

"Keep marching, recruits!" Sergeant Singh barked. "Follow!"

They passed through the metal gates, entering the base . . . and began their training to become killers.

If RASCOM had been a massive hive of concrete, towers, roaring engines, screaming jets, and confusion, Fort Djemila was a desolate wasteland. There were barely any buildings here within the fence. Marco saw one concrete building that might have been a mess hall, a smaller building that could have been showers, and a few trailers, but that was about it. The rest was just rocky fields, dunes, hills, and boulders. He could just make out rows of tents in the distance past marching soldiers. No tanks or jets, no towering barracks of concrete and metal, no jungles full of rude monkeys. Sand, stone, tents, heat, and searing sunlight—that was Fort Djemila somewhere here in North Africa.

"Form rank!" Singh barked, forcing them to repeat the drill several times as he timed them. Whenever they were too slow, he had them drop and give him twenty push-ups. When finally they stood in rows of three, Singh shouted, "Attention!"

The recruits stood stiffly. As they would do back in RASCOM, Addy, Marco, and Elvis formed one trio. At his one side stood another trio: Lailani, Caveman, and the hulking Beast. At Marco's other side stood a far less appealing trio: the smirking Pinky and two of his henchmen, both brutes of the type seen on wanted ads.

As the recruits stood under the searing heat, Sergeant Singh saluted, and Ensign Ben-Ari approached. The young officer turned her cold green eyes upon the platoon. Even in the heat, Marco felt a chill. For the first time since assuming command of the Dragons Platoon, the officer spoke to her soldiers.

"Welcome to hell," she said. "Welcome to ten weeks that will break your body and spirit. I will shatter you here. I will mold you into killers. You will become scum-slayers. Is that understood?"

"Yes, ma'am!" they shouted.

Ensign Ben-Ari nodded. "Not all of you will survive this training. Fewer will survive the scum. I have ten weeks—that is all—to turn you from soft boys and girls into soldiers. And I've brought help."

On cue, an armored jeep rolled up, belching out fumes and casting clouds of sand. Three soldiers hopped out, dressed in battle fatigues. They wore helmets and body armor, and they carried heavy assault rifles—not sleek plasma weapons like the one Ben-Ari carried but crude, rude bullet-sprayers. All three soldiers were young, and their insignia displayed two chevrons on their sleeves. Marco recognized that rank already; they were corporals.

They're one rank below Sergeant Singh, Marco thought. *And far below Ensign Ben-Ari. Yet infinitely higher than us recruits.*

If Ben-Ari was a goddess, and if Sergeant Singh was her angel of wrath, corporals were holy knights—and the recruits were mere peasants.

The three corporals stood at attention and saluted Ensign Ben-Ari. She returned the salute. "At ease," she told them, then turned back toward the recruits. "I'm dividing this platoon into three squads. A corporal will lead each one. You will report to your squad leaders, who will report to Sergeant Singh, who reports to me. Understood?"

"Yes, ma'am!" the recruits shouted.

"These corporals have fought the scum," said Ensign Ben-Ari. "They killed scum. They saw friends die in scum claws. And they will teach you how to kill them too. Each squad commander will teach his or her recruits how to clean, fire, and love your weapon, how to love killing the enemy." The officer turned toward her corporals and raised her voice. "Corporal Railey Webb!"

One of the three corporals stepped forward and saluted. "Yes, ma'am!"

Corporal Webb was a slender woman with brown skin and dark eyes, and black curls peeked from under her helmet, just long enough to cover her forehead. Her battle fatigues were sandy, and her T57 assault rifle hung across her back, nearly as tall as she was. She moved effortlessly on two prosthetic legs. Marco had known amputees—there were many back in Toronto, victims of the scum attacks—who wore realistic prosthetics that looked almost identical to actual limbs. Corporal Webb wore something different. Her prosthetics were thin, curved, and metallic like blades, built not for realism but speed. Marco had heard of such prosthetics—Blade Runners, they called them. They let their owners run and leap faster than they ever could on real legs. Marco wondered if Webb had lost her legs in a great battle, had come here to train new warriors while nursing her wounds.

"Corporal Webb, you'll command the first squad," said Ensign Ben-Ari. The officer pulled on augmented reality sunglasses and read out names, and fifteen recruits went to stand behind Corporal Webb.

"Corporal Fiona St-Pierre!" Ben-Ari called out.

Another corporal stepped forward and saluted. She had dusty yellow hair, a prominent nose, and a bad case of acne. Cruelty filled her blue eyes, and her lips were a thin, bitter line. Fifteen other recruits joined her squad. Marco was grateful he wasn't among them. He didn't like that bitterness in St-Pierre's eyes.

"Corporal Emilio Diaz!" Ben-Ari said.

The third and last corporal stepped forward and saluted. He was a tall, muscular man with black eyes and a wide jaw. He moved with grace that belied his size, and his assault rifle hung across his hip. An ugly scar ran up one of his forearms. Marco felt small, thin, and young by this scarred warrior.

"All of you who remain," Ben-Ari said to the recruits, "join Corporal Diaz's squad."

Marco was glad that he had stood by his friends. It meant he would share a squad with Addy, Lailani, Elvis, Caveman, and even Beast; the hulking Russian had been growing on him. Unfortunately, Pinky and his henchmen were in the same squad. The fifteen recruits took formation behind Corporal Diaz.

Ensign Ben-Ari faced the three squads of her platoon. "You come to me scared, weak, and confused. But we will make you warriors. This is an ugly war. This is a vicious enemy. This training will be the hardest ten weeks of your lives. But know this, soldiers of Earth: I am proud of every one of you, and I will do everything that I can to help you succeed."

With that, Ensign Ben-Ari and Sergeant Singh entered the jeep and drove off in a cloud of dust, leaving the recruits with their corporals.

"All right, you sacks of shit!" Corporal Diaz said, pacing in front of his squad. "Goddamn. Ensign Ben-Ari might be proud of you, but you'll have to prove your worth to me." He raised his submachine gun. "You see this son of a bitch? This is a T57 assault rifle, capable of firing in semi-automatic or automatic modes to a range of fifteen hundred meters and powerful enough to tear through solid steel. It fires good old bullets. That's right, bullets, same as you see in two-hundred-year-old John Wayne movies. It did the job back then, and it does the job now. Plasma blasts and lasers might be good for fancy officers. But this bad boy is going to kill the scum in the field." The corporal cocked his rifle. "This specific bad boy tore through three scum warriors and spilled their insides across the Appalachian Trail. And I'm going to show you how to do the same."

Elvis called out, "Question, sir!"

Corporal Diaz turned toward the boy. "I'm not an officer, soldier. Don't you sir me. You will call me Corporal or Commander."

"Yes, s—I mean, yes, Commander!" said Elvis.

"What's wrong with your sideburns?" Corporal Diaz asked.

Elvis had shortened his sideburns at RASCOM, but they still grew impressively long. "Sorry, si—Commander! I was born with long sideburns, Commander."

Diaz stepped closer to the recruit. "Get those things shaved off, or you're likely to trip on them. What's your question?"

Elvis cleared his throat. "With all due respect, si—Commander, you fought the scum in the Appalachians. You killed the scum. Why are you here, training us miserable recruits, when you could be spraying bullets into alien guts?"

"Excellent question!" said Corporal Diaz. "Did everyone hear Recruit Sideburns? You want to know why I'm wasting my time with you babies instead of killing scum? We'll, I'll show you why." The corporal slung his weapon across his back and pulled up his shirt. Two ugly, apple-sized scars appeared on his chest. When the corporal turned around, he revealed two matching scars on his back. He pulled his shirt back down. "Scum bastards got me in the mountains. Two claws like scimitars tore through me, shattering four segments in my spine. You might think you know pain, but you don't truly know pain until scum claws shatter your spine, pierce your lungs, snap your ribs, and nearly rip out your heart. I got titanium bones in my spine now and an artificial lung, and I thank God Almighty every day, because my squad buddies weren't as lucky. Their teeth had to be fished out of scum shit to be identified. My fighting days are over now, but I can still train new killers to pick up where I stopped."

They all stared at him with wide eyes.

"Corporal Diaz is a fucking badass," Addy whispered to Marco.

The corporal spun around and marched toward her. "Name, recruit!" he barked.

"Addy Linden, Commander!"

"Did I ask you a question, Linden?"

"No, Commander!"

"Down! Forty push-ups and extra guard duty tonight."

"Yes, Commander!" Addy said, dropped down, and shouted out forty push-ups. She rose, panting and glistening with sweat. "Question, Commander!"

"What is it, Linden?"

Addy's eyes shone. "When do we get our guns, Commander? I want to spray scum with bullets."

"Right now you don't spray spit without an order from me." Diaz looked across his squad. "I'd sooner trust my grandmother with a Behemoth tank than you lot with a peashooter. You'll get your weapons once you've proven your worth. You can start now, all of you, by running three kilometers. Go."

They ran.

Marco had never been much of a runner, and he was soon wheezing, sweat soaking his uniform. He understood now why battle fatigues were opened at the armpits. Caveman and Elvis wheezed at his sides, faces red, hair soaked with sweat. Clouds of dust rose all around them. Addy, meanwhile, seemed to have no problem with the run. She was leisurely jogging at the front of the line, right behind Corporal Diaz, and hadn't even seemed to break a sweat. Pinky, that little lunatic, was so fast he ran past the corporal. Even Lailani de la Rosa, the smallest recruit in the platoon—a couple of inches shorter than the diminutive Pinky— was racing ahead.

When the three kilometers had finally ended, Marco found no relief. Corporal Diaz was crueler even than Sergeant Singh. He had the recruits do push-ups, sit-ups, jumping jacks, then repeat the cycle. Marco imagined that, yes, this had to be as bad as scum claws in your spine.

"You want to eat again?" Diaz said. "I'm not tossing apple cores your way until you give me another kilometer."

They ran again.

Finally, coated in dust and sweat, Diaz nodded. "All right, soldiers. You've earned your breakfast. Come with me. You have fifteen minutes."

They walked toward the largest building in the base, the mess hall. It was smaller than the one back at RASCOM and just as crowded. Hundreds of other recruits filled it, turning toward the new arrivals, and murmurs rose across the tables.

"How much you wanna bet they're calling us fresh meat?" Marco said.

Addy licked her lips. "Mmm, fresh meat. I could go for some Spam."

They lined up to grab their trays.

"You can't possibly enjoy Spam," Marco said. "Or call it fresh."

She knuckled his head. "Fresh from the can, old boy." She reached into her pocket and pulled out a can of Spam. "I swiped this little guy from the RASCOM kitchen."

Marco examined the can and groaned. "Addy! This can is thirteen years old. It wasn't fresh back during the Panama Assault."

"So long as it's younger than the Cataclysm, I'm a happy diner."

They got their chow—gray gruel, gray slop, gray soup, and slices of—thankfully not gray—Spam. Marco sat at a table with his usual group. Caveman was tucking in, and even little Lailani seemed to be enjoying the fare. Elvis winced with every bite.

"So did you see those two hot corporals?" Elvis said, forcing down a spoonful of gloop. "Fucking hot, both of them."

Pinky walked up toward them, slammed his tray down onto the table, and sat to eat. He brayed like a donkey, crooked teeth thrust out. "That blond corporal's got a face like pizza." He laughed at his own joke. "Corporal Pizza! You like fucking pizza, Elvis?"

Elvis shuddered as he swallowed another bite of slop. "I'd rather eat pizza."

"I bet you would." Pinky brayed, then turned toward Marco. "What about you, Poet? You got the hots for Corporal Diaz, don't you? Bet you can't wait to shower with him. Just don't drop the soap."

Marco tilted his head. "Did somebody hear something? I thought I heard a cockroach squeaking."

Rage suffused Pinky's face. The little soldier leaped right onto the table, scattering trays, and lunged at Marco.

Marco leaped back, surprised at the attack, and fell down hard onto the floor. Pinky jumped onto him, only for the rest of the platoon to grab the little recruit and pull him back.

"Down, Pinky!" Elvis said. "Down!"

Addy grabbed the little soldier's arm. "Cool it, runt! Corporal Diaz is right over there."

Indeed, the tall corporal marched toward them across the mess hall, face red. "What the fuck is going on?" he said.

"I—" Marco began.

"Silence!" Diaz barked. "Stand at attention when your commander approaches."

Everyone at the table rose and stood at attention. Across the mess hall, all eyes turned toward their squad. Marco's tailbone screamed in agony, but he forced himself to stand still. Pinky was muttering, standing at attention between Addy and Elvis.

"What happened?" Diaz began.

Everyone started talking at once.

"Stop!" Diaz barked. He pointed at Beast, the massive Russian, who stood nearby. "You, Mikhailov. You saw the whole thing. What happened?"

The giant bald Russian gulped. He looked from one soldier to another, then back to Corporal Diaz. "*Ya ne znayu.* I don't know, Commander. I no see."

Corporal Diaz looked across the squad. "Then maybe every one of you sorry buggers needs to serve kitchen duty all week. Maybe—"

"It was Pinky, Commander!" rose a voice. "That is, Recruit Peter Mack, Commander. Him, the little guy. He started it all. He just lunged at Emery, Commander."

Marco turned toward the voice. It was Lailani who had spoken. The tiny recruit emerged from behind Beast, pointing at Pinky. She gave Marco a little nod.

Oh fuck, Marco thought. He didn't want Lailani implicated in all this. If movies had taught him anything, it was that in prison and the military, rats were not treated well. He could already see socks full of bars of soap in Lailani's future.

Pinky fumed and began to howl. "She's fucking lying!" He made to lunge toward her. "You fucking little China whore, I—"

For a man with a metal spine, Corporal Diaz moved amazingly fast. He grabbed Pinky, twisting his arms behind his back.

"You just earned yourself a few hours in the brig, Mack," the corporal said.

The platoon's other two corporals approached—the blond, hard-eyed St-Pierre and the dark, small Webb on her prosthetic blades. Both helped drag Pinky out of the mess hall.

"You're fucking dead!" Pinky shouted as they dragged him out. "Both of you, Emery and de la Rosa! You're fucking dead!"

For a moment all the recruits stood in stunned silence.

Then everyone got back to eating, talking, and laughing.

"You going to eat your Spam, Poet?" Addy reached toward Marco's plate.

He let her take the slice. He turned toward Lailani.

"You didn't have to do that, Lailani," he said.

The little soldier snorted. "Why not? Fuck that prick. I'm not scared of him."

"He'll be out of the brig tomorrow and pissed off," Marco said.

Lailani scoffed. "Eh, fuck him. I grew up in the slums of Manila. Never had a roof over my head, had to fight for every scrap of food. On good days we slept by the train tracks. On bad days on the landfills. I've fought rapists and murderers before Pinky even learned how to jerk off. Let him come at me then. I hate assholes like him." She looked at Marco. "How he talked to you is wrong. He's a bully. A nasty one. And I don't tolerate bullies, whether they're aliens or little punks like him." She looked across the table. "You hear that, boys and girls? Any one of you has a problem with me ratting on a fellow recruit, you tell me now, and I'll shove my boot up your ass. If you wait until I have a gun, it'll be worse."

They all stared at her, then looked back at their trays.

At that moment, looking at Lailani—even with Kemi's photo in his back pocket—Marco was deeply, madly in love.

Addy nodded. "Yep. As I said. I like this one." She turned toward Elvis. "Yo, Elvis, you gonna eat that Spam?"

Elvis pulled his plate back. "Away with you, ravenous beast!"

The recruits soon forgot about Pinky, talking instead about their corporals, but Marco was silent. He kept thinking about the scars on Lailani's wrists, about Kemi back home, and about what would happen when Pinky returned to the platoon.

CHAPTER NINE

The first day of basic training was just as long and exhausting as RASCOM.

For what seemed like hours, they practiced their marching and formations.

They ran. They jumped. They climbed ropes. Push-ups, again and again.

Five minutes to run to the latrines—nasty, horrible holes in the ground without a toilet seat to be found.

Five minutes to gather around a single, leaky tap that rose from a rocky field, to fill their canteens with a few drops per soldier.

Ten minutes to shovel more gray slop and Spam into their mouths.

It all blurred together to Marco—the marching, running, push-ups, and everywhere the shouting, standing at attention, dropping down, rising, crawling through the dust, jumping, forming ranks, breaking ranks, an endless confusion, all in the sweat and dust and heat of the desert. His copy of *Hard Times* still bulged in his back pocket, but Marco couldn't even imagine finding the time to read a book here, and he realized the folly of his plan, his hope to find some comfort in a book. If they had only a moment without a commander shouting at them, they used that moment to pee, race to the tap and refill their canteen with a few drops—never time for more than a few drops—or gulp down a few bites. Then the shouting, racing, electrical prods, falling, jumping, all jumbled together into a mishmash that spun Marco's head.

"Fuck this shit," Addy said, doing sit-ups at his side in the sand.

"Yeah," Marco said, panting, awash with sweat. Suddenly the words blurted out from him. "I miss my library. I miss my father. I miss Kemi. I miss being a human. I feel like an animal here. Fuck this shit indeed."

Addy raised her eyebrow. "What? Poet, it's only been two days! I'm talking about guns. Fuck this no guns shit! Let me shoot!"

Lailani jogged up toward them, plonked down, and began her sit-ups. "I agree. I want to blast aliens. Pew pew pew."

Marco sighed, rose to his feet, and began his jumping jacks. "You girls are insane."

At least Pinky wasn't here today. The little delinquent was still cooling off in the brig. If Pinky had been here, had heard Marco's moment of weakness . . . Marco didn't even want to think about that. He silently vowed to keep his weakness to himself. He would tell nobody else about his homesickness, his fear. If Addy and Lailani were so motivated, so tough, Marco would learn from them, would become as strong as they were.

It seemed the passage of years, generations, ecological epochs before dinner. In the darkness, they filed into the mess hall, collected their dirty plates and mugs, and accepted their meals.

"Mmm, Spam!" Addy said, sitting down at their table. "Poet, can I have your Spam?"

"Stop that!" Marco slapped her hand away and shoved the mystery loaf into his mouth. "I'm hungry enough to eat even this, and it's probably made out of scum asses."

"I want to kick their asses, not eat them," said Elvis, sniffing at his meat.

Marco groaned and looked over to the commanders' table at the back of the mess hall. Sergeant Singh, the corporals, and Ensign Ben-Ari were sitting there, enjoying sandwiches. Sandwiches weren't fine dining, perhaps, but compared to this gray slop and gooey meat, it would have felt like a king's feast.

"Why do they do this?" Marco said, looking at his friends. "Why the sleep deprivation, the shouting, the marching, the drilling, the inspections, the slop . . ." He let the goo plop from his spoon back onto his plate. "How does any of this help us fight the scum? Lailani is right. We should be learning how to fight, not suffering through this nonsense."

Lailani spoke softly. "Because they want to break you."

"Oh, they've broken me," Marco said.

Lailani stared at him, and Marco was taken aback by the rage that flared in those dark eyes. "You think this is hard, Canada? What do you know of hardship? Did you ever rummage through trash bins to survive? Did you ever sleep in gutters as hundred-peso whores pissed around you, screaming as it burned them? Did you ever live along the train tracks where thieves, rapists, and murderers lurked at every corner, where thirteen-year-olds whored out their bodies, where they had daughters with American soldiers, and—" Lailani stopped suddenly and looked down at her plate. "Forget it. You wouldn't understand. You think you're broken now, but you know nothing." She rose from her seat. "I'm done eating." She tossed her Spam at Marco. "Eat it. And don't ever fucking complain about it again. It's more than many people have."

With that, eyes damp, Lailani de la Rosa marched away.

All the recruits sat in silence for a moment.

"Say," Elvis said, "do we have ranks?"

Addy looked at him. "What?"

"Do we have ranks?" Elvis said. "Are we privates or what? I think we're privates, if Diaz is a corporal and Singh is a sergeant."

"You're not a fucking private!" Addy said, tossing slop at him. "You're just a pissant recruit. All of us are. We ain't got no ranks yet. Not until we're done with boot camp."

"But we have to have ranks!" Elvis said. "You can't be a soldier without a rank."

"Well, then, you're ranked Pissant Elvis, how about that?"

As the squad all began to argue about whether they had ranks or not, Marco sat silently, staring at Lailani's empty seat. He thought about how, only yesterday—or was it this morning?—she had stood up for him, had faced Pinky for him. He had thought they would become friends. Right from the very start, seeing her jog up to their platoon at RASCOM, Marco had felt instant affection toward Lailani Marita de la Rosa. What had he done to sour things so badly?

He thought about how her life must have been. His life had been hard in Toronto—losing his mother to the scum, spending his childhood and youth racing into bomb shelters and subway stations, seeing death, fire, disease. One summer, he had spent three whole months underground with a gas mask on as the scum had relentlessly pounded the city. Not an easy life, not as easy as lives in pre-Cataclysm books. But it seemed downright idyllic compared to what Lailani had described. Marco had never had to eat from garbage bins, sleep on trash heaps or train tracks, or deal with rapists and murderers.

Who are you, Lailani? he wondered. She had mentioned being only half Filipino, that her father was an American soldier. That's how she was able to serve here in the Western Command. So why had she grown up homeless in Manila? Had her father died fighting the scum, or had he abandoned her to poverty?

Marco thought he understood the scars on her wrists a little better now, how that sort of life could have driven her to cut herself.

"I'm done." He rose to his feet and stepped out of the mess hall. He wanted to find Lailani, to apologize to her, to comfort her somehow, but within moments Sergeant Singh was ordering the platoon into formation again, and Lailani was careful to stand as far away from Marco as possible.

After lunch, when Marco was bracing for more exercise, Ensign Ben-Ari returned to lead them to a rocky field, where they sat facing the concrete wall of an armory. The officer clicked on a projector, and the words *Why We Fight* appeared on the wall over a background of fluttering HDF flags. The title faded away, replaced with a woman, ten feet tall, smiling sweetly and saluting. A butterfly pendant hung around her neck.

"Well, if it isn't our old friend, Captain Butterflies," Addy whispered to Marco.

In the video, the pretty young soldier smiled, dimples deep and teeth sparkling. She wore a white uniform with three golden bars on each shoulder.

"Hello, soldiers of Fort Djemila!" she said. "I'm Captain Edun, happily here to serve the Human Defense Force!" She gave an adorable salute. "Did you know that every day across the galaxy, soldiers of the HDF—just like you—kill over a thousand *scolopendra titania* aliens? That's right! With proper training, you'll learn how to defend Earth and make your families proud!"

Images appeared in the reel, showing sickeningly sweet families—all with blond hair, blue eyes, and bad tans—smiling and waving to the camera in suburban yards. A golden retriever wagged his tail, and a happy mailman tipped his hat.

Captain Butterflies appeared back on screen, more somber now. "Fifty years ago the *scolopendra titaniae*, a predatory alien race from the Scorpius system, launched a surprise attack against

Earth." Images appeared on screen, showing flaming purple balls hurling down toward Earth, followed by cities collapsing and forests burning. Butterflies spoke over the images. "Six billion lives were lost, more than half the world population. Entire cities were laid to waste. Humanity seemed close to extinction."

Images showed hungry, skeletal survivors searching through ruins for food, and Marco thought about Lailani. He sought her in the platoon, saw her sitting on the other side by a few soldiers whose names Marco hadn't yet learned. Lailani was staring at the reel, face blank, but her tiny fists were clenched.

Captain Butterflies continued speaking, this time more firmly. "But humanity did not fall. The armies of the world gathered together in the ruins, forming the Human Defense Force, an alliance of humanity's best. We launched our own spacecrafts, repurposing vehicles previously used for exploration and tourism. We launched a desperate attack on Abaddon, the *scolopendra titaniae*'s planet. Many of our brave pilots perished. But one courageous pilot, the hero Evan Bryan, reached the enemy planet and successfully launched a hydrogen missile."

The film showed a grainy photo of a handsome young hero in an old-fashioned uniform, saluting the flag. The image changed to an animation of a starfighter raining down death onto an enemy planet.

"Millions of *scolopendra titaniae* died that day," said Captain Butterflies. "The HDF struck back! Since that day, the aliens have never dared destroy entire Earth cities again. For fifty years they've been trying to break our spirit with a War of Attrition, killing us one at a time. For fifty years they believed they could shatter our resolve, that our civilization would collapse like cobwebs if terrorized enough. But humanity still stands!" The images now showed proud children, mothers, fathers, and senior citizens saluting flags of the HDF. "Thanks to soldiers like you, your families can sleep well tonight. Thanks to the HDF, Earth and her colonies across space thrive. The HDF—defending our species, defending our hope, defending our civilization. That is why we fight!"

The camera zoomed out, revealing a crowd of smiling children, all raising toy guns. They stomped centipedes—these ones Earth centipedes, only a couple of inches long—under their shoes. "That is why we fight!" they chanted.

The images crackled, then faded, leaving only the concrete wall.

A few soldiers clapped politely.

"Play 'Freebird'!" Addy cried out, earning a glare from Corporal Diaz and an extra hour of kitchen duty the next morning.

After the brief indoctrination, Ensign Ben-Ari faced the soldiers again.

"Are you ready to learn how to kill these creatures?"

They all shouted, "Yes, ma'am!"

Their eyes all shone, but Marco felt queasy, and he kept seeing it again and again—the pods slamming into the Earth, millions dying, and his mother in the snow.

CHAPTER TEN

The recruits marched through the desert base, heading past boulders, crossing a dune, and walking along a barbed wire fence. A vulture circled above. Two rusty bins rose ahead in the sand, each the size of an automobile. The smell of oil and metal hit Marco's nostrils, and the sun baked their helmets.

"All right, recruits!" shouted Sergeant Singh, his teeth brilliantly white against his black beard. "Grab your body armor and grab your guns."

"Fuck yeah!" Addy shouted, earning an hour of kitchen duty.

"Yes, Commander!" shouted the others.

They stepped toward the closer bin. Inside, they found knee and elbow pads made from hard green plastic. Marco strapped them on.

"I feel like a Ninja Turtle," he muttered.

"Ninja what-the-fuck now?" Addy said.

"You know, Ninja Tur—" He sighed. "Forget it. Kemi was obsessed with the twentieth century."

Addy rolled her eyes. "Kemi this, Kemi that. Forget about her."

Elvis, Beast, and a few other male recruits whistled and stepped closer.

"You got a girlfriend back home, you hound dog?" Elvis said.

"I bet she's very beautiful." Caveman sighed wistfully.

"Does she have big hips like Russian woman?" said Beast, largest in the platoon. "You sleep with her yet? You make her a woman? In Russia, you not real woman till man fuck you."

Marco groaned. "Can we stop this?"

Addy nodded. "He did! He slept with her."

The boys' eyes all lit up. At once, hands were slapping Marco on the back, and a few other recruits approached, adding their congratulations.

"You make me proud!" said Beast, his slap to Marco's back nearly knocking him down. "We drink vodka later."

"Marco is a pimp!" Elvis announced. "He—"

"Recruits!" Sergeant Singh shouted, marching toward them. "Shut your mouths. I don't care who Recruit Emery used to fuck, so long as he can fuck up scum with his T57 machine gun. Now go grab your weapons."

The recruits' eyes lit up, Marco's conquests immediately forgotten. They raced toward the farther bin, and Marco followed reluctantly. He wasn't comfortable with the boys talking about Kemi that way. Sure, their appreciation of him seemed earnest, and maybe he had earned some respect among then.

But I don't want that respect to be at your expense, Kemi, he thought. He remembered how they had made love that last night, the worst and best night in his life.

Fuck, I miss you, Kemi, he thought, surprised at the thought. He had never cursed before joining the HDF, and now he was cursing even in his thoughts.

The second bin was full of oil—a giant, metal bath of odorous oil. Addy leaned over the bin, reached inside, and pulled out a dripping assault rifle. Her eyes gleamed, and she seemed about to shout out in joy when she saw Singh and shut her mouth. Other recruits followed her lead, pulling out weapons. Marco rolled up his sleeve, reached into the oil, and felt a weapon. He pulled it free. It dripped, splattering oil onto his pants and boots.

"These here are your T57s," said Sergeant Singh. "They're almost four feet long, weigh nine pounds, and will fire a thousand rounds a minute to tear scum apart from a kilometer away. These guns are now your lovers, your best friends, your gods, and dearer to you than your dicks."

"I don't have a dick, sarge," Addy said.

"You do now," he replied, pointing at her gun.

Marco hefted his weapon. The weight was comforting—heavy enough to have substance, light enough to easily wield. The handguard was a good foot long, ridged and black, hiding most of the barrel. The stock flared out, just the right size to press against Marco's shoulder. He gripped the hilt with his right hand, held the handguard with his left, and peered through the front sight at a distant dune. There was no magazine loaded into the gun, but Marco already felt stronger than he ever had. He tried to imagine a scum crawling over the dune and his bullets spraying the alien.

"Soldiers, lower your weapons!" Sergeant Singh shouted. Several other recruits had raised their guns. "Grab straps and sling them across your backs."

They grabbed straps from a bucket, attached them to the guns, and slung them across their backs. With their helmets, knee and elbow pads, and machine guns, they looked almost like real soldiers.

The muzzle of Lailani's gun nearly touched the sand; the weapon was almost as long as her. Marco tried to meet her eyes. She had not spoken to him since their awkward exchange in the mess hall. But the short recruit kept avoiding his gaze. Her chin was raised, her lips tight. The dragon tattoo on her collarbone, her hard eyes, and her massive gun made her seem like the toughest soldier in the platoon, Marco thought—despite her height.

I'm sorry for offending you, Lailani, he thought, though he wasn't even sure what he had done.

"Hell yeah, this is more like it!" rose a hoarse voice from behind, and Marco's stomach sank.

Fuck me.

He turned around, his belly soured, and he had to curb the instinct to grab and aim his new gun.

Peter "Pinky" Mack was sauntering back toward the platoon, grinning and showing nearly all his crooked teeth.

Corporal Diaz was walking with him, escorting the runty recruit toward the bins.

"Watch it, Mack," the corporal said. "Unless you want to spend the night in the brig too."

Pinky snorted. "No, Commander. A few hours in that fucking cell were enough for me. I want to shoot scum!" He reached into the oily bin, pulled out a weapon, and mock-fired toward the dunes. "Pow, pow, pow! Dead fucking aliens! Pow! Emery killed by friendly fire! Pow!"

"Recruit!" shouted Diaz. "You will respect your weapon, and you will respect your fellow soldiers, or you will spend your five years of service in the brig."

Pinky nodded and slung the gun across his back. "Sorry, Corporal. Just excited to fight for the HDF. I want to kill scum like you did. I'm tough. Not like some." He shot Marco a withering glare, then barked a laugh.

"Lovely," Marco muttered, leaning toward Addy. "Give the little psychopath a gun. Makes perfect sense to me."

Addy patted his back. "Don't worry, Poet. Little dude's so insane he'll probably end up shooting off his own balls. That'll save us from a future Pinky."

"Latrine duty!" Sergeant Singh shouted, reeling toward them. "Both of you, Emery and Linden. Tonight. Next time you'll keep your mouths shut."

This elicited groans and laughter from the recruits. Marco and Addy cringed, but all they could do was nod and shout out, "Yes, Commander!"

As if kitchen duty wasn't bad enough, Marco thought, heart sinking.

"Now march, platoon!" Sergeant Singh shouted. "In formation! Recruit Ray, call out the march!"

"Yes, Commander!" Elvis said and began to march, shouting out. "Left, right, left, right!"

The rest of the platoon followed, marching across the sand, as Elvis cried out time.

As Marco walked, sudden pain stabbed his back. He cringed. He turned around to see Pinky walking behind him, pointing his gun forward. Marco realized the source of pain; Pinky had jabbed him in the back with his muzzle.

"You better watch your back, Canada," Pinky said. "Might end up with a bullet in it someday."

Marco wanted to reply, but Corporal Diaz was walking closer, and Marco didn't relish double latrine duty. He walked silently, trying to ignore the jabs in his back. As if Pinky's jabbing wasn't enough, Marco's muscles ached from hours of training. Blisters were blooming across his feet, and the damn heat was baking him. It was hard to believe that this was only his second day in the military. He felt as if he'd gone through months of deprivation.

They climbed a hill and descended into a valley. A concrete platform stretched across the sand like a boardwalk, and a few hundred meters away rose—

Scum! Marco thought, heart thudding, sure that the aliens were invading. But he quickly relaxed and cursed his antsiness.

Those were only wooden figures in the desert, carved into the shape of rearing centipedes, ten feet tall and lined with claws. Paper bullseyes were plastered onto the wooden figures.

"This guy almost pissed his pants!" Pinky said, pointing at Marco as their commanders conferred together. "He thought they were real!"

"Fuck you, Pinky," Marco said.

Pinky's face flushed, but before he could reply, the platoon's three corporals approached them, carrying sacks full of magazines.

The platoon split into its three squads, and they all sat in the desert. Each corporal spent a few moments displaying their own weapon—loading, unloading, clearing out jams, flicking the safety off and on.

"Remember, soldiers," said Corporal Diaz. "These weapons were built to kill scum, but they'll kill humans too. Never point them at another soldier. Not on purpose, not by accident, not if your gun is slung across your lap—never. Not if the safety is on. Not if you're *sure* the gun isn't loaded. Not if you hate your comrade's guts. I see anyone pointing a muzzle at another soldier—you'll spend a month in a reeking dungeon with no company but your own shit. You have these guns to protect life, but they'll just as easily take it. Understood?"

"Yes, Commander!"

"Good." Corporal Diaz slammed a magazine into his gun. "To fire these bad boys, you load, then charge with two fingers." He raised rabbit fingers, grabbed the charging handle, and tugged back until the gun clicked. "This weapon is now loaded, but the safety is still on. In this military, you will fire *only* in semi-automatic mode. *Never* in fully automatic."

Addy raised her hand. "Why not, Commander?"

Diaz turned toward her. "Because automatic is a good way of getting all your buddies killed. You fire these T57s in automatic, they'll spray out bullets like a machine gun so long as the trigger is pressed. In the heat of battle, with scum charging toward you, with the kick of a thousand rounds per minute driving into your shoulder, you're likely to lose control. The gun will start spraying everywhere like a loose hose. Automatic mode kills more soldiers with friendly fire than it kills scum. Semi-automatic only!"

Caveman raised his hand. "What's semi-automatic, Commander?"

The other recruits turned toward Caveman and guffawed. The heavyset brute was a humorous sight, perhaps. His bottom lip was thrust out, his brow furrowed in confusion, his heavy eyebrows pushed low over his beady eyes. His fatigues were in disarray, and polka-dot underwear thrust out from his pants.

"Silence!" Corporal Diaz shouted, glaring at the laughing soldiers. "I bet half of you don't know the answer to this question." He turned toward Caveman. "When the safety switch is on, the gun won't fire. When it's set to automatic, it fires like a machine gun; you'll empty an entire magazine within seconds. With semi-automatic, your weapon will fire one bullet at a time. Each time you pull the trigger—and you wait two seconds between trigger pulls to let these babies cool off, unless you want them to jam—a bullet fires. Now remember! Semi-automatic means new bullets are always being loaded. You only have to load the first bullet. After each bullet is fired, a new one is automatically loaded into the chamber for you, no need to cock the charging handle again. Once you're done firing, you'll have one last bullet in your barrel. You remove that bullet yourself, manually, after every firing session, or you're likely to blow your own brains out next time you put down your gun." He pulled open the barrel of his gun, exposing its innards, and fished out the bullet he had loaded. "Like this. Remember—each time you fire one bullet in semi, another is loaded. *Never* forget to remove your last bullet from the gun. Understood?"

"Yes, Commander!" they shouted.

Diaz tossed them a sack. "Now put on these earmuffs. This is going to get loud."

Hearing "earmuffs," Marco imagined pink fluffy things for warmth. But here were hard, plastic devices that looked like heavy headphones.

When everyone's ears were covered, the three corporals stepped toward the concrete platform. They lay down on their bellies, propped up on their elbows, their machine guns pointed toward the distant wooden targets. They cocked their weapons, pressed the stocks into their shoulders, and gripped the handguards. The recruits watched from behind.

Elvis leaned close and pulled Marco's right earmuff off his ear. "Corporal Pizza's got a nice ass," he whispered.

Marco glared at him. "Don't call her that. And don't say that."

Elvis grinned and punched Marco's arm. "I can't believe you fucked Kemi, you player, you. Proud of you, brother. I—"

The corporals fired, and furious, roaring, impossibly loud sound flared.

Marco and Elvis cringed and pressed their earmuffs against their ears.

Bullets roared.

Fire blazed.

Empty casings flew.

The sound was so loud that even with his earmuffs Marco winced, and his ears rang, and he swore that he'd kill Elvis if he suffered hearing damage from that first bullet.

Holes appeared in the wooden targets. The corporals shot again, waited two seconds, again, again. Bullets peppered the scum. One of the wooden targets spun, its mock claws whirring, and collapsed into the sand.

The corporals lowered their guns. All three removed their magazines, pulled open the barrels, and fished out the last loaded bullets.

The three corporals returned to their platoons, guns smoking. The recruits removed their earmuffs.

"Bad. Ass," Addy whispered.

Caveman whimpered, eyes screwed shut, pressing his hands hard against his earmuffs and pounding his feet. Marco tilted his head. He wanted to approach the heavyset recruit, to comfort him, but Corporal Diaz stepped back toward them.

"There are three ways to fire your T57s," Diaz said. "Lying on your stomachs, kneeling, and standing. We'll start from the ground up. When you lie on your stomachs, you want both elbows on the ground, one hand on the gun's handguard, and the magazine pressing against your forearm. And don't forget to keep that stock against your shoulder unless you want the gun to kick back into your nose. Now go kill those wooden scum."

The soldiers stepped onto the platform, where they took magazines of bullets from crates. They spread across the platform, facing their targets.

"Magazines—in!" barked Corporal Diaz.

With clicks, the recruits slammed their magazines into their guns.

"On your stomachs!"

They flattened themselves on their stomachs. Marco lay between Addy and Caveman. He peered over the latter's back, trying to meet Lailani's eyes, but the little recruit was staring ahead at her target, oblivious to all else.

Caveman let out another whimper. "It was so loud," he whispered.

"Cock your guns!" shouted Diaz.

Marco grabbed the charging handle and tugged back. He heard a click as a bullet left the magazine and entered the chamber.

"Switch to semi-automatic!"

Marco flipped the safety switch to semi, careful to avoid the automatic mode.

"Aim!" shouted Diaz. "Fire!"

Forty-five recruits pulled their triggers. Bullets roared out toward the scum targets.

Marco missed his first shot. The bullet hit the sand by his wooden scum. He frowned, stared through the sight, and adjusted the stock against his shoulder. He pulled the trigger again. He couldn't tell for sure from this distance, but he thought he hit. No sand, at least, flew this time. He fired again. Again. Across the platform, the other recruits were firing too. Empty casings flew from the chambers. When one shell grazed Marco's hand, he winced. The damn thing was *hot*.

"Die, you fuckers!" Addy was shouting as she fired bullet after bullet.

"Die, fucking scum!" Lailani could be heard shouting.

Caveman was wailing. The stocky recruit dropped his gun and scampered back.

"Halt your fire!" Corporal Diaz shouted. "Platoon, halt your fire!"

A few more bullets rang out, and they lowered their guns. Still lying on his stomach, Marco turned to see Caveman retreating several steps from the platform. Corporal Diaz approached him. The two soldiers stood a few feet behind Marco.

"I'm sorry, Corporal." Caveman mewled. "It's just so loud. So loud! Even with my earmuffs, I can't take it!" He seemed close to weeping. "I'm sorry."

Corporal Diaz had spent the day shouting, berating, and cursing his recruits, but now the soldier's face softened. He placed a hand on Caveman's shoulder.

"You did well, soldier," the corporal said. "I'm proud of you."

Marco's eyes widened. He had already admired Diaz for killing scum in the Appalachian Mountains, for suffering horrific wounds but remaining in the HDF to train new soldiers. Now his admiration for the wounded warrior grew further.

"Fabian, we need a soldier to guard the perimeter of the firing range," Diaz said to Caveman. "Go patrol the field. You'll fire your gun again tomorrow."

Caveman gulped and saluted. "Yes, si—"

Corporal Diaz, suppressing a smile, pulled the beefy boy's hand down. "Don't sir or salute me, I'm not your ensign. Now go."

"Yes, Commander!" said Caveman and lolloped off, face red.

They spent another hour firing their guns, lying, kneeling, standing. After each magazine emptied, they headed toward their targets, and soon Marco was able to hit the wooden scum every time. But wooden stationary scum were one thing. Marco had seen the creatures move, scuttling at incredible speed. Next time he encountered a living one, would he be able to even load and aim in time, let alone hit it?

At sunset they left the field. Marco tried to think how many days he had been here. When was the last time he had slept—back in RASCOM? He couldn't remember sleeping here at Fort Djemila yet, but it seemed like he had been here for days, weeks already. Time moved differently in the army. He was a veteran of two days, but he could barely remember his life as a civilian. Toronto now seemed a different world, different life.

As the soldiers headed toward the mess hall for dinner, Sergeant Singh stopped Marco and Addy.

"Not you two," the turbaned sergeant said. "You two don't eat tonight. You start your latrine duty. I want them spotless by the time the rest of your platoon is done eating."

Marco groaned inwardly. He wanted to object, to blame Addy, but refusing this stern commander seemed a bad idea.

Sergeant Singh isn't here to lead us like Ensign Ben-Ari or teach us like the corporals, he thought. *He's here to discipline us, and if we argue back, we'll end up in the brig like Pinky.*

"Yes, Commander," both Marco and Addy said.

The sergeant led them toward a small concrete building. They entered to find showers and rows of toilet stalls.

At least these weren't just outhouses like back in RASCOM. They had spent the day pissing in the open desert, and just the sight of actual stalls was such a relief that Marco almost—*almost*—didn't mind having to clean them. Again there were no toilet seats; the HDF was all about squatting over holes, it seemed. At least those holes weren't in the open, which already put the army ahead of prison, which was a little something to be grateful for.

Sergeant Singh handed them bottles of ammonia and mops.

"Clean the showers and the toilets. You see all that mold? I want it gone. I want this place clean enough to eat off."

"So, cleaner than the plates in the mess?" Addy said.

"Watch it, Linden."

With that, the sergeant left, perhaps to join the rest of the platoon at dinner. Marco and Addy remained here, holding mops.

"Thanks a lot, Addy," Marco said. "You just had to talk while we were getting our guns. Was it so important to tell me Pinky will shoot off his balls?"

She nodded. "Yes! It was." She kicked open a toilet stall, covered her mouth, and grimaced. "Oh, God! It's like a scum took a shit here." She closed her eyes, blindly splashing ammonia.

As they worked, cleaning the stalls and showers, Marco looked at her—this girl he had known all his life, who had grown up with him, who infuriated him, yet whom he loved with all his heart.

"Addy," he said. "I want you to know something. This place is a nightmare. It's an absolute fucking nightmare. I thank God, Cthulhu, and the Flying Spaghetti Monster that you're here with me. I'd have gone mad here without you."

She winked at him. "Even if I got you latrine duty?"

"Well, not that part. Addy . . . how are you?"

She cocked her head at him, scrubbing a shower's floor. "What do you mean?"

"I mean—are you really having fun here? Like you said earlier?"

Addy put down her mop. She turned toward Marco and held his arms. "Marco, I'm fucking terrified, all right? There are about a million scum up in the sky, desperate to kill us, and we just spent hours talking to a corporal who got half his guts torn out, and I can't stop thinking about my parents, and I just want to go home. I just want to go home, Marco." Suddenly tears were flowing down her cheeks. "I'm scared and homesick and I hate this place. But . . ." She sniffed. "But I want to fight. Yes, I still want to fight. I want to kill the scum—all of them. So I'm glad I'm here. And I'm glad you're here with me." She smiled, tears on her cheeks. "You're just a silly little thing, but I can think of no better friend to fight aliens with."

When finally the place was clean, they washed ammonia off their hands. They walked back out into the desert to find it dark, a million stars above.

And it was cold.

It was damn cold.

All day, Marco had been sweating in the heat, but now he shivered. Addy's teeth chattered.

"Did we just spend six months cleaning and it's winter now?" she said.

"We're in a desert," Marco said. "It's like that here. Deserts are just dry emptiness, and they let all the heat escape into space at night. Sun goes bye-bye, so does the heat."

They spotted their platoon ahead in a field, assembling tents in the sand. Addy and Marco joined the work, stomachs growling and teeth chattering. They set up three tents, one for each squad, and a ring of stones to define the perimeter of their platoon. Around them, across the desert, several other platoons were setting up their own tents. When the tents were up, the recruits assembled rows of cots inside, each topped with a thin mattress. Each tent included fifteen cots, enough for a single squad.

When the tents and cots were finally up, Marco was yawning. He had barely slept his last night in Toronto, and he had only slept an hour overnight at RASCOM. He didn't expect to get a full eight hours of sleep in the military, but a decent, solid six hours would do him wonders.

Yet before he could hit the mattress, Ensign Ben-Ari returned to them. Sergeant Singh walked with her, carrying a projector.

"Attention!" the sergeant called. "March!"

Marco groaned, looking back longingly at the tents and cots within. They marched through the desert under fields of stars. When no commanders were looking, Marco glanced at his watch. It was 10:00 p.m.

I still haven't had time to even read my book, he thought. *Let alone work on my novel.*

They returned to the armory, and the soldiers stood in a semicircle outside, facing the armory's windowless wall. Ensign Ben-Ari switched on the projector, and a flickering image appeared on the wall. Good old Captain Butterflies walked into the frame, smiling her sweet, dimpled smile.

"Hello, soldiers of the HDF! Captain Edun reporting for duty!" She gave an adorable salute, her smile blinding, and her butterfly pendant gleamed. "Did you know that for fifty years Earth's scientists have been studying the anatomy of the *scolopendra titaniae*? In this video we'll review their basic structures, describing how they eat, mate, and . . ."

Marco yawned, his attention waning. His eyelids felt like weights. His T57 hung across his back. It weighed only nine pounds, but right now it seemed heavy enough to crush his spine.

"Soldier!" Sergeant Singh said, marching toward Marco. "Was that a yawn? Does this bore you?"

"No, Commander!"

The bearded sergeant stared at him, seeking conceit, then spun toward Elvis, who was scratching his side.

"Stand still, soldier!"

They all stood at attention, watching the video, as Sergeant Singh assigned various punishments—ranging from push-ups to kitchen or latrine duty—to anyone who yawned, swayed, so much as slouched or scratched. Meanwhile, on the armory wall, the projector was showing scientists in lab coats dissecting the scum. Marco tried to focus on footage of a mother scum coiled around her maggots, but the vision kept blurring. His eyelids kept closing on their own, and once—when they closed for too long—he earned an electrical shock from Singh's baton. He kept his eyes open after that, using all his willpower just to stare ahead, to absorb those images. A scientist was pulling entrails out of a scum, then testing a severed claw by plunging it into a hog carcass.

Finally, at eleven at night, they marched back to their tents and took formation.

"All right, soldiers," said Sergeant Singh. "In one hour—at midnight on the dot—you come back here and take formation. Anyone who's late lands in the brig. For the next hour—you're free. I suggest you use this hour to attend the toilets, to shower, to write home, to cry for mommy if you like. If you use the showers, you get a friend to guard your gun. Anything else you do— anything, even sleeping—that gun stays on you. Come back here in the fanciest pajamas you've brought from home. Go."

With sighs of relief, the soldiers broke formation. Some headed to their tents for a nap. Others ran toward the showers and toilets. Marco looked at Addy.

"A full, free hour," he said. "Damn, we haven't had a free hour since, well . . . that hour we slept back in RASCOM."

She nodded and stretched. "I'm going to shower. I didn't clean the showers just for Pinky to foul them up again. You coming with?"

Marco hesitated. There were stalls around the toilets— thank goodness—but the showers were public. To shower in front of Pinky and the others . . . and Addy? Marco had grown up with Addy in the same apartment, but he didn't even like her seeing him in his boxer shorts. Yet when he sniffed his armpits, he recoiled. After running around for a day in the Chilean jungle, then training for a day in the North African desert, he smelled like the innards of a scum.

"All right, let's go," he said, hoping for a whole lot of steam in those showers.

One recruit, the scrawny boy Marco had seen reading *The Lord of the Rings* back at the recruitment spaceport, volunteered to guard the guns while his comrades showered. Marco and Addy took spare clothes from their duffel bags and stepped into the showers. As they walked past the toilet stalls, Marco realized that he hadn't emptied his bowels since Toronto, two days ago. With the lack of toilet seats and lack of privacy, he wasn't quite ready to attempt the feat yet, deciding to hold off for as long as possible.

They reached the showers. Most of the platoon was already there, naked under the hot water, boys and girls alike. If anyone was too shy, they'd have to stink. There would be no privacy in the army. Few people seemed to mind. Even Caveman seemed happy now, smiling and whistling as he shampooed. Elvis was singing "Suspicious Minds" as he soaped up. Marco was just glad the boy hadn't chosen to sing "Love Me Tender."

Addy went first, stripping naked and stepping under a showerhead. Marco caught a glimpse of her body, then quickly looked away. He didn't like how Addy made him feel. She was like a sister to him . . . wasn't she? He didn't want to think about her like that. Not here.

He removed his clothes and stepped into the shower too—thankful that he had brought flip-flops from home. A few soldiers were joining Elvis in song, and Marco noticed that Lailani was showering here too, singing along with the others. He hadn't noticed her before. She was so short she nearly vanished among the other soldiers. He looked at her, for just a second, unable to help but notice her slender, wet body, and—

Lailani looked at him, and he quickly looked away, his cheeks flushing. He finished washing quickly, toweled himself off, and dressed in his sweatpants and T-shirt. Clothes from home. Clothes that still smelled of his old apartment.

And suddenly, here in the showers, it all hit him.

Home. The library. His favorite books. His father in the kitchen, cooking a meal. Kemi smiling, hugging him, walking through the city with him. And suddenly there were tears on Marco's cheeks, and he was thankful for the steam that rose around him.

There was steam on the mirrors too, obscuring his reflection. He shaved by sense of touch, not wanting to risk Sergeant Singh's wrath. The sergeant, of course, had a full beard, but Marco imagined that he'd have to convert to one of the world's fine bearded religions before he could give up shaving in the military. After cutting himself in the steam, he wasn't sure that was a bad idea, and he was already trying to decide between joining the Amish or Orthodox Judaism.

"Get out of my way, Beast!" Lailani said, walking around the massive Russian. "Move it or I'll dunk your bald head into the toilet."

"In Russia," he began, "toilets so powerful they would rip off your head. Not like these silly American toilets."

Lailani groaned. "We're not in America!"

The towering Russian shrugged. "Not Russia. Close enough."

Groaning, Lailani came to stand at a bench near Marco, still naked and drying her short hair. Her dragon tattoo coiled from her navel up to her collarbone, and the rainbow shone on her other arm. As she dressed, she spoke.

"You're trying awfully hard to ignore me, Emery. Not like back in the shower."

He rummaged through his duffel bag. "I've got other things to worry about, de la Rosa."

Lailani snorted, looked down at his copy of *Hard Times*—he had placed it on the bench—then grabbed it. She tugged out the photo that peeked between the pages. The photo of Kemi.

"Hey, stop that!" Marco said.

Lailani's eyes widened. "This is your girlfriend?" She whistled. "She's hot. I'm jealous."

"Give it back!" Marco reached toward the photo, but before Lailani could return it, Beast grabbed it from the little Filipina. The Russian stared at Kemi, and his eyes widened too.

"That your girl?" he said. "She almost pretty like Russian woman!" He whistled. "*Krasivaya*. Beautiful. Here, wait a moment. Here picture of my girlfriend." He pulled a photo out from his duffel bag, and Marco found himself staring at a smiling woman with pigtails and a missing tooth. "She prettiest woman in Russia."

The other soldiers gathered around, passing the photos back and forth, and finally Marco managed to grab Kemi's photo and return it to his book.

"He fucked her, you know," Elvis was telling people. "Made her a woman." He patted Marco on the back. "My man."

"Stop saying that," Marco said. "I, we . . ."

We broke up, he wanted to tell them. *Kemi was accepted to military academy. She's going to be an officer like Ensign Ben-Ari. And she has no more room for me in her life.*

Yet he could say none of those things, so he simply stepped back outside into the night. His eyes stung again, and even with an assault rifle across his back, Marco felt weak as a child.

CHAPTER ELEVEN

Sergeant Singh met them outside their tents at midnight. Three tents rose here, low and olive green, for the platoon's three squads.

"Your first day at Fort Djemila is over," the bearded sergeant said. "Wake up call is at 4:30 a.m."

The recruits stood in formation in the sand, wearing sweatpants and T-shirts, and Marco cringed. After two sleepless nights, four and a half hours didn't seem like nearly enough. It would beat the single hour from last night, but Marco could imagine many yawns tomorrow.

"Your corporals will assign you guard duty for tonight," Sergeant Singh said. "That's right. You are soldiers now—soldiers with weapons. Every fifteen minutes, I want one guard outside each tent. When your shift is done, you return to your tent and wake up the next soldier. If you see anything suspicious at night— any strange lights in the sky, any giant centipedes crawling over the dunes—you raise the alarm. If you hear a siren blaring, everyone puts on their uniforms, grabs their weapons, and kneels between the cots—*inside* your tents, still and silent. Understood?"

"Yes, Commander!"

"When you sleep tonight," Singh said, "you keep your T57s under your pillows, your boots and uniforms beside your beds. If the scum attack, I need you uniformed and ready to fire your guns within seconds. For morning inspection, you present yourselves with polished boots, made beds, and oiled guns. You'll find oil and shoe polish in your duffel bags. Understood?"

"Yes, Commander!"

Sergeant Singh nodded, turned, and walked away, soon vanishing in the night.

The three corporals, commanders of the platoon's squads, approached and read out names, assigning guard duty to each tent. In his squad, Marco was set to guard fourth—right after Addy and before Pinky.

"Lovely," he muttered. "I get to have a crazy hockey player waking me up, then get to wake up a psychopathic jockey."

He stepped into his squad's tent and his heart sank. It was small. It was stifling. Fifteen crude, rusty cots spread here in two rows, barely any space between them, topped with narrow mattresses. If you could call them mattresses; they were no thicker than his thumb and barely wider than a coffin. At once, recruits rushed toward the four bunks at the edges of the tent, those with only one neighbor. Addy was one of the lucky four. Marco resigned himself to a cot beside hers. He was thankful that, at least, Pinky had chosen a cot on the other side of the tent.

Marco dropped his duffel bag between his and Addy's cots, slid his T57 under his pillow, and lay on the mattress. He could feel the cot's metal bars through the thin mattress, but after days of exhaustion, he couldn't complain. He closed his eyes.

He didn't remember falling asleep, but he found himself floating through a dream world, a black desert whose dunes rolled beneath him like waves. Kemi was there, naked in the night, beautiful and seductive like an Arabian princess in an old tale, and Marco kissed her, made love to her on a cot, but she became Lailani, and the steam of the showers rose around them, and Elvis was there, singing "Love Me Tender" and patting Marco on the back.

"Poet!" Through the darkness, Pinky approached, sneering, and the tiny recruit grew taller, sprouting claws, becoming a centipede.

"Scum attack!" Marco shouted, firing at the alien, but his bullets kept missing, and the scum grabbed him, shook him, called his name.

"Poet! Poet, damn it."

Marco opened his eyes. Addy was leaning above him, shaking him. He blinked, rubbed his eyes, and checked his wristwatch. He'd been sleeping for half an hour.

"Your guard duty, little buddy." Addy yawned. "Go out and watch for scum. Fifteen minutes, then wake up . . . next . . . guard . . ." She yawned, landed on her cot, and snored.

Marco rose, shivering in the cold, and pulled on his fatigues and helmet. He slung his gun across his back and hung four magazines full of bullets from his belt. He stepped past the other recruits. Beast was mumbling in his sleep, something about a girl named Oxana, while Elvis was actually singing—singing in his sleep!

As Marco walked by Lailani, he paused for just a moment. He looked down at the young soldier. During the days, Lailani Marita de la Rosa was all grunts, growls, and guts, but at night she seemed so peaceful, a fragile doll. She seemed so young, so beautiful, and Marco remembered making love to her in his dream.

Shame filled him. This felt wrong. Why was he thinking about Lailani like this? Not here. Not now. He had a war to worry about. And he still had some hope of seeing Kemi again. He walked by Lailani, pulled open the tent flap, and stepped outside into the cold desert.

The stars shone, and Marco stuffed his hands into his armpits and circled the tent. Other recruits were patrolling around their own tents. When Corporal St-Pierre walked by in the distance, they all stood at attention, guns at their sides, then resumed their patrols. Marco looked up at the stars as he walked. He sought Antares, a star in the Scorpius constellation, the scum's star. Humanity had a few colonies in space—mostly military compounds these days—but the scum had spread across many star systems, destroying entire civilizations in their path.

And now they have their eyes on Earth, Marco thought. *But so long as the HDF stands, Earth will stand too.*

He looked across the other stars. There were other sentient civilizations out there, distant galactic empires. Some were barely more than myths, so distant humanity knew little about them. The Guramis, aquatic aliens who lived in a watery world with no land. The Silvans, dwellers of trees as tall as skyscrapers. Hundreds, maybe thousands of other civilizations, some of them predatory, others benevolent. But they were all far. Too far to help humanity. Earth alone would have to hold back the scum, or Earth would fall. Marco gripped his gun, wishing he could go back in time, could fire bullets into the scum that had killed his mother.

When his fifteen minutes were up, Marco returned into his tent.

He approached Pinky's bed.

Oh fuck, Marco thought.

Peter "Pinky" Mack was snoring, his gun's muzzle peeking out from under his pillow. His face was gaunt, the nose thin, the eyebrows sharp, his black hair spiky. His crooked teeth thrust out like a donkey's.

Who are you, Pinky? Marco thought. He knew nothing about the boy—where he had come from, how he had become this creature. Marco could almost imagine the boy growing up in some subterranean cavern, twisted with hatred, fearing the sunlight, changing year by year into a monster, perhaps obsessed with a precious ring.

"Pinky," Marco said. "Pinky, your turn."

The recruit would not wake.

"Pinky, man." Marco shook him, daring not speak louder for fear of waking the rest of his squad. They were all sleeping in their cots around him. "Guard duty."

But Pinky turned away, still snoring. Marco cursed. Fuck it. He'd had enough. He wouldn't go out and guard for Pinky's shift too, and if St-Pierre or another commander walked by again, saw no guard outside their tent . . .

Marco grabbed his flashlight from his belt, pointed it at Pinky's face, and flicked it on and off. The light hit Pinky's eyelids, and finally the runty recruit groaned, opened his eyes, and stared into the light.

Pinky groaned loudly, rose from bed, and shoved Marco.

"What the fuck are you doing?"

"Guard duty," Marco said.

Pinky's groans woke up soldiers across the tent. A few pillows were tossed their way.

"Shut up!" rumbled a muffled voice.

"Pinky, I'm not taking your guard duty," Marco said. "It's your fifteen minutes. It's—"

But the small soldier returned to his bed and closed his eyes.

Marco trembled with rage.

"Just take his shift too, Poet," Beast muttered from his cot. "Little fucker will not wake. Sleeps like Russian bear in winter."

"I'm not taking his shift," Marco said. "Nobody is taking his shift. He's going to wake up and—"

"I'll take double shifts," rose a voice, and Marco turned to see Lailani approaching, pulling on her fatigues and strapping her gun across her back. "It's my turn after him anyway, and I'm already up." She passed by Marco, then looked at him and touched his arm. "You fought well against the Evil Pinky, but sometimes the goblin wins. Get some sleep, Poet."

She stepped outside the tent into the night.

Marco returned to his cot and closed his eyes.

Losing to Pinky hurt. But Lailani talking to him, touching his arm, had felt wonderful.

He sank back into an exhausted dreamworld. He stood on a distant, dark planet, wearing a spacesuit, holding his gun. Canyons, craters, and caves surrounded him, a rocky wasteland, the stars foreign. His platoon stood with him, and they were all wearing metal suits like mechanical exoskeletons. A clattering rose. From around them, hundreds, then thousands of scum were racing forward, and they fired their guns, and the bullets roared out, and—

Sirens blared.

Marco bolted up in bed.

The siren wailed, up and down, mournful, warning. *Scum. Scum. Scum.*

Across the tent, the squad leaped up in their cots—even Pinky. Marco tugged on his fatigues so quickly he nearly tore them, strapped his helmet onto his head, and grabbed his gun. He knelt between two cots, reaching down to touch the magazine of bullets that hung from his belt. The other soldiers knelt too, shadowy lumps, guns in hand. The siren gave one more wail, then fell silent.

The squad remained still.

For a long time they waited.

"What's going on?" Elvis finally whispered. "Is it over?"

Marco shook his head. "No continuous tone siren yet. Wait for the all clear."

They waited. The minutes ticked by. The world was silent.

"It's got to be over, whatever was happening," Elvis said. He crept toward the edge of the tent and peeked outside. "Hey, Beast! Beast! You see anything?"

The Russian, who was outside on guard study, stuck his head into the tent. "I no see shit. No all clear yet. Stay on alert. Corporals walking around outside. If they see you leave tent, they smash you. Might be a fucking scum somewhere in sand. In Mother Russia we'd have killed it already." He closed the tent flap, remaining outside.

Inside the tent, the recruits waited.

Marco checked his watch. 3:15 a.m. The minutes ticked by. Soon it was almost four in the morning.

"I got to piss," Elvis said. "I'm making a run for the latrines."

"You can't go outside," Marco reminded him. "Remember about the smashing?" He imitated Beast's accent. "Corporal smash you."

Elvis groaned and rose from between the cots, gripping his groin. "I'd rather get smashed than piss my pants. If the scum are attacking, I ain't dying with piss on my pants."

Caveman raised a bottle of orange juice. "Here, piss in this," he said. "Wait." He gulped down the juice. "Now piss."

Elvis grabbed the bottle. "How did you even get this, Caveman?" he asked, then shook his head. "Never mind. Guys, look away."

They all groaned and looked aside. Elvis filled the bottle, then placed it near the tent flap. Marco grimaced to see droplets drip onto the floor only a foot away from his cot.

"Fuck, I gotta piss too," Lailani said. "Caveman, got another bottle?"

Caveman shook his head but offered her a milk carton. "Use this. Wait." He chugged down the milk. "Here."

Lailani grabbed the carton. "Perfect."

Soon three more soldiers had filled cartons and bottles, placing them by the tent flap—uncomfortably close to Marco.

"Marco, you want this Tupperware?" Caveman asked, handing him a container.

"I'll hold it in," Marco said. "How do you even have these things, Caveman?"

Caveman grinned. "Easy, I—"

The siren wailed again—a long continuous tone. All clear.

The recruits all exhaled in relief. When Marco checked his watch, he saw that there were only thirty minutes until the morning inspection. He had slept . . . how long so far? An hour? Two? Not even? Since joining the military, he hadn't slept more than three hours, he estimated, and had barely slept the night before the army too.

He flopped down onto his cot, remaining in his fatigues, boots on his feet. Yet exhausted as he was, he couldn't fall back asleep, not with the knowledge that any minute now, Sergeant Singh would be rousing them, inspecting them, shouting, push-ups, another day in hell.

In the darkness, a voice rang out.

"Up, up! Morning inspection!" Sergeant Singh pulled open the tent door and stomped inside. "Morning inspe—"

The sergeant's boots hit the bottles and cartons, and piss spilled across the floor.

The recruits all stared.

"Fuck," Lailani whispered.

Sergeant Singh stood very still for a long moment, then looked up at the recruits. "Well, you've all just earned an hour of latrine duty tonight. You have sixty seconds to present yourselves outside the tent. And somebody mop up this piss."

Marco groaned. Tonight? It was 4:30 a.m. He didn't know if "tonight" meant now, the next time it went dark, next week, this month, back in time—the entire concept of day and night was a blur now. Somewhere in the back of his mind, Marco thought that dawn was soon coming, that it was his third day in the army, but that seemed impossible. He had always been trapped here. The old Marco Emery, the boy who had lived in Toronto, who had been writing a novel, that was just a past life or a dream.

"Sixty!" Sergeant Singh shouted outside. "Fifty-nine!"

Elvis rose and stretched. "Goooooooooood morning, 4th Platoon!" he roared out, then shook his head at the perplexed looks. "What, no classic film buffs? Philistines."

Marco was thankful that he had slept in his fatigues. He splashed his boots with polish, straightened his shirt, hurriedly made his bed, and rushed outside for inspection. The recruits lined up. Caveman was still wearing his pajama bottoms—this time they were covered with little dinosaurs.

Only four recruits passed inspection that morning. Marco failed on account of his rifle; he had forgotten to oil the chamber. All those who failed lay down in the sand for their push-ups, then tried again, again, finally passing inspection—uniforms and beds neat, boots polished, faces shaved, guns oiled, helmets on straight.

"Sergeant Singh!" Elvis dared to say. "Commander! The alert last night. Did the scum—"

"False alarm, recruit," Singh said. "A scum pod was spotted in the sky, but it landed in the nearby town, skipping our base."

"Nearby town, Commander?" Elvis said. "Where are we?"

"You're in hell, recruit, and I'm the devil," said the sergeant. "That's all you need to know. Now run—all of you."

In the darkness, they began to jog around the camp. Another day in Fort Djemila, AKA hell, began.

CHAPTER TWELVE

Running.

Push-ups. Sit-ups.

A breakfast of gray slop—and finally a quick, queasy foray into the toilet stalls to expel it.

Gathering around the tap in the desert, waiting for the drip, drip, drip of water into the canteen.

Running. Heat. Sweat.

One soldier passed out from heat stroke. Another threw up his breakfast. They ran some more.

They sat outside the armory, watching Captain Butterflies speak of the scum menace and the glory of the HDF. They fired their guns. They tossed grenades. They ate, and another race to the latrine, and rumbling stomachs and shuddering and exhaustion and more sweat.

When it wasn't Sergeant Singh shouting at them, it was the three corporals. When the corporals weren't around, the sergeant was back. Ensign Ben-Ari rarely saw them, only to deliver a quick sermon on the pride of the military, indoctrinate them with a propaganda reel, then head off to wherever officers spent their days.

Whenever Marco was on his feet, he hoped, wished, prayed to sit down. His leather boots were so rough his blisters were growing blisters. He had developed a limp, and his lower back soon cried in protest too. It was only his third day in the military, but aside from two or three hours of sleep since leaving Toronto, he'd been running, exercising, training, sweating, shouting, and being shouted at, and he had never felt so weary. As they jogged around the base, as they stood firing their guns, as they marched in formations, as they stood for inspection—the thoughts kept racing. *Please let us sit. Please let us rest.* Often he felt close to collapsing, as if the blazing sunlight could knock him down.

Yet whenever they sat—to watch a reel, listen to a corporal's combat lesson, even just eat—Marco kept praying to please stand up. Sitting was agony. Whenever he sat down, his eyelids felt like weights again, and sleep kept creeping up on him. Yet whenever his eyes began to droop, somebody was there— their sergeant, a corporal, even Ensign Ben-Ari—to shout, to rouse him, to threaten him with more latrine or kitchen duty or push-ups. As Marco sat watching films of soldiers battling scum, or watching a corporal demonstrate how to assemble a rocket launcher, Marco could barely focus, had to divert all his energy to his eyelids, this war to keep them peeled.

And whenever they rose, he felt such relief—finally he could walk off his sleep!—only to instantly feel that agony in his back and legs, to keep praying to sit again.

Whenever I stand, I want to sit. Whenever I sit, I want to stand. If Marco had to summarize his third day at Fort Djemila, it was like that.

In the afternoon their corporals led them toward a canvas pavilion near the barbed wire fence that surrounded Fort Djemila. A few screens stood at the back of the pavilion, showing propaganda films and historical footage of the Cataclysm. The hero Evan Bryan was smiling on one screen, describing his mission to nuke the scum's home planet. Twenty or thirty massive radios sat in the shade by the screens, each the size of a duffel bag, with two leather straps like those of a backpack. The machines looked two hundred years old, like a relic from the great wars of the twentieth century. Rust coated their dials and switches.

"Field radios," said Corporal St-Pierre, gesturing at the bulky machines. The recruits stood before her under the canvas pavilion. "With these machines you'll learn how to communicate with your fellow soldiers."

"Corporal St-Pierre," said a recruit, "they're a bit . . . large. And rusted. And ancient. Doesn't the HDF use electronic earpieces?"

The blond, stern corporal glared at the soldier. "Earpieces can be hacked by the scum. These radios are over a hundred years old. The scum don't expect us to use technology so primitive. You will learn to use these radios, and you will spend the next twenty-four hours patrolling the camp's perimeter with them. Is that understood?"

"Yes, Commander!" they cried out, all but Pinky, who shouted a "Yes, pizza!"

A few recruits turned toward Pinky and smirked. Marco winced. He was sure that Corporal St-Pierre, whose face was badly pimpled, had heard Pinky's insult. Indeed, her eyes hardened and her lips tightened. But the corporal said nothing, perhaps too ashamed, and Marco felt sudden pity for her.

Their corporals were lords and masters to the recruits, but Marco realized that St-Pierre couldn't have been more than a year or two older than them, just a girl far from her own home. Maybe she too was afraid. Maybe she too cried in the shadows. She too was human.

"You will take shifts," said St-Pierre. "Half of the platoon will patrol the entire fence of Forth Djemila, carrying the radios on your backs, then hand them over to the other half. Each patrol should take two hours. Then you will rest for two hours. Then you will do another patrol. You will continue to do this for a full twenty-four hours. During your two-hour resting periods, you're free to rest in this pavilion—and I strongly suggest you use those hours to *rest*." St-Pierre nodded toward the cots in the pavilion. "Remember. There are cameras all around this base. We will be monitoring your patrols. If anyone so much as stands in place for a minute, let alone sits down during a patrol, that's a serious strike against you. Too many strikes, and you will fail to complete basic training. Unless you want to fly back to RASCOM and start over, I suggest you take these patrols seriously. Now pair up! I want each pair to walk side by side, the next pair walking several feet behind."

Marco glanced toward Lailani, hoping—daring to hope—that maybe, just maybe, the two could be paired up, could patrol together. He just wanted to learn more about her, about her past. That was all, he told himself. It wasn't at all the warmth when she looked at him, or how she wouldn't leave his mind, or the memory of—

"Pairsies?" Addy said, reaching out to grab Marco's hand. The rest of the platoon hooted and whistled.

"Romantic stroll!" Caveman said, chortling. "They're going to kiss!"

"Remember, Marco," Elvis said, "Addy likes to be spanked."

Addy rolled her eyes. "I'm going to spank you, Elvis, right on your big fat ugly face." She grabbed one of the radios. "But first patro—whoa!" Addy swayed, clinging to the boxy radio. It was larger than her torso. "Thing weighs a fucking metric ton."

Marco grabbed his own radio. Addy was stronger than him, and he struggled to even lift the damn thing. He needed Elvis to help strap it across his back. At once, Marco's spine—already aching after days of basic training—screamed in protest. When he took a step, a blister burst. Across the tent, other pairs were lifting their own radios, swaying under the weight. Lailani had paired up with Beast. It was hardly fair, Marco thought, watching the massive Russian and the tiny, four-foot-ten Filipina carrying the same burden. Lailani was barely able to stay standing, but she tightened her jaw and stepped out of the tent, the radio—it must have weighed more than her—across her back.

"Come on, soldiers!" Lailani said. "Let's patrol these fences for fucking scum. Just . . . without . . . talking." She wobbled under the weight.

Half the platoon headed out, leaving the other half behind in the pavilion to rest and absorb some propaganda films. Each pair walked side by side, the other pair walking several paces behind.

They began their patrol, circling the base, carrying their burdens. Every step was a nightmare. Every step was an inferno. Every step was the Cataclysm. Every step was scum claws tearing into Marco's spine. Every step was scum piercing his feet. Every step was the distance back home. The sun beat down, and sand blew into their eyes, and their guns banged against their hips. Their helmets wobbled on their heads. The straps of their radios tore into their chests, ripping, digging through, pulling down, pressing the segments of their spines together.

"Do these radios even work?" Marco said, trudging forward.

"Doubt it," Addy said, gleaming with sweat. "They're relics."

"So why the hell are we carrying them?" They walked around some thorny bushes, among the only vegetation in the base.

Addy spat. "Same reason they barely let us sleep, feed us slop, and shout at us all day."

"Because they're assholes?" Marco said, wiping sweat from his eyes. The barbed wire fence stretched ahead, endlessly long.

"Because they need you to forget who you were," Addy said. "They need to shock you, to shatter you, to break your body and spirit, before they can rebuild you into a soldier."

"I'm not going to forget who I was," Marco said. "I don't want to forget home. To forget the boy I was."

"Marco, sweet darling, the boy you were wouldn't be able to kill a spider, let alone a ten-foot-tall centipede predator from deep space. To survive in this war, we're going to have to change. All of us. We're no longer the kids we were, a writer and a hockey player. We're soldiers."

"Well, nobody asked me if I wanted to be a soldier," Marco said.

Addy glared at him. "Nobody asked the Earth if it wanted space scum to nuke it, but them's the breaks."

Marco was too weary to keep arguing, and in truth, Addy was right. Marco focused only on walking now, one foot after another. Addy began to sing but soon gave up, conserving her breath for the journey. The other recruits walked ahead and behind them, trudging with the radios on their backs. Whenever they so much as slowed to wipe their brows and drink from their canteens, cameras on the fence moved, and voices blared out from speakers.

"March!"

They kept marching.

An hour stretched by, and they had only patrolled halfway around the camp. Every step now felt like a war against a horde of scum. The sand kept stinging, the wind blasting them, the sun burning them. Marco shook the last few drops from his canteen, blinked, and trudged on. Addy was walking ahead but slowing down. Caveman was last, sweating and drooling and wailing as he walked, mumbling something about flowers and scum and bullets being so loud. Lailani walked near him, encouraging the brutish soldier onward, patting his arm. The smallest soldier in the fort looked just as exhausted, however, her face dripping sweat, her eyes sunken.

"Two thirds of the way there!" Marco said. "I can see the mess hall. Come on, soldiers. We've got this."

They kept walking. Another platoon was doing their jumping jacks in the yard; they gazed at the Dragons with pity. As they trudged by the gates, a rocket roared and slammed down, and new recruits emerged, but everyone was too tired to even talk about fresh meat.

After ninety minutes of carrying the radios, with the pavilion already in sight in the distance, Lailani collapsed.

At first her knees buckled, then hit the sand. An instant later, her face followed her knees. The massive radio drove into her back, crushing her.

"Lailani!" Marco called. He removed his radio and ran toward her. "I need some help!"

Caveman was already grabbing the radio on Lailani's back. They had to cut through the strap to pull it off, then drop the heavy device into the sand. Lailani lay on her stomach, moaning.

"I'm all right," the tiny soldier muttered. "I just tripped on a rock. I'm fine."

She tried to rise, then groaned and fell back down.

"You're not all right, de la Rosa," said Marco. "They shouldn't make you carry the same weight as us. I'm twice your size, and Beast is twice my size, but the radios are all the same." He placed a hand on her shoulder. "Careful. Don't try to rise. Your back might be—"

"I can carry the same weight as anyone!" Glaring at him, Lailani sat up, wheezed for a moment, coughed, and then struggled to her feet. "You don't know what I've been through, Emery. I used to walk the slums of Manila for days without rest. I—" She turned green, leaned over, and vomited into the sand.

"She's dehydrated," Marco said. He looked at one of the cameras in the fence. It was staring at them. "She's dehydrated and hurt! We need a medic!"

The camera looked away. Marco cursed.

"Bastards," Addy muttered, gazing toward the distant, shady pavilion. It still lay a couple of kilometers away.

"Recruits, anyone got any water left in your canteens?" Marco said.

They stepped forward, radios still on their backs. Nobody had more than a few drops of water left, but they shared even these drops with Lailani. She drank and slowly the color returned to her cheeks.

"I'm going to finish this patrol," Lailani said. "I'm a soldier. Just like anyone else. I didn't join this army to die in basic in some godforsaken desert. If I'm going to die, it'll be shooting scum on their planet." She grabbed her radio and pulled it onto her back. "Let's march."

Marco walked at Lailani's side, close enough to let her lean against him.

"I need to lean on you," he said. "Will you help me?"

She leaned more heavily against him, panting now, sweat dripping from the tip of her nose. "Sure thing, Emery."

They trudged on, breathing heavily, the sun shimmering. Finally Marco spoke again.

"De la Rosa, I'm sorry for yesterday. If I insulted you in the mess."

She looked at him, snorted, and leaned back against him. "You didn't insult me. I'm crazy, Emery. You should know that. You don't want to be my friend. You certainly don't want to fall in love with me. I'm fucking crazy. Army shrink said so."

"They don't give guns to crazy people," Marco said.

"Crazy people make the best soldiers. What is war but madness?" She paused for a moment and looked into his eyes. "Emery. Understand something. I joined this army to die. I'm going to die in glory, like the heroes of the old war, blasting the scum apart. You don't want to get close to me. I'll just break your heart."

She turned and walked on, leaving him behind, and Marco thought about the scars on her wrists.

When they finally returned to the pavilion, having completed a patrol of Fort Djemila in two hours, they lowered their radios and all but collapsed onto the cots in the shade.

"Have fun, boys and girls," Addy said, covering her eyes with her arm, as the other half of the Dragons Platoon lifted the radios. Groaning, they headed off on their own patrol.

Marco panted for long moments, sleep creeping up on him, but forced himself to stand, to trudge two hundred meters to a tap that rose from the sand, and fill his canteen—a long process, drop by drop, as the other recruits lined up behind him and howled for their turns. Marco wanted to rinse out his canteen, but when the others began pelting him with pebbles, he just drank and let the others fill their own canteens.

I joined the army to die.

The words wouldn't leave him even as Marco lay on a cot in the pavilion, the propaganda reels flashing around him. He rolled aside and saw Lailani lying on another cot, curled up on her side. He wanted to go to her, to comfort her, to tell her that things would be better—but his weariness was too great.

He slept.

After two hours, another shift began.

Once more, Marco, Addy, and the others lifted the radios. They walked out, ready for another patrol under the devastating sun.

Two hours later they returned to the pavilion more weary, broken, and haunted than they had thought possible.

Marco collapsed onto his cot, gasping for breath, his back, legs, chest, and head screaming in agony.

"They say war is hell," he rasped. "War would be easy compared to boot camp."

"War's a whorehouse compared to this," Elvis agreed.

Whistling sounded, and Marco turned to see two recruits stepping into the pavilion, carrying plastic bags. Pinky walked at the lead, and behind him walked Nick "Dicky" Dickerson—a brute who idolized his little master, one of the bullies who had attacked Caveman back at RASCOM. Both delinquents opened their plastic bags.

"We've got lunch!" Pinky said. "We met Sergeant Singh on the way to the mess hall, and we got everyone some grub. Spam sandwiches galore!"

At that moment, Marco would have eaten scum sandwiches. With the others, he limped toward the food, his blisters protesting every step.

"Spam sandwich for you, Spam sandwich for you . . ." Pinky tossed them from the plastic bag toward the recruits, all the while munching on his own sandwich. "Here, have two sandwiches, Beast. One for you, one for you." He took another bite. "Hell, I'll even toss one to Tiny de la Rosa and Maple Syrup here." He lobbed sandwiches at Lailani and Addy. "And . . . I'll keep this last one for myself."

Marco stomped up to him. "Fuck you, Pinky. You already ate. Hand that sandwich over. That one's mine."

"Is that so?" Pinky swallowed the last bite of his own sandwich and unwrapped the last one. "Think I'll have two sandwiches today."

"Pinky, I don't want to fight you," Marco said. "But I'm taking that sandwich if I have to rip it out of your intestines."

Pinky bit into it and licked his lips. "You gonna fight me for the rest?"

"Knock his fucking teeth in!" Addy shouted.

"Kick his balls!" shouted Lailani.

"Kill the poet, Pinky!" chortled Dickerson.

The other recruits gathered around, laughing and shouting, and Marco made a lunge for the sandwich. Pinky pulled back, took another bite, and Marco—exhausted and in pain as he was—leaped forward and barreled into the smaller recruit.

Pinky landed punches and kicks. He was amazingly strong for his small size. Marco had seen him do a hundred push-ups before, a feat even Beast and Addy couldn't accomplish. The little bastard fought like a honey badger, but Marco was not letting this one slide. He took the punches, swung at Pinky's wrist, and knocked the sandwich out.

The sandwich flew through the air and landed in the sand.

Pinky brayed out laughter, spraying saliva. "You win, asshole. Go enjoy your sand sandwich."

Marco straightened, his face stinging from Pinky's blows, and salvaged what he could of the meal. He ate sullenly, not sure if he had lost pride or won it.

"Pinky," Marco said when they were all sitting on their cots, "what the fuck is your problem?"

Elvis nodded, coming to sit by Marco. "Yeah, what's your deal? Why are you, well, an asshole? Now don't come lunging at me! We all know you're an asshole. You know it. The commanders know it. Hell, the scum probably know it."

Sitting on his cot, Pinky stared at them all. The pavilion shaded the sun, but it was still blazing hot, and sand kept blowing in from the desert. For a long time Pinky just sucked on his crooked teeth, then he laughed.

"Hell, they tried everything with me," Pinky said. "My god, they tried. My grandmother. My teachers. My shrinks. Fuck, they spent a lot of hours on me, trying to save me. That's what they all called it. Saving me." He laughed bitterly. "Didn't work. When your dad's in prison, and your mom's a junkie and alcoholic, and you're more afraid of the gangs on your street than the scum, well . . . you turn into old Pinky here."

"Bullshit." Lailani rose to her feet and spat.

"It's true," said Pinky. "Granny thought the army could save me. See, now, normally they don't put kids like me here. Not when you've spent years in juvy. Nah. Usually they ship us off to special units in the army—where the criminals go, you know, the delinquents. But even the army shrink thought he could save me. They thought that if they could put me with normals—you know, normal sons of bitches like Poet here, college kids—that it would rub off. Hopeless. If my own dad's belt couldn't beat sense into me, this place sure as fuck can't."

They all stared at Pinky for a moment, silent, and Marco felt . . . It shocked him, but there it was.

He pitied Pinky.

The kid was a psychopath, a criminal, as loathsome as scum, but damn it, Pinky had lived the sort of life Marco—even after the loss of his mother—couldn't imagine.

But Lailani seemed to feel no such pity. The small recruit trembled, fists clenched, teeth bared. "That is a crock of shit," she said.

"Is it?" Pinky said.

Lailani nodded and pointed at him. "Shitty childhoods don't have to turn you into an asshole. Your sob story doesn't work on me. Your dad was in prison? At least you had a dad. My father was an American soldier who left me when I was still a fetus. Your mom was a junkie? My mom was a thirteen-year-old prostitute. You grew up in a tough hood? I grew up on a trash heap. I rummaged through landfills for bits of food, for chicken bones with some meat on them, for rotten fruit. You were scared of gangs? I was scared of adults raping me and rats infecting me with disease and starving every day when thousands of others rummaged through the trash. By the time my mother died, I was eating paper, and I did this." She raised her wrists, showing the scars, tears in her eyes. "So don't you talk to me about your fucked-up childhood, Pinky, because I'd have loved to have that life. And I didn't turn into a sick bully like you."

Tears now flowed down Lailani's cheeks. Lips trembling, she turned around, walked to the farthest cot, and lay down.

For a moment the recruits were all silent, and the only sound came from the propaganda reels. On the screens a quadruple amputee was talking about how the scum had taken his limbs but couldn't break the spirit of humanity. He gave a prosthetic thumbs-up.

"So, Corporal Pizza's got a nice ass, right?" Elvis said.

Beast groaned. "You no idea what nice ass is. Only in Russia you see nice ass." He pulled out the photo of his girlfriend. "Take my girlfriend Ludmila, for example."

"Her name was Oxana yesterday," Elvis said.

"What?" Beast shook his head, his cheeks flushing red. "No. No. She is Ludmila. Look. Let me show you. Look at Ludmila. I have more photos."

Marco rose from his cot and walked toward the back of the pavilion. From here he could see the rocky field spread toward the barbed wire fence and the rolling dunes beyond. He could just make out distant yellow mountains. Lailani lay on her cot, curled up into a ball, staring into the distance. Marco sat down beside her.

"Hey, de la Rosa," he said.

"What do you want, Emery?" she said, voice choked.

He fished through his duffel bag and pulled out a crumpled granola bar, its silvery wrapper bristly with dirt. "I brought this all the way from home. Beats Pinky's Spam sandwiches. Want to share it?"

She said nothing.

Marco wiggled both the limp bar and his eyebrows. "It's got raisins!"

Lailani said nothing, just stared ahead at the desert and barbed wire fence, eyes red. "I wish the scum would break in already," she said softly. "I keep waiting for them to come at that fence. For us to fight them. I want to fight. To die in battle—a heroine in a war. Not to die crushed under some radio. Not to die with slit wrists in an alleyway. That's why I didn't cut deep, you know. Because I didn't really want to die like that. I wanted a good death."

Marco hesitated, then touched her shoulder, surprised by how dainty that shoulder was, and he marveled again at how she had carried the massive radio. "How about this, de la Rosa? We become war heroes and survive, then die in eighty years, shriveled up like these raisins, rocking in some rocking chairs on some patio facing a duck pond, laughing about how Pinky got his balls chopped off by the scum."

Lailani finally cracked a smile. "I bet they're small and shriveled up like raisins too."

He peeled open the granola bar, broke it in two, and gave her the larger portion. "Mmm, Pinky balls, appetizing!"

They ate, and Lailani's eyelids drooped, and she leaned against him and slept. Gently, Marco lowered himself onto his back, and Lailani slept against him, her head on his chest. In an hour they would rise for another round of patrols, crushed under their radios, but for now—at this moment, for this hour—Marco felt peace for the first time since leaving home.

Before he drifted off to sleep, he turned his head, and he saw Addy standing in the pavilion, staring at him and Lailani, a strange look in her eyes. Then his tall, crazy foster sister turned away and lay on her own cot, and for an hour Marco knew nothing but the languorous heat and Lailani's breath against him.

CHAPTER THIRTEEN

After the longest, most painful twenty-four hours of Marco's life, the Dragon Platoon's recruits finally abandoned their rusty, antique radios and hobbled back toward their tents. Marco had never imagined that a tattered old military tent in the desert would ever seem beautiful, but right now it looked like an oasis. He yearned to lie on his old cot between Addy and Lailani, rest, and maybe finally—after days of this hell—get a chance to write a few paragraphs in *Loggerhead*.

When he saw the corporals standing outside the tents, he knew it was not to be.

All three of the Dragons' corporals were there: the slender and dark Webb, the stern St-Pierre, and the tough-as-old-leather Diaz. All three held their guns in hand.

"Attention!" Corporal Webb shouted, pacing on her bladed prosthetics. For somebody barely larger than Lailani, she had a voice that made even the mighty Beast stiffen and raise his chin.

"Formations!" St-Pierre shouted, and the recruits— blistered, sunburnt, parched, and famished—formed rank in the sand.

"All right, recruits!" Corporal Diaz said, stepping toward them. "Now that you're back from your little vacation, we've got a treat for you. You're about to fight some scum. March behind me! Emery—you call out time."

Marco could barely walk. His back screamed with every step. His feet felt shattered, not only blistered but crushed, the bones ground to shards. But he followed. After the pain of carrying the radios for a day, he would tolerate this too. The platoon formed two lines and marched behind the corporals. Marco walked by Corporal Diaz, calling out time.

"Three, two, one, march! Three, two, one, ma—"

"Louder!" Diaz said.

Marco shouted as loudly as he could—which wasn't, he thought, nearly as commanding as the corporals' voices. "Three, two, one . . ."

They marched on, leaving the tents behind. Many of the soldiers lagged, limped, and broke formation, only for the corporals to shout and goad them back in line. With every step, as his feet and back ached, Marco looked at Corporal Diaz. The veteran had suffered three scum claws ripping through him, shattering his spine. That spine was now bolted together. If the corporal could march here in the sand, Marco—who had never suffered an injury aside from Addy knuckling his head—certainly could.

Corporal Diaz survived the Appalachian Trail, one of the worst battles of the decade, he thought. *I can survive basic training.*

They marched toward a sandy field, and Marco nearly lost his count.

"Fuck me," Addy whispered behind him.

Three scum—actual, real scum, not just wooden figures—rose in the sand ahead, balanced on their bottom segments.

Marco reached for his gun. A few other recruits did too. Curses rose across the platoon.

"Calm down, soldiers," rose a voice from ahead. "They're dead."

Ensign Ben-Ari emerged from behind the massive black centipedes. The officer's silver plasma gun hung on her hip. The weapon looked far more elegant than the crude, bullet-spraying machines the other soldiers carried. Ben-Ari wore her helmet, and dark shades hid her eyes.

"Attention!" Corporal Diaz shouted, and all three corporals saluted their commander. Ben-Ari nodded and returned the salute.

"We collected these buggers in the sands of the Algerian desert," Ben-Ari said, gesturing at the creatures. "These are just their exoskeletons. Their innards were sucked out and buried. Just a whiff of what's inside them can kill a soldier, and their blood and meat will melt the flesh off your bones." She tapped one of the claws. It thrust out like a scimitar. "There are tiny holes on the tips of these claws. They won't only slice you apart. They'll inject you with poison that'll have you screaming and begging for death."

Corporal Diaz nodded, rolled up his sleeve, and revealed a nasty scar. "She's right. I know."

Marco cringed, looking at the three exoskeletons. Each one dwarfed Ensign Ben-Ari. Eighteen hard black segments formed their bodies, each sprouting two claws. At the top of the creatures, mandibles—smaller but just as sharp as the claws—rose like horns.

"These aliens aren't just ugly," said Ensign Ben-Ari. "They're also intelligent. More intelligent than we humans are. We've colonized a handful of planets. They control dozens of star systems. They can build organic starships using biotechnology we can't even understand. They can clone humans from a single hair follicle, indoctrinate them, and send them to Earth as spies. We still can't communicate faster than light. They can communicate instantly at any distance using quantum entanglement technology beyond anything we have, making their communications impossible to intercept. In every way, they are superior to us humans. And you will learn to kill them—without even using bullets."

"No bullets, ma'am?" Addy said, gasping.

"Maybe we can feed them Spam sandwiches and they'll choke to death," Elvis offered, earning a laugh from his friends, forty push-ups, and an hour scrubbing pots that night.

Ensign Ben-Ari approached a wooden crate and cracked it open. Bayonets gleamed inside.

"Fuck yeah!" Addy said. "Brutal. Now *these* are weapons."

Marco frowned at her. "We fired assault rifles and tossed grenades, and you're impressed by knives?"

Addy nodded. "Anyone can pull a trigger or toss a bomb. It takes balls to fight an alien up close with a sharp piece of steel."

"Not steel, soldier," said Ensign Ben-Ari, stepping closer. "Steel would shatter against the scum exoskeletons. These bayonets are made from a diamond-iridium composite with a coating of graphene, developed by HDF scientists. These blades can saw through a tank—and they'll cut the scum here." She lifted a bayonet and tapped one of the towering exoskeletons. "See where their segments meet? That's where their armor is weakest. That's where you fire bullets, and that's where you stab them. That is if you can avoid their claws." The ensign slapped the exoskeleton, and it spun on a hidden axis, claws whirring.

"Ensign, ma'am," said Elvis, looking queasy, "why approach the scum? Our guns can hit them from a kilometer away."

Ensign Ben-Ari stepped toward the recruit, removed her shades, and stared into his eyes. "How many bullets are in a magazine, recruit?"

"Sixty, ma'am."

"And how many magazines do you carry?"

"Six, ma'am."

"According to HDF statistics, two hundred thousand bullets are fired for every dead scum. How many scum can you kill with your bullets?"

Elvis thought for a moment, counting on his fingers. "Two hundred thousand per dead scum . . . sixty bullets per soldier . . . carry the one . . ." He scrunched his lips, then sighed. "Not many, ma'am."

Ensign Ben-Ari nodded and turned toward the rest of the recruits. "In battle you'll run out of bullets. Sometimes your gun will jam. Sometimes a scum will leap onto you in close quarters— among trees, inside a building, inside a scum hive—and you'll be too close to even load, aim, and fire. Sometimes your bayonet will be the difference between a dead scum and you in the belly of one." She turned toward Corporal Diaz. "Corporal, care to demonstrate?"

"My pleasure, ma'am," said the corporal, smiling thinly. He lifted a bayonet from the crate, snapped it onto his T57 assault rifle, then charged with a howl. Dust flew under his boots. Ensign Ben-Ari hit the exoskeleton again, spinning it madly on its axis. Corporal Diaz swung his weapon sideways, catching a claw's blow on his gun's stock. More claws lashed. Diaz swung his gun the other way, blocking the claws on his barrel.

He pulled his gun back. With a roar, he shoved the muzzle forward.

The bayonet hit the centipede between two segments. The exoskeleton cracked. The blade sank all the way down. The scum stopped flailing.

Diaz pulled his gun free, then thrust it again, shouting wordlessly. The bayonet slashed between two other segments, cutting deep. A third blow sliced off a claw, and a fourth finished

195

the job. The top half of the centipede, large as a man, cracked off and thumped onto the sand.

"Dead scum," Corporal Diaz said.

"It was already dead," Addy whispered to Marco, then fell silent when Ben-Ari's eyes flicked toward her.

"Linden!" Ben-Ari barked. "You seem to think this was easy. Step up and grab a bayonet." The officer pointed at a second scum exoskeleton. "You're next."

"Gladly, ma'am," Addy said. "Just like beating up hockey players back home."

She snapped a bayonet onto her gun, roared, and charged toward the scum.

Ensign Ben-Ari hit the exoskeleton and stepped back. The massive centipede spun on a hidden axis, claws lashing.

Addy reached the alien and thrust her bayonet. A flailing claw caught the barrel of her gun, knocking it aside. The stock rose to hit Addy's chin, knocking her head back. The claws spun again, driving into her side.

"Addy!" Marco cried, leaping forward.

Corporal Diaz grabbed him. "The claws are dulled, soldier. Stay where you are."

Addy fell into the sand, lip bloody. Indeed the claws had not cut her—but they'd leave ugly bruises the next day. Addy struggled to her feet, cursing and grumbling.

"Real scum don't move like that, Commander," she said to Ben-Ari.

The lieutenant nodded. "Real scum are three times as fast, and they're racing all around you as they lash their claws." Ben-Ari pointed at another recruit. "You, Dickerson. Go."

Nick "Dicky" Dickerson, one of the burly brutes who followed Pinky, grunted and grabbed a bayonet. He too charged at the scum. He too fell into the sand, bleeding from his temple and elbow.

One by one, the recruits charged toward the exoskeleton, lashing their bayonets. Beast was nonchalant as he slammed at the creature, managing to cut off one claw, but finally the remaining claws knocked down even the mighty Russian. Lailani screamed as she charged, landing furious blows, and it looked like she would slice the scum in two, but a low claw finally hit her legs, and the little soldier rolled.

"One dead varmint coming right up," drawled the lanky Sheriff, grinning toothily. They called him Sheriff partly because he was from Texas, mostly due to the sheriff's star he had drawn onto his helmet with permanent marker. Defacing military property had earned him kitchen duty all week, but they let him keep the helmet. "Just like rustling cattle back home."

Hooting and hollering, Sheriff raced toward the scum, suffering a blow to his jaw so bad it knocked out two teeth. Corporal Webb had to accompany the Texan to the infirmary across the base.

Pinky stepped up next. He passed a hand through his hair, spat, scratched his balls, and grabbed a bayonet. With a hoarse scream, he charged.

The exoskeleton spun.

Screeching, Pinky leaped into the air and swung his T57. The stock slammed between two claws, halting the creature's spin. Pinky slashed the gun the other way, driving the bayonet between two segments. The exoskeleton cracked. Laughing and cursing, Pinky pulled the gun back, leaped into the air, and drove the bayonet into the crack. He kicked against the claws, twisting the gun, and leaped back.

The exoskeleton cracked in two, exposing hollow innards. Another blow sent the top half falling.

"Fuck yeah!" Pinky said, strutting like a rooster. "That's how it's done!"

The recruits whistled, applauded, and patted Pinky on his back. All but Marco and his friends. They stared, sullen.

"Lucky bastard," Addy said. "We softened it up for him."

Elvis nodded, rubbing his side where the dulled claws had struck him. "We added a thousand little cracks. He just needed to give the last one."

"Emery!" said Ensign Ben-Ari. "You're up." She pointed at the third and last scum.

Marco gulped. This was a fresh exoskeleton, no cracks or crevices on it. He wouldn't have Pinky's advantage, and he certainly lacked Corporal Diaz's battle experience. Marco approached the crate and pulled out the final bayonet. The graphene blade was black and glimmering like obsidian. Marco almost felt like a character in some fantasy novel, given a magical blade to slay the mythical ice-zombies.

Maybe I should write that kind of book instead of Loggerhead, he thought, attaching the bayonet to his assault rifle. He stepped toward the scum.

"Kick its ass!" Addy shouted.

"It doesn't have an ass!" he called back at her.

"Carve out its heart!" Lailani cried.

Marco wasn't sure scum had hearts either, but he'd take whatever encouragement he could get. Unlike his comrades, he didn't charge toward the exoskeleton but approached slowly, weapon raised. Ensign Ben-Ari slapped the scum, and it began to spin, claws lashing.

Those claws were as long as his gun. To cut the creature, Marco would have to step into their range. He stepped closer, then leaped back as the claws lashed. Pinky, Dickerson, and a few others scoffed behind him. Marco tightened his lips.

Careful, he thought. *Don't charge like a brute. Slowly.*

He approached again, thrusting his weapon.

A claw hit the barrel, nearly yanking the gun from his hand. If not for the rifle's strap, it would have flown from his grip. He stepped back again.

"It doesn't have an ass!" Pinky said behind him, speaking in mock falsetto, and laughed hoarsely.

Marco tried to ignore the goading, the mocking laughter of the other recruits. He narrowed his eyes, staring at the scum. Its claws were still swiping from side to side like a boxer's swinging fists. Suddenly Marco no longer stood in the African desert. Suddenly he was back in the snow, in the frozen streets of

Toronto, and the scum was scuttling toward him, killing his mother, eating her corpse, killing Addy's parents, and Marco screamed and lashed his gun forward with all his strength.

The bayonet slammed between two segments so powerfully it crashed through them, and the barrel of the gun followed, sinking deep, halting only at the handguard. Claws slammed into Marco's side with the might of swinging hammers, cracking against his ribs, and he screamed in pain but wouldn't release his gun. He pressed his boots against the scum and yanked mightily, ripping the bayonet out, tearing through more of the exoskeleton. A claw slammed into his helmet, ringing his head like a bell.

Marco fell back onto the sand.

Before him, the scum cracked in two. Marco rolled aside, and segments of hard exoskeleton and claws fell, piercing the sand inches away.

For a moment Marco lay in silence. Nobody was laughing now.

He stood up and stared down at the torn scum. He kicked sand onto it.

Finally Pinky broke the silence with a snort. "Big deal. It was already dead."

"So was yours," Addy said, earning a glare from the little soldier.

That night at the mess hall, Marco earned pats on the back from his comrades—aside from Pinky and his gang. Beast even offered to let Marco borrow his photo of Oxana—or was it

Ludmila?—just for the night, to keep him company during his guard duty. Marco politely declined, but he did accept Sheriff's dessert. It was more wet sponge than cake, but Marco was grateful for any sustenance. After only a few days in the military, he was already down a notch in his belt.

"Well, we're all expert scum killers now," Addy said as they ate. "I'm ready to win the war."

Elvis made his best war face and stabbed his Spam. "Pow! I'm Marco Emery, scum killer!" He bit into the meat. "Tastes like chicken."

That night, as Marco lay on his cot in his squad's tent, he felt somebody watching him, and he turned to see Lailani looking at him. She quickly closed her eyes and rolled away, and Marco spent a moment looking at the back of her head, at her buzzed black hair, and he remembered holding her in the pavilion, how she had slept against his chest.

"Goodnight, Lailani," he whispered before Addy slapped him with a pillow.

"Guard duty," she said, and Marco trudged outside into the night, gun in hand, bayonet sheathed at his side. The stars spread above, and somewhere among them lurked millions of the scum.

CHAPTER FOURTEEN

"You just had to call her Corporal Pizza," Marco said, trudging through the desert, holding one side of the trash bin.

Addy shrugged, holding the other side. "I didn't know she was listening! And besides, everyone calls her that. Elvis came up with it."

"Yes, but you're not an idiot like Elvis," Marco said.

Addy bristled. "Yes I am!"

Marco groaned. "Her name is Corporal Fiona St-Pierre, and you hurt her feelings." He leaned down to pick up a candy wrapper, then placed it in the bin. "And now we have to clean the whole base. And I didn't even do anything! You're the one who called her Pizza. I was just listening to you."

"Well, I'm glad her feelings are hurt. She's a nasty, unpleasant woman, not nearly as nice as our other commanders. Her personality's worse than her skin. Hell, even Sergeant Singh is more pleasant, and he's always scowling under that big black beard of his." Addy lifted an old pair of underwear. "Eww!" She shuddered and tossed it into the bin. "Eww, eww, eww, scum streak marks!"

Marco shuddered as he saw a condom in the rocky field. He used the candy wrapper from before to lift it, then quickly tossed it into the bin, cringing. "Disgusting." He struggled not to gag. "Anyway, look, it's St-Pierre's job to be tough, and—" He grimaced. "What the hell—is that a dead rat?"

They had been carrying the garbage bin through Fort Djemila for the past hour, punishment for insulting the corporal. The recruits had brought an assortment of personal items from home—toiletries, snacks, undergarments—and the garbage littered the base, rolling through the rocky fields and sand. Their bin was large enough to stuff Beast into and already half full.

"Poet, none of this would have happened if you hadn't asked me what food I miss most," Addy said. "You made me think of pizza. You see, it's your fault. If not for you, we'd be at the firing range now, blasting wooden scum. Instead we're picking up dead rats and underwear and—"

"Addy," Marco whispered.

"—and candy wrappers and tampons and—"

"Addy, look," he whispered again, eyes dampening. "Oh God. Oh God."

"What, Marco? What? I'm trying to—"

He grabbed her cheeks, forced her head sideways, and her jaw unhinged.

"Fuck me," she whispered.

Marco nearly wept. "It's beautiful. It's so beautiful."

Holding the bin between them, they began to run.

It rose from the desert like a temple, like a holy monument, like the burning bush Moses had seen. Marco heard the song of angels. It was impossible, *had* to be impossible, just a mirage—yet there it stood before him in all its glory, promising to deliver manna from heaven and all the sweet sins of hell. Beaten up, red and gray, covered in scratches but still full of delights, the vending machine glistened, calling to him.

Marco placed his palms against the transparent plastic, gazing at the treasures within.

"Gooble-drops!" he whispered. "Fizz-wizzlers! Almond Crunchers! They're all here!"

Addy drooled. "Bags of Hickory Chips. Bottles of icy-cold Forest Dew. And . . ." She gasped and tears filled her eyes. "Ice cream, Marco! Bars of delicious, completely unnutritious maple-flavored Hockey Puck ice cream, just like at home! Oh mama. Marco, my dear old boy, today we feast." She rummaged through her pockets. "You have any money?"

"I think so. I still have my wallet from home."

They pulled out their wallets and produced a few hundred dollars, just enough to buy two or three items. They chose two Hockey Pucks—rich maple ice cream between two large cookies—and a bottle of Forest Dew to share. They sat in the shade of the holy vending machine, here at the far edge of the camp, only the sand and barbed wire for company. For a few blessed moments, they ate and drank.

"I almost feel human again," Marco said and took another bite.

"A little taste of civilization." Addy devoured the last few bites of her ice cream and took a swig of pop. "I missed this."

"Me too," Marco said. "If I were back in Toronto now, I'd guzzle down ten of these."

"I don't just mean the ice cream," Addy said. "I miss just talking to you. About things other than war." She pulled a pack of cigarettes from her pocket and lit one.

Marco raised an eyebrow. "Addy, for the last couple of years at home, you barely talked to me. You spent all your time with what's his name, the hockey player? Butch? Buck? Bubba?"

"Steve," she said.

"Ah, that was it."

Addy rolled her eyes. "He was an idiot anyway. Good in bed, that was all."

"Addy!" Marco winced. "I don't want to think of you like that."

She stuck her tongue out the side of her mouth and winked. "Jealous?"

"Of course not."

"Why not?" Addy placed a hand on his thigh. "You don't *looove* me like you love de la Rosa?"

Addy had never touched him like that before. She had often knuckled his head, twisted his arm, elbowed him in the ribs, but now she rested her hand on his thigh, dangerously high up.

He stood up—too quickly, he thought. "Very funny, Addy," he said. "You're a real joker." He snorted. "You've been living in my home since we were both eleven. We're practically brother and sister now."

"And Lailani is an exotic flower of the Orient, and your cock longs for her like your stomach longs for ice cream." Addy nodded and blew a smoke ring. "I get it."

"Now who sounds jealous?" Marco said. Suddenly he wasn't enjoying this time away from the platoon. Addy had always been a strange one, but now she confused him more than ever. And suddenly—damn it, he couldn't help it—he remembered seeing her in the shower, glimpsing her naked body, and the water dripping down her, and—

He swallowed and looked away, pulled a last bill from his pocket, and stuck it into the vending machine. He bought an Almond Cruncher bar and placed it into his pocket.

"You're not going to eat it?" Addy said. "You're saving it for de la Rosa, aren't you?" She grinned. "Marco and Lailani, sitting in a tree, f-u-c—"

"Addy!" He grabbed one side of the garbage bin. "Shut it and help me. Let's get this over with."

She waggled her eyebrows. "So you can get back to de la Rosa faster."

They walked through the camp, picking up the last pieces of trash. Marco wanted to tell Addy that he was still in love with Kemi, but he said nothing. He didn't want to dredge up that memory. For the first few days in the HDF, he had thought of Kemi constantly, but now—six days into his service—he was thinking about her a little less. So much of that old world seemed like a distant, hazy memory. Six days. Six eras ago.

They were walking back toward their platoon when they saw the second miracle rising from the desert.

Marco and Addy paused and stared silently.

For a long moment they said nothing.

"It's . . ." Marco approached slowly and touched it. He looked back at Addy. "It's a public telephone. I think."

Addy stepped forward too. She raised her hand and touched the metal box on the pole. Neither had seen a public telephone in real life before, only in old movies. For over a century the world had used nothing but portable phones—the devices getting smaller and smaller every generation. But no electronics were allowed in Fort Djemila. At first Marco had assumed the ban was meant to prevent the recruits having any contact with the outside world—to make them forget their old lives, to isolate and break them here within this prison. But he remembered the rusty old radios, the crude bullets. Scum were technologically advanced, but they had trouble with old technology. They couldn't hack old technology, not as easily as they could hack humanity's cutting-edge gadgets. At least that was the story their commanders told. And here before them—an old phone with actual numbers you had to press, an actual receiver to speak and listen, an antique. Yet when Marco lifted it, he heard a live line.

He quickly placed the receiver back.

"Should we . . . call anyone?" Marco said. "Should—"

"Soldiers!" rose a shout, and Marco and Addy looked up to see Sergeant Singh in the distance.

Both recruits stood at attention. Singh approached them, frowning.

"Commander!" Marco said, standing stiffly, gun pressed to his side, chin raised.

"If you're done with your cleaning duties, place this bin back at the gates, then report to exercise yard."

"Yes, Commander!" they said.

Singh nodded. "And don't let me catch you lazying around again, or I'll have you mopping the latrines for the rest of your training."

As Marco and Addy hurried back to their platoon, they kept glancing at each other, and Marco knew that Addy was thinking about that phone too. A chance to contact the outside world. To speak to Father . . . and to Kemi.

They spent the rest of the day training with their corporals—crawling under barbed wire, climbing over wooden walls, firing their guns, and battling dead scum. All the while Marco thought about the holy artifacts he and Addy had found—both links to the outside world, one of taste and smell and memory, the other promising actual voices from their old lives.

"I kill you!" Beast shouted, ripping Marco away from his thoughts. The massive Russian, sweat glistening on his bald head, charged toward one of the scum exoskeletons in the training yard. He thrust his bayonet again and again, finally piercing the shell, then fell to his knees as the recruits cheered. Beast pulled out his photo of Oxana, his pigtailed girlfriend, and kissed it. "For you, Lud—I mean, Oxana."

Elvis leaned toward Marco. "Psst. Show me that photo of Kemi again, will you?" He whistled. "Hot."

"No, fantasize about St-Pierre if you must," Marco whispered back, falling silent as the corporal walked closer.

They waited until St-Pierre walked by, then Elvis leaned close to Marco again. Another recruit was now attacking a dead scum.

"Say, Poet," Elvis whispered, "you think your friend Maple might be interested in a guy like me?"

Marco raised his eyebrows. "Addy? Addy Linden? She'd rip your balls off. You have better chances wooing Ensign Ben-Ari."

They both turned to look at the officer. Among their commanders—Sergeant Singh, the three corporals, and Ben-Ari—they saw the ensign the least amount of time, knew the least about her. Yet whenever he met Ben-Ari's eyes, Marco thought he saw sadness there, perhaps as great as the pain inside of him, of Lailani, of the rest of them.

Who are you, Ben-Ari? he thought, looking at their platoon's commander. *What brought this pain to your eyes?*

"Look at those green eyes," Elvis said, looking at the officer. "That golden hair. That smile."

"She's not smiling," Marco said.

"I've seen Ben-Ari smile before! In the mess hall, when she's with the sergeant and corporals and thinks we're not looking. Beautiful smile." Elvis sighed. "If Maple's out of my league, you think that maybe Ben-Ari would—"

"Ben-Ari is your commanding officer," Marco reminded him.

Beast stepped toward them, wiping sweat off his brow, still holding his photograph of Oxana. He patted Elvis on the back. "What you need is good Russian woman. Blond. Can drink lots. Strong like ox. You date Russian girl, she treat you like king." He kissed his photo. "Like my Ludmila."

"Your Oxana," Marco reminded him.

Beast nodded. "Yes, yes, of course. Russians always have two names, you know. Not like you Americans with your one puny name that means nothing."

Marco wanted to remind the towering Russian that he was Canadian but decided to drop the subject.

That night, at eleven, Sergeant Singh granted them a free hour again before lights out. Marco was exhausted—he had guard duty in three hours, then had to wake up for morning inspection shortly after that. He hadn't showered in three days, though, and he was beginning to smell like scum shit. Speaking of which, gray slop and Spam didn't sweat their way out. Abandoning his cot, Marco raced toward the showers and grabbed a last toilet stall. The door didn't offer much privacy. An inch was exposed on each side, a full foot below, and he could see the other recruits walking to and from the showers and changing at the bench. Only a week ago Marco would have been mortified by this lack of privacy, but after days with these people, he allowed himself to finally—for the first time—spend a few minutes reading *Hard Times*.

Thankfully, neither Lailani nor Addy were in the shower today to confuse him. There were other females in the platoon, some of whom were showering now, but Marco placed himself behind a few of the guys and washed while listening to Elvis croon "Always on My Mind."

As Marco was heading back toward his tent, he paused in the darkness. Under the stars, he stared west. It was still a kilometer away, but maybe if Marco ran, if he didn't encounter any commanders, he could make it to the phone. He could call Kemi tonight.

He took a step in that direction. He paused, looked around him, seeking commanders, seeing none. He stood in flip-flops, sweatpants, and a T-shirt, a submachine gun on his back, shivering in the cold, exhausted, wanting nothing more than to sleep, but that phone beckoned.

He took another few steps, heading into deeper shadows, when he heard the weeping.

Marco froze and frowned.

A shadowy lump rose ahead beyond the lights that hung around the tents. Marco walked toward it, and the weeping grew louder.

A figure leaped up ahead. Metal clattered. "Who's there?" A barrel of a gun rose.

"Whoa, calm down!" Marco raised his hands. "It's me. It's Marco. Beast, that you?"

Marco stepped closer and saw him there. Sasha "Beast" Mikhailov cast an impressive figure in the night, standing six and a half feet tall, all muscle, his neck as wide as his bald head, his gun in hand. And yet tears now shone on his cheeks.

"Look away," Beast said, turning aside. "I am ashamed."

Marco approached slowly. "Hey, Beast, it's all right. I think every one of us has cried here by now. Well, maybe not Pinky, but I'm still convinced he's a baby scum."

Beast nodded and wiped tears away. "I hate this place. Hate it! I miss home. I scared here."

Marco hesitated, then placed a hand on the burly recruit's arm. "You'll see home again. This isn't forever. You'll see your family, you'll see Oxana again. Sometimes they let soldiers visit home for Christmas, and—"

"There is no Oxana," Beast blurted out. "Okay? There is no Oxana. There is no Ludmila. I made her up." He lowered his head. "It picture of my sister, not my girlfriend. I don't have pretty girlfriend like you. I lied."

"Why?" Marco said. "Just to impress the guys?"

Beast was trembling—actually trembling. He reached into his wallet and pulled out a piece of paper. He unfolded it, revealing a photograph. "This is who I love. His name is Boris. But I can't tell that to the guys. What you think Elvis and Dicky and Pinky and everyone say? You think they let me shower with them?" Beast scoffed. "They be even more scared of me than they are now. They don't know I'm scared of them. But you, Poet, you all right." He gave Marco a crooked look. "You all right, yes?"

Marco again patted Beast's arm. "We're both all right. You keep that photo of Boris, and let that be your strength, that he's there waiting for you."

Beast nodded. "Like Kemi waiting for you."

Marco said nothing. Nobody here knew that Kemi had joined Julius Military Academy, that he wouldn't see her for years, that they had essentially broken up on his last night home. It was still too painful to talk about. Only Addy knew. He would reveal this terrible truth to nobody else.

We all have secrets here, he thought. *Beast, Lailani, Pinky, Ben-Ari—we're all just wearing masks. Let me wear mine a little longer.*

Marco returned to his tent, lay on his cot, and placed his gun under his pillow. He turned on his flashlight and looked at the photo of Kemi.

He put the photo aside and switched off his flashlight. He could just make out Lailani sleeping on the cot next to his, a small lump of darkness. Gently, Marco placed the chocolate bar on her duffel bag, a surprise for her to find when she woke up for guard duty. He closed his eyes and slept for two hours.

CHAPTER FIFTEEN

On Sunday morning a miracle occurred at Fort Djemila.

Sergeant Singh stood before the recruits, delivering the good news.

"All right, soldiers. It's Sunday. You've completed your first week of basic training. You still have nine weeks to go before you become proud privates in the HDF. But today—for the rest of the day—you rest."

Marco blinked, disbelieving.

"Commander," he said, "you mean we watch reels all day between exercises?"

"I mean," said the bearded sergeant, "that you sleep. You write letters home. You pray. You do your laundry in the sink. You jerk off in the toilets. You do whatever the fuck you want so long as you report to three meals in the mess, are in your tents for lights out at eleven, and pass morning inspection tomorrow morning." He smiled thinly. "Though if you insist, I can have you run through the obstacle course a few more times today."

"Letters and laundry sound excellent, Commander," said Marco, scarcely believing his good luck.

And Sergeant Singh left.

He left!

The corporals, the sergeant, the ensign—they were gone.

For the first time in a week, the recruits of the 4th Platoon were alone.

Marco felt magnanimous, and he shared news of the vending machine behind the chapel, only a kilometer or two away, and soon the soldiers were back in their tent, carrying their bounty: a feast of candy and chips and pop and melting ice cream. They all ate in their tent, and even Pinky seemed in a decent mood. They told the crude stories of soldiers, the boys boasting of women they had conquered—most of those stories lies, no doubt—and gossiping about their commanders. Beast spoke about how drill sergeants in Russia beat recruits who failed morning inspection, didn't just give them kitchen duty, breeding real warriors. Elvis did a spot-on impression of their corporals and sergeants, eliciting laughter so loud Marco had to hush them, fearing one of the commanders would hear.

"Fuckin' whorehouse here," Elvis said, flopping down onto a cot. "Sundays at boot camp, yeah!" He yawned. "Now shut up, all of you. It's time to sleep and dream of home."

Bellies full, they slept.

For a week now the recruits had really just catnapped, constantly being woken for guard duty, and three times already— sirens in the middle of the night and a long hour at high alert, kneeling between the cots until the all clear was given. Now on this searing Sunday, they lay on their cots, and for a few glorious hours, Marco was lost in darkness.

A pillow hit his head, waking him. Marco opened his eyes to see Addy standing above him, her T57 slung across her back.

"Hey, Poet." She raised a soccer ball. "Look what I found. We're going to eat lunch, then play ball. You in?"

He groaned and checked his watch. It was 2:00 p.m. He had slept for six wonderful, blessed, dreamless hours. He looked back at Addy. The other recruits were lacing up their boots and heading toward the exit. One grabbed the ball from Addy and kicked it across the tent.

"Muhmmm, go away," Marco muttered.

"Lunch!" she said. "Delicious Spam!"

Marco groaned, grabbed her pillow, and placed it over his head. "I still have a bag of Hickory Chips. Let me sleep."

"Fine, tubby." She poked his belly button, then turned away. "Lailani, you in?"

Lailani sat up on her cot, yawned, and stretched. "I'm staying too. I ain't leaving this tent until tomorrow's inspection. Enjoy your game. Try not to kick your ball into any ammunitions warehouses."

The recruits whistled and hooted.

"Poet and Tiny, alone in a tent!" said one.

As Elvis walked by, he slapped Marco's shoulder. "Remember, de la Rosa likes to be spanked."

Marco lobbed the pillow at him. "You already told that joke about Addy."

The recruits filed out, leaving Marco and Lailani alone in the tent. He could hear them arguing about who was history's best soccer player. There seemed to be two camps, one supporting Santos, the others championing Alvarez. The voices soon faded into the distance. Marco lay on his back, closed his eyes, but couldn't fall back asleep. Finally he sat up, made the trek to the latrines, and came back with an empty bladder and shaved face. Lailani was sitting on her cot, oiling her gun.

Marco opened his bag of Hickory Chips and held it out to Lailani. "Chip?"

She looked up from her gun. "It's not true, you know."

"What?"

"What Elvis said. How they laughed about us." She pulled off her buttoned shirt, remaining in a white tank top, and showed him the rainbow tattoo on her arm. "I like girls."

"Oh," Marco said. He hated the feeling of disappointment that filled him. "That's great."

Lailani shrugged. "Figures. I hate men anyway. I saw how they hurt my mother, how they hurt me." She stood up, walked toward Marco's cot, and sat down beside him. "You're different, though. You're not like any other boy I've known. I like you." She leaned against him.

"I like you too." His arm felt awkward, pinned to his side, and he slung it around Lailani. She nestled closer to him.

"Tell me about your book," she said. "Addy said you're writing a book. *Jarhead?*"

"*Loggerhead*," Marco said.

Lailani grabbed a chip. It crunched between her teeth. "What does that mean?"

"It's a type of turtle," Marco said. "A large sea turtle."

"You're writing a book about turtles?" Lailani grabbed another chip.

"No," Marco said. "It's only a plot device." He spoke as Lailani snacked. "You see, it's about a man."

"A turtle man?"

"No, not a turtle man. Just a man. He lives on a beach, homeless, friendless, mentally challenged. Mentally he's like a child."

"Like Caveman," said Lailani, nodding.

"Worse," said Marco. "A lot worse. He just lives on the beach, and he suffers from amnesia. He doesn't remember his name, where he comes from, how he got here. He has only vague memories of a family he lost. Gangs bully him. His life is sad."

"So where does the turtle come in?" Lailani said. "I like turtles."

"Sometime before the book begins, the man saw a giant turtle—a loggerhead—wash onto the shore, still alive. The man watched as scientists attached a tracking device to the turtle, then released it back into the water. The man on the beach begins to write letters to the turtle, which he places into glass bottles, which he tosses into the water. He tells the turtle—and the reader—his story. Each chapter is a different letter the man writes. It's written with spelling mistakes and grammatical errors on purpose. That's how the man writes." Marco smiled thinly. "Makes my job easier too. No need to fix typos."

Lailani looked up at him. "And what story does the man tell the turtle?"

"At first the man only talks about his daily struggles, addressing them to the loggerhead. But more things happen, all described in the letters. One day a young woman arrives on the beach. She claims to be the man's daughter. The man gets scared and chases her away. She comes back. She tells him that he was a successful doctor, that he was in a car crash, that he injured his head and forgot who he was. The man remembers brief images of his previous life, which scare him. Again he chases the woman away. Slowly it begins to return to him. He used to be intelligent, successful, rich—but then a crash. Fire. Blood. And him here on the beach. He's scared. In his last letter, he tells the turtle that he'll swim out to find him, even if he drowns, but that he hopes he'll find a magical underwater kingdom where no pain or memory exists, where he and the turtle can be together. The novel ends with him swimming out into the ocean with his last letter, implying his death." Marco was silent for a moment, then cleared his throat. "At least I think the book will end like that. I've only written the first few chapters."

Lailani thought for long moments. "It's sad," she finally said. "I like it. Can I read the first chapters?"

"When they're done. They still need some revising."

"I wish I could write and be creative," Lailani said. "I'm not much good at anything other than moping and being depressed. It's why I like the HDF. I think I'm the only one here who likes it. There's not much time to think here. I like that. Thinking can hurt. Memories and too many thoughts."

Marco brushed crumbs off her shoulder. "Addy told me something. She said that here in the army, they want us to forget who we were. They break us and rebuild us. We're new people here. What happened to us in our past lives—that still matters, and it still hurts, and it'll always be a part of us. They can't take that away. But we have new lives now. Blank slates."

Lailani nuzzled him. "You're definitely not like the others. You're smart. I like you." She stood up, pulled off her clothes, then lay down on her stomach, naked on the cot. She looked up at him. "You can have sex with me if you want. The others won't be back for a while."

He blinked, shocked, but couldn't look away from her dark, slender body stretched out on his cot. He caressed the rainbow tattoo on her arm. "I thought you don't like boys."

"I don't. Just you." She buried her face in the pillow. "I ruv you."

He lay down beside her and stroked her buzzed black hair. "You ruv me?"

She nodded, still pressing her face against the pillow. "I don't want to say it properly. I'm shy." She took his hand. "Let's do this."

Marco hesitated. Here, in the army tent, with the others about to return any moment? And with Kemi still fresh in his mind?

We might all die tomorrow, he thought, looking at Lailani, and suddenly he "ruved" her too. Not loved. No. They didn't know each other enough for that. But he ruved her—a mumbling, hesitating, awkward sort of feeling, full of shyness and uncertainty. He undressed, and he held her, and he made love to her, but this too was awkward, clumsy, not at all like his time with Kemi. Lailani wouldn't kiss him, perhaps feeling that was too intimate, too scary. She turned her head away whenever he tried to kiss her lips. Their sex was all banging elbows and gasps and giggles when things didn't quite work. Finally he lay at her side, not sure what had happened, feeling disoriented as after a long run, and she lay in his arms.

Did that even work? Marco thought. *What just happened?*

"I liked having sex with you," Lailani whispered into his neck, still shy, not meeting his eyes. "I like you."

Yes, Marco thought. *Whatever just happened, it worked. It was right.*

He stroked her hair and kissed her forehead, and at that moment, Marco loved her—fully, with every beat of his heart, this precious, fragile doll, this broken thing, this fierce warrior.

They heard voices from outside.

"No way," somebody was saying. "Santos is the greatest player of all time."

"You're crazy," rose another voice, moving closer to the tent. "Alvarez is always going to be the greatest. Santos is just famous for modeling and selling hair gel. Alvarez can score."

Lailani hopped back onto her own cot and pulled her blanket over herself. Marco covered his own nakedness. Both pretended to sleep as two recruits entered the tent, now arguing about who should have won the World Cup of 2078. Lailani peeked from under her blanket at Marco. She gave him a tiny smile and a wink, then closed her eyes and slept, and soon sleep covered Marco again, and even in the sweltering heat of the desert, he missed holding Lailani in his arms.

* * * * *

On Sunday night, with another hour of freedom left—at least, as much as one could have freedom within barbed wire fences—Marco walked toward the beacon that rose in the dark desert.

He paused. Sand blew around him, and the distant shouts of "Yes, Commander!" rose from somewhere in the camp behind him. Marco took a deep breath and walked on. In a rocky field, he reached the phone.

His hand brushed the receiver.

It won't work, he thought. *It's just an antique like the radios we carried. It can't actually call home.*

Yet he found himself dialing with shaky fingers, and the phone rang.

"Hello?" sounded a voice on the other end.

The lump that grew in Marco's throat wouldn't let him speak.

Again the voice sounded. "Hello?"

"Dad," Marco said.

"Marco! Marco, how are you? Is everything all right?"

"I'm fine, Dad. Everything is fine. I . . ."

And suddenly tears were flowing down Marco's cheeks, and he hated himself—for being so weak, for being just a boy. He was a soldier now. He was training to kill scum. He had made love to two women. He had fired guns and thrust bayonets. And now he couldn't speak, couldn't breathe, could barely see through his tears.

"I'm so glad to hear you, Marco," said his father. "Hang in there, buddy. This isn't forever. The first week's the hardest, you know that, right?"

"Yeah. I know." Marco cleared his throat. "I just called to say hi, to tell you I'm all right, to see how you are."

It was stupid. It was so stupid. Why had he called? Why was this so hard? Why was this bringing tears to his eyes, making his voice shake?

I miss home, he wanted to say. *I'm scared. I want to come back. I just want to come back home. I miss you.*

But Marco could say none of those things, would not have his father worry. So he only repeated, "I'm good. I'm learning new things. And I'm looking after Addy."

"Your old room is waiting here for you," Father said. "Next time they let you out—whether it's this Christmas or another holiday—it's all here waiting."

Marco didn't want to hear that. Thinking about his old home was too painful, and he began to understand why electronics and any contact with the outside world were forbidden here. It wasn't because of any scum spies. It just hurt too much to think of your home. Heaven burned the eyes of those in hell. This was Marco's home now, this desert, and his fellow recruits were his family now. This was all he was, all he could be, or he'd be torn apart.

"Dad, listen, I have to go now. I'm not sure when I can call again. I'll try to call soon. Addy is fine too. Goodbye, Dad."

"Goodbye, Marco. Love you."

"Love you too." Again his voice choked, and his tears fell. He hung up. He walked away, blinking rapidly.

"Poet!" Elvis ran toward him. "Poet, Poet! Come see! Beast is doing push-ups with Addy standing on his back. You have to see this! Hurry!"

They ran together back toward their tent, and Marco allowed himself a small smile. Tomorrow at 4:30 a.m. another day of hell would begin, but right now he had a home here. He had friends. And he had Lailani.

Let me have this day, he thought, *before the world collapses again.*

CHAPTER SIXTEEN

The days stretched on, blurring together into one endless nightmare of heat, of burning sunlight, of vomiting from dehydration, of crawling under barbed wire, of running through sand, of climbing fences, of firing guns, of fighting exoskeletons, of shouting. Always shouting. Always heavy eyelids and falling asleep and please, please let us stand up, but the eyelids were so heavy, and the batons of the commanders shocked them, and the radios broke their backs, and finally standing—finally walking— only to find that even then, the eyes began to close, the mind began to drift into sleep, and their backs ached and feet screamed, and please, please let us sit, and the sun still burned, and their bodies broke. And down another notch on Marco's belt, and more runs to the latrine to expel the gray slop and Spam, and another notch down, and his fatigues—once tight—now loose around his body, and his face haggard, his eyes gaunt, and still shouting.

There was no shame, no modesty in the HDF. They pissed side by side in the sand. They huddled together for warmth in the freezing nights, sleeping in fields, trudging in patrol around the fence. There were long nights in guard towers, staring out into the dark desert, nights of no sleep, watching the darkness, counting the stars. There were long nights alone by the gates, guns in hand, the desert storms stinging. Guarding. Always guarding. Every hour at night—guard duty or more sirens, more scum spotted in the distance, and days of firing their guns, and the smell of gunpowder always on them.

No days, no nights, just an endless, eternal loop, a cycle of heat and cold, light and dark, pain and exhaustion, thirst and nausea.

Marco did not read his book. He did not write. He did not think of home, did not worry about the scum, did not remember Kemi. There was no more time to think. Every waking, sleeping moment—a sergeant shouting, shocking him, or corporals punishing them, or Ben-Ari with her icy eyes, and more push-ups, another kilometer to run, another round with the radios. Never time to think. Marco no longer thought, no longer had thoughts, no longer had a mind. He was his rifle. All he was—an organic machine attached to the metal, trained only to obey, only to kill. He no longer knew how to read or write or be human. All he knew—to polish his boots, oil his gun, stand at attention, march, drill, shout, fire, obey, kill, kill.

Obey.

They ran, marched, shouted.

Kill.

They fired. They screamed.

Kill.

Kill. Kill.

Sometimes when they marched, ran, climbed, crawled, fired, Marco turned to look at Lailani. But she rarely looked his way, and at night they collapsed exhausted into their bunks. He tried to talk to her again, but she seemed shy around him, looking away, distant, afraid.

Was it just a one-night stand? Marco thought, trying to catch her gaze, to speak to her. *It wasn't one for me, Lailani.*

But whenever he tried to approach, a commander walked by, and they stood at attention, and the training resumed. Marco began to feel like a fool. He had shared his novel and his cot with Lailani, but now she seemed intent on avoiding him, not even meeting his gaze, not even giving him a smile, and washing on the other side of the showers.

She had lied to him, Marco had begun to realize. For days she dodged him. She didn't truly like him—"ruv" him, as she had called it. She liked somebody else, or she liked nobody here, and maybe that time in their bed had been only a weak moment for her, one she now regretted.

"Goodnight, Lailani," he said once at night, but the others laughed, mocked him, imitated him. And Lailani ignored him, wouldn't even meet his gaze.

A one-night stand, he thought. *That's all I was to her.*

Marco decided to push Lailani out of his mind, to focus only on his training, only on surviving this training. Yet whenever he lay on his cot, he couldn't help it. He imagined that Lailani lay in his arms again, and when he dreamed, he dreamed of her naked with him, of making love, of scum racing across the desert, and of the endless darkness of space.

* * * *

"Battle formations!" Corporal St-Pierre shouted. "Go! Faster! Now!"

The platoon scrambled into fireteams of three, the first gunner at the lead, two others flanking their leader. Marco slammed a magazine into his gun and stood, weapon raised. Addy and Elvis, part of his trio, knelt at his sides. Other fireteams loaded their guns around them.

"Fire!" St-Pierre shouted.

Marco cursed. He had forgotten to load his gun. He loaded now, and he cursed again. He had forgotten to pull on his earmuffs too. The bullets blazed around him, and he grimaced, the sound deafening. He fired. His gun rang out.

"Hold your fire!" St-Pierre cried. "Hold your fire!"

Another two shots were fired, and the guns fell silent. Corporal St-Pierre approached, pulling off her earmuffs, her face red, her blue eyes blazing.

The rest of the 4th Platoon's commanders were away today, perhaps resting from the vigors of basic training, but there was never any rest for the recruits. For twenty hours a day, they trained for war. Some days of training were not so bad. Whenever

Corporal Webb trained them, she was kind enough. As it turned out, Webb had lost her legs in battle only six months ago; the injury had given her compassion to the new warriors she was preparing for battle. Corporal Diaz was harsher but still fair, and while he did punish errant recruits, he never seemed to delight in the task.

But Corporal Fiona St-Pierre lacked all compassion. Days with St-Pierre were different. Marco often thought that scum would be kinder.

"Pathetic!" St-Pierre spat, moving between the recruits. "Mikhailov, you're supposed to rest your magazine against your forearm. Yours is dangling in the air like your cock." She moved toward Noodles, the scrawny and spectacled *Lord of the Rings* fan, and yanked his helmet up. "How do you expect to see the scum devouring your entrails?" Finally she came to stand before Marco, and she glared, blue eyes blazing with hatred. "You fired too late, Emery. You forgot your earmuffs. You nearly got your whole platoon killed." She spat on his boot. "You are a pathetic worm. You are all pathetic worms! What are you?"

"Worms, Commander!" they shouted.

"Worms, Pizza!" shouted Pinky with the group, and Marco shot him a glare.

"She can hear you," Marco hissed.

Pinky grinned at him. "Good."

The practical joke had begun to spread through the platoon. Whenever they shouted "Commander!" to St-Pierre, Pinky would shout, "Pizza!" The first few times, Pinky's voice had drowned in the crowd, but slowly more and more recruits were imitating him, calling out the cruel taunt, a reference to St-Pierre's complexion. And Marco knew that the corporal could hear it, that she knew of the nickname. St-Pierre was too proud to admit it, but every time she trained them, she was meaner, more vindictive, determined to punish the platoon for Pinky's prank.

St-Pierre now pointed at the ground. "Crawl then, worms! Crawl through the sand like the worms you are."

They flattened themselves on the ground and began to crawl, guns held before them. The sand was hot, the rocks stabbing, and they had not drunk water for hours.

"Faster!" shouted St-Pierre, and her baton crackled with electricity as she drove it into the backs of recruits. "Under that barbed wire!"

Marco bit down hard and nearly screamed as her electric baton slammed between his shoulder blades. He crawled faster.

Elvis crawled at his side, soaked with sweat and matted with sand. "Never thought I'd say this, but I miss Sergeant Singh," he said. "I—" He screamed as St-Pierre placed a boot on his back and shocked him with her baton.

"Crawl under that barbed wire, worms!" St-Pierre shouted.

They crawled under a low net of barbed wire. It stabbed at their backs and helmets. As Marco crawled, he suddenly froze and stared.

A scorpion scuttled across the sand before him.

Wails of protest across the platoon—everyone was now under the barbed wire—confirmed that the others had met their own arachnids.

"There are scorpions here, Commander!" Elvis cried.

"Good," St-Pierre said, walking outside the barbed wire. "Let them sting you. Crawl until you're covered with stings. Go! Faster!"

They crawled. Marco swung the barrel of his gun before him, flicking the scorpion aside, then crushing it under his muzzle. A scream rose nearby.

"The son of a bitch stung me!" Sheriff wailed.

"It hurts!" cried Caveman.

"Crawl!" shouted St-Pierre.

Finally they emerged from under the barbed wire. Sheriff and Caveman and three others clutched swelling scorpion bites, and several other recruits were bleeding from the barbed wire.

"We have to see the medics," said Sheriff. "We—"

"You will keep training!" said St-Pierre. "The scum won't give you time to see medics, and their stings are worse. Battle formations! Scum ahead! Go!"

They formed fireteams again. This time Addy took the lead, and Marco and Elvis knelt at her sides. All three pointed their guns forward.

"Fire!" shouted St-Pierre, and Marco pulled his trigger, and hot casings flew, and—

"Halt!"

As soon as St-Pierre's voice rang out, Marco realized his error, and terror froze him.

Fuck. Fuck.

He wasn't the fireteam leader in this exercise. And yet, instead of merely providing backup to Addy, he had fired his weapon with her.

They were firing blanks in this exercise, but had these been live bullets, Marco realized that he could have—in the heat of battle—shot Addy in the back.

St-Pierre stepped toward him, silent, but her eyes showed her fury.

Marco straightened and stood at attention. "I'm sorry, Commander. I was imagining the scum, and—"

She drove her baton into his belly, and electricity crackled. "Down!" she shouted. "Fifty push-ups, shout out each number!"

Marco dropped and began his push-ups. He had been able to do forty before, never fifty. He began.

"One!" he said, rising up again.

St-Pierre kicked him down again. "One, *Commander*, and shout it. Start over."

"One, Commander!" He pushed himself up, then down again. "Two, Co—"

"Louder!" The baton hit him again, knocking him down. "You will shout, or you will do this all day. Start over. Shout!"

"One, Commander!" Marco shouted, repeating his push-up. "Two, Commander! Three—"

"Louder!" she shouted, pressing her boot against his back, shoving him down. His face hit the dirt. "Faster!"

As the other recruits watched, Marco kept doing his push-ups, St-Pierre pressing her boot against his back all the while. Finally he rose, arms trembling.

"You will complete your training for the day, Emery, then report to the brig," St-Pierre said. "You will sleep there tonight. Is that understood?"

"Yes, Commander."

St-Pierre turned toward another recruit. "I did not let you wipe sweat off your forehead, maggot! Run! A full loop around the base. Go!"

The training with St-Pierre continued for hours of agony, electricity, barbed wire, scorpions, thirst, and burning sunlight. Marco soon missed Sergeant Singh too.

That night, Marco walked across the base, heading toward the brig—an underground cell he had managed to avoid until now. He took a shortcut, walking around a fenced lot where several armed vehicles parked, topped with .50-caliber guns. Before boot camp ended, the recruits were to train with the weapons, a day which Marco both feared and looked forward to.

Marco was walking by one of the heavy, olive-green vehicles when he heard voices.

"I can't do this anymore, ma'am." The voice was soft, pained. "They mock me. They mock me all the time. They don't respect me like they respect Emilio or Railey or Amar."

Daniel Arenson

Marco froze, suddenly worried he was walking on forbidden ground. It took him a moment to recognize that voice. It was Corporal St-Pierre who was speaking. Marco had never heard her speak so softly, with such vulnerability. He inched forward, peered around a vehicle, and saw the corporal standing on the lot, facing a shadowy figure.

Who was she talking about? Then it dawned on Marco. Corporal Emilio Diaz. Corporal Railey Webb. Sergeant Amar Singh. Marco had heard their first names weeks ago, had forgotten them.

"You will earn their respect, Fiona," replied the shadowy figure, and Marco recognized Ensign Ben-Ari's voice. "This is new to all of us."

"Not to Emilio," said Corporal St-Pierre. "Not to Amar. Not to Railey. They all fought scum, killed scum. What do I know?"

Ensign Ben-Ari stepped into the light, and her eyes were soft. She placed a hand on St-Pierre's shoulder. "As much as I do, Fiona. I hadn't yet seen action either. I was just a cadet at Officer Candidate School a month ago. Just a hurt, frightened girl with a famous father, trembling to follow in his footsteps."

"The recruits respect you, ma'am," said St-Pierre. "You're a commissioned officer. And your father was a famous colonel. I'm nothing but a joke to them." Suddenly tears were on her cheeks. "I've failed you."

234

"No," said Ben-Ari. "Fiona, you are capable, strong, intelligent, and ambitious. You are my soldier, and that makes me proud."

Fiona raised her chin, eyes damp, and saluted. "And I'm proud to serve you, ma'am."

Ensign Ben-Ari returned the salute, and both women parted, going their separate ways. Marco hid in the shadows, waiting until they were gone. Then he walked onward to the brig, reported to the guard, and spent the night in the dark, moldy cell, thinking about the conversation, vowing to work a little harder tomorrow with his commanders.

CHAPTER SEVENTEEN

Hope "Jackass" Harris joined the Dragons Platoon two weeks into their training, a force as loud and furious as a scum invasion.

"Hello, you sons of bitches!" she cried, grinned, and gave a pirouette. Her voice was raspy as gravel spilling over beaten leather. "Aren't I cute? Aren't I just the most fucking adorable princess you've ever seen?"

"Looks like a goddamn ogre," muttered Dickerson, standing at Marco's side in formation.

"Be nice," Marco said, but when he looked back at Recruit Harris, he cringed. He had to admit, Dickerson was right.

Marco wouldn't win any beauty contests himself, and he never judged people by their looks, preferring to judge them based on their taste in music and literature like a civilized person. But even he found Hope Harris's appearance intimidating. Her nose was a massive beak, and a thin mustache topped her upper lip. A unibrow like a furry black caterpillar formed a V over that nose. Her eyes were beady and black, her cheeks pockmarked, and her hair was a frizzy mess that looked like black iron wool. Her forehead sloped backward, and she had no chin to speak of. Dickerson was right. She looked like an ogre, and Marco hated himself for agreeing with such a cruel thought.

"Recruit Harris!" Sergeant Singh shouted. "Go form rank with the others."

Harris curtsied. "But of course! I know the boys here at Fort Djemila have been waiting for a cutie like me to join their ranks. I tells ya, my good looks and lovely aroma were wasted in the brig. Wasted! A month of nothing but rats for company." She walked toward the platoon, reaching up to stroke Singh's arm as she passed by him. "Aren't you a handsome one, and—"

"Harris, if you don't shut your mouth, you'll spend the rest of your military career in the brig, not just a month."

"They call me Jackass," Harris said. Her voice was so raspy and deep it could have belonged to an aging, three-hundred-pound truck driver with emphysema. "Nobody calls me Harris. Jackass! Must be because I have such a cute little bottom." She emitted a braying, heehawing laughter that hinted at another origin of her nickname. "I'll show you my bottom if you like. I—"

"Harris!" Singh shouted. "Form rank!"

Harris, AKA Jackass, sighed theatrically and went to fill the gap in the Dragons' ranks. "Not appreciated in my time, just like my doppelganger, Marilyn Monroe."

Marco and Elvis glanced at each other, cringing.

"We lost Noodles for her?" Elvis muttered.

David "Noodles" Greene had been an awkward recruit who had spoken little in the Dragons Platoon—a scrawny boy with huge glasses, a concave chest, and an encyclopedic knowledge of Tolkien's Legendarium. After finally collapsing in the obstacle course, the HDF doctors had given Noodles—

nicknamed for the thinness of his limbs—a discharge from basic training. He would spend his five years of service working behind a desk. That left a gap to fill in the platoon, and who better to fill it than one who had already completed two weeks of basic training at another fort only to then spend a month in the brig?

"Hey, sweetie." Jackass batted her eyelashes at Marco. "You're cute. Aren't you just glad to serve with a hottie like me?"

"March!" Sergeant Singh commanded, and the platoon continued their day's training.

Throughout the day Jackass could not go five minutes without getting into trouble or annoying her new comrades. With every push-up, she grunted like a beast. Whenever the commanders weren't looking, she danced instead of marched. As they cleaned their weapons, she drew naughty drawings on the ground with her gun oil. One time she planted a kiss on Caveman's cheek, drawing awkward laughter from the platoon. By lunchtime, Jackass had earned ten hours of kitchen duty, three hours of latrine duty, and was doomed to spend next Sunday laundering sheets and cleaning the old machine guns rusting in the armory. Yet with every punishment announced, Jackass only sounded that braying laughter.

As they ate lunch in the mess, Jackass cannibalized all conversation. She stuffed two slices of bread into her mouth, forming a duck's beak, and quacked around the table. She guzzled down yogurt straight from the tin and gave an enormous belch.

"Fucking freak," Pinky said, pelting her with a spoonful of slop.

"She's an ogre all right," Dickerson muttered. A few more recruits laughed.

If Jackass noticed the mockery, she gave no sign of it. She curtsied for the onlookers. "Now now, boys, I know you all have massive crushes on me, but try not to tease me so much." She brayed out laughter and covered her mouth. "Aren't I cute?"

Addy, normally the vocal one in the platoon, was subdued today, watching Jackass with wide eyes.

"There's something wrong with her," she said to Marco. "Must have hit herself too hard on the head."

Marco began to think that Addy was right. Perhaps Jackass was mentally challenged, maybe even worse than Caveman. The soldier seemed oblivious to her ridiculous behavior and appearance. She was now giving a horribly offensive imitation of Sergeant Singh, complete with a thick Indian accent, seemingly unaware that the others were mocking her and pelting her with food.

"Harris," Marco said, gently pulling her back into her seat. He wanted to save her from this self-inflicted humiliation. "Tell me more about the brig. A month must have been horrible. Pinky once spent a day there and nearly broke."

"I did not!" Pinky said. "Fuck you, Emery."

"My name is Jackass," Jackass said. "Harris is my family name. Hope is the dumb name my parents gave me. I'm only Jackass now because I'm cute like a little donkey." She brayed.

"All right, Jackass," Marco said. "Tell me about the brig. Quietly. The commanders can hear you from across the hall."

Jackass sighed and pressed her palms together. "Oh, the brig is lovely! Lovely, Marco! There are no sergeants breathing down your neck. There are no corporals shouting at you. There are no fancy officers with fancy orders. They leave you alone all day long, and you can rest. No push-ups. No jogging. Just quiet." Her eyes lit up. "You think Sergeant Singh will send me back? Maybe if I'm really a horrible soldier, they'll send me back."

"You *want* to go back to the brig?" Addy said. "You're mental."

Jackass blew her a kiss. "Don't hate me because I'm beautiful, darling." She leaned against Marco and kissed his cheek. "Or because I'm stealing your boyfriend."

Addy snorted. "He wishes he were my boyfriend."

Marco glanced across the table, trying to meet Lailani's gaze. She was looking straight at him, met his eyes for just an instant, then looked away.

I ruv you, she had said, nestling against him, her body warm in his arms—a memory seared inside him, a memory that hadn't left him since that day over a week ago. And since then—barely more than this glance.

"Not bad, this Fort Djemila," Jackass said, interrupting his thoughts. "Chow's all right. Over in Fort Timgad, the food's like shit. Sarge here ain't bad either. And you should have seen the sergeant at Fort Setif. The woman had a bayonet stuck up her ass, I swear."

Elvis reached across the table for a jar of jam made from indeterminable fruit. "You were at two other basic training bases?"

Jackass brayed out her laughter. "Two? I've been to six already. Never last more than a week anywhere."

"I can't imagine why," Addy muttered under her breath.

"I've been in the HDF for six months now," Jackass said. "Maybe a year, I'm not sure. Mostly in various prisons. I hope they send me back soon. Not a bad way to go through your service, the brig."

Finally Lailani, who had been silent all this time, rose to her feet. She pointed a butter knife at Jackass. "Don't you want to kill scum?" Lailani said, glaring. "Don't you want to finally complete basic training and fight for your species?"

"Darling!" Jackass held up her hands. "I'm a lover, not a fighter! Besides, I'd serve the troops much better by singing and boosting their morale." She launched into a song, her voice deep, hoarse, and as pleasant as glass smashed against gravel.

They continued their training.

Gunpowder, blisters, torn muscles, the breaking down of the soul.

Fainting in the heat, crawling in the sand, battling the scum skeletons, forgetting who they were.

Another day in Fort Djemila. Another day as recruits. Another day waiting for these ten weeks—this eternity—to end, to emerge from the crucible as soldiers.

That night, Corporal Diaz read out the guard shifts. Marco pulled third guard, after Caveman and before Lailani. Following a day of training and firing and fighting, his body ached, and his soul felt blank. After lights out, he slept, a dark, pitiless sleep like drowning in oil.

I'm okay, Dad, he said in his dream. *I'm okay. I'm scared. I'm hurt. There are scum after me. There are scum everywhere. I'm on a dark planet. I'm stuck here.* He clutched the phone. *I want to go home.*

A hand touched his shoulder.

"Poet. Poet, your turn to guard."

He opened his eyes, and he saw Caveman looking down at him through the shadows.

"Poet, have I ever told you about that time I visited Greece?" Caveman said, and his eyes lit up. "Oh, the flowers I picked there! If I were in Greece right now, I would pick such a bouquet for this tent!"

Even as he struggled to rise from his nightmare, Marco couldn't help but smile. He sat up and patted Caveman's shoulder. "Maybe we'll visit together someday, after this war. I can work on my novel there, and you can pick flowers."

"I'd like that. I'll find you some beautiful flowers." Caveman yawned. "Goodnight, Poet."

Marco patrolled outside the tent for fifteen cold, shivering minutes, teeth chattering, and it seemed as if he were still in that dream, standing on a dark planet, that the scum would soon appear, swarming over the dunes toward him.

When his shift ended, he returned into the tent. Fifteen cots stretched here in two rows, and the squad's recruits slept. Jackass was snoring. Marco walked between the cots and knelt by Lailani. He touched her shoulder.

"Lailani," he whispered.

She opened her eyes.

"It's your shift," he said.

She left her bed, pulled on her fatigues and helmet, grabbed her gun, and stepped outside, silent all the while. Marco stood for a moment, then followed her. He stood outside in the night beside her. She stared ahead into the darkness, silent, facing away from him.

"Lailani, is everything all right?" Marco said. "Did I do anything to hurt you?"

She turned toward him. "You should sleep. Inspection's coming soon."

"Lailani, you've barely spoken to me all week. What happened between us . . . did it mean nothing to you? It meant something to me. Is this because of Kemi? We broke up, Lailani. I—"

She pressed a finger against his lips, hushing him.

"It meant something to me too," Lailani whispered. "It meant a lot. It meant too much. And that's why you need to stay away from me."

"I don't understand." He tried to hold her hand, but she took a step away.

"Marco, I'm bad news," Lailani said. "I'll hurt you."

He smiled thinly and rubbed his side. "More than St-Pierre's baton?"

Lailani nodded. "Much more." She turned away from him, staring into the darkness. "Marco, for you, for everyone else, basic training is a nightmare. It's deprivation and hardship and despair. But not for me. Because this is so much easier than my old life. I have food here. I have a cot to sleep on. I have friends. I'm not always afraid. But I still remember the old days. I still remember the men paying my mother a handful of pesos for her body. I still remember my little cousin starving to death. I still remember rummaging through filth in a landfill, a thousand other starving souls around me, seeking banana peels and rotten old chicken bones to eat. I still remember being so sick, throwing up so much, wanting to die until I cut myself. When I said I joined the HDF to die, I meant it. I'm four feet ten and weigh ninety-three pounds. They wanted to exempt me, saying I'm too small, too weak. When they saw the scars on my wrists, they absolutely refused to let me join. But I insisted. I kept showing up at the recruiting center until they let me enlist—and only because my father was a soldier and killed scum. I joined to die in battle, Marco, and that's what I intend to do as soon as basic training is over. This is my suicide. And I don't want you to love me. I don't want your heart to break." She touched his cheek. "You're too sweet for that."

He held her hands. "You don't have to die, Lailani. We can live, both of us. Together."

"And what, get married after the army, have babies? I would never have babies. I don't want to give them my depression. I wouldn't know how to live happily with you. There's something broken inside me, something that cannot heal. But I can still become a heroine. I can die a heroine—for humanity. It would be a good death."

Marco wanted to pity her, but instead he found anger inside him. "Well, it's too late. Because I already love you. I already fucking love you, Lailani. I want you to live, and I want you to know that you matter. That somebody loves you. That there is still a good life for you to live. It's hard to see here, but there is still goodness in the world. Don't die before you claim some of it. Let me help you. Let me show this to you."

Lailani looked away from him, eyes damp, then whispered, "I hate you. I hate you for doing this. For making me care about you. For confusing me so much."

"And hey, I need somebody to share chips with, and Addy just eats the whole bag."

For the first time since Marco had known her, Lailani smiled—not just a thin, hesitant smile but a huge, real grin that showed her teeth. She embraced him and leaned her cheek against his chest. Their rifles and magazines of bullets clattered together.

"I do want to read your novel when it's finally done," Lailani said, "and it'll probably take you years to write."

He pulled her helmet back and kissed her forehead. "So do you still ruv me?"

She nodded. "I ruv you."

"Ruv you too." He kissed her nose, then pulled her helmet down over her eyes.

He returned to his cot. Just as he was drifting back to sleep, as Lailani returned from her guard shift, he felt a gentle kiss on his lips, then saw Lailani crawl into her cot. He slept and no longer dreamed of scum.

CHAPTER EIGHTEEN

Marco and Elvis stood in the guard tower, watching the dark desert, their guns in hand.

"It's a scum!" Elvis pointed. "Look!"

Marco rolled his eyes. "Elvis, it's the same boulder from before. Calm down."

The guard tower's turret was small, cold, and exposed. Behind them spread Fort Djemila, and before them rolled the desert. Elvis seemed miserable here, hopping from foot to foot, tapping the railing, and nibbling his lip. But Marco liked it up here. In the night, it felt like floating above the world, like a sailor in a crow's nest on some ancient sailing ship. There were no shouting commanders up here, no Pinky, no kitchen duty or exercises or screaming bullets. Just a tiny enclosure and darkness.

"Sorry, Poet." Elvis lowered his gun. "I'm a bit jumpy. There's scuttlebutt."

"What scuttlebutt?" Marco raised an eyebrow.

"Scuttlebutt about a scum invasion."

Marco sighed. "Elvis, there are no electronics on this base. How did you hear scuttlebutt? And why do you even call it scuttlebutt?"

"Oh, I have my sources," Elvis said. "You know my sources, right? Remember when you lost your beret?"

Marco nodded. "I was terrified Sergeant Singh would murder me."

"And who got you a new beret the next day?"

"You did," Marco said.

Elvis nodded. "Through my sources. And they've heard scuttlebutt. Scum coming. And—" He gasped and loaded his gun. "Scum!"

"Elvis!" Marco pushed down his friend's barrel. "Boulder. Boulder!"

With a shudder, Elvis nodded, opened his gun, and fished out the loaded bullet. "Sorry, the whole jumpy thing."

"We're all jumpy," Marco said. "You and Addy and me. The three Canadian kids. We've seen our share of scum. Well, I suppose the whole world has." He looked at his friend. "Whereabouts back home are you from anyway?"

"If nowhere has a middle," said Elvis, "that's where I'm from. Farmlands. Nothing but soybeans for kilometers around. Not even any good plants like corn, just fucking soybeans, and the damn things taste horrible. Had to drive an hour just to see my girl."

Marco's eyes widened. "You have a girlfriend? All this time, when the boys were sharing photos of our girls, you didn't say anything."

Elvis nodded, quiet for a long moment. Finally he reached into his back pocket, pulled out his wallet, and opened it. Inside was a photo of a young woman waving at the camera. "That's her. Ellie."

"She's beautiful," Marco said.

"The most beautiful girl in the world," said Elvis. "She died seven months ago."

"God." Marco lowered his head. "I'm sorry, Elvis. That's horrible. Did the scum . . .?"

"Nah." Elvis returned the wallet to his pocket. "Car crash. Just before she died, we talked about getting married after the army. We already planned it all out. Would have helped us get through these five years, you know? We already named our future kids."

"I don't know what to say." Marco touched his friend's shoulder, then pulled his hand back, feeling awkward, feeling like the movement was too cliche, meaningless. "I'm sorry, again."

"When I came here," Elvis said, "I decided to be happy when I remembered her. To remember our good times. To still let her memory help me."

"I understand why you didn't say anything about her until now," Marco said. "But I'm glad you told me."

Elvis shrugged. "I don't like talking about home much. I think about it a lot. Don't talk about it much. I'm a different person here. I was just Benny Ray back home, just a dumb farm boy. Here you guys call me Elvis. Here I have my sources. Here I have my gun. Here I mean something."

Marco couldn't help but grin. "And there, my friend, you are wrong. Here we are cogs in a machine. Ensign Ben-Ari is an officer. She means something. We're peasants!"

Elvis groaned. "Great, so even here I'm a farmer!" He peered into the darkness. "God, I hate that boulder."

"We'll blow it up tomorrow with grenades," Marco said.

In the darkness, Elvis began to croon, and they stood in the guard tower until dawn spilled across the desert like liquid fire.

* * * * *

"Meet the sand tigers," said Ensign Ben-Ari. "They are nasty beasts. They are deadly. They are nearly indestructible. They can survive in desert, forest, and on the surface of almost any planet we operate on. In battle they are your best friends."

The platoon's recruits stared, silent.

"They're a bit rusty, ma'am," Addy finally said.

"This isn't the goddamn Space Territorial Command, Maple," Elvis said. "This is a training base. We get the rusty old leftovers."

"Watch it, recruits," Sergeant Singh said, reaching for his baton.

As Marco stared at the sand tigers, he tended to agree with his friends. The machines on the lot—he counted twenty of them—looked a century old. At a glance, the sand tigers looked like tanks. They were large, cumbersome, and covered with armored plates. Instead of wheels, their bodies were mounted on caterpillar tracks. But they were smaller than the Behemoth tanks Marco had seen back in Toronto, and they had no cannons. Instead, machine guns thrust out of turrets at their tops. They looked less like tigers to Marco, more like clumsy old rhinos who wanted little more than to spend the day lounging in the sun.

Ensign Ben-Ari stepped toward one of the machines. The top of her helmet reached about halfway up the vehicle's armored body.

"Sand tigers," she said. "Produced by Chrysopoeia Corp since 2112. Each one of these machines is eleven feet tall, weighs sixty metric tons, and can race across almost any terrain at sixty kilometers per hour. That's fast for a machine this heavy. They are topped with .50-caliber, stinger-class machine guns." She reached toward the back of the armored vehicle, grabbed a handle, and pulled open a hatch, forming a ramp. "Inside, they comfortably seat one driver, two gunners, and nine infantry troops. These babies will drive over scum, crushing their exoskeletons, and take you deep into enemy territory without a scratch."

"But do they have a cup holder?" Elvis asked, earning thirty push-ups from Singh.

When Elvis stood up again, Ben-Ari walked toward him. She stared at the recruit, eyes hard. "You're a joker. It's funny to mock these machines. To call them leftovers. To call them rusty. But these machines mean something, Recruit Ray. They mean that humanity still stands. That we survived. That we fight back. That we rose from the ashes of the Cataclysm that wiped out most of our species. You see rust. I see humanity rising from ruin. And I'm proud of that. Because fifty years ago, you wouldn't be looking at rusty machines of war. You'd be looking at burnt corpses."

Elvis lowered his head. "I'm sorry, ma'am."

Ben-Ari walked away from him, pacing along the lines of troops. "Today you'll get to drive these sand tigers. Some of you might even go on to serve in them after basic. Form into fireteams: one driver, two gunners."

The platoon performed many exercises in trios called "fireteams." They grouped into threes when forming rank, when firing their guns, even for kitchen or latrine duty. While squads and platoons were official and unchangeable, the recruits could technically form any trios they liked, changing them each exercise. Yet over time, common trios had begun to emerge in the platoon, friends sticking with friends. Pinky always joined with his friends Dicky, a hulking brute, and Marfa, a snickering girl with shaggy brown hair. Beast and Caveman had become close friends, and Elvis often joined them—smaller and shorter and seeking their strength. As always, Marco paired up with Addy. At first, the third soldier in their fireteam was always different; sometimes Elvis (before he abandoned them to the taller, stronger recruits), sometimes Noodles (before he got kicked out of basic), sometimes Sheriff with the star on his helmet.

Today it was Lailani who approached them.

"Mind if I join in, kind sir and kind madam?" she asked.

Marco nodded, feeling his cheeks heat up. "You may, kind lass," he said.

Lailani tipped her helmet at him and came to stand between Marco and Addy; she didn't even reach their shoulders.

"Hey, Poet, Maple," Pinky called out, pointing at them. "You two adopt a little boy?"

"Watch it, Mack," Sergeant Singh warned.

Marco had to admit—with her buzz cut, slender frame, and short stature, Lailani did look like she could be their son. Even the diminutive Pinky was tall in comparison.

"Hey, Pinky," Lailani said. "Do they call you Pinky because of your height, or because that's the size of your dick?"

"De la Rosa!" the sergeant said. "Enough. Into your sand tigers. Move it!"

Face red, Pinky flipped them off, then turned to join his friends. They stepped into one of the armored vehicles. The other fireteams were doing the same. Marco, Addy, and Lailani walked toward a sand tiger and pulled open the back door. It creaked downward with a shower of rust, forming a ramp. Ben-Ari had claimed that a vehicle could hold a dozen troops, but even for just the three of them, it was a tight squeeze.

"These things are a lot bigger on the outside," Addy muttered.

"Sort of the opposite of a TARDIS," Marco said.

"What did you call me?" Addy frowned at him.

"I said TARDIS. You know, from the show?" Marco sighed. "Never mind.

"These walls are *thick*," Lailani said, looking around. "It's a mobile castle. Half this beast is just the armor."

Equipment filled the chamber, taking up a lot of the space. Two litters hung from the walls. Metal boxes were piled up, labeled *Medical Supplies, Ammunition,* and *Battle Rations.* A bench stretched between them. There were countless dials, buttons, cables, monitors, and pipes everywhere, and no fewer than three fire extinguishers. A narrow opening led to the driver's seat at the front, and a ladder rose toward a hatch in the ceiling.

"I call gunner," Marco said.

"Me too!" said Lailani.

"Me too!" said Addy, then cursed. "Fine. Fuck it. I'll drive. I'm a better driver than Marco anyway." She climbed over the boxes and under hanging cables, making her way toward the driver's seat. She pulled on a lever, and the engine coughed, sputtered, then growled before easing into a purr. Sixty tons of reinforced steel vibrated.

Marco climbed the ladder, and Lailani followed. They pushed open the hatch and reemerged into the sunlight. They found themselves standing in a gunner's turret. It offered only minimal protection—a ring of iron plates that rose to Marco's chest and Lailani's chin, leaving the rest of them exposed. From the ground, the machine gun mounted here had seemed small. But standing here in the turret, Marco realized how large the gun was. The barrel was longer than Marco was tall. No, this wasn't a tank, but it came damn close.

There were two places to stand in the turret. One gunner could hold the gun and pull the trigger. The other could turn a wheel, spinning the turret from side to side. Lailani took wheel duty. It was the right height for her, and she'd have to stand on her tiptoes to reach the machine gun's trigger. When Marco placed his finger on that trigger, a shudder ran through him. Firing his T57 was one thing, but this gun seemed powerful enough to knock down buildings.

Ahead of him, he saw Ensign Ben-Ari emerge into the turret of another sand tiger.

"We head out!" Ben-Ari said. "Drivers, follow me. Keep your speed slow and steady until we leave the camp—ten kilometers per hour, no faster. Once we're in the sand, we'll see some speed."

Ben-Ari's sand tiger began to move first, rumbling across the lot on its caterpillar tracks. The machine was so heavy that even in first gear it sprayed sand and pebbles like a car spraying water from puddles. One by one, the other sand tigers followed, moving in single file out of the lot and across the base.

Fort Djemila was several kilometers long, most it just empty space. The line of armored vehicles rumbled along, spraying sand and belching out smoke. Marco watched the base roll by: rows and rows of tents, drilling platoons, the concrete mess hall, the trailers where the commanders lived, the bulky armory, the firing range, the infirmary and the chapel, and mostly just sand and stone and heat. From here in the gunners' turret, the base seemed somehow smaller. The soldiers jogging, doing their jumping jacks, or marching seemed like mere toys. When Marco had first come here, he had been so terrified, so disoriented, that Fort Djemila had spun around him, had seemed like a swirling nightmare he couldn't escape. Now it had form, had internal logic to the madness.

This must be how the commanders see the fort, Marco thought. *Not as a frightening, dizzying dream, full of pain and danger, but just a stage. Just a stretch of desert. Just an illusion.*

As he watched a few new recruits marching into the base—"fresh meat," he could imagine Elvis muttering—Marco knew what they were experiencing. They saw only the blinding sun and burning sand. They heard the roaring engines, the shouting sergeants, the gunfire from the range. They didn't perceive the base as Marco could, with weeks of experience under his belt. All they had was the world in their heads, filtered through the pain and sunlight and sound. It seemed to Marco as he rode here that reality was fluid, that so much existed simply in the mind, open to many interpretations.

His thoughts were cut short as the sand tigers reached the barbed wire fence enclosing the base. The guards opened the gates, and the armored vehicles rolled out into the open desert. They rumbled past the small spaceport—the new recruits' rocket was still smoking here—and over a hill. The dunes rolled endlessly before them.

And they began to charge.

Sixteen sand tigers roared, racing over the dunes. Sand rose in great clouds around them. As they rose and fell over the dunes, the gun turret rocked, and Marco had to cling onto the railing with one hand. Lailani swayed at his side, grinning, clutching the gun's wheel with both hands. Inside the vehicle, Addy was whooping as she pressed down on the gas.

"Hold on tight!" Addy cried. "We're going all the way up to sixty!"

Sixty kilometers per hour wasn't very fast on a highway, definitely not very fast for a jet. But in a rusty, clanking, massive machine of metal and chains rumbling over dunes, it seemed as fast as a rocket leaving the atmosphere. The engines bellowed. The sand flew. Marco was nearly tossed from the turret as they crested a massive dune. For a moment the front of the vehicle hovered in the air before slamming down with a shower of sand.

"Hey, Poet!" Pinky shouted from the turret of a nearby vehicle. "Race you, asshole!"

"Faster, Addy!" Lailani shouted.

They seemed to go even faster. The caterpillar chains blurred. Sand gushed out in storms. Marco felt as if he were riding one of the sandworms from *Dune*. They raced for half an hour across the desert until they crested a hill, and Ensign Ben-Ari shouted into a megaphone, calling for them to halt. They arranged themselves along the hill in a row. Below in the rocky valley rose a hundred or more scum—just exoskeletons, still and propped onto metal rods.

"Gunners!" Ben-Ari spoke into her megaphone. "Aim!"

Lailani spun the metal winch, and the gun turret creaked as it turned, facing the scum exoskeletons. Atop the other sand tigers, the turrets creaked too, moving into position. Both Marco and Lailani pulled on their earmuffs.

"Fire!" Ben-Ari said.

Gripping the machine gun with both hands, Marco fired.

Even with his earmuffs, the sound was deafening. Blazing-hot .50-cal cartridges flew into the air. The bullets—each like a dagger—flew through the massive barrel, twenty firing per second, raging with fury. Marco clung to the gun, jaw clenched, body rattling. He had never even fired his T57 in automatic mode, let alone a machine gun with a barrel longer than his body. He shouted wordlessly, clinging on, as the ammunition belt raced through the machine.

The scum exoskeletons shattered. Claws, abdomen segments, and mandibles flew through the desert. As the guns kept firing, the recruits cheered.

"Die, assholes!" Lailani shouted at Marco's side, wheeling the turret toward a second target.

"Hell yeah, fuckers!" Pinky was shouting, firing his machine gun.

Marco remained silent, firing until the ammunition belt was done. The gun clicked to a halt, smoking. Hot shells sizzled around his boots.

"Who needs tanks, right?" Lailani said. "Give me machine guns over cannons—any day."

As the recruits were cheering and pointing at the shattered scum exoskeletons, Marco remained silent. He had seen live scum before. Live scum didn't stand upright and still, waiting for bullets to riddle them. They moved faster than the sand tigers. They leaped through the air. Their claws could pierce through armor— maybe even the armor of these vehicles. If Marco ever met them in battle, he doubted Lailani could turn the turret fast enough, doubted he could hit them as they swarmed from all sides. But he said nothing.

After basic, just give me that nice, cushy office job, he thought, *so I never have to fire these guns in actual battle. Maybe I'll get to share an office with Noodles and spend the war dissecting* The Silmarillion.

They turned and rolled back toward the base, and Lailani kept talking about how many scum she'd kill in the war, and Marco listened and nodded silently.

That night, as the squad slept in their tent, Marco couldn't fall asleep even after his guard duty. He looked at Addy sleeping at one side, Lailani at the other, and his friends deeper in the tent. He imagined them in battle, scum tearing through the camp, ripping open the sand tigers, dodging their bullets, their claws sinking into flesh. When he finally slept, he dreamed of that day long ago in Toronto, but it wasn't his mother dead in the snow. It was Addy, Lailani, Elvis, and the rest of his friends as the scum fed upon them, and even as Marco fired his gun, they closed in around him, as plentiful as grains of sand in the desert.

CHAPTER NINETEEN

They were five weeks into basic training, halfway through, when Ensign Ben-Ari gathered the Dragons Platoon and told them, "Today we are leaving our base. Follow me. Leave your duffel bags."

Marco stood with the fifty soldiers of his platoon in the rocky fields of Fort Djemila. His heart burst into a gallop. The scum! The scum were surely attacking! Just last afternoon the sirens had blared for three hours, and they had crouched between their cots with their guns, waiting for a battle that had not come—that, perhaps, was now here.

"Are we going to fight already, ma'am?" Elvis said.

"We're not ready, ma'am!" said Elvis. "We're only halfway through training."

"I'm ready." Addy hefted her gun. "Time to kick scum asses."

"For the millionth time, Addy," Marco said, "they don't—"

"Shut the hell up, soldiers!" Sergeant Singh shouted, drawing his baton. The tip crackled. "*You* do have asses, and next soldier to speak gets this rammed up theirs. And no, you're not going to fight today. You're still good for nothing but scum food—which would be a good use for you, if you ask me." The sergeant pointed at Addy and Marco. "You two just earned extra guard duty tomorrow night."

Ensign Ben-Ari waited until the soldiers were all silent, then spoke again.

"Earlier this week, HDF special forces launched a brazen attack on a scum laboratory deep in the Scorpius system, destroying a particularly nasty virus the enemy has been developing for biological warfare. We haven't struck this deep into their territory since the Cataclysm. We don't like to escalate the conflict, but this was an action that had to be taken. We're expecting the scum to retaliate—on Earth."

The ensign paused, giving the soldiers time to digest the news. Marco felt a chill even in the heat of the desert. He knew that the scum dared not gas entire Earth cities again like they had fifty years ago, not since humanity had developed the technology to leap through space and nuke their world. But since the Cataclysm, the War of Attrition had ebbed and flowed, some days quiet, others devastating. Would the war now escalate, perhaps even into another Cataclysm?

"Ensign," he said, "if we're not about to fight, what will we do?"

Ben-Ari looked at him. "The scum have already increased their sorties against our cities, landing ten times the usual number of pods. But we predict a larger retaliation sometime within the next few weeks. We believe the scum are planning the operation now. In preparation, cities across the world are conducting

261

disaster relief exercises. Drills. Today you'll become actors. We head out to Greece this morning, where HDF medical forces will seek casualties within yards, streets, and ruins." She pointed at the recruits. "You will be the casualties. Some of you will be missing your legs. Others will be infected with scum venom. Others will be burnt. Sergeant Singh will hand out cards with your acting roles on the way there."

"Now march!" Singh shouted. "Linden, call out time!"

"Left, right, left, right!" Addy cried, and the recruits marched, heading out the gates of Fort Djemila for the first time in five weeks.

Five weeks? *Impossible,* Marco thought. It had been five years. Five generations. Five epochs. He felt like a man who had languished all his life in a dungeon, finally emerging into the light.

"There's actually a world still outside," he whispered to Elvis.

His friend marched behind him, looking around at the dunes. "I just see sand and a dick-shaped airplane."

Caveman grinned at them and clasped his hands together. "We're going to Greece! Flowers!"

A heavy HDF plane waited on a slab of concrete. A company of recruits soon exited the camp, two hundred soldiers in all, and they entered the aircraft. Several rows of benches filled the interior, and Marco took a seat between Addy and Elvis. He was careful not to sit too close to Lailani; gossip had been spreading through the platoon, which Marco didn't want to fuel.

But he sat close enough to meet her eyes, to nod at her. She made a goofy face at him, eyes crossed and cheeks puffed out.

As they flew over the desert, Sergeant Singh moved down the fuselage, pushing a bin full of civilian clothes.

"All right, soldiers!" the sergeant said. "For this exercise, you'll be emulating civilians, and I want you to look the part. Remove your uniforms and choose civilian clothes from this cart. You'll be leaving your uniforms, your helmets, and yes—your guns—here on the plane."

"And if the scum attack for real while we're there, Commander?" Addy said.

"Then they'll enjoy a delightful snack. Now off with your uniforms!"

There wasn't much time to rummage through the bin. The sergeant gave them each only a few seconds to grab whatever they could. Marco managed to pull out white sneakers, a pink button-down shirt, and green pants—not just olive drab like a military uniform but actual leprechaun green. He wanted to find a different outfit, but Singh rolled the bin away.

With a sigh, Marco pulled off his fatigues, remaining in his boxer shorts and undershirt. The green pants were too short, revealing half his shins, and loose around the waist. He reused his uniform's belt, hoping the sergeant would approve this single usage of military equipment. The shoes were too large, and the pink shirt was tiny. Marco was barely able to squeeze his arms through the sleeves, and there was no way he was buttoning the thing.

When Addy looked at him, she burst into laughter. "You look like an old lady whose clothes shrunk in the dryer!"

Marco grumbled. "Well, you look like a soccer hooligan."

Addy had managed to grab a soccer jersey, jean shorts that fit well enough, and flip-flops. She grinned and spun around, showing him the word "Alvarez" printed across the back of her jersey. "But I *am* a soccer hooligan! Alvarez—best player in the world!"

Elvis groaned, stepping toward them in a leather jacket and tight leather pants. "I told you, Maple, the best player is Santos."

Addy and Marco's eyes widened.

"Holy mother of God," Marco whispered.

Addy blinked and pointed at Elvis's outfit. "Leather daddy!"

"Hey!" Elvis bristled. "It's *Elvis*. The real Elvis. His Comeback Special, 1968." He gave a karate chop. "Thank you, thank you very much."

"I thought Elvis wore white jumpsuits with rhinestones," Marco said, thinking back to the classical music Kemi would play for him. "You look more like Rob Halford."

"Elvis wore leather too." Elvis grumbled and walked away down the fuselage.

Jackass pirouetted toward them in a frilly pink dress. Her unibrow was raised in delight, and her buckteeth thrust out. "Aren't I a pretty princess?" She danced through the fuselage, merely giggling as recruits tossed clothes at her.

"Great, it's an ogre in a dress," Addy muttered.

"She's not an ogre," said Marco. "Just a bit odd. She's a nice person."

Addy shuddered. "She eats dry paint she peels off the walls, Marco. She eats paint to get sick and spend days in the infirmary. She's a weirdo."

Marco shrugged. "I like weirdos." He thought about how the recruits mocked Corporal St-Pierre, how he had later seen her crying, confessing her fear to Ensign Ben-Ari. "Maybe there's more to Jackass than others see."

"Oh god, there's more?" Addy cringed. In the back of the plane, Jackass was now braying like a donkey and letting another recruit ride her. "Thank you, I've seen enough."

Soon all the recruits were dressed in an assortment of secondhand, discount-bin clothes. Marco had never seen a more ridiculous group of people. Nobody's clothes fit right, and no outfit seemed newer than two generations. Caveman wore a flowery Hawaiian shirt and kept stroking the fabric. Beast looked miserable, wearing a yellow suit that was several sizes too small. Pinky wore a bandanna and a jeans vest, and he was busy sawing through his sweatpants with his knife, shortening the legs.

"Holy shit," Addy whispered. "Would you look at that. It's true. She's actually a girl."

Marco turned around, and his jaw unhinged.

Wow, he thought. *Just . . . wow.*

At first he didn't recognize her, was sure it was a different recruit. But it *was* her. It was Lailani. She walked toward them in a blue dress that actually fit, white slippers, and a wide hat that hid her buzz cut.

Elvis approached, whistling. "Wow, de la Rosa is hot. Who knew?"

Lailani grumbled and kicked him hard, knocking him back. "Shut up, Leatherface." She came to stand before Marco, grumbling. "I look fucking ridiculous."

"You look like Audrey Hepburn," Marco said.

She raised her fists. "Don't insult me. Who the fuck is that? Some princess?"

Marco smiled thinly. "Think of it this way, Lailani. It's a disguise. Your enemies won't expect a petite, beautiful woman in a summer dress to slaughter them."

Lailani groaned. "I don't want to be a petite, beautiful woman. Fuck this shit. Yo, Elvis! I'll switch clothes with you."

His head appeared over a seat. "What? I look glorious! Get lost, de la Rosa." His head vanished behind the seat, then popped up again. "Seriously, you look like a princess."

Lailani groaned and tossed one of her slippers at him. "Fucking ridiculous," she muttered, stomping off. "I look like a goddamn doll. I didn't join the goddamn army for this shit . . ."

Marco watched her leave. Addy grinned and elbowed his ribs. "Poet's in love!" She waggled her eyebrows at him.

He pushed her elbow away. "Shush, hooligan."

There were no windows on the plane, but Marco guessed that they were flying over the Mediterranean by now, heading toward the Greek isles. Marco had read many books about Old

Europe, a place of civilization, art, culture, architecture, a rich history of both beauty and bloodshed. Half that continent had been destroyed in the Cataclysm, and many of the old landmarks from the books—the Eiffel Tower, the Big Ben, the Leaning Tower of Pisa, the Dio Statue of Rome—were gone. But still Marco vowed to soak up whatever he could of this continent, even if they spent only a day here, even if he saw nothing but a few old buildings. It was better than looking at barbed wire and sand.

Sergeant Singh returned with a bag, handing out laminated cards that dangled from lanyards.

"These are your acting roles," said the sergeant, giving a card to each recruit. "You're already experts at acting like scum killers, so you might as well act like scum victims now. Once we land, we'll distribute you across the city. Wear these cards around your necks. Rescue forces will be along to save your miserable asses."

Marco accepted one of the cards and read it. "I have two broken legs."

Addy whooped, raising her card overhead. "Nice! Choking on scum miasma." She began to cough theatrically.

"Crushed by a collapsed building," said Elvis, slipping his lanyard around his neck. The card dangled.

"What?" Lailani exclaimed, staring at her card. "Impaled by a scum claw? No way I'd let those buggers get close enough."

Across the plane, they began to act out their roles. Recruits moaned, rolled on the ground, yowled in pain, coughed, choked, and begged for help. Caveman delivered a powerful performance of a burnt man, earning applause. Marco even caught Singh smiling, but the sergeant soon scowled again, and Marco realized that Singh too was an actor, had always been acting.

"All right, enough!" Singh said. "You've all won your Oscars. Wait until we land before you act up again. We're descending now. And remember, you might look like a bunch of idiots, but you are still soldiers of the HDF. You will conduct yourselves with dignity among the locals. You represent me now, represent your officer, and represent the entire Human Defense Force. So act like it. Even if you're dressed like a bunch of morons."

They landed on the runway and emerged from the plane, leaving their uniforms, helmets, and weapons behind, taking only their dog tags. They found themselves in an HDF airport, and buses pulled up to the runway. Each platoon filed into one bus, and they left the base, heading—for the first time in six weeks—into the civilian world.

They drove down a road between palm trees and a beach. Hills rose to one side, lush with pines, fig trees, and cypresses, and many white and blue houses grew among the greenery. Soon the buses were heading through the city itself, and on the sidewalks, they saw people—real people, civilians with real lives, shopping, chatting, laughing, eating. Inside the bus, the recruits of the Dragons Platoon pressed themselves against the windows, staring at the city rolling by. After two months in hell, it seemed impossible that this world could be real, that it wasn't just another propaganda reel.

Addy leaned across Marco, pressing herself against the windowpane. "It's real. It's beautiful. People. Food. Life."

"Get off!" Marco tried to shove her back into her seat. "Your knee is digging into my groin."

She ignored him, leaning over his lap, her elbow now pressing against his ribs as she stared outside. "I see a cafe, Marco. A cafe that serves real food, not just Spam."

"I thought you liked Spam." He struggled to pull her off him. She was all poking elbows and knees. "God, you weigh more than a scum queen."

Addy finally sat back down in her seat, eyes shining. She clasped his hand and squeezed it, and as she gazed at him, her smile faded.

"Marco, do you remember how at school we learned about . . . what was it called? The great tragedy before the Cataclysm. The one with the Nazis."

"The Holocaust?" he said. "From two hundred years ago."

Addy nodded. "Yes, that one. One story stuck with me. It was about a class of children from a ghetto. The ghetto was inside a normal city, but concrete walls surrounded it, and nobody could leave. It was like a prison inside the city. For years the children lived in that ghetto, starved, beaten, tortured. Finally they were loaded into trains, taken out of the ghetto, a journey toward death camps outside the city. As the trains pulled out of the ghetto, the children looked outside the carts, and they saw the actual city around the ghetto. They saw real life, people who weren't starved, beaten skeletons, people who had normal lives. The children realized that not all the world was hell, not everyone had been reduced to an animal state. Just them. And yet that world was beyond their reach. They could see it, but they could never live it. And the train rolled on. That's like us. We can see real life, but it doesn't belong to us."

"Grim story," said Marco. "And not at all like our story. Those children were taken to death camps. They were gassed to death."

"And we're being trained to become scum fodder," said Addy.

"No. We have guns. Helmets. Grenades. Brave commanders. We're being trained to kill scum." Yet his words sounded unconvincing to his ears. Perhaps Addy was right. Perhaps those people outside the windows—enjoying the day, walking with friends, eating, laughing—perhaps that was something he and Addy could no longer become, would never have again. Perhaps they were like those children, having a mere glimpse of another, older world before the poison and fire.

They drove up piney hills, moving higher. Between the trees and homes they could see the Mediterranean. White and azure buildings rose around them, some with arched windows, some with domes. The buses rattled along a cobbled street, then finally entered a war zone.

It wasn't a true war zone. Marco saw no scum, heard no bullets or bombs. But it looked the part. An entire neighborhood had been converted into a massive ruin. Ambulances flashed their lights. Medics were setting up tents. Buildings lay fallen, and bricks, uprooted trees, even bent bicycles littered the streets. Water gushed out from a smashed fire hydrant, and smoke unfurled from burning tires. The buses traveled through the ruins, and everywhere swarmed the rescue services of the HDF, wearing hazmat suits. Marco had grown up in war. He had seen scum attacks and their aftermath. But those had always been localized to a couple of blocks. Here was street after street of mock ruin.

"It looks like the Cataclysm," Addy muttered.

"Minus all the corpses," said Marco.

Addy grinned. "That's us."

They spilled out of the buses, three hundred of the oddest characters the town had ever seen. With saggy pants and tight shorts, with clattering flip-flops and shoes that clowns would think excessive, with frilly dresses and Hawaiian shirts louder than artillery, they walked through the town. Marco kept tugging up his sagging green pants, and his pink buttoned shirt was so small it was cutting off circulation to his arms. His shoes kept falling off his feet. His card hung around his neck on the lanyard, denoting him a man with broken legs—which could very well become reality if he kept tripping over his shoes.

"Spread out!" shouted Singh. The sergeant still wore his uniform, complete with a military turban, and carried his T57. "We begin in ten minutes. Find a place and stick to it."

Marco walked down the cobbled street, past parked ambulances, around a medical tent, and along a row of willows and pines. Even as radios hummed, hundreds of people bustled back and forth, and helicopters hovered above, Marco inhaled deeply, reached out, and let his fingers run between the willow leaves. He knelt and lifted a pinecone.

There's a world here. There is Earth. There is still beauty.

Lailani knelt before him, and Marco gazed at her dark face, her almond-shaped eyes, her somber mouth. She held out her hand, and on her palm stood a tiny turtle.

"Loggerhead," she said. "Thought you'd like it."

Marco smiled.

Yes, there is still beauty in the world.

They gently placed the turtle among the pines, then walked until they saw a pile of bricks and tires between three crumbling walls. It seemed like a good place for the scum to shatter a man's legs and impale a woman's chest. Marco and Lailani lay down on the rubble, and soon Addy and Beast joined them. Across the ruins, other recruits found their own places. Some lay on the street, a few recruits climbed onto a roof, and Elvis climbed onto a tree and slung himself across a branch.

And they began to act.

"My skull is cracked like melon!" cried Beast. "Feels like Russian tank drove on it! Not puny American tank, they can't break walnut!"

Addy was coughing and rolling around. "Help, I'm poisoned! Scum miasma! Evil scum butt gas all up in my lungs!" She coughed and made gagging sounds. "Almost as bad as Marco after eating cheese!"

"Help, a scum claw skewered me!" Lailani cried. "Though I don't know how, because there's no way they could have come close enough! Because I'd kill them in half a second!"

Marco, for his part, did not join the orchestra of voices. He lay on the rubble, trying to convey broken legs as best as possible, which just involved bending them and giving the odd grimace.

After a few moments of this, Addy said, "Well, where are the medics?"

Marco shrugged. "It's meant to be a realistic drill. The scum just devastated Greece. It'll take the medics a while to organize."

"But nobody's appreciating my performance!" said Addy.

"It's lovely," said Marco. "Encore, encore."

"Don't you talk fancy French to me," said Addy. "I'm not Corporal Pizza."

Marco had taken his copy of *Hard Times* with him. Before the military, he would read a lot. He had read exactly five pages in the past five weeks of basic training. When he opened the paperback, Kemi's photo fell out. He looked at her for a moment. For two years Kemi had been his girlfriend—the girl he loved, wanted to marry. The girl who was now at Julius Military Academy, training to become an officer, to have a military career. Marco looked over the photo at Lailani, who lay on the rubble nearby, moaning about the scum claw, which had inexplicably pierced her despite her fierceness.

"It's only because I dived in front of it to save Marco's life!" Lailani was calling out. "Otherwise I'd never get stabbed!"

Lailani was an odd one, a broken bird Marco wanted to heal, whom he loved, a woman who shouted about killing scum and dying in battle, yet one who was soft, loving, kind.

You brought me a turtle, he thought. *That means more than you know.*

He stuck Kemi's photo between the back pages of the book, then returned the book to his pocket.

Air blasted the ruins as three medical helicopters hovered down toward them. They landed by the rubble, red lights flashing. Medics leaped out, wearing gas masks and carrying stretchers. They wore white HDF uniforms, and patches on their arms displayed serpents coiling around staffs.

"Triage and take the most serious cases you can save," rose a voice from inside a jet. "Leave the mortally wounded. We have no room for them."

Marco lost his breath.

"You can save me!" Addy said, coughing. "My goddamn lungs are full of—ow!" She yowled as a medic stabbed her with a needle. "Hey, what the fuck, man, this is pretend!"

"I'm done for!" cried Lailani. "Gored! Skewered! Leave me. Save the others!"

Marco frowned and pushed himself onto his elbows. He recognized the voice that had come from the chopper . . .

"Get them on litters." A woman emerged from the helicopter, wearing a white uniform, a blue beret, and a gas mask.

"Not that one. She's a goner. Take the poisoned woman, and that one, his legs are—"

She stopped talking.

Marco's heart pounded in his chest.

"Kemi," he whispered.

She stared at him across the ruins. She pulled off her gas mask, revealing wide eyes and a gaping mouth.

"Cadet Gray?" asked a medic, standing by Marco with a litter.

Kemi stared at Marco, gasping, then collected herself. "Take him, Doc. Load him into my chopper. Go, move! Another scum attack is imminent."

The medics lifted Marco onto the litter. He wanted to leap off, to run toward Kemi, but they strapped him in place and carried him into one of the medical helicopters. Kemi entered after them. Other medics carried Addy and Beast into the two other choppers, leaving the mortally wounded—including Lailani—behind.

With roaring engines, the helicopters rose.

As they flew over the city, Marco managed to rip off the straps binding him to the litter, ignoring the medics' protests. He stepped toward Kemi, and she stared at him, frozen, face hard, a cadet in training dedicated to her task. Then her eyes dampened, and she laughed, and she pulled him into an embrace.

"Marco," she whispered and kissed his cheek, then his forehead, then his lips. "Oh, Marco, it's really you. I can't believe it. I can't believe it!" A tear flowed down her cheek. "It's a miracle. It's a miracle from heaven, it has to be."

"How—" he began. "What—" He laughed, holding her hands. "I don't know what to say."

Kemi grinned—that huge grin he loved so much. "I've only been in military academy for three weeks, but it feels like an eternity. This is our first time outside of the academy, our first taste of command. I'm a cadet now, Marco. And look at you!" She tugged at his tiny pink shirt and baggy green pants. "Is this your uniform?"

"Well, they don't give us peasants fancy uniforms." He looked at Kemi's uniform—sensible white trousers, a blazer with brass buttons and cuff links, and a beret with a golden pin. A plasma pistol, sleek and silvery, hung from her belt. She still wore the pi pendant he had given her. "You look beautiful, Kemi. I missed you. You—"

He bit down on his words. What was he doing? Had he forgotten that Kemi had broken up with him, had chosen a life in the military? Had he forgotten Lailani—the woman who "ruved" him, who had slept with him, had gifted him a turtle only moments ago—a simple gift yet one that meant so much to him? Yet standing here with Kemi, as the helicopter hovered over the city, was so surreal it spun his head.

I'm a soldier, he thought, *wearing a tiny pink shirt, with my ex-girlfriend as a cadet saving me from a fake disaster zone.*

This was not how he had imagined the HDF.

The helicopter descended and landed by the medical tents Marco had seen from the bus.

"Soldier, return to your litter," said one of the medics. "Our exercise isn't over."

"Wait," Kemi said. "One more moment. Please." She turned toward Marco, bit her lip, then hugged him again. "Hey, I'll be in these ruins all day. I'll see you again here. All right?"

He nodded. "Yeah." And he refused to acknowledge the terror that this—here in this helicopter, with the medics tapping their feet—could be goodbye forever.

Kemi kissed his lips. "I love you, Marco Emery. I'm sorry for how we parted last time. I love you."

"I love you too," he whispered, and he was speaking the truth. He lay back on his litter.

Tears in her eyes, Kemi watched the medics carry him outside. As the helicopter rose again, she stood at the open door, watching him until she vanished behind a hill.

CHAPTER TWENTY

One by one, medics carried more recruits into the medical pavilions, where nurses and doctors bustled around them. Marco found himself with splints on his legs, and eventually Addy was carried in, an oxygen mask on her face.

"They stuck me with a needle, Poet!" she said, ripping the mask off. "A real needle. They're experimenting on me!"

"Maybe you have superpowers now," Marco said.

She punched him. "Yeah, super strength, so watch it."

The medics carried in the other recruits, some still acting their parts, others sleeping on their litters. Many were bandaged. The medics moved among them, consulting with doctors, discussing each case. Outside the pavilion, Marco could see guards with guns and armored jeeps. Helicopters kept buzzing overhead and lights flashed.

Two more medics entered the tent, carrying a body bag on a litter. The zipper was opened just enough to reveal Lailani's face. She stuck her tongue out at Marco and crossed her eyes.

"Dead!" she said. "I told you I wouldn't make it." She winked and flashed him a grin.

But Marco couldn't smile back. Not after knowing about Lailani's earlier suicide attempt and death wish. Not after falling in love with her. Not after meeting Kemi here, feeling so confused.

They waited in the medical pavilion for an hour, maybe two, when nature began to call in earnest. To all of them.

"I gotta pee so bad it's coming out of my nose," Caveman said, wiping snot on his sleeve.

Addy nodded. "Same here." She hopped off her litter. "Let's find a place."

Marco looked around him. He couldn't see any of their platoon's commanders. No corporals, no sergeant, no Ben-Ari, only a few medics smoking in a back chamber. He nodded. He himself was feeling the pressure.

"Let's go," Marco said. "Let's find some food too. I'm famished."

Addy raised an eyebrow. "Famished? What the fuck is that, British?"

"It means he's hungry," Lailani said. "He's an author. That's how authors speak. He's writing a book about a turtle. He told me all about it."

Addy's eyes widened, and she spun toward Marco with a grin. "You told her about *Jarhead*!"

"*Loggerhead*, Addy. *Loggerhead*. Come on."

They exited the pavilion and searched for a porta-potty but found none. They walked along the cobbled street, navigating between soldiers, other recruits in secondhand civilian clothes, and local Greeks who had exited their homes to gape at the affair.

Those homes rose along the road, built of white stone, some topped with domes. The recruits spotted a low brick wall around a garden. Two oaks and a pine grew from the yard, shading a house.

"Let's go water those trees," said Elvis.

"That's somebody's yard," said Marco.

Addy was already climbing over the low wall. "Well, I hope they're not doing any gardening today."

As his friends climbed over the wall into the yard, Marco sighed and followed them. Lailani and Addy went behind the bushes, while the boys stood by the trees. Only a few weeks ago, Marco would never have been able to pee in public. Five weeks in the army had taken his shame, and he watered the tree with the rest of them.

As he was zipping up, Marco noticed the old woman sitting on the porch.

She was staring at the recruits, eyes wide, clutching a bible to her chest.

"Sorry, granny!" Addy cried, emerging from behind the bushes. "Bunch of soccer hooligans, these ones are."

"Go Santos!" said Elvis.

Addy punched him. "Alvarez!"

The grandmother rubbed her eyes and stepped into her home. The recruits were about to leave when the old woman returned, carrying a pot full of peppers stuffed with rice, beef, and diced tomatoes. Soon the recruits were sitting in the grass, feasting on the best damn meal they had eaten in six weeks—the best meal, Marco thought, he had eaten in his life.

"It's a damn whorehouse here," Elvis said, reaching for another pepper.

Beast nodded. "Whorehouse." The unfortunate slang had been spreading through the platoon.

Addy puffed on a cigarette. "We just need beer."

Lailani, despite her size, scarfed down four stuffed peppers. She leaned against Marco, patting her belly, her lips stained with tomato juice.

"This is the best day of my life," she said.

Marco slung his arm around her, remembered kissing Kemi, and hated the guilt inside him.

Soon Lailani was asleep, leaning against him, and they still hadn't seen any commanders. As Marco sat in the yard, he noticed Jackass sitting under a tree—thankfully not one of the trees the recruits had dampened. For once, the girl was silent and still, not braying, dancing, or shouting hoarsely about how dainty and adorable she was.

Gently, Marco laid the sleeping Lailani down on the grass. She mumbled and stirred but didn't wake. Marco walked across the yard and approached Jackass.

"Hey, Hope, what's up?" he said.

"Jackass," she said. "That's what everyone calls me. Only my mom calls me Hope." She raised a book—a copy of *The Sun Also Rises*. "Just reading."

Marco's eyes widened. "You like Hemingway?"

Jackass nodded. "I do. It's a good book. I've been reading Hemingway this summer. Have you read him?"

And now more guilt filled Marco. With Jackass's appearance—the beaked nose, the unibrow, the crooked teeth—and with her hoarse voice, braying laughter, and long stints in the brig, he had assumed her uncultured, perhaps illiterate. He nodded and sat down beside her. "I've read *The Old Man and the Sea.*"

"You'll like his other books too," Jackass said. "They're good."

Marco pulled his copy of *Hard Times* from his pocket. "I've been reading Dickens. Well, trying to read it. I've only read a few pages so far. Not much more time in the army."

"I love Dickens," said Jackass. "*Great Expectations, A Tale of Two Cities, Oliver Twist* . . . But my favorite is *David Copperfield.*"

"Mine too," said Marco. "I read that one last year."

"The way he just chronicles life," Jackass said. "The way he captures the society, those characters, immortalizing them on the page . . . that really inspired my own writing. Well, I'm not nearly as good, of course. My novels are shit compared to his." She shrugged. "But I like writing. I like reading. Passes the time, you know?"

Marco nodded. He knew. "Do the other recruits know that you're so well read, that you've written books?"

Jackass snorted. "Nah. They just think of me as the cute, adorable princess that I am. They don't know about my books or about the poems I sold to magazines. Besides, who cares? I won't know any of you for long. They always end up sending me to some military prison, then transferring me to another base." She shrugged. "Another reason I like books. They don't change on you."

They sat for a long time, talking about reading and writing. Marco had grown up in a library, was a self-professed bookworm, yet Jackass was better read, had written more words, had published poems, and Marco thought again about how St-Pierre had confessed her weakness to her officer, how Addy had slunk into his bed at night, shivering and afraid, how Beast missed his boyfriend and wept at night, how Sergeant Singh sometimes stifled a smile between shouts, how they all wore masks in this war. How they all hid behind armor.

"Why do you let them call you Jackass?" Marco finally asked, able to resist no longer. "You're intelligent, cultured, and—"

"And ugly," said Jackass. "I look like an ogre. I know what I look like, what I sound like. I hear what the others whisper." She shrugged. "So I embrace it. I play the jackass for them. I could cry all day, but I'd only be miserable. If I take it from them, if I claim that name, that character, then I have strength. Then I can't be hurt. It's what Lailani does too." Jackass nodded. "She's scared, Marco. She's so afraid. She's so sad. So she pretends to be so strong." She patted his knee. "You're a good boy, Marco. Look after Lailani. Look after all your friends."

Finally it was Corporal Webb who came walking down the street, moving gracefully on her metal prosthetics, and spotted them in the yard.

"Soldiers!" she barked. "Follow me. Regroup with our platoon. We've got new cards for you. We're doing another drill."

Throughout the day, Marco kept looking for Kemi, but there were thousands of people here, and he didn't see her again. At sundown, a captain—an officer with three bars on his shoulders—marched their company's four platoons toward a school gymnasium. Sergeants stood here, handing out blankets and wrapped sandwiches. Marco was unsurprised to discover they were Spam sandwiches.

"Seems like we're spending the night," Marco said to Addy.

She looked around at the large gym. "Just the right size for a soccer game. Maybe we'll play tomorrow morning."

Two hundred soldiers lay down on the laminate floor, wrapped in their blankets. After the long day, Marco would have given his left foot for a hot shower, a toothbrush, and even just a thin army mattress, but those were luxuries. He had already spent one night on the cold, stone floor of the brig. Laminate was softer than a water mattress.

Addy slept at his one side, her cheek resting on her palms. Lailani slept at Marco's other side, close enough for him to feel her warmth, not so close as to rouse hoots and hollers from the others. Yet as the lights turned off, plunging the gymnasium into darkness, Lailani's hand reached out in the darkness and held his.

284

This is the best day of my life, Lailani had said. Yet as Marco lay in the darkness, he remembered what Ensign Ben-Ari had said. The war was escalating. The scum were beefing up their attacks, preparing for a massive retaliation. Very soon this drill might become reality. These wounds—Addy choking, Beast crushed, Lailani dead—might soon be real. Marco held Lailani's hand more tightly, never wanting to let go, never wanting the dawn to come.

CHAPTER TWENTY-ONE

"Damn it, Harris!" shouted Sergeant Singh. "Your boots are dusty. Your shirt's not tucked in. Your gun's dry. Get back into your tent, then come back here in your sleepwear. Go!"

"Aye, aye, Captain!" Hope "Jackass" Harris gave a mock salute, then disappeared back into the tent.

The Dragons stood outside their tents in the predawn darkness. At 4:30 a.m., the North African desert was cold, dark, and miserable. But finally their hell at Fort Djemila was nearing an end. After nine weeks of training, they had only a week of hell left.

In one week, Marco thought, standing at attention in the cold, *we'll become privates. In one week we'll be true soldiers of the HDF.*

Marco suppressed a shudder, not wanting to risk Sergeant Singh's wrath. As horrible as basic training had been, there was safety here. There were his commanders to guide him. Out there in the war, he wouldn't be shooting at wooden targets. Marco didn't know where he'd be stationed. He would be sorted after receiving his rank. He could be sent to guard some gate in the middle of a desert, perhaps given a cushy office job analyzing deep space data, or maybe even sent into space itself to defend the colonies and fight on the front lines. He had little say in the matter, but one thing was certain: his enemies would be a little more ruthless than Pinky.

"Captain Blackbeard, sir!" Jackass emerged from the tent, wearing her pajamas again—pink and embroidered with hearts. She held a teddy bear, and she gave a little curtsy. "Do you think I'm sexy, Sergeant?"

Behind his beard, Sergeant Singh's face turned red. "Harris! You've spent six months bouncing from one basic training base to another. Are you determined to spend your five years of service as a recruit? Get back into your tent, and come out here—presentable as a soldier—on my countdown. If you fail inspection this time, you'll spend the next week in the brig, then have to start your basic training from scratch."

"Jackass, just listen to him!" Addy blurted out. "One more week. You can do this."

Jackass danced back into her tent. Sergeant Singh called out the countdown. Finally Jackass emerged from the tent, wearing her uniform. Shoe polish stained her pants, which weren't bloused. Her gun wobbled between her legs like a tail, and her helmet was crooked.

Sergeant Singh sighed. "Do you think you look like a soldier, Harris?"

Jackass shook her head. "No, Sarge. But I think I'll be wonderful as an entertainer for the troops. You know, sort of like Marilyn, my idol." She began to sing. "Happy birthday, Mr. Sergeant, happy—"

"Shut up!" Pinky shouted from the ranks. "For fuck's sake, you fucking retard."

Even Elvis grumbled. "Jackass, just shut up and act like a soldier. You want to spend your life in the brig?"

"Ogre," muttered another recruit.

"Freak," spat another. "Get her out of our platoon."

Jackass only laughed and pirouetted. "It's all right! I love the brig. Nice and quiet, and nobody bugs me, and I can catch up on my beauty sleep."

"That one would need to sleep for a century," Pinky said.

Risking Sergeant Singh's fury, Marco stepped out of formation and approached Jackass. He placed a hand on her arm. "Hope, let me help you, all right? Come on, buddy. One more week. You've got this." He looked into her eyes. "All right?" He dropped his voice to a whisper. "You're not this person. I know the real you. I know the intelligent, sensitive Hope. Not just the Jackass. You don't have to be the Jackass anymore."

Her eyes dampened, and she shook her head. "This is all I can be," she whispered back.

But Sergeant Singh had heard enough, it seemed.

"Emery, back into line!" the sergeant said, then turned toward Jackass. "That's it, Harris. I warned you. Report to the brig, and tell them you're to spend a week there. You won't receive your rank with your comrades next week. When the week is done, you'll report back to RASCOM and be assigned to start basic training again at another fort. Is that understood?"

"Aye aye, Captain Blackbeard!" She gave an exaggerated salute, chest thrust out. "Reporting to the brig!"

Jackass began dancing her way through the darkness, whistling a tune, her gun dangling between her legs.

"Good riddance," Pinky said. "Retard."

Marco sighed. He had hoped that finally, after half a year of bouncing from fort to fort, prison to prison, Jackass would finally complete her basic training with the Dragons Platoon, then maybe be assigned to guard some gateway or bridge and stay out of trouble. He shuddered to imagine having to start boot camp from scratch.

"All right, soldiers," said Sergeant Singh. "Settle down and present your rifles for inspection."

They held out their guns, and Singh moved between them, checking the chambers for oil.

"Good work, Fabian," said the sergeant. "Not oiled enough, Ray, that's your second time. Linden, why—"

A gunshot rang across the camp.

Marco started. He turned in the night. "That came from the brig," he whispered.

Sergeant Singh nodded. "Inspection is over. Linden, lead the morning exercises." He began walking toward the brig. "Stay here, and—Emery? Emery! Halt!"

But Marco ignored his sergeant. He ran through the darkness, his rifle clattering across his back. The gunshot still echoed in his ears. He raced through the sand, down a rocky path, and toward the brig.

A dark lump lay on the ground, a few feet away from the concrete prison. Marco raced forward and knelt.

"Hope," he whispered. "Oh god, Hope."

Hope "Jackass" Harris lay on her back, her rifle across her chest. Her jaw, her face, and half her skull were gone, splattered across the sand. Marco was thankful for the darkness.

"Hope," he said again. "Oh, damn it, Hope, why did you do this?" He lowered his head, shuddering, eyes damp.

He started when he felt a hand on his shoulder.

"You tried to help her, Marco. Come now. Come with me."

Marco looked up to see Sergeant Singh standing above him. Medics were already rushing forward with a litter, but it was too late for Hope. In the distance, Marco could just make out the Dragons Platoon doing their morning jumping jacks.

"Come on, Marco." The sergeant's voice was kind; Marco had never heard him speak kindly before. "Let's give the medics room."

The sergeant led Marco through the base, leaving the tents far behind. They walked through a gateway in an iron fence, entering a gravelly compound. Several trailers stood here. Dawn began to rise in the east, casting pink and yellow light across the desert. They stepped into a trailer. Inside, Marco saw a cot, a desk, two chairs, and a cupboard—a simple box of a home.

"Wait here," Singh said, patted Marco's shoulder, and left the trailer.

Marco waited for a long time, standing in the chamber, pacing, struggling to breathe. His mind was a roaring storm. The walls of the trailer seemed to close in around him. That gunshot kept echoing, and he knew he'd never forget that sound, never forget seeing that lump in the darkness.

It must have been an hour before the door to the trailer opened. Ensign Ben-Ari entered.

Marco stood at attention and saluted her. The young officer returned the salute. Standing close to her, Marco realized how young, how small their platoon's commander really was. He doubted she was much older than twenty.

But wars are fought by the young, Marco thought. *It's always been so.*

"Sit down, Marco," Ben-Ari said.

Marco sat on the bed.

"On the chair," Ben-Ari said, pointing.

Marco stood up quickly. "Sorry, ma'am." He sat on the small plastic chair by the bed.

Ensign Ben-Ari walked across the trailer, gazed out the window at the yard, then turned back toward him. "Marco, I come from a long line of soldiers. My father was a colonel in the HDF. My grandfather was an officer as well. His father before him too. For generations, the Ben-Ari family has fought against our enemies, going all the way back to my ancestor, a partisan who fought the Nazis in the forests of Eastern Europe."

Marco nodded. "Yes, ma'am. The scum destroyed your country. Your nation found a new home in the HDF. I know the stories."

Ben-Ari sat down on the second chair. "I was born to become a soldier, Marco. Born to lead men and women in battle. Maybe even born to die in battle." She sighed. "But the recruits I command . . . they have homes, all but one or two of them. They're teenagers, fresh out of high school, who never wanted to fight a war. You and your friends are not volunteers. You were drafted, and we had to break you here, to turn soft souls into soldiers—souls that were never meant to fight. My job is to train you, to harden you, to turn you into motivated soldiers eager for the fight."

"You've trained us well, ma'am," Marco said, and he meant it. "I'm proud to have you as my commanding officer."

Ben-Ari gave him a hard, blank stare. "Marco, when we return to our platoon, we'll tell them that Hope accidentally discharged a bullet into her leg while tripping. We'll tell them that she's in an infirmary off base. Is that clear?"

Marco gasped. He leaped up, banging his chair against the wall. "But ma'am! How can we lie to them?" He shook his head. "Hope was my friend. And she died. She deserves to be mourned. She—"

"She will be mourned." Ben-Ari stood up too and placed a hand on Marco's shoulder. "You and I will mourn her. Her family will mourn her. But right now I need my platoon to be strong, to be motivated. In only a week, Marco, you will all leave me. You will all become privates. Many of you will move on to receive specialized training. Some will be ready to start fighting. And your friends will all need to believe that this is a just, noble army, not an army where . . ." She looked out the window again. "Where this happened."

Marco clenched his fists at his sides. His breath shook. "I can't just sweep this under the rug. It happened. I saw it happen."

"What you saw, recruit, is classified. If you speak of it, you will be court-martialed, and you will spend the next five years rotting in a military prison." Her voice softened. "I don't want that for you, Marco. You're a good soldier. You would make a good candidate for officer school, if that's a path you choose to pursue. I would recommend you myself. Sometimes good soldiers need to take hard paths like this one."

"To lie," Marco said.

Ben-Ari nodded. "Yes. To lie."

Marco stood still for a long moment, looking at his boots. Finally he raised his head and looked back at Ben-Ari. "Commander, I will remain silent, but I ask for a favor in return. I don't want to lose any more friends. In a week we're all going to be reassigned. If you have any sway at all with our sorting officers, please speak to them. Ask to keep this platoon together. Let me keep serving with Addy, with Elvis, with Caveman, with Beast." His voice dropped. "With Lailani." He thought for a moment, then quickly added, "But maybe not with Pinky."

Ben-Ari seemed to be struggling to remain stern, but a smile finally tugged at her lips. She nodded. "I'll see what I can do. No guarantees."

Marco nodded, remaining somber. "I'll miss Hope. Always."

Ben-Ari's smile faded. "You will lose more friends, Marco. Not all of us return home from our service. But I want you to know this. Look into my eyes." Ben-Ari stared at him, solemn. "I am proud of you."

He nodded, eyes suddenly damp.

"Dismissed," she said—softly, kindly. "Go back to your friends."

He saluted and left the trailer. He returned to his platoon. His last week of training began.

CHAPTER TWENTY-TWO

For their last week of training, they stepped outside the base, but this time no rocket, no airplane, no buses awaited them—only the cruel, vast expanse of the desert.

The entire Dragons Platoon stood here. Ensign Ben-Ari, clad in battle gear, her blond ponytail emerging from under her helmet, her plasma gun in hand. Sergeant Singh, tall and turbaned, his beard as black as his sunglasses, his ceremonial dagger gleaming. The three corporals: the tough and scarred Diaz, the small and deadly Webb on her metal legs, and the hard and cruel St-Pierre. And with these commanders stood the platoon recruits. All wore their fatigues, helmets, and padded armor. All carried their guns, vests laden with magazines, heavy duffel bags stuffed with equipment, and canteens full of water. The sun beat down with a fury.

Ensign Ben-Ari spoke to them. "Seventy-five kilometers from here, an air-conditioned jet awaits you. That's forty-seven miles, for the Americans among us. That is a long way, soldiers. That's nearly the length of two full marathons. You will cross this entire distance, carrying all your equipment, within twenty-four hours. Is that understood?"

A few "Yes, ma'ams!" were sounded, but other recruits grumbled.

"It can't be done," Elvis muttered.

"Nobody can walk that far in a day, ma'am," said another recruit.

"Two marathons in a day?" said another. "Carrying all this? In this heat?"

Addy snorted. "Piece of cake. I can do this in my sleep."

"Silence!" shouted Sergeant Singh, reaching for his baton. "Your officer did not ask your opinion. You *will* complete this journey if I have to shock you the entire way."

Marco was already exhausted—just from standing here in the heat of the desert, his equipment weighing him down. He couldn't imagine traveling two entire marathons across the dunes. He tried to do the math in his head. If they had twenty-four hours, that meant they needed to cross over three kilometers per hour. He could remember walking from the library to Lake Ontario within an hour, a distance of two or three kilometers. Of course, that had been on a paved road, not a searing death-desert, and it wasn't carrying these heavy magazines, this massive gun, a gas mask, a canteen, and a duffel bag the size of a scum queen, but . . . yes. It should be possible. Just barely, agonizingly possible.

"Is that understood?" Ensign Ben-Ari asked again.

"Yes, ma'am!" This time they all understood.

Ben-Ari nodded. "Good. Since you seem so eager, I'm going to make the task a little harder for you. Sergeant?"

Singh nodded, approached a truck parked in the sand, and opened the back door. He and the corporals began pulling out litters. On each litter lay a dummy dressed in a military uniform.

"These dummies represent wounded soldiers," said Ben-Ari. "Your comrades. Each one weighs two hundred pounds. You will carry these litters—four soldiers each—to our destination."

This elicited more groans.

"Ma'am, we're already carrying a ton!" Elvis said.

Marco was inclined to agree. His back already ached from his burden—and that was before lifting a litter.

"In actual battle, you'll have to carry this much," said Ben-Ari. "And you'll have to carry your wounded too. Who will you whine to then? The scum? Will you complain about a wounded comrade's weight as he lies dying, desperate for medical attention? Will you complain about the distance as the scum drive you from their strongholds, as you must seek aid across the wilderness? The scum will be far less merciful than I am."

This was greeted with silence.

Ben-Ari nodded. "Good. You understand now. The harder the training, the easier the battle. Now form teams of four—and lift those litters. We begin."

Marco nodded, choosing Addy and Lailani to be on his team. He wanted Elvis as a fourth, but the rock-loving recruit bit his lip and shook his head.

"Sorry, buddy," he said to Marco. "I'm with Beast, Caveman, and Pinky. Dudes are fucking strong, even the little one." He glanced at Lailani, then back at Marco. "I'm sorry."

Marco groaned. He looked around, hoping to find another recruit—preferably one with some muscle, maybe Sheriff or even the brutish Dickerson—but they were all forming their own quartets. They were left without a fourth. Even Sergeant Singh and the three corporals formed one unit, lifting a litter of their own.

Marco's jaw fell open as Ensign Ben-Ari—his commanding officer herself!—stepped toward them.

"I'm with you," Ben-Ari said.

Marco saluted clumsily. "Yes, ma'am."

Ben-Ari grabbed one end of their litter. "Go on, help me lift it. I'm not carrying this thing myself."

Marco, Addy, and Lailani lifted the other three corners of the litter. Marco walked at the front with his officer. Addy and Lailani brought up the rear. They placed the poles on their shoulders. The damn thing was heavy, digging into Marco's shoulder and bending his arm.

"The two-hundred-pound dummy that broke the camel's back," he muttered, then glanced at Ben-Ari. "Sorry, ma'am. Bad joke."

Their journey began . . . at a run.

The sergeant and corporals took the lead, racing across the sand. When Ensign Ben-Ari began to run too, Marco had no choice but to match her speed. The dummy wobbled on the litter. When Marco glanced behind him, he saw Addy and Lailani running too, faces determined. Marco began to doubt this configuration; Addy towered over Lailani, a full foot taller, and the litter tilted, putting most of its weight on Lailani. Finally Addy had to lower her end of the pole under her arm instead of carrying it on her shoulder. It was clumsy, and Marco wanted to stop and fix things, but Ben-Ari kept running, and they all scrambled to keep pace.

"Come on, soldiers!" Ben-Ari said. "We're not letting Sergeant Singh beat us."

"I'm fine with him beating us!" Marco said.

Ben-Ari glared at him. "I'm not. Hurry. We're going to win this."

"It's a contest too, ma'am?"

The ensign nodded. "Everything is a contest."

Sand flurried around them. A dozen other teams ran around them, carrying their own litters. Beast, Caveman, Pinky, and Elvis were quickly moving ahead, taking third place, then bypassing Marco's team to trail behind Singh and the corporals.

The sun beat down. The sand stung them. Their lungs ached, and they ran onward.

The base became but a smudge behind them, then a glint, then vanished. Everywhere around them was just the desert, dunes and rocky hills and barren valleys. The horizons shimmered with heat, and the sun was as cruel as the litters and duffel bags and unrelenting pace. Finally, even Ben-Ari could no longer run, and they trudged on, breathing heavily, sweat soaking them.

"We can do this, soldiers," Ben-Ari told them, and Marco wondered if she was speaking to them or to herself. "You're doing great. You can do this."

"Ensign Ben-Ari?" Lailani said, panting at the back. "Do you think maybe the dummy can take a turn, and I can ride on the litter?"

The journey continued. They walked across sheets of stone, over rocky hills, and down a narrow path that sent stones tumbling down a cliff—and nearly a few recruits. They ran through a canyon, walls of stone soaring at their sides. Boots sinking, they slogged through sand, climbing dune after dune. Every hour, Ben-Ari allowed them a quick rest—to drink, to breathe, to quickly eat their battle rations. Then they moved again, carrying the litters, alternating between walking and running.

Marco had thought that the day carrying the radios had been bad, but now he missed that day. Back then, they had alternated between shifts of walking and resting, and the terrain had been easier. Here was an unforgiving, relentless torture, the sun whipping them, burning their skin, burning their lips. The weight creaked their bones. The sand gushed around them.

A few hours into their journey, their first recruit collapsed. They had to radio in a medical helicopter from Fort Djemila to pick him up. An hour later, another two recruits fell. The helicopter returned. Teams were broken up and reformed. The platoon continued.

As the hours stretched by, it wasn't the weight, wasn't the distance that brutalized them. It was the terrible heat. They refilled their canteens from jerrycans on the litters, but soon that water ran low too, and the sun kept pounding them, and they kept sweating. Atop a rocky hill, the massive Beast collapsed, vomiting.

A helicopter arrived within moments, carrying the dehydrated giant back to the infirmary. Some litters were now carried by only three soldiers.

The sun was setting when Lailani collapsed.

Her littermates lowered their burden, rushed toward her, and Marco let her drink the last few drops from his canteen, and he fed her his last energy bar.

"I'm all right," Lailani said, rising to her feet. "I'm fine."

"You're dehydrated," said Marco.

She shook her head. "Just got the wind knocked out of me. The heat. I'll be fine now that the sun is setting."

She grabbed her corner of the litter. But Marco saw her exhaustion, saw how she swayed.

"Addy, mind trading places with me?" Marco said. "I'd like to walk at the back."

Addy herself looked more exhausted than Marco had ever seen her. Her face was sunburned, her eyes sunken, her lips bleeding. She nodded silently. She moved to stand by Ensign Ben-Ari. They lifted the litter together. They walked on.

As Marco walked at the back with Lailani, he made sure to carry most of the weight, to let the dummy slide toward him. If Lailani noticed what he was doing, she didn't mention it. She trudged on, swaying, limping, her lips a tight line. The tiny recruit nearly vanished under her duffel bag, her gun, her helmet, and the litter.

She's working the hardest here, Marco knew.

The sun vanished, and they walked through the cold of night. Sergeant Singh was still at the lead, navigating in the darkness, holding a flaring beacon. The others followed like weary pilgrims chasing a star. The wind gusted and the temperatures plunged. They no longer ran. Every step was a battle. Every dune crested was an army of scum defeated.

For hours they traveled through the night, their flashlights casting thin beams through endless darkness. The stars shone above, and Marco felt as if he were walking through space, as if he were fighting the scum in their constellations. He looked up at the stars. Right now the elite forces of the HDF were fighting up there. The STC, the Space Territorial Command, operated in that vast darkness, defending Earth's colonies and even venturing deeper to hit the scum in their own territory. As painful as this march was, Marco knew it was nothing compared to what the STC commandos were doing. As cruel as this desert was, it was kind compared to space.

As they entered the fiftieth kilometer of their journey, Addy began to sing. Voice hoarse, lost for breath, she belted out, "You'll Never Walk Alone." Marco had heard her sing it while watching soccer games at home. He knew the words. He added his voice to hers.

A verse in, Lailani joined them, then Elvis, and then dozens of other recruits were singing too. Marco was shocked to see that even Ensign Ben-Ari sang with them. Their voices grew louder, filling the night.

When they reached their destination—a pavilion and jet on a sandy field—they collapsed, laughing in the dawn. Addy rolled around in the sand, laughing, singing, weeping. Lailani lay under the pavilion on her back, just staring, just breathing, a smile on her lips. They cracked open jerrycans of water, spilled it over their heads, drank, hugged. The recruits who had collapsed on the way awaited them here—some grumbling, others ashamed that they had failed, but soon they too laughed and sang and embraced those who had conquered the distance. Marco walked with a limp, his head spun, his lips bled, and his skin was peeling, but he had never felt better.

Ben-Ari faced them. They all fell silent, watching her.

"Ten weeks ago," she said, "you came to me scared, soft children from across the world. Today your training is complete. Today you are warriors."

Daniel Arenson

CHAPTER TWENTY-THREE

After ten weeks of sand and sweat and screaming bullets, the recruits of the 42nd Company marched through Fort Djemila toward the courtyard, prepared to receive their insignia of rank.

Marco marched with his platoon, his rifle held at his side. For the first time, the recruits weren't wearing their tattered, shabby combat fatigues. This night, the night they graduated from Fort Djemila, they wore fine service uniforms their sergeant had brought them. Like their fatigues, the uniforms were olive green, but these were woven of rich cotton, neatly ironed, and didn't smell like sweat and dust. On their heads, they wore their berets, and their guns and boots gleamed.

Ensign Ben-Ari marched ahead of the platoon, leading them into a sprawling courtyard. A wooden stage, still empty, stood at the back between towering speakers. The company's four platoons arranged themselves in the courtyard and stood at attention.

Marco stood stiffly, chin raised, gun pressed against his side. Addy stood beside him, and he glanced at her. She gave him the slightest of smiles, not turning her head.

Ten weeks ago we were two terrified kids from Toronto, Marco thought. He remembered arriving at RASCOM, disoriented,

304

horses galloping through his belly. He remembered the exhaustion, the pain, the tears at night.

You were always at my side, Addy, he thought. *We did it.*

He glanced to his other side. Standing there, Lailani was staring ahead, chin raised, lips tight. Beyond her, Marco could see his friends. Elvis, his sideburns growing too long again. Caveman, lips tight, eyes shining with pride. Beast, towering over the others. They had become Marco's friends, his family. He loved them as if he had loved them all his life.

Yet not all of us made it, he thought, and he remembered that time sitting with Hope under the tree, talking to her about books. *I won't forget you, Hope. You will always be one of us, a soldier of the Dragons Platoon, 42nd Company. You will always be my friend.*

The platoon commanders stood ahead of the recruits—three corporals, one sergeant, and one ensign each. They too faced the stage.

A drum beat and a trumpet blared through the speakers. Years ago, Marco knew from the books, armies had employed many actual bands; they still had one at RASCOM. But a galactic war was expensive and speakers were cheap. Two sergeants stepped onto the stage and saluted, and two officers followed them on stage. One was a captain, his insignia displaying three bars on his shoulders, and Marco recognized the commander of his company. He remembered the burly man accompanying the troops here from RASCOM ten weeks ago. A second officer was a tall, middle-aged man with red hair and two stars on each shoulder—insignia that Marco hadn't seen before. The sergeants on the stage saluted their officers, and the red-haired man began to speak.

"Good evening, soldiers of the HDF! I am Lieutenant Colonel Murphy, commander of Fort Djemila. It has been my honor to watch you come here as green boys and girls, train with your commanders, and become warriors. Tonight you will receive your insignia, will be promoted from recruits to privates. Tonight you are ready to serve humanity and fight the enemies that seek to destroy us. Thanks to your courage, your discipline, your strength, and your fighting spirit, Earth will stand, and your families will be safe."

It was, perhaps, more propaganda, not much different than the one Captain Butterflies spoke in the reels. But at the moment, Marco felt just a little bit of pride.

The speakers began to play "The Phoenix," the anthem of the Human Defense Force. It was not an upbeat marching song. It was not about glory in battle, about victories won. The song told of Earth's green hills and blue oceans, of humanity's rise, and of the Cataclysm, of Earth's fall into darkness, then of a world that rose from the ashes, stronger than before. The soldiers stood at attention, saluting the flag until the anthem ended.

"Your platoon leaders will call your names," said Lieutenant Colonel Murphy on the stage. "Walk up to them, salute, receive your insignia, and be proud. Tonight you are soldiers!"

The company's four ensigns stepped closer to the stage, then swiveled on their heels, facing their platoons. They began to call out the names of their soldiers.

"Recruit Benny Ray!" said Ensign Ben-Ari.

Elvis left the formation, walked twenty steps toward the ensign, and saluted. Ben-Ari returned the salute, they spoke for a moment, and she pinned his insignia to his uniform. Private Benny Ray returned to the platoon, beaming, a chevron on each of his sleeves. He winked at Marco.

"Recruit Addy Linden!"

Addy too stepped toward the ensign, saluted, and received her insignia.

"Recruit Lailani de la Rosa!"

As Lailani returned with her insignia, she looked at Marco. He nodded at her, and she made a silly face, cheeks puffed out like a blowfish and eyes crossed.

One by one, the recruits stepped toward the ensign and became privates. Ben-Ari called Marco's name last.

He walked up to her and saluted. She looked into his eyes for a moment, silent, and he saw sadness there. She nodded, a barely imperceptible gesture, and returned the salute.

"Hello, Marco," she said.

He nodded. "Ma'am."

Ben-Ari held out the insignia of a private, and she pinned a chevron to each of his sleeves. When she stepped back, she smiled at him, and now her smile was warm and filled her eyes.

"You did well, Marco. I stand by what I told you last week. You would make a good candidate for officer school. If you choose, I would be glad to recommend you. The HDF needs good officers, and not just from the military academies. We find good commanders among the enlisted too."

Marco nodded. He had been thinking about that offer all week. But becoming an officer meant at least ten years in the HDF. It wasn't just a war, it was a career, one Marco wasn't ready to pursue.

"Thank you, ma'am," he said. "But I'm an author and librarian, not an officer. I'll continue to serve as an enlisted soldier."

Ben-Ari nodded, still smiling, and her eyes only grew warmer. She placed a hand on his arm. "I hope we get to serve together again. And maybe someday I'll read your book. Good luck, Marco. I'm proud that I had you as a soldier."

He saluted her, his officer, perhaps his friend, and returned to his platoon.

That night in their tent, the recruits did not go to sleep. They all sat on their bunks, uniforms unbuttoned, feasting from the vending machine. They had been saving their candies, chips, and drinks for weeks, and tonight they dined. It was past lights out, but when Corporal Diaz stepped into their tent, the wounded warrior did not shout or order the recruits into their cots. Instead, the squad's commander actually joined them at the feast, laughing with them.

"You're privates now!" Normally so stern, Diaz patted Marco on the back. "Don't look so shocked to see your commander here. You're true soldiers tonight, my brothers and sisters-in-arms."

"I'm not so sure about that," Marco said. "We can't compare to you. You fought the scum, Commander. You killed several of them. You survived horrible injuries and still came back a warrior."

Corporal Diaz munched on potato chips. "And they're nasty buggers, I can tell you." He nodded and looked into Marco's eyes. "You'd be good as an infantryman. When you meet your sorting officer tomorrow, you can put in requests, you know. They don't always listen, but sometimes they do. You can ask to serve in the infantry like I did. It's a tough gig, but you'd do well."

"Thank you, Commander," said Marco. "I've thought about it, and . . ." He sighed. "You taught me well. Truly you did, and I'm proud to have trained with you. But my father served in the archives. We're a family of librarians. Nobody in our family has ever served in a combat role. I'm hoping to work in the archives myself, to help manage the military information. It's an important job too. Information is power."

Corporal Diaz nodded. "Of course, Emery. You deserve it. Maybe even a job with Military Intelligence. You're not just a dumb grunt like us."

"I don't mean it that way, Commander!" said Marco. "Please, forgive me if I sounded condescending."

Diaz shoved the bag of chips aside and rose from the cot. He glared down at Marco. "So you think I'm just a dumb brute, is that it? Capable of nothing but marching and shooting, too stupid to work in the archives like you?"

Marco was flummoxed. "No, Commander! I only—"

Diaz burst into laughter, grabbed Marco around the neck, and knuckled his head just like Addy used to. Across the tent, the squad roared with laughter.

"I got you there!" The corporal released Marco, then turned solemn. "I know, Emery. You're a smart soldier and can do whatever you want in the HDF, even serve in space on the front lines. I'm proud to have trained you."

The tent's flap opened. A hush fell as Sergeant Singh entered, his eyes stern under his impossibly black and bushy eyebrows. His face twisted with anger beneath his beard. Elvis gaped, crumbs falling from his mouth.

"You sons of bitches," the sergeant grumbled, then pulled out two bottles from behind his back, and a grin split his face. "I brought champagne!"

As cheers filled the tent, the tough sergeant, the same man who had spent ten weeks drilling and disciplining them, uncorked the bottles and sprayed the squad with fountains of champagne. The soldiers howled with laughter and reached for the bottles, trying to salvage the drink. Elvis leaped onto a cot and began crooning "Are You Lonesome Tonight?" while Caveman and Beast drew cheers by slow dancing.

Nobody knew where they'd be assigned tomorrow. Some would be sent for further training, learn to fire artillery, drive tanks, fix jets, analyze intelligence data, or a host of other possible jobs. Most would serve here on Earth. Perhaps a select soldier or two, those with recommendations from Ben-Ari, would be sent into space to defend the colonies outside the solar system. They were all afraid, Marco knew. In many ways, this was like the last night before traveling to RASCOM. But tonight, for a few hours, they placed aside the fear. They celebrated.

But Marco soon had enough of the festivities. He had always been one for quiet introspection and reading, not social events. He glanced at Lailani across the crowd. She sat at the back on a cot, crossed-legged, looking at him. Marco excused himself and left the tent, and when Lailani followed a moment later, he heard the "oohs" and whistles from within.

Elvis's voice followed them. "Remember, Poet, de la Rosa likes to be—"

"Shut it!" Marco shouted back.

Marco and Lailani walked through the darkness, leaving the company's tents. The stars shone above, and Marco could see the Scorpius constellation, the center of the scum's empire. It was many light years away, but standing here, Marco almost felt like he could reach up and touch those stars.

Lailani and he walked until they reached the fence that encircled the camp, metal bars topped with barbed wire. They stood and looked out into the dark desert. For a long time they were silent, staring at the darkness. From the distance they could hear Elvis's crooning and the odd gale of laughter.

Finally Lailani spoke. "Is this goodbye?"

"Maybe not," Marco said. "We might end up serving together."

Lailani turned toward him, eyes damp. "In the entire HDF, an army of millions?"

"I spoke to Ben-Ari," he said. "I asked to remain with you, even after basic training. She'll speak to her superiors. It might work."

Lailani nodded and lowered her head. "And it might not. I didn't want this."

"Want what?" He touched her cheek, felt a tear, and she pulled away from him.

"To like you," she whispered. "To like anyone. You always lose them. Always."

Marco thought of Kemi, thought of how he had seen her again in the helicopter, how he might not see her again for a decade.

"I love you, Lailani," he said. "This is . . . this is probably just my fear talking." His voice suddenly shook, and his heart pounded. "I'm scared, Lailani. I'm terrified. Of the scum. Of going to war. Of what might happen tomorrow, maybe even being sent into space. I'm so scared, and this is the worst possible time to say this, to tell you this. But maybe it's also the best time." He reached out to hold her hand. "I want to be with you. I want to marry you. If we don't see each other again for years, I'll wait for you, and I will see you again. I want us to spend our lives together."

The words were just spilling out from him. He had not planned this. Had not intended to say any of it. It all just came out on its own, and he felt stupid. He felt like a lovesick boy, blabbering in terror, clinging to the nearest soul for comfort.

"I'm sorry," he said, cheeks burning with shame. "I was scared. I said something stupid. I know I've only known you for ten weeks. I know that you normally like girls, not boys. I know that—"

Lailani grabbed him, pulled him into an embrace, and pressed her damp cheek against his chest.

"I love you too, Marco," she whispered. "I used to be so afraid. So hurt. For so many years, I . . . I did things that I can't speak of. Things were done to me. Things that I can't tell you. Not yet. Maybe not ever." Her tears fell. "But with you, I feel a little safer, and the monster inside me is a little smaller. Yes. Yes. I will marry you." She looked up at him, smiling, her eyelashes spiked with tears. "I can even help you write *Loggerhead*. I'll find you turtles for inspiration."

They kissed in the night, then stood holding each other, gazing at the dark dunes and stars.

They're somewhere out there, Marco thought. *The scum. Billions of them, colonizing the galaxy, planning their next assault against us. Planning our destruction. I don't know what future Lailani and I have, what future humanity has, and I don't know if I'll live to be old or live to be nineteen. But right now I'm happy. Right now I have Lailani in my arms and more joy than I ever felt.*

They were walking back to the tent when the sirens blared across the camp.

Lailani sighed. "Fuck me. Another drill. On our last night too."

Marco groaned. "Come on, let's get back and wait it out."

They had suffered through a dozen drills by now. They were always at night. The commanders always had some excuse—suspicious movement spotted from a guard tower, chatter on the airwaves, a report of escalation at some world city. Each drill had ended peacefully, and Marco was convinced—everyone was—that drills were just a planned part of their training.

Marco and Lailani began to move faster toward their tent, where they expected to spend an hour or two crouched between the cots, holding their guns.

They had crossed half the distance when the purple light flared.

Marco and Lailani spun around, and the light washed across their faces, and the sirens blared, louder, louder, crying out for aid.

Hundreds of pods were raining from the sky, flaring out with white, lavender, and indigo light. The air crackled and lightning flashed and the sound of them rose louder than sirens, screaming, screaming, tearing over them. The desert rose, waves of sand like an ocean, burning, cracking, as the pods slammed into the dunes, as the miasma spread, as the creatures emerged from within.

The sirens wailed, and guards in the towers fired their guns, shouting, "Scum! Scum!"

CHAPTER TWENTY-FOUR

The sky shattered.

The world burned.

Marco and Lailani stood in the desert, holding hands, as death rained and hundreds of spinning pods, veined in purple and wreathed in flame, slammed down from the sky.

At once Marco was back there, back home in Toronto, an eleven-year-old boy. At once he heard his mother scream, saw her burn, and as the earth shook, he fell, and in the sky he saw them hail down.

"Marco!" Lailani cried. "Gas masks!"

As the pods hit the sand, lavender smoke emerged—the miasma that had slain millions, that deformed babes in the womb, that twisted humanity into dying, servile wretches with shrunken heads. Marco held his breath. He tore his gas mask off his belt, tried to put it on, forgot that he was still wearing his helmet. Lailani was struggling with her own mask.

Screeches filled the desert. Shadows scuttled. The creatures emerged from the pods. The scum.

Thousands. Thousands.

This can't be happening.

Marco tugged at his helmet's straps.

This is a dream. This isn't real.

A creature scurried over the snow toward a mother and her child. A creature raced across the sand, rearing, claws stretching out like swords. As fire blazed, as gunfire crackled across the camp, the scum leaped into the air, a god of wrath and retribution, claws gleaming, flying toward Marco.

Join your mother. Join her. He heard it laugh in his mind. *Join her, Marco. Scream with her. Scream—*

Marco dropped his gas mask; he had no time to put it on. Still holding his breath, he knelt. He slammed the stock of his gun against his shoulder, gripped the handguard, inserted a magazine, cocked the loading hammer, flipped the safety off—a ritual that he had performed a thousand times in training, that only took a second or two, that seemed to take an era.

The scum swooped toward him.

His bullet rang out, slammed into the creature, cracked the skeleton, and blood spurted out, black and hot, and Marco screamed as the droplets seared him. He fired again. Again. White-hot casings flew. The creature fell into the sand, and Marco rose, emptying his magazine into the scum, and Lailani rose at his side, gas mask on, firing too. The scum kept writhing. It tried to rise. It managed to rear like a cobra. Their bullets slammed into its head, cracking more of its exoskeleton, and still its claws lashed, and still they fired, and Marco emptied his second magazine, and finally the creature fell and rose no more.

Ringing.

Nothing but ringing in his ears.

He had no earmuffs, no earbuds, only the pain, blazing, thudding, ringing thickness like cotton stuffed into his ears. More pods rained down. More scum screeched.

This can't be real. A dream. A dream. Any moment now, Addy will wake me for guard duty. A nightmare. Just a nightmare.

"Marco, your mask!" Lailani cried, and though she stood near him, she sounded miles away. The purple smoke wafted around them.

He finally managed to pull on his gas mask, and he gasped for air. His breath rattled through the filter. When he tried to take a step, his leg nearly buckled; it was burnt, bleeding, sizzling. The ringing in his ears rose higher, a single note like a siren calling the all clear. All clear. All clear.

"We killed one," he said, voice muffled, as if it spoke inside his head. "We killed one!"

"And thousands more are here!" Lailani said, gun in hand.

They stood back to back, guns raised. All around them, the base crumbled. Scum were scurrying up a guard tower as the sentry screamed and fired his gun. One of the scum fell, but the other centipedes reached the tower top, and screams rose, and the structure collapsed. The fence fell. Tents burned, and a massive blast rose from the base's chapel, shaking the desert. Flames lit the camp, revealing countless aliens racing across the desert. More pods kept streaking through the sky like red and purple comets, whistling down, slamming into the desert, releasing more of the creatures.

It's a dream, Marco thought. *I'm back in my tent. I'm asleep. This has to be a dream.*

A soldier ran toward them, shouting something, but Marco couldn't hear. Before the soldier could reach them, a scum leaped onto him, severing the man's legs, then cracking the head open. Another soldier ran, burning, a living torch, and the scum leaped onto her, ripped her apart, and the woman collapsed into burning pieces. A jet was trying to rise from the port outside the fence, engines roaring, only for a pod to slam into it. As the jet dipped, scum leaped from the sand, grabbed its wheels and wings, and the vehicle shattered and blazed and lit the night. Soldiers fell from the jet, still alive, screaming, burning, falling into the waiting jaws of the scum below.

This is hell, Marco thought. *The world is gone. All is darkness and fire.*

"They're the sky," Lailani whispered. "They're the desert. They're everything. They are gods."

Two more scum raced toward Marco and Lailani. They fired, but the bullets glanced off the creatures' claws, and the aliens kept racing forward. Marco ran out of bullets, and he pawed for another magazine. Lailani cursed.

"My gun's jammed!" she shouted, desperately pulling the barrel down to fish out the stuck bullet.

The two scum leaped into the air toward them, and Marco stared up at his death.

White fire.

Blazing, stinking, searing plasma tore forward, ionizing the air, and washed over the two scum. The creatures screeched, torn apart, and both of them fell, shattered and burnt and writhing. Marco finally loaded another magazine and emptied bullets into their twisting forms.

He turned toward the source of the plasma. He saw Ensign Ben-Ari standing there, her silvery plasma gun—the weapon of an officer—in hand.

"Emery!" she cried, voice barely audible past the ringing in Marco's ears. "De la Rosa! To your platoon, now! Move it, soldiers!"

He nodded and ran toward his officer. Lailani ran with him. All around them, soldiers were firing guns, falling, screaming, dying. A man crawled toward Marco, reaching out his hand, begging for help. He ended below the ribcage, his legs, his pelvis, his stomach gone, spilling out organs. A girl curled up in the sand outside a burning tent, weeping, desperately trying to stuff entrails back into her slit belly.

"Papa!" she called. "Papa, please, I want to go home." She fell silent as the scum rose behind her, as the claws impaled her neck.

"Emery, de la Rosa, form rank!" Ben-Ari shouted. Marco saw the rest of his platoon standing outside their tent. A scum still twitched nearby, only one claw still moving, the head gone. Three recruits—no, they were privates now—lay dead around the creature. They were his friends, the people Marco had trained with. He couldn't even tell who they were. Their faces were gone, they were barely human, they were lumps of flesh peeking from tattered green rags, they were teeth stuck in strands of hair and red mush.

"Marco!" Addy cried, bleeding from a gash on her arm, her gas mask muffling her voice. "Last to the party as always, Marco!" But he heard the terror in her voice, saw the tears in her eyes.

"Battle formation!" Ben-Ari shouted. She fired plasma at a scum that raced toward them, burning the creature. Thousands more were scurrying everywhere. Gunfire and screams filled the camp. "Fireteams of three, move!"

The Dragons Platoon took formation as they had trained a thousand times, as the tents burned, as another pod slammed down a hundred meters away, as the fences collapsed, as the mess hall crumbled, as explosions from the trailers rocked the camp, as thousands of scum raced across the sand. A platoon. Three of its soldiers dead. Forty-seven soldiers. Forty-seven friends—terrified, guns raised, lost in a world of hellfire and death and alien vengeance. Marco, Addy, and Lailani formed one fireteam. At their side, Elvis, Beast, and Caveman formed another trio. Other trios stood together, guns raised, gas masks on, helmets on heads.

"He's dead," Sheriff said, pointing at one of the corpses, voice shaking. "Nick is dead, and—"

Three scum raced toward them, screaming, human flesh dangling from their claws, a head impaled on one. Ben-Ari fired her plasma gun, tearing into one alien. Dozens of privates fired their rifles, tearing into the other two aliens. One creature managed to reach the platoon, riddled with bullets, and grabbed Tamara, a private from Squad 2. She screamed as the claws ripped her open, tore out her ribs, tore out her organs. Marco screamed and fired his gun, and the others fired with him, and bullets tore into the scum, tore into Tamara, shattered both corpses until they melted together, fusing in death.

"Soldiers!" Ben-Ari shouted. "Hear me! Our jets are lost, but help is on the way. Transporters will be here in fifteen minutes. We're going to evacuate and bomb this base from the air."

"We won't last fifteen minutes!" Sheriff said, weeping, shaking. He fell to his knees. "We won't last one min—"

"We're seven hundred meters from the sand tigers," Ben-Ari said. "We'll fight from the armored vehicles. Behind me now. Charge!"

She turned and began to run through the base, firing her plasma gun.

"Charge!" Marco shouted and ran after her, firing bullets.

The survivors of the Dragons Platoon ran, howling, firing their guns.

Seven hundred meters away, Marco could see the lot of armored vehicles—the massive sand tigers. A battle seemed to rage there. He saw fire, heard screams, heard bullets. Seven hundred meters. Five minutes of running, maybe four. An eternity. The distance to the heart of the galaxy. And across the sand, countless centipedes, each twice the size of a man, reared, lashed claws, fed on corpses. And still more rained from the sky, burning the sand, melting stones, emerging with the poison miasma to leap onto soldiers, to rip them apart.

"Charge!" Ben-Ari shouted, running at their lead, her white plasma carving a path ahead, shattering scum. Severed claws flew through the air.

"Charge!" the privates shouted, running with her, firing their guns.

Marco screamed as a stray bullet, fired by a fellow Dragon, seared across his arm. Another soldier screamed and fell, a bullet in his leg. Friendly fire claimed a third solider. The rest kept running, firing their guns at the scum that leaped toward them. A centipede reared, grabbed a soldier, and ripped him apart. The alien tossed aside the legs and fed upon the still-living torso and head. Another scum rose from the sand, grabbed a private, and pulled the woman down, twisting her head until the neck snapped, then cracking open the skull. The bullets shrieked everywhere.

A nightmare. Just a nightmare. Just keep running. Just run until you wake up.

Addy screamed as flying debris—a chunk of exoskeleton—scraped across her hip, tearing her uniform, tearing her skin. But she kept running. Lailani knelt, fired her gun, ran onward. A scum leaped toward her, and Lailani fired, knocking it back, suffering a blast of venom against her thigh. She screamed and fell, leaped up, kept running. Marco fired his bullets as the sand rose everywhere, and the fire lit the night, and the aliens tore into the troops.

"Scum, scum!" Caveman shouted, running nearby. "Scum attack!"

"We know!" Addy shouted. "Fire your gun!"

Caveman fumbled for his weapon, still running. "So loud. So loud!" He dropped his rifle and covered his ears. "I can't take the noise. I—"

"Keep running!" Marco shouted, reaching toward his friend, but it was too late.

A scum raced toward Caveman, seeing an easy target. Marco fired, and his bullets glanced off the scum, unable to crack the exoskeleton. The creature leaped toward Caveman. The heavyset soldier made a desperate attempt to raise his gun, to pull the trigger, but the scum was faster. Mandibles grabbed Caveman's leg, tearing deep into the flesh, and the bone shattered, thrusting out from the wound. Caveman screamed and fell.

"Caveman!" Marco cried and ran, firing his gun. From closer range, his bullets tore between the scum's segments, digging deep into the creature. It squealed and released Caveman, and a bullet into its head silenced it.

"Keep running!" Marco shouted to Lailani and Addy. Both had paused and were approaching him. "Get to the sand tigers!"

"Fuck you, Poet!" Addy shouted, firing her gun at a scuttling scum. Lailani was screaming, firing in the other direction, holding off the creatures.

As the women covered him, Marco grabbed Caveman. The brute was wailing, covering his ears, calling for his mother.

"I want to go home," he blubbered. "Mama. Mama. I want to go home. I want my flowers. I want my mama."

"I'm taking you home, buddy." Marco groaned as he lifted the heavy soldier. Caveman easily outweighed him by seventy or eighty pounds. "Come on. Come on!"

He managed to sling Caveman across his shoulders. Stooped, Marco trudged toward the lot of armored vehicles. The weight threatened to crush him, but Marco had walked two marathons through the desert, carrying all his equipment and a litter. He could now carry his friend.

Ensign Ben-Ari's words returned to him. *The harder the training, the easier the battle.* Marco had hated the past ten weeks, but right now he was thankful for every sweaty, horrid moment.

There were perhaps a hundred meters left to the sand tigers. Ben-Ari had already reached the lot, and blasts of plasma lit the night. The battle raged ahead between the massive metal machines. Marco concentrated on walking, one step at a time, carrying the wounded Caveman. Addy and Lailani flanked him, firing their guns, emptying magazine after magazine, clearing a path for him. More venom sprayed Addy, and she bellowed and cursed but kept walking even as her leg sizzled.

Finally they reached the lot. The metal fence had collapsed. The scum had overwhelmed the place. The giant centipedes were racing across the asphalt and over the armored vehicles. One scum was tearing off a sand tiger's .50-cal gun. Three other scum had managed to rip open a vehicle, and they were tearing apart its engine. Soldiers knelt between the sand tigers, firing their guns.

Marco saw Corporal Webb running between two vehicles on her metal legs, screaming, firing her gun. Before Webb could reach new cover, a scum leaped at her from a sand tiger's turret. Corporal Webb fell, and the scum ripped off her metal legs, then ripped off her arms, then died in a hailstorm of bullets. Webb screamed beneath the corpse, limbless, falling silent when a twitching claw sank into her chest.

Marco refused to let the horror overwhelm him. Horror would come later. For now he had to survive, to save his friends.

"There, that one!" Marco said. "543A!"

Carrying Caveman, he pointed at a sand tiger near the back of the lot, the serial code 543A painted on its rusted hull. The scum had not yet disabled it. He trudged forward. A centipede raced across the asphalt toward him, but Addy and Lailani blasted it. Severed claws clattered across the lot.

We just have to last ten more minutes, Marco reminded himself. *Ten minutes until help arrives.*

The battle had been raging for only a few minutes, though it seemed like hours already. Corpses lay everywhere. Marco focused on walking. Nearby, one armored vehicle began to move, then another. A third vehicle's engines rumbled to life. Marco spotted Beast rising into one sand tiger's turret, grabbing the machine gun, and firing. Massive bullets tore into scum on the lot.

Finally Marco reached sand tiger 543A. He paused, sweating and panting, Caveman still slung across his shoulders.

"Addy, the door?" he said.

"Ladies first," she said, tipping her helmet. She grabbed the armored door on the sand tiger's rear. It was large as a garage door and thick as a man's fist. She pulled it open, and a scum spilled out.

Addy screamed, fell onto her back, and fired her gun as the scum leaped. Bullets tore it in two. Both halves of the creature fell, still alive, still scurrying. Lailani screamed and fired her gun, slaying one half. Addy jumped back, spraying bullets, and killed the other half. Both women stared into the armored vehicle.

"Fuck me, it laid eggs inside!" Addy said. She gagged.

Marco could barely keep carrying the heavy Caveman. He stepped toward the vehicle and gazed inside. A handful of eggs, football-sized, lay in the cramped interior of the sand tiger. He placed Caveman down beside them. The soldier was shivering, his leg blasted open, the bone sticking out. His face was ashen, drenched with sweat.

"Marco," he whispered. "Marco, I need you to promise me something, Marco . . ."

"Soon, buddy," Marco said. He looked around at the yard. A few other sand tigers were moving. Corpses of both scum and soldiers lay on the asphalt. Gunfire blazed.

"Addy, you want to drive?" he said.

She nodded, leaped over Caveman and the eggs, and propped herself into the driver's seat. "You man the turret!"

Marco noticed that Lailani was still outside the vehicle, panting, shivering. Marco leaped out toward her. She looked up at him, pale, eyes damp.

"I can't climb," she whispered.

For the first time, Marco saw it. A scum's severed claw was embedded in Lailani's thigh. Around it, the wound sizzled, turning purple, infected with scum venom.

"Just a mosquito bite," Marco said, terror pounding through him, his eyes filling with tears.

He lifted Lailani. He carried her into the sand tiger. He laid her down beside Caveman.

Scum screeched, racing toward them across the lot, and Marco fired his gun, then pulled the door shut. The scum slammed into the metal.

"Addy, drive!" Marco shouted.

As the vehicle began to move, Marco rummaged through his pack and pulled out two bandages. He slapped one onto Caveman's wound and secured it with duct tape. He grimaced, inhaled deeply, then pulled the claw from Lailani's thigh. It came free with a spurt of blood and venom. Fingers shaking, Marco pressed the second bandage against the gushing wound. Lailani shivered.

The sand tiger rocked as scum slammed into it, then jolted, rose, landed hard, rocked again. A small screen revealed a view of the outside, and Marco saw the centipedes slamming into the armored car. The door dented as claws bashed into it.

"This'll help." Marco pulled out the needle from his first aid kit. Lailani's eyes widened, and Marco slammed the needle into her thigh, right into her wound.

She screamed.

Marco's fingers shook, but he managed to pull a second needle from Caveman's pack, then punch it into the heavy soldier's leg.

Caveman bellowed, then lost consciousness.

Marco felt close to fainting too.

"What the fuck was that?" Lailani said, shivering and pale.

"Antidote to scum poison," Marco said. "You must have fallen asleep in first aid class." He smiled and stroked her cheek. "Typical."

Lailani coughed. "I only care about killing scum. I—"

"Marco, man the fucking turret!" Addy shouted from the driver's seat. "They're climbing up!"

Marco nodded. Leaving Caveman and Lailani, he approached the ladder in the center of the armored vehicle. His legs shook. His heart thrashed.

No terror. Climb. Fight.

He had climbed halfway up when, below him, the scum eggs began to crack.

"Oh, fucking hell," Marco muttered.

The sticky ovals dripped slime as they bloomed open. Scum the size of garden snakes emerged.

Grimacing, Marco leaped down, crushing one creature beneath his boots. Its claws reached out, ripping his trousers and skin. Other eggs were opening; Marco counted seven of them. He dared not fire his gun here within the armored vehicle.

"Marco, the turret!" Addy shouted again. She looked over her shoulder from the driver's seat, a cigarette dangling from her lips, and paled. "Fuck me. Baby scum! Forget the turret! Kill those things!"

Marco leaped over the wounded Caveman and Lailani, pulled open the back door, and kicked the hatching eggs. They tumbled outside onto the sand, spilling out the spawn. Three of the clawed creatures were still inside, fully hatched. Lying down, Lailani kicked one with her good leg, shoving it out. Marco swatted the others with his gun's barrel, finally driving them out.

One adult scum raced across the sand after the vehicle. It leaped toward them. Marco fired a bullet, knocking it back outside. He slammed the door shut.

"Addy, reverse!" he said.

She nodded, and the sand tiger rolled backward, crushing the spawn beneath its tracks.

"Now get up there!" Addy said. "There are scum climbing the goddamn sides! Shoot them off."

Without time to bandage his burnt leg, Marco grabbed the ladder. He climbed into the turret, his head and torso emerging into the night. A massive stinger-class .50-cal gun was mounted here, but this was a two-man job: one soldier to fire the gun, the other to operate the wheel that turned it from side to side. Resigning himself to firing in only one position, Marco grabbed the heavy weapon and pulled the trigger.

Marco's personal weapon, a T57, was a deadly piece of technology, able to slay three men with a single bullet, tear through brick walls, and even crack the exoskeleton of a scum. The sand tiger's machine gun made it look like a peashooter. The stinger's muzzle lit the night. The bullets tore into scum, shattering exoskeletons. The sand tiger, weighing in at sixty metric tons, crushed the dying creatures beneath its tracks. At his sides, Marco saw other armored vehicles leaving the lot. Corporal Diaz stood in one turret, firing another machine gun. Dickerson stood beside him, wheeling the weapon from side to side. Beast was shouting in another vehicle, muscles bulging as he fired a second stinger, tearing into other scum.

Addy drove their sand tiger onward. It moved at a slow, rattling pace. Another scum raced forward, and Marco fired his gun, but he couldn't hit it. Damn it! He needed a second person here, somebody to turn the winch, to aim the gun, and the scum leaped up the side of the vehicle, and—

The gun spun sideways. Marco fired, blasting the scum apart. He turned his head to see Lailani in the turret beside him. She gripped the winch, already spinning the gun in the other direction.

"Fire!" she shouted.

Marco pulled the trigger, and hot casings the size of sausages flew. Bullets tore into the scum ahead.

"Lailani, back inside!" he said. "You're wounded."

She scoffed. "Fuck you, Emery. I'm not missing this."

They drove over the broken fence, leaving the lot, plowing over scum. The aliens cracked under this massive box of steel. Lailani kept spinning the gun, and Marco kept firing, slaying the scum in the desert, bullets ripping off claws and chunks of exoskeleton.

"Marco!" He heard Ensign Ben-Ari, and he turned to see her in the turret of another sand tiger. "Marco, make to the spaceport! Transport should be here in five minutes."

Marco nodded. "Yes, Commander!"

"Duck!" Ben-Ari shouted, raised her plasma gun, and shot at him.

Marco winced and ducked.

The plasma blasted over his head, hitting a scum that was leaping from a guard tower. The creature fell down dead. Marco looked back at Ben-Ari, helmet seared, only to see her firing in another direction. Beneath the officer, her sand tiger crawled onward, crushing more scum.

"Addy!" he shouted down into the vehicle.

"I heard!" she shouted from the driver's seat. "Limo service straight to the port!"

As they drove onward, scum kept climbing the vehicle. Lailani wheeled the .50-cal stinger with one hand, firing her personal rifle with the other hand. The bullets screamed across the armored facades, ripping off the scum. The heavy caterpillar tracks finished the job.

The spaceport lay a kilometer away. They had crossed only a hundred meters when Marco shouted, "Addy, stop!"

She pressed down on the brakes. "What?"

Marco pointed. "Fuck."

Three soldiers stood in the desert, forming a ring, firing their guns at a hundred or more scum that surrounded them. Marco recognized two of the soldiers. One was Sheriff, the Texan with the star on his helmet. Another was Corporal Fiona St-Pierre. Marco barely had time to see the third soldier before a scum grabbed the woman, pulled her down, and ripped out her ribcage. Sheriff and St-Pierre screamed, firing in automatic.

"I see 'em," Addy said, and she directed the sand tiger toward the two soldiers. The aliens screamed as they died beneath the caterpillar tracks. More scum kept climbing the vehicle, only for Marco and Lailani to shoot them down.

"Fuck, out of ammo!" Lailani said, placing down her T57.

"Grab the stinger!" Marco said. He leaped down from the turret, slipping back into the cabin. Above him he heard Lailani fire the machine gun.

"Addy, can you help Lailani up there?" he shouted.

Addy grumbled, leaped out of the driver's seat, and began to climb the ladder. Her rifle dangled across her back. "Fuckin' hell, who made you officer? It's do this, do that, stop here, go there . . ."

Soon Marco heard her shouting as she fired her rifle above, helping Lailani clear out the enemies. That left the vehicle without a driver, idling in a sea of scum.

Marco quickly checked on Caveman—he was still alive, but barely—and then pulled open the heavy back door of the sand tiger.

A scum leaped in, then another. Marco fired, shooting in automatic. The sound echoed inside the vehicle, and his ears screamed, rang, tore.

"Inside!" Marco shouted, not hearing himself, and gestured for Sheriff and St-Pierre. Both soldiers leaped in, only for the scum to grab Sheriff, pull him back, and begin to devour him. Corporal St-Pierre scurried across the cabin, bleeding from gashes on her legs.

"Sheriff!" Marco shouted from the hatch, chest shaking. "God, Sheriff!"

The Texan screamed, reaching out to him in the sand, only for the scum to rip off his legs, crack open his back, and pull out the spine. Marco stared in horror, tears on his cheeks.

"Sheriff . . ."

No. No horror now. Horror later. Survive now.

Marco was about to slam the door shut, then keep driving toward the lot, when he saw him there in the field, standing alone.

Fuck.

It was Pinky.

CHAPTER TWENTY-FIVE

The little soldier stood out in the open, firing two rifles, one in each hand, howling. Yet as Marco watched, one gun ran out of bullets, and a scum grabbed Pinky's legs. With a scream, Pinky fell, still firing one weapon. The scum wrapped tighter around his legs.

Fuck. Fuck. Fuck. Fuck.

There was no driver in the seat now, and Pinky was a good ten meters away—and had maybe two seconds to live.

Cursing, Marco leaped out from the vehicle.

He fired at one scum, at another, a third, knocking them back. As he reached Pinky, he emptied his last magazine into a fourth alien.

"Emery, help me!" Pinky said. "Get it off!"

One of Pinky's legs was missing. The scum was wrapping around the second leg. The creature turned toward Marco, hissing.

Marco drew his bayonet from his belt.

The scum leaped toward him.

Marco snapped on the blade and raised his gun.

The scum impaled itself on the graphene blade, screeched, and lashed its claws. One claw slashed across Marco's arm, spurting blood. He kept holding his gun. He twisted the blade, pulled back, and thrust the bayonet again. The blade crashed into the alien's head.

Marco let the gun hang on its strap. He grabbed Pinky and lifted him. Pinky's one remaining leg dangled loosely. The stump spurted, and Marco grimaced and reached into the wound. Pinky howled in agony as Marco found the vein and pinched it shut. He trudged back toward the sand tiger.

"Marco, you fucking idiot!" rose Addy's voice. She was back in the driver's seat, backing up the sand tiger toward him.

He leaped inside, carrying the wounded Pinky. He placed the little soldier—by God, he barely weighed a thing—on the floor, then slammed the door shut, crushing a scum that was trying to enter. The sand tiger rolled onward, plowing through centipedes, moving toward the spaceport.

"You should have left me," Pinky rasped. "Emery . . . you should have left me."

Marco was already forming a tourniquet from his belt. "Pinky, you're an asshole, but you're an asshole in my platoon. So don't you fucking die now. Because I intend to remind you of this for the rest of your life."

Shivers seized Marco. He retched. As his vision blurred, he rummaged through his first aid kit, found another needle of antidote, and slammed it into his wounded arm. He gritted his teeth, agony blazing across him until the pain of his scum venom faded.

Arm numb, Marco climbed back up into the turret, rejoining Lailani at the gun. He looked around. The base was in ruins. Tents blazed. The mess hall was gone. As Marco watched, three pods fell from the sky, slammed into the armory, and a massive explosion rocked the desert. Fire blazed. Both Marco and Lailani covered their heads, wincing as the flames roared. A series of explosions followed, so loud Marco covered his ears. Rocks and sand and bricks pelted them. When they looked again, the armory was gone. A mushroom cloud rose where it had stood.

"They nuked it," Lailani said.

Marco could barely hear anything over the ringing in his ears. "No. They didn't have to. There go Fort Djemila's armaments. Boxes of bullets and grenades all gone in a flash."

Lailani gasped and pointed the other direction. "Look, Marco! Help! Transport jets!"

He turned and looked. Five massive cargo jets, each large enough to hold hundreds of troops, were descending toward the spaceport. Guns blazed on their sides, destroying the scum that covered the landing strips. Several sand tigers were racing toward the jets. A voice blasted out of speakers.

"All soldiers of Fort Djemila, evacuate at once! Enter the transport jets in the spaceport! Evacuate the base!"

The first massive jet landed, and soldiers ran toward it, raced up a ramp, and vanished inside. Other jets were busy firing on the scum, then landing among the corpses, accepting more soldiers.

"The cavalry's arrived!" Addy shouted from the driver's seat of their tiger. "We're getting the hell out of here."

When they reached the spaceport, Marco opened the door. He shouted, "Medics! We need medics!"

Wind blasted him as more jets landed, and scum were still clattering across the tarmac. There were two litters inside the sand tiger, one hanging from each wall. They placed Pinky on a litter first. His wounds were the worst, one leg gone, the other dangling by loose scraps of flesh. The little soldier had already lost consciousness, and they carried him outside. Medics emerged from one of the transport jets, grabbed the litter, and carried Pinky into the vessel.

St-Pierre was wounded too, but well enough to limp toward the medics herself. She all but collapsed onto a litter, where the medics placed an oxygen mask on her, then rushed her into the jet.

Marco, Addy, and Lailani returned into the sand tiger to fetch Caveman.

"Come on, buddy," Marco said, helping Caveman onto the last litter. "Time to visit the doctor. Might be you'll get ice cream."

Caveman was ashen, eyes sunken. The bone still thrust out from his broken leg.

"Wait," he whispered. "Marco. Promise me something, Marco."

That was when Marco noticed the blood darkening Caveman's shirt. He frowned, pulled off Caveman's vest of magazines, and lost his breath.

A scum's claw had pierced Caveman's torso. The tip emerged just over the navel.

"Marco," Caveman whispered. He gripped Marco's hand. "Go to Amsterdam. See the floating flower market. Buy a bouquet for me."

"You'll go there with me," Marco said. He lifted the litter. Addy and Lailani helped him carry it outside. "Caveman, we're going to go there together, all right? We'll go to that floating flower market of yours, and you'll tell me the names of the flowers. So shut the fuck up now."

Perhaps, if Marco had known that was the last time he'd speak to Caveman, he'd have chosen a better parting sentence. Perhaps if he had known that Caveman would die right there on the tarmac, before the medics could even take him into the jet, Marco might have hugged his friend, said farewell. But the last he saw of his friend was the medics above him, slapping his chest, trying to restart his heart. The last thing he heard was a medic sighing and muttering, "Well, fuck it, move on to the next one."

Marco stood on the tarmac, silent.

Then he looked back at the sand tiger.

"Addy, Lailani," he said. "Can you still fight?"

Both women were about to enter the jet. Farther back, one of the transport vessels was already rising into the air, carrying survivors. Other jets were still on the ground.

"What?" Addy glared at him, panting. Blood stained her leg, and burns covered her arm. "Why? You forgot your wallet?"

"There are still soldiers back there," Marco said. "Not everyone made it out. We can still squeeze a few more people in the back."

Addy stared into his eyes, conflicted for just a second, then tightened her lips and nodded. She returned into the sand tiger and took the wheel.

Marco and Lailani climbed back up into the turret. They left the spaceport behind, returning into the inferno of Fort Djemila.

As they were driving back toward the tents, they passed by a second sand tiger, which was rolling across a field strewn with scum. Ensign Ben-Ari stood in the turret.

"There might still be soldiers back there!" Marco cried to her.

Ben-Ari nodded. She raised her plasma gun, fired into the air, and shouted, "Dragons Platoon! With me! Back to the tents! Dragons Platoon, follow me, in your sand tigers!"

Marco saw his friends in other sand tigers, joining them. Elvis. Beast. A few other survivors. They had six sand tigers, that was all. Yet they left the transport jets behind, and they drove back into the inferno.

When they rolled between the tents, Marco saw burnt bodies everywhere, but he still heard gunfire. They followed the sound to see a squad of soldiers standing back to back, firing at the scum. They were mere recruits, maybe a week into their training—"fresh meat" who had barely learned to fire their guns. Their friends lay dead around them, and Marco opened the sand tiger's door, gesturing for them to enter. Addy fired at his side, holding back the scum as the soldiers leaped inside. They drove to the spaceport, and the recruits leaped out of the sand tiger and into a jet. Another jet, full with survivors, rose into the air.

Once again, Marco and his friends returned into hell, firing their guns. More pods kept raining down. One crashed onto the sand tiger's hood, and the scum emerged from within, spraying venom. The acid stung Marco's arms, but he fired, killing the creature. He returned to the tents. He found three more recruits. He pulled them inside, returned to the port, and another jet rose.

It was dawn, and Marco lost track of how many times he had driven back and forth, when he could find no more survivors. Speakers thrummed.

"All remaining soldiers—evacuate now! Five minutes to nuclear detonation. All remaining soldiers—evacuate now."

Marco looked at the base from the turret. Thousands of centipedes had claimed it, crawling over the remaining buildings, coiling in the desert, laying eggs in the sand, screeching. Hundreds of the aliens began to race toward the port.

Addy drove their sand tiger toward the last jet. The soldiers leaped out, guns firing, and raced onto the ramp. The jet began soaring even while the ramp was still closing.

Marco stumbled across the fuselage, found a window, and watched fighter jets streak through the sky below. Mushroom clouds rose over Fort Djemila, growing smaller, smaller, mere puffs below as the transport jet rose high over the desert and the stars spread around them.

Marco fell to his knees, then to his side. He closed his eyes.

"Marco?" Lailani grabbed his hand. "Marco!"

All was darkness. He lay in a boat at sea, endless constellations floating around him.

CHAPTER TWENTY-SIX

"Wake up." Hands grabbed and shook him. "Wake up, moron. You're not unconscious, just sleeping, so wake up."

Marco moaned. Weakly, he swatted at the figure shaking him. He wanted to sink back into darkness, into a land with no pain, no memory.

"Marco!" Weight pressed down onto his torso, driving the air out of him. "Wake up or I'm going to squish you."

Marco groaned, pain stabbing through him, and opened his eyes. He was lying in bed, actual white walls around him—not tent walls but walls of real stone. And Addy was sitting on him.

"Get off!" He shoved her. "You weigh more than a sand tiger."

Addy grinned—a huge, toothy grin—and began showering him with kisses, covering his cheeks, forehead, even his lips. "You're alive! You're alive!" She frowned, then spat. "Gah! You taste like scum."

"Get off!" He finally shoved her off him and inhaled deeply. "Everything hurts."

Bandages covered his arms, and a blanket was pulled up to his chest. He was in a hospital, monitors and charts and machines beeping around him. Addy was dressed in a hospital gown.

Bandages covered her hip, left arm, and shoulder, and scratches and bruises coated her skin, but she still beamed.

"How bad was I hurt?" Marco said. He tried to rise from the bed, then yelped and pulled the blanket back over him. "And where are my clothes?"

Addy stuck her tongue out at him. "Your clothes took the brunt of the attack." She grabbed a hospital gown from the wall and tossed it at him. "Your body is fine. Well, it's still too short and scrawny, but it didn't get any centipede claws in it, if that's what you mean. Mostly you're just worn out and bashed up, some burns that'll heal. Could have been worse." Her smile faded and her eyes darkened. "It was worse for many of us. Half our platoon . . ." She lowered her head.

Marco nodded and lay back down, remembering how Sheriff had died in the sand, how Caveman had died on the tarmac. "Is Lailani . . ." He was unable to complete his sentence.

"She's fine. Bashed up too, and that claw in her thigh will leave a scar, but the little bugger's a fighter." Addy hopped toward the door and hollered. "Hey, guys! Poet's awake! Come bug him!"

Patients tumbled into the room, leaped onto the bed, and began bouncing.

"Marco, you lucky dog!" Elvis grabbed him and knuckled his head.

"Can people please stop doing that?" Marco said, but he couldn't suppress a smile.

More recruits kept pouring in, discussing the battle, patting Marco on the back, mussing his hair, laughing. Beast stood on crutches, shaking his head. "That was not real battle," he was saying to nobody in particular. "In Russia, we fight *real* battles. Not these small American scuffles." But even the massive, bald Russian was eventually laughing with the others and sharing stories of killing the scum.

Marco kept waiting for Lailani to join them, but she was nowhere to be seen, and he wanted to ask about her, but everybody was too busy speaking, laughing, play fighting. He wished she were here. He wished all those who had fallen could be here.

"I wish Caveman could laugh here with us," Marco finally said. "And Sheriff. And Corporal Webb. And the others we left behind."

Now the laughter died, and they all grew solemn. For a long moment, they stared in silence at their feet. Finally it was Addy who grabbed a paper cup from a dispenser, filled it with water, and raised it.

"To our fallen friends."

The others took their own cups and raised them. "To our friends."

It was only water they drank, but after months in the desert, water was a precious drink, symbolizing life more than wine.

"To our friends," rose a hoarse voice from the doorway, and Marco turned to see Pinky entering the room.

At once, Marco's heart twisted, and all the hatred he had harbored for long weeks melted. Peter "Pinky" Mack sat in a wheelchair, face ashen, eyes sunken, both his legs gone. Bandages wrapped around the stumps, and an IV bag dangled above him, connected to his arm.

"Pinky," Marco said, sitting on his bed.

Pinky rolled his wheelchair toward him. He stared, eyes hard, and Marco cringed, mentally preparing for Pinky to insult him, to shout, maybe to weep, but instead Pinky grabbed his hand.

"You saved my life, Poet," Pinky said. "You goddamn Canadian, you saved my life." He squeezed his hand. "You're my brother."

Marco nodded. "Brother," he said.

"All right, all right, everyone out!" Addy said, wiping a tear from her eye. "Pinky needs to rest. Poet needs to work on his book. Tomorrow they'll probably ship us off to another battle. Out, out, everyone!"

The soldiers shuffled out, still swapping battle stories, until only Addy remained. She stood still for a moment, then sat on the bed beside Marco, and she simply embraced him. They sat silently for long moments, cheeks pressed together, and he realized that she was crying. Marco stroked her long blond hair and kissed her cheek.

"It's all right, Addy," he whispered.

She looked at him, tears in her eyes. "None of this is all right. None of this." She let out a soft sob. "I miss home. I'm scared, Marco."

He pulled her back into his arms, and they sat together, comforted by each other's warmth.

"Hey, Addy," he finally said. "Remember that time Elvis peed in the milk carton?"

She let out something halfway between sob and laugh. "How can I forget? He sprinkled all over the floor around my cot." She laughed again. "Remember that time Beast and Pinky arm wrestled? My god, I couldn't believe Pinky won! He's smaller than one of Beast's entire arms."

"That little dude is strong!" Marco said. "Hey, Addy. I wonder if Dad has stories like this too from his time in the army. When we go back home for Christmas, we'll talk to him about it. He'll bake his famous ham, the one with maple syrup and those little potatoes."

Addy licked her lips. "And we'll watch a Leafs game. They'll finally win the Stanley Cup this season, you know."

Marco snorted. "No way. They haven't won in over two hundred years."

"They'll win the year we go home," Addy said. "We'll go to a game. You and me and your dad. Maybe Lailani will join us if she has leave and nowhere else to go. And we'll buy those giant hot dogs and beer—yes I'm going to make you drink a beer, *make* you!—and we'll cheer, and we'll know we made the world safe. We'll know that we made it possible. And we'll . . . we'll forget everything that happened here." She nodded and wiped away her tears. "We'll forget."

But Marco knew that he would never forget. He knew that for the rest of his life, he would still see the scum rip into Sheriff and dismember Corporal Webb, that he'd always remember Caveman's last words to him, that he'd wake up from nightmares, even as an old man, seeing the thousands of scum still swarming.

Maybe someday the world will be saved, Marco thought. *Maybe someday the world will be good, and all these things Addy talks about will happen. But some scars don't heal. Some pain never leaves you. Some soldiers are buried in the battlefield, but others carry that battlefield with them for the rest of their lives.*

He wanted to say all these things but could not, so he simply held Addy, and she leaned against him. Finally, with the sun setting outside the window, she rose to her feet, stretched, and cracked her neck.

"All right, old buddy boy, it's almost seven, and we have a foosball game starting in the hospital lounge. You in?"

Marco shook his head. "I think I'll finally write a chapter in my book."

"Oh, right!" Addy nodded. "*Jarhead!*" She turned to leave.

"*Loggerhead!*" he called after her. "It's about a turtle! A—" He sighed as she vanished into the corridor. "Never mind."

His duffel bag lay by his bed, still sandy. He rummaged inside, found his sheaf of paper and a pen. He looked over the first few chapters of *Loggerhead.* A story written in another life, by another person, before everything had changed. It had been his dream to become a writer. Who was he now? He looked at his hands, once soft, now callused, hands that had killed. *Loggerhead*, by Marco Emery. He did not know who that was.

"Marco."

A soft voice, almost timid, almost afraid.

He looked up from his book. Lailani stood in the doorway, dressed in the blue summer dress and hat from their drill in Greece.

"Lailani," he whispered.

She gave him a half smile, looked down at her dress, then back up at him. "I look fucking ridiculous. I hope you like it."

He couldn't help but grin, and his eyes stung. He leaped from his bed, and she crashed into his arms, and he held her close against him. She kicked the door shut as they kissed.

"You look beautiful," he said.

Lailani snorted. She tossed aside her hat, revealing her buzz cut. "I don't want to look beautiful. I want to look like a warrior. I—" She leaned her head against his chest. "Okay, maybe for you I want to look beautiful." She grinned and nibbled her lip. "I ruv you, after all."

He tilted his head. "You know, maybe you should remove the dress."

She nodded. "Yes! Finally." She tossed it off.

When they had first made love, it had been awkward, all banging teeth and jabbing elbows, but this time it was smooth, pure, good, it was perfect, and afterward he held her in his arms, and he kissed her over and over, and he whispered, "I love you."

She closed her eyes, nestling against him. "I wish we could stay like this forever."

"We have tonight." He kissed her cheek. "Memories stay with you. Always. The bad memories hurt you, but the good ones warm you in the cold. This night will be one of our good memories."

They made love again, then slept in each other's arms until dawn.

CHAPTER TWENTY-SEVEN

The next morning, Marco began to explore the hospital, which was located on a North African coast with a view of the sea and ancient Roman columns. He discovered a copy of *The Sun Also Rises* in the hospital's library, and he even lost a game of foosball to Addy. Their wounds were healing fast. Within a few days, they would be ready to continue their service.

"Marco." Corporal Diaz stepped into the lounge, moving on crutches, a bandage around his head. The gruff warrior barely seemed to notice the wounds; they were but scratches compared to what he had suffered in the Appalachians last year. "You're wanted. There's a car waiting for you by the exit."

Marco placed down his cup of instant noodles. "Commander?" he said, frowning.

The corporal smiled thinly. "I told you, Marco. We're no longer at Fort Djemila. You can call me Emilio now."

It still seemed strange to be on a first-name basis with the scarred warrior. For ten weeks of training, Marco had seen Corporal Diaz as an impossibly powerful, wise deity. It was hard to believe that Emilio Diaz was only nineteen, that he loved video games, that he couldn't wait to go home to his parents, brothers, and pets. Again Marco had learned a lesson about perception.

"What is this about, Emilio?" he said.

The corporal shrugged. "No idea. Order came from above."

Marco headed to his room, where he dressed in the new military uniform they had given him, his new rank of private sewn onto the sleeves. He walked through the hospital and took the elevator down to the exit. A military jeep idled there, a corporal smoking in the driver's seat.

"Cig?" the young man said, holding out a box.

Marco shook his head and stepped into the jeep. The corporal shrugged and began to drive. They left the hospital behind. The driver took him through a crumbling, ancient city of brick homes, pale domes, narrow alleys, and virtually no vegetation or color.

Finally they headed toward a military base by the sea. An ancient Roman aqueduct and amphitheater rose by a barbed wire fence. Soldiers stood at the gates, armed with T57s, and waved them in. The jeep stopped by a concrete building, where a portly guard escorted Marco inside, down a corridor, and toward a closed door.

"Enter and salute," the guard told him, sweat glistening on his upper lip. "Answer every question with 'Yes, ma'am' or 'No, ma'am.'"

Marco narrowed his eyes. "What is this? Am I being court-martialed?"

"None of my business," said the guard and left.

Marco frowned. Had he done anything wrong? Was he in trouble? He opened the door and stepped into a small, simple chamber.

Einav Ben-Ari sat here at a desk.

His confusion only grew, and Marco stood at attention and saluted. "Private Emery reporting, ma'am."

Ben-Ari rose from the desk, returned the salute, and gestured at a second seat. Marco noticed that new insignia shone on her shoulders, two bars on each. She was no longer Ensign Ben-Ari, fresh out of officer school, but a full-fledged lieutenant.

"Hello, Marco." Her voice was kind, and Marco exhaled in relief. He wasn't in trouble after all. "Have a seat."

He sat down. "Hello, ma'am."

Ben-Ari picked up a framed shadowbox from the table. Inside were antique medals. Ben-Ari gazed at them and spoke softly. "These are two hundred years old, Marco. They belonged to one of my ancestors. He fought the Nazis in the Second World War, a partisan in the forests of Poland. It wasn't a real army, but after the war ended, they gave him these medals. I look at them sometimes to remind myself of why I fight. Most of my family died in the gas chambers in that war, but the survivors fought on. Since that day, Marco, every person in my family has fought in a war. Many have died in wars. We were once a family of singers, poets, and playwrights. We became a family of warriors." She put down the shadow box. "Marco, now it is our generation that must fight against annihilation. It is we who must become warriors."

Marco nodded, not sure what to say. "Yes, ma'am. I understand."

Ben-Ari rose from her seat. She walked toward a map that hung on the wall, a massive star chart detailing Earth's galactic neighborhood. When she turned back toward him, her eyes were haunted. "Marco, the war against the scum is going to escalate further. We're going to retaliate for what they did to Djemila. They will retaliate in turn. The vicious cycle will spin faster. Like the wheels of a scythed chariot, it will cut all those in its path. We're putting together a new brigade to fight the scum on the frontier—right at our most distant colonies in deep space. I'm going with them. And I want you with me."

"But . . . ma'am!" Marco stood up so quickly he nearly knocked back his seat. "I'm not a warrior. I know you think I am. But I'm not like Pinky or Beast or Addy. I'm a librarian. I fought one battle, yes, but I need a job like my father had. To work in the archives. To protect knowledge. To—"

"Marco, you're the finest warrior in my platoon," said Ben-Ari. "Because you're careful. You're wise. You're decent. Violence is not your nature, and that's the kind of soldier I want fighting for me. That's the soldier we all need up there in space. A man who values peace more than war."

Marco turned away. He lowered his head. This was not what he had wanted. Basic training was supposed to be the hard part. After that, he had hoped to spend his service in the archives, maybe analyzing data from deep space, hell, even mopping floors or making coffee for officers in a cozy, safe base somewhere quiet. Not to leave Earth. Not to fight on the front lines. The memory of his battle still spun his head. He didn't think he could tolerate more violence.

He thought of Caveman, dying on the tarmac. He thought of his mother, dying in the snow. He thought of the billions lost fifty years ago when Earth had fallen into darkness.

And he thought of home—of his books, his father, his city, of that hockey game he had promised to see with Addy, those hot dogs they would eat, that laughter that would fill their days.

But there would be no more books, he knew. There would be no more laughter, no more family or friends, if the scum won.

He turned back toward Ben-Ari. Toward his commander. His officer. His friend.

"I never wanted any of this," Marco said. "I never wanted to join the army. I never wanted to fight. I never wanted to be anything but a writer. But I think that your ancestor didn't want to fight in the forests. And my friend didn't want to die on that tarmac. And millions of people who fought evil throughout history wanted nothing more than to sit at home with a book, a fire in their hearth, family around them. But they all went out and fought, because they knew something." He nodded, eyes damp. "They knew that the world is beautiful, but that it stands on the shoulders of those bleeding, those hurt, those crying out in pain so that others can laugh, love, give us something to fight for. So I will fight. But I have one condition. I'm just a private, and you're my commanding officer, but I make of you this demand. I'll fight for you, ma'am, but not alone. Not without my friends. Not without Addy, Lailani, Elvis, Beast . . ." He thought for a moment. "That is, if they want to come. If they want to fight. If they're braver than I am."

"If they are half as brave," said Ben-Ari, "they will come."

"Ma'am, may I speak freely?"

She nodded. "Go for it."

"I'm so fucking terrified I'm ready to piss my pants," Marco said.

Ben-Ari stared at him, frowning, then sighed. "Go back to your friends, private. We deploy in forty-eight hours. Oh, and . . . bring an extra pair of pants. Just in case."

He saluted. "Lieutenant."

She returned the salute, the hint of a smile in her eyes. "Dismissed."

* * * * *

They sat in the rocket, strapped into their seats. They wore battle fatigues and helmets, and their guns hung at their sides. The rocket idled on the tarmac, waiting for the signal to lift off.

"Poet, move your knee!" Addy shoved him. "You're hogging all the space."

Marco shoved her back. "Then move your elbow. It keeps poking me."

Addy groaned and shoved him. "It's not my fault I've got long arms."

"Will you two hush?" Lailani said. "Be like me and just stay in your seats."

"Easy for you!" Addy said. "You're about the size of my left butt cheek."

"She's a lot smaller than that," said Marco, earning an elbow straight into the ribs.

Sitting across from them, Elvis began to croon. Apparently, he couldn't help falling in love.

"No discipline in this army," Beast muttered, sitting by the singer. "Not like Russia. There is *real* army."

Fifty soldiers filled the rocket—some survivors of Fort Djemila, others gleaned from other units. None had been to deep space before. All had lost somebody to the scum. None were older than nineteen.

A young officer—only a year or two older—came climbing up the rocket. Her blond hair was gathered into a ponytail, and her green eyes were wise and strong yet carried hidden sadness.

"Listen up, soldiers!" Lieutenant Ben-Ari said. "Are you ready to hit the scum where it hurts?"

"Yes, ma'am!" they shouted.

"Right in the ass!" said Addy.

Marco groaned. "Addy, I told you, scum don't have—"

A voice rose from the speakers, interrupting him. "Ten. Nine. Eight . . ."

They all gripped their seats, inhaled deeply, and raised their chins. Ben-Ari hurried through the hatch above into the officers' deck.

"Two . . . One . . . Blastoff."

The engines roared, and with fury and flame, the rocket flew. They blasted through the atmosphere, and Marco looked out the viewport to see the northern coast of Africa, then the Middle East and Europe, then the vast hinterlands of Russia, and finally the entire Earth, a sphere in the blackness. He had never been so far from home.

For a moment, they all stared in awe. Then Elvis returned to his crooning. Addy was soon arguing with Lailani about who the greatest soccer player was. But Marco remained silent, watching the view, watching the Earth grow smaller and smaller, becoming a blue marble, floating through the black.

"A mote of dust suspended in a sunbeam," he whispered.

Addy turned toward him. "What's that, Poet?"

"Something somebody else wrote," he said. "Long ago."

Addy leaned her head on his shoulder, watching the view with him. Lailani did too. Soon they were all silent, staring out the viewport as the only world they had ever known grew smaller in the distance. They flew onward into the deep, unforgiving darkness. To the colonies. To war. To a dream of home, friends and family, and a precious blue marble in an endless black sea.

THE END

NOVELS BY DANIEL ARENSON

Earthrise:
Earth Alone
Earth Lost
Earth Rising
Earth Fire
Earth Shadows
Earth Valor
Earth Reborn
Earth Honor
Earth Eternal

Alien Hunters:
Alien Hunters
Alien Sky
Alien Shadows

The Moth Saga:
Moth
Empires of Moth
Secrets of Moth
Daughter of Moth
Shadows of Moth
Legacy of Moth

Kingdoms of Sand:

KEEP IN TOUCH

www.DanielArenson.com
Daniel@DanielArenson.com
Facebook.com/DanielArenson
Twitter.com/DanielArenson

Made in the USA
Middletown, DE
21 January 2017